Last Letter Home

Rachel Hore worked in London publishing for many years before moving with her family to Norwich, where she teaches publishing and creative writing at the University of East Anglia. She is married to the writer D J Taylor and they have three sons.

Also by Rachel Hore:

The House on Bellevue Gardens
A Week in Paris
The Silent Tide
A Gathering Storm
A Place of Secrets
The Glass Painter's Daughter
The Memory Garden
The Dream House

RACHEL HORE

Last Letter
Home

SIMON &
SCHUSTER

London · New York · Sydney · Toronto · New Delhi

A CBS COMPANY

First published in Great Britain by Simon & Schuster UK Ltd, 2018
A CBS COMPANY
This paperback edition published 2018

1 3 5 7 9 10 8 6 4 2

Simon & Schuster UK Ltd
1st Floor
222 Gray's Inn Road
London WC1X 8HB

Simon & Schuster Australia, Sydney
Simon & Schuster India, New Delhi

www.simonandschuster.co.uk
www.simonandschuster.com.au
www.simonandschuster.co.in

A CIP catalogue record for this book
is available from the British Library

Paperback ISBN: 978-1-4711-5696-0
eBook ISBN: 978-1-4711-5697-7

Typeset in the UK by M Rules
Printed and bound by CPI Group (UK) Ltd, Croydon, CR0 4YY

MIX
Paper from
responsible sources
FSC® C020471

Simon & Schuster UK Ltd are committed to sourcing paper that is made
from wood grown in sustainable forests and support the Forest Stewardship
Council, the leading international forest certification organisation. Our
books displaying the FSC logo are printed on FSC certified paper.

To Sheila
and in memory of Ann

One

They call it a storm and after days of it she felt storm-tossed, clinging to the wreckage of her life, each new attack dashing against her with a force that left her bruised and gasping. She might have borne it if it had simply been words, painful, devastating words though they were, words that cruelly shredded her self-worth, her professional reputation, her trust in her own judgement, her identity as a woman, but it was more than that; her sense of safety was threatened.

It had been her first time in a television studio, Jolyon Gunn's late night chat show, and she'd been invited on at the last minute because one of his guests had been taken ill. Probably with fear. Narcissistic Jolyon was not known for his charm, though this seemed only to boost the ratings.

'And we welcome historian Briony Wood, who is writing a book about World War Two, is that correct, love?'

'Yes, it's to be called *Women Who Marched Away*. It's about the ATS, the women's infantry service during—'

'Sounds smashing,' he cut in. Jolyon did not have a long attention span. 'Briony's here to talk about the news that lady soldiers will now be fighting on the front line. Briony, I know this will be contentious but, really, war is a job for the lads, isn't it?'

'Not at all. There are plenty of examples of fighting women going right back to the Amazons. Or think of Boudicca or Joan of Arc.' Briony tried not to sound strident, but the sight of so many men in the audience, some of whom had nodded in agreement at Jolyon's words, meant she had to speak with confidence. Dazzled by the studio lights, she blinked at her host, who lounged lord-like in his leather director's chair with his short legs spread, suave in a designer suit, his fat Rolex watch glinting. He smirked back at her and rubbed his neat black beard.

'Surely they're exceptions, though, Briony, and we remember what those Amazon ladies had to do to use their bows, don't we?' He made a slashing gesture to his chest and winked and there were shouts of male laughter. 'You see it's not natural, women fighting, they're not *shaped* for anything apart from pulling out each other's hair.'

More bayings of amusement.

Briony drew herself up and glared at him. 'That simply demonstrates their determination. Anyway, just because something is "natural" doesn't make it right. Warfare itself is natural, after all. But, Jolyon, surely our discussion should be about psychology and the social conditioning around gender . . .'

The word gender made Jolyon straighten and his eyes filled with a mad light. Briony realized she'd walked right into a trap. This was a populist show and outspoken Jolyon had a huge following among a certain sort of male, but it was too late to retract her words, she'd look weak and stupid. She was suddenly acutely aware of how schoolmarmish she must appear, her light brown hair tied in a knot at her nape, her charcoal-coloured sheath dress smart and understated rather than fashionable, even with the soft blue scarf coiled about her shoulders.

'The girls aren't tough enough, Briony. They'll cry, and fuss about their lipstick.' The audience howled with laughter at this, though there were one or two hisses of disapproval as well.

'I'd like to see you on a battlefield,' she snapped. 'You'd not hack it for a second compared to some of the brave women I interviewed for my book.'

There were shouts from the floor and several men rose to their feet. One shook his fist at Briony. Jolyon himself stared at her with a pasted-on grin, for a moment lost for words. Only for a moment, though.

'Thank you, Briony Wood,' he pronounced with mock surprise. 'I think she's just called me a coward, guys! Isn't that smashing?'

Escaping into the rainy night, Briony switched on her phone to be greeted by a tattoo of alerts as the messages flew in. She opened her Twitter app with trepidation. As she read the first notifications, her eyes widened with horror.

You ugly cow cum the war you'll be first against the wall.

Our Jolyon's tuffer than any wimmin.

The third was merely a string of obscenities that brought her hand to her mouth.

The phone then rang. A name she recognized. She swiped at the screen.

'Aruna?' She glanced about the lonely South London backstreet and began to walk briskly towards the main road.

'Don't look at any messages. Especially not Twitter.' Briony heard the panic in her friend's voice.

Too late. 'Oh, Aruna. Why did I say it? How can I have been so stupid?'

'It's not your fault, he was awful, the pits. I'm sorry I ever gave his people your name. Listen, where are you?'

'Clapham. I've just left the studio.' Briony turned onto the high street and startled at a trio of youths in leather jackets who swaggered, laughing, out of a brightly lit pub. They brushed past, not even seeing her. 'What did you say?'

'Don't faff about with public transport. Get a cab.' Aruna sounded urgent. 'Go straight home, then ring to tell me you're safe.'

Men from Jolyon's audience were beginning to emerge from the studio front door. They hadn't spotted her yet, but their coarse gestures and rough laughter frightened her. Briony pulled her scarf up over her hair and began to hurry.

Aruna came to her flat in Kennington that night, and Briony was glad because the next morning the abusive messages were still pouring in. At first, despite Aruna's protests, she read them, answered the more reasonable or supportive ones, deleted others, sobbed with rage, but on they came. Finally, Aruna made her suspend her Twitter and Facebook accounts and told her to avoid the internet altogether. She did read a blog piece Aruna found, from a female politician who'd suffered similar attacks. 'Eventually the cyber trolls will tire and retreat to their lairs,' the woman concluded. The advice was to 'stay strong'.

'It's all very well to say,' Briony sighed. She wished her father and stepmother weren't on holiday. She could have done with a bolthole.

The 'staying strong' strategy might have worked had not the furore been stoked by Jolyon Gunn himself. When she sneaked back online that evening it was to find some stinging comments about her 'prudish' appearance being the reason she was still single in her late thirties. His fans, thinking this hilarious, all joined in.

'Prudish? When have I ever been prudish?' Briony gasped. Never mind Aruna's reassurances, this was unfair.

It had been a quiet Easter for news and the second morning after the ill-starred chat show she emerged, a bag of student essays in hand, to hear a man bellow, 'Briony! Over here!' She turned and was blinded by a camera flash. 'Give us a quote about Jolyon, love,' he said, with a cheerful grin. Panicking, she tumbled her way back indoors and watched him drive off. She'd leave going in to college till tomorrow.

Later that day Aruna rang to warn that someone had posted her home address on Twitter. They knew where she lived now, the trolls. On the third morning, an anonymous postcard with a picture of a clenched fist on it arrived in the post. She was now too frightened to go out and made Aruna, who'd popped by with some shopping, tell a group of teenagers loitering on the pavement to clear off. Aruna's dark bobbed hair flew in the wind as the youngsters stared back in innocent puzzlement at her earnest, pointed face. Briony realized with embarrassment that she was being paranoid. After Aruna had gone, an avuncular policeman showed up and settled his bulk on Briony's sofa, where he sipped tea and recited comforting platitudes about the online threats.

She rang Gordon Platt, her department head, for advice, but he sounded flustered, muttered about the college's reputation and told her not to come into work for a few days 'for security reasons'. She ended the call feeling let down and marooned. 'It'll all go away soon,' Aruna told her again. 'If you keep your head down they'll soon get bored.'

Aruna was right. The attention melted away as quickly as it had begun. There was other news. The trolls found new victims. It was safe for her to come out.

The trouble was that for a long while after that she didn't feel safe at all.

She still dragged herself into work, but felt overwhelmed. It wasn't simply the usual heavy workload, the administration she had to do on top of teaching and her own research, it was anxiety about getting any of it done. The headaches that had been bothering her for some time became more frequent. They would start at the base of her skull and creep up to her temples and behind her eyes so that sometimes students or colleagues might find her collapsed on the tiny sofa in her office, as she waited for the painkillers to kick in.

Eventually her doctor referred her to a counsellor. A few weeks later, she found herself in a peaceful upstairs room scented with lavender, sitting opposite a supple, elegant woman with a thin, wise face. Her name, appropriately, was Grace.

'I feel I've struggled so hard all my life,' Briony told Grace when she'd finished explaining why she'd come. 'Now I don't know what it's *for* any more. I've lost all my confidence.'

Grace nodded and made a note, then looked at Briony with eyebrows raised, waiting.

'Everything's a huge effort.' Her voice caught in her throat, so that 'effort' came out as a whisper.

'Tell me about the other things in your life, Briony; your family, for instance, what you enjoy doing when you're not working.'

Briony briefly covered her face with her hands, then took a breath so deep it hurt. 'My mum died of cancer when I was fourteen. She wasn't ill for long, but it was an awful time and then she simply wasn't there any more. It was like this huge hole.'

'That must have been dreadful.' Grace's sympathy encouraged her.

'What was worst was there was no one I could talk to. Dad thought we should just get on with things, be practical, and I tried to be like Mum with my brother, which he hated. Will's younger than me. He's married with two kids and living up north because of his job. We're fond of each other, but we're not close.'

'And you don't have a partner of your own? Children?'

Briony shook her head. 'I ... it simply hasn't happened for me, I don't know why. Nothing's quite clicked. It doesn't bother me, exactly, I have lots of friends but, well, sometimes I think it would be nice.'

Grace stirred and smiled. 'If you are open to it, then it might happen,' she said, her eyes shining.

'What do you mean?' It sounded mysterious and a little patronizing, to tell the truth. She explained crossly how relationships had fizzled out, though she'd felt perfectly 'open' to them continuing.

Grace simply smiled in that slightly maddening way. 'We can talk more about that. I think you should slow down a bit, Briony. Say "no" more often and try to do things that you enjoy. And perhaps the next time we meet we should start by talking about your mother.'

Briony nodded, wondering how all this could help her, but the doctor had said Grace was good, and she liked the sense of peace that the room imparted, so she agreed to visit again.

Over the course of the next few months she found herself telling Grace about how abandoned she'd felt by her mother's death, how it had been the sudden end of her childhood. Grace pointed out the importance of other losses – her mother's parents only a few years before, how her brother Will had learned self-sufficiency and their father had finally married again. Perhaps, Grace suggested gently, Briony had developed her own defensive shell that stopped her letting anyone in. And the trolling experience had traumatized her so much because of the stress she was already under.

After her eight weeks of seeing Grace, she sensed that something tightly coiled, like a steel spring, inside her was beginning to unfurl. There were still days when she would relive her ordeal, and feel frightened and powerless again, but these became fewer. She was beginning to come through.

Two

Several months later

'Stop it, Zara. You're driving everyone crazy.'

'Apologize then, Mike. Say you're sorry.'

'I'm not saying sorry for something I haven't done . . .'

The angry voices faded as Briony tugged shut the door of the Italian villa with the tiniest of clicks. Her sigh of relief sent the gecko in the porch darting into the eaves. A fellow escapee, she thought, watching it vanish but, unlike her, it wouldn't feel guilty. How long did she have before the others stopped bickering and noticed she'd gone? Perhaps they'd think she'd retired to bed early and lock up. Well, she didn't care. Three days into their holiday and she was already tired of their company. Of Mike and Zara, anyway. Aruna and Luke weren't to blame. At least, they didn't *mean* to make her feel the odd one out.

The evening was thick with the late July heat. Briony sniffed at the savoury smoke from their barbecue still hanging in the air as she set off over the rough ground between the olive trees to the gate. When she gained the leafy coolness of the lane, a fragrance of resin replaced the pungent smoke and she breathed it in gratefully.

Which way now? Downhill the road led back through the hamlet with its bar and shop, then across a bridge over a babbling river where light dazzled off the water, a beautiful spot where children paddled. That way meant other people, though, and she wanted to be by herself. So she struck out left, up the hill towards the dying sun. It was a direction she hadn't taken before.

The going was easy despite the warmth and it wasn't long before the lazy atmosphere of the Italian countryside and a pleasant stretch in her calves calmed her ruffled mood. She hated any form of conflict since the trolling, even when she wasn't directly involved. It made her want to run and hide.

Soon, the gritty road crunching under her trainers became a soft grassy track that drew her up between terraces of fruit trees where the air smelled fresh with citrus. Minutes later she came to a bend in the path above a sharp drop. She stopped, then stepped out onto a rocky crag to stare at a sudden breathtaking vista of the valley. Up and beyond the encircling hills were the folds of other hills and other valleys, a view that lifted her mood, it was so beautiful.

Beneath the gold-streaked sky all was peaceful. The air was so still and the valley so deep that the smallest sounds echoed up. Briony narrowed her eyes and listened. Far away, a dog yapped a warning in canine Morse code. The strains of a car engine competed with the putter of a tiny plane passing overhead. Close by, a lone cicada tried a hesitant note like a violinist testing a string. Another, and then, as if at the drop of a baton, a whole orchestra of them started up around.

Briony's gaze rested on the terracotta roofs of a small town clinging to the neck of the valley. Tuana. She recalled a fragment of conversation she'd had with her dad the week before. She'd rung him to let him know where she would be staying.

'Tuana?' Martin Wood had said. 'That rings a bell. You know your mum's dad, Grandpa Andrews, was stationed there during the war?' The reminder was enough to send her online to look for pictures of the town, then to the college library for a couple of books about the Second World War in Italy that she'd brought with her. Her grandfather had died when she was ten, silent about his war experiences to the last.

They had stopped in Tuana for supplies on the day they arrived and found it a tranquil place with tight winding streets and a public square dreaming in the sun, but after they'd visited the little supermarket, Mike had been impatient to drive on to the villa and crack open the local vino he'd bought, so there'd been no time to poke around.

The valley was idyllic; well, it appeared to be. Just as Briony knew that the grey haze crowning the furthest hills must be the pollution of Naples' industrial belt, and the distant twin peaks wreathed in smoke was Mount Vesuvius, so did the thought of Mike spoil her pleasure. She yanked a tendril of bindweed from a nearby bush. It snapped, flailed the air like a whip, then lay limp in her hand. She let it fall.

There must be something wrong with her to feel this way. Anyone else would consider themselves lucky. Two weeks' summer holiday at a villa in the mountains of Italy! It was Aruna who'd asked her along. Lovely Aruna, who since they'd found themselves sharing a student flat together, years ago, had been her best friend.

Apart from Aruna, the holiday party were comparative strangers to Briony. Aruna's colleague Zara and hospital doctor Mike were the couple in full spate of a row. Then there was Luke, a tall, gentle, laid-back man in his late thirties who was Aruna's boyfriend of six months and whom Briony found considerate and easy to talk to.

Briony stepped down from the rock and continued along the narrow path around the shoulder of the hill, treading carefully; one wrong step could send her tumbling. When she next looked up it was to see an escarpment ahead. Among trees crowded against the hillside above, her sharp eyes could make out part of the roof and upper storey of a sizeable house. How did one get to that, especially by car? There must be a road from some other direction.

The footpath led more steeply uphill now, zigzagging between trees, but, curious about the house, Briony began to climb. She reached a ridge, hot and out of breath, to find that there was indeed a rutted earth road, snaking off right towards where she'd seen the house.

Someone must have come this way because there were tyre marks in the dust. The owner of the house, presumably. But who would live up here, in such a lonely spot?

She followed the car tracks for a couple of minutes before the road suddenly broadened out then ended abruptly at a pair of sagging wrought-iron gates bound by a rusty chain. A creeper with tiny red flowers twisted through them. It must have been a long time since they'd been opened. Of a car there was no sign, only soil thrown up on the road where the vehicle must have turned in impatient movements. Reaching the gates, Briony grasped the bars and stared, like an outcast, into the lush greenery beyond.

Because of one of those odd tricks of perspective, she could no longer see the house. Such an air of dereliction and loneliness lay over the place that she felt an answering melancholy. She yearned to slip between the gates or attempt to scale the crumbling wall that ran at head-height on either side, but she did not dare. Suppose the owner caught her and accused her of trespassing? Although she could read some Italian, she stumbled to speak it, and she'd have difficulty explaining herself. She smiled, imagining trying to charm some furious Mafioso type. The place appeared to be deserted, but the vehicle tracks told her she couldn't be certain.

The sun was dipping behind the hills and the sky bloomed crimson. Soon it would be dusk. With reluctance, Briony turned from the gates. As she scrambled her way down the hillside, tiny bats teased the edges of her vision as they swooped for insects.

At the crag where she'd paused half an hour before, she was surprised to see someone else standing there, staring out across the valley. The sunset dazzled, but then she recognized that lanky figure, his hands in jeans pockets, that mane of nut-brown hair. It was Luke. 'Hello,' she called as she drew close.

The light glinted off dark glasses as he turned. 'Hey.' He smiled his quirky smile. 'Isn't this amazing? I was trying to orient myself.' He pointed over the valley. 'Do you suppose that's the road we came in by, Saturday?'

Briony squinted at the silver ribbon winding down the hill-side towards Tuana. 'It must be.'

'What did you find up there?' Luke nodded in the direction she'd appeared from and she described the wild garden, and tried in vain to point out the roof of the old villa. Now, in the dying light, the trees appeared to be fused together in a dark slab.

'Never mind. Perhaps another time.'

'Yes.' They stood quietly for a while watching a tiny train cross a distant hillside, then she asked, 'Were you taking a walk, or did you come to find me?'

'I saw you slip out earlier and . . . well, you were gone a long time. Aruna wondered if you were OK.' Luke's forehead wrinkled in a frown. 'Are you?'

'I'm fine. Just needed some peace and quiet.'

'Ah. Sorry, I didn't mean to intrude.' He raised his sunglasses and looked rueful.

'You weren't, honest.'

'Good. The lovebirds have made it up, by the way. It's safe to go back in the water.' This last he said in a stagey whisper with an ironic twist of his eyebrows, and she burst out laughing. As he led the way back down the narrow path towards the villa, she felt happy because someone understood.

'Mike's all right really,' Luke remarked. 'He enjoys upsetting people with those grisly hospital tales. It's best not to rise to it, then he'll shut up.'

'I think it's horrible to talk like that about your patients.' *I do sound prim*, Briony told herself, but to her relief, Luke nodded.

'He's an idiot. I don't think Aruna realized exactly what she was taking on when she invited them. He was all right in London. Isn't it strange when you see people out of their normal context? You notice new things about them.'

'About how they really are?'

'Different sides, perhaps. You still have to consider them as a whole.'

She envied Luke his laid-back attitude. 'I suppose so.' Mike was affable enough, she had to admit, and could be amusing company, but when he'd had a drink or two he became loud, boorish. And – she felt a flash of anger – it was their precious holiday he was spoiling.

'So, what about me?' she said lightly. The path had widened and they were walking side by side now. 'Am I different out of my milieu?'

Luke didn't answer for a moment. 'Yes and no,' he said finally, as though choosing the right words. 'I think in London we instinctively act in a certain way; it's a kind of armour, but here it's easier to see behind that to the person beyond. A nice person in your instance, of course.' He glanced at her with a grin.

'That's all right then. Sometimes I suspect the person inside me is a poor shrivelled thing.'

'We all feel that about ourselves sometimes. I know I do. I suppose, since you asked, you seem a little ... careworn. I'm sorry if I'm saying the wrong thing ...'

'You're probably right,' she admitted. 'I'm still unwinding, I think.'

They trudged on in silence, Briony's feeling of anxiety returning the closer they got to the villa. She was faintly alarmed now by the concerned glances Luke was throwing her. Perhaps she'd made a fool of herself by flouncing out and he thought her bonkers? But when they came to the door and he stood back to let her go first, their eyes met briefly. He did not smile, but his grey-blue eyes under the mop of springy hair danced with good-humoured complicity.

'Thanks for coming to find me.'

'*No problemo,*' he said. 'Aruna was worried.'

'It is called the Villa Teresa,' the stout barman of the tiny local tavern pronounced loftily the following day in answer to Briony's question. He gave the round zinc table a deft wipe with a cloth and set before her a cappuccino and a glass of iced water. Then he glanced about the sunny terrace and lowered his voice. 'No one lives there now, *bella*. There is, how you say, a difficulty.' He spread his fingers to indicate a web of intrigue.

'But who does it belong to?' Beautiful, he'd called her. The way he'd spoken almost made her feel it. She lifted her sunglasses up onto her head and blinked up at him and ran a smoothing hand over her long hair, released from its usual neat chignon. The sun was lightening the pale brown to blonde, she'd noticed happily in the mirror that morning.

More customers arrived, distracting him. 'I do not know, *signorina*, sorry.' With a bow of his head he stepped over to serve a silver-haired American couple who were settling themselves at a table nearby, the woman fanning herself with a tourist pamphlet, and her husband calling impatiently for *acqua minerale*.

Briony sipped her coffee and flicked through the book she'd brought down with her. It was an illustrated account of the Allied forces' liberation of Italy. Round here must have been quite a battleground, she realized as she examined the photographs, fought over by the Germans and the invading Allied forces. It was difficult to imagine now, sitting outside this pretty ochre-roofed café with its view of the arched bridge and the chattering river, though this terrace would have been the perfect lookout spot. 'The Germans retreated, blowing up transport links as they went . . .' she had begun to read, when—

'*Scusi, signorina.*' A soft female voice from the table behind, where previously there had been no one.

She twisted round to meet the almond-eyed gaze of a fine-boned, middle-aged Italian woman in a long-sleeved top of royal blue who was sitting in the shade over a coffee. It took a second for Briony to recognize her as Mariella, the maid for their villa. Only yesterday she and her shy grown-up daughter had driven up with piles of fresh sheets and snowy towels which they had stowed in a cupboard before restoring the kitchen to order with tactful efficiency.

'*Buongiorno*, Mariella, I'm sorry, I didn't see you before. *Sono Briony.*'

Mariella acknowledged this with a nod, but her eyes were on the book. '*Per favore, Briony*, the book?'

Briony showed her the cover, then when Mariella reached

out a beckoning hand, passed the volume to her. She watched the woman turn to the pictures with her long fingers, and was struck by the passionate expression in her eyes.

'You, you know about this here?' Mariella said, tapping the book, and Briony caught her meaning.

'I'm a historian,' she explained. 'What happened here is fascinating to me. I write about the Second World War,' and she explained about *Women Who Marched Away*, while the woman listened, examining Briony's face with calm eyes. 'Also,' Briony added, 'my grandfather, *mio nonno*. He was a soldier here, a British soldier.'

At this Mariella stiffened and her stare intensified, leading Briony to wonder if she'd unwittingly given offence. The war might be history to some, but she knew that for others it had left wounds that would never heal, with repercussions that affected their children, of whom Mariella might be one. She was still troubled when Mariella returned the book with a simple, '*Grazie.*' The cleaner switched subjects. '*La casa?* The house? You are happy?'

'Oh, very happy,' Briony hastened to say. 'Everything's lovely, thank you.'

'*Prego*,' the woman replied vaguely, glancing again at the book. Then, '*Signor Marco*,' she called over her shoulder and the proprietor appeared in the doorway to the kitchen, drying his big hands on a towel, his bald pate shining under the electric light. She spoke several sentences of Italian to him, too fast for Briony to follow, but the words 'Villa Teresa' kept being mentioned. Signor Marco replied with the same rapidity and Briony looked from one to the other trying to make sense of it all. Finally he retreated to his kitchen and the woman arranged her cardigan around her shoulders, collected a black tote bag from the floor and stood up to go. '*Ciao, bella.*'

'*Ciao*. Good to see you,' Briony mumbled, still wondering what the conversation with Signor Marco had been about, and she watched Mariella call goodbye to him and wander out into the sunlight.

There was something puzzling going on here, she reflected. Mariella, her slender frame bowed, walked slowly, deep in thought. Suddenly she paused, turned and stared back up at the café, a watchful expression on her face. Then she seemed to come to a decision, for with purposeful stride, she crossed the road and set off along a narrow footpath that vanished up the hill behind the village shop opposite. Briony stared after her, feeling considerably disturbed by the whole encounter. Had she unintentionally touched upon some secret trouble?

Three

The following morning Mike announced an outing to a nearby vineyard. Briony immediately elected to stay behind. 'I'm feeling a bit tired,' she lied. 'You all go. I'll do some shopping and book us a table for tonight.' They were going to try a restaurant in the next village, which Aruna had found recommended in the visitors' book.

'Are you sure you're OK?' Aruna asked, her face worried. Since Briony had returned from her evening escape the atmosphere in the house had been subdued and everyone except Luke had been giving her wary glances, which she hated.

'I'm absolutely fine,' she said, trying her best to appear cheerful. 'Really. I'm just not sleeping that well. It's the heat.' This was true, but so was the fact that she felt embarrassed by their concern and simply yearned for her own company.

Aruna nodded, but she didn't look convinced.

After she had waved them off, Briony made the restaurant reservation then walked down the hill and bought a few supplies at the local shop, which she lugged back to put away in the kitchen. Then she made a pot of gorgeously scented coffee.

Settling herself on a sunbed by the pool, she picked up a novel she'd bought at the airport. The pleasure of being by herself, with the thought of olive bread, soft cheese and fruit in the kitchen awaiting her, was immense. Then she heard the sound of a vehicle stopping outside in the lane. Surely they weren't back already.

There was a hammering on the front door. Surprised, Briony opened it to find an overgrown youth of about eighteen standing in the porch. At his feet lay a big cardboard box. He'd left his car with the engine turning and its ugly chugging annoyed her.

'*Buongiorno*. For you,' he said in heavily accented English, indicating the box.

Briony glared at it with suspicion. It was grimy and bore a picture of a food mixer on its side.

'For you,' he repeated, his huge, dark-lashed eyes pleading. 'My mama give.'

'Sorry? *Non capisco*.'

The boy waved his arms in frustration, then spun on his heel, pushing his hand through his thick black hair as he searched for words. He turned to face her again and tried a charming lopsided grin.

'For you to see,' he said. 'Like TV. Thank you.'

She studied him for a second, then hunkered down and pulled up the flaps on the box. Inside was a machine of some sort, though not a food mixer. An old film projector, she realized, and a couple of round shallow tins – old-fashioned film canisters. 'I don't think this can be for me,' she said, miming 'no' with palms raised.

'*Si, si*,' he insisted. 'Mama, she, she . . .' He rubbed the air vigorously as though with a cloth on a window.

'Cleaning? Oh, your mother is Mariella?'

'*Si*, cleaner. Very good. This for you. I go now. *Arrivederci*, *signorina.'* And he set off down the garden, stopping only to wave one last time.

'What is it for?' Briony called, too late. She watched him jump into his car, execute a hurried three-point turn and accelerate away with a screech of grinding metal, leaving a cartoon cloud of dust.

Briony wriggled her bare toes, her arms folded, and stared down at the box. Why on earth had their cleaner sent them an old film projector? She sighed. Whatever the answer, she couldn't leave it on the doorstep. She dragged the box into the kitchen where there was enough light to inspect the contents. She picked out one of the canisters. The slim round tin was so tightly closed that it took a few goes with a coin from her purse to prise it open.

She was no expert, but the film inside appeared to be in usable condition. She found the end of the tape, unwound a long strip and held it up to the light, examining the place where the photographic film began, but could discern no identifiable image. She thought for a moment, then wound it up and returned it to its case.

The presence of the box on the floor troubled her as she sat on a stool to eat her bread and cheese, hardly noticing the taste she'd so looked forward to. It occurred to her eventually that there might be an explanatory note with the gift. She hefted the machine up onto the table. The second tin contained only an empty reel. There was nothing else in the box nor anything written on the side. If only she had some idea of how to operate the wretched machine. Usually a technician would set film up for her if she needed it during research.

She was still puzzling over it when, in the early afternoon, the others returned from their expedition, hot, bothered and, in Zara's case, much the worse for the wine-tasting. 'She drank it instead of spitting it out,' Aruna whispered, as they watched Zara haul herself upstairs to lie down.

Mike, carrying a box of clinking bottles into the kitchen, noticed the projector at once. 'Hello, where did that come from?' He set down the case next to it and picked up the canisters. He was breathing heavily and his fleshy face dripped with perspiration underneath his short thinning hair, but his eyes brightened as he examined the machine.

'The cleaner's son brought it over, I've no idea why.'

'I might just be able to get this baby going,' Mike murmured as he fitted the empty reel onto a sprocket. 'My dad had one. He used to show us Charlie Chaplin films at Christmas. It was brilliant when he made them go backwards.'

'Ladies and gentlebums,' Mike's deep voice boomed out of the shuttered darkness of the sitting room late that evening after they'd returned from the restaurant. 'With any luck the show will now begin.'

The white bed sheet Luke had rigged up as a screen caught a sudden square of winking yellow light that leaped from the projector.

'There's a spider on the sheet!'

'Don't be a wuss, Zara,' Mike sighed.

'Come on, little guy. It's not your turn for the limelight.' Luke nudged it to safety.

The machine's whirring loudened as the sprockets began to turn. A series of grainy black panels flickered over the sheet and then came a quivery black and white image. It took a moment for Briony to make it out. 'A plane.' It was tiny, flying smoothly in a cloudless sky, then suddenly it began to emit flames and black smoke and dipped and weaved, coming in and out of focus as the camera swooped to follow it. There were gasps from everyone in the room.

'Any sound there, Mike?' Aruna said urgently.

'Can't get any.'

The plane dropped silently behind a hill and everyone groaned.

'Ah,' Mike said as the image changed. A panorama shot of a large, untidy garden, a couple of parked trucks.

'Army, or something?' said Luke.

'There are no markings, but could they be British?' Briony moved to a better vantage point, trying to see the details more sharply. Two men in uniform were unloading boxes from one of the vehicles, then there was a close-up shot of the soldiers' faces, grinning for the camera. One made a V for Victory sign and his lips moved. 'Definitely British,' Briony muttered, seeing a badge on a sleeve.

There was a whitish building of some sort in the background. Briony hoped the shot would pan out so she could see what it was, but instead it hovered over the boxes, then swooped round to show a small group of men sitting on crates playing cards and smoking. One made a monkey face, another waved, but a third hid his face with his arm. The camera zoomed in on the cards in his hand and then there must have been a scuffle after that because the picture spun chaotically towards the sky, and then there was a sudden glimpse of the white building again as it was righted. Window shutters, a pantiled roof.

'A villa,' Luke said quietly. 'British soldiers at a villa here during the war.'

'Seems like it,' Briony agreed. The screen went dark then brightened again. This time the picture appeared to be a peaceful scene across a valley with all its terraces and groves of trees. 'It's our valley!' Then she breathed in sharply. 'Oh no.'

'The bridge!' They all spoke at once as they pointed out landmarks and noticed with dismay the wartime damage. A bomb crater; terraces ravaged by vehicle tracks; the shell of a burned-out house, charred rafters swaying in the wind; finally a shot of an overturned tank. A scrap of a boy with a rapturous smile stood balanced on the black cross on its side, one raised arm punching the air.

And then, 'Those gates,' Briony cried out, when the picture changed again. 'Luke, it's the place I came across the other evening.'

It made sense suddenly. 'I was asking Mariella about the villa I saw up the hill,' she explained. 'Where I walked before Luke found me. That must be why she's given us the film. But,' she wondered, 'where did she get it from?'

'Sshh, there's more,' Luke said.

They found themselves staring at two men in khakis weeding a patch of earth studded with tender little plants.

'Potatoes!' he pronounced knowledgeably.

'Tatties, eh? Ooh ah!' Mike's teasing voice.

The camera zoomed in on one of the hoes working briskly between the plants and a hand reaching down to yank out a weed, then moved upwards. The man's open jacket revealed a vest stretched over a tanned, muscled chest. His head was lowered as he concentrated on his work, and his arms glistened with sweat. As though noticing the camera for the first time, he looked up and straight at the lens, pushed his cap back and wiped his forehead with his arm. Short, springy dark hair grew above a high forehead and laughing eyes in a narrow, tanned face.

Surprise raced through Briony's whole body.

She knew that face, those eyes.

There came a loud ripping sound, the picture flew away in a rag of ribbon and the screen glared yellow once more.

'That's it, folks,' Mike said, switching on the lights. 'Can't see what the fuss is all about, personally.'

There were general murmurs of bewilderment. Why had Mariella given Briony this film? 'It was of round here,' Aruna said, 'so perhaps she thought we'd be interested. Hey, Briony, are you OK?'

Briony blinked and realized that everyone was staring at her. 'Sorry,' she said, then after a moment, 'I wonder if Mariella meant it for all of us, or maybe ... well, I don't know. Listen, guys ... Mike, sorry to be a pain, but I need to see it again.'

There were groans, but she didn't care. She had to. She knew without doubt that the film had been for her and her alone.

The soldier's face was as familiar to her as her own.

'He was exactly like my brother. I didn't mean it was Will, of course,' Briony told Luke and Aruna, 'it would have been my grandfather. Mum always said Will took after him.'

It was later in the evening and she had stepped out to join the others in the gloom of the vine-canopied patio, hesitant until they welcomed her. Astringent smoke from a candle on the low table filled the warm air, its flickering flame throwing restless shadows up the leafy wall and reflecting off beakers of the ruby wine they'd bought at the vineyard. With Mike's help she had watched the film again, making him slow it right down when they reached the shots of the man who looked like her brother.

'I did see what you mean about him being vaguely like Will, though the clip was so grainy. Do you know for definite your grandfather was here during the war?' Aruna asked.

'According to Dad he was in this part of Italy.'

Aruna looked sceptical. 'It would be an amazing coincidence if it was him, Briony. I mean, those men all looked alike, especially in khaki with those savage haircuts.'

'Mmm.' She wouldn't let Aruna sway her. The man's eyes had looked out across the years into her own in a way that had tugged at her heart. She had only been ten when Grandpa Andrews died and could not remember him clearly, but she'd seen pictures. She was possessed by the desire to know if this man was him.

The obvious thing would be to ask Mariella, but she wasn't due for a day or two and Briony couldn't wait. In the morning she'd find out where she lived and visit her.

After Aruna and Luke had retired to bed she sat alone for a while in the candlelight watching the shimmering reflection of stars on the tranquil surface of the pool and thinking. Grace, her counsellor, had encouraged her to talk about her mother, and in the course of these conversations Briony had come to understand the true extent of her loss. With her mother's death she had lost that entire side of her family. Maybe, just maybe, she'd been handed a chance to recover something.

Four

It was to a modest farmstead that Signor Marco at the café directed Briony the next morning, on the side of the hill directly above the village, the path a slog to climb in the heat. Behind the yard gate, a heavy muscular dog of uncertain breed and doubtful friendliness broke into deep barks at her approach, but at a sharp command from Mariella it slunk back to its kennel.

Mariella invited Briony through into a cool, tile-floored kitchen where she was glad to sit at a wooden table and sip water. Of the boy who had given her the projector and the mysterious cine film there was no sign.

Mariella continued with her tasks, tidying freshly ironed laundry into a basket with deft movements. The back door stood open to a view of the terraced hillside and from the yard came the contented *chook chook* of chickens scratching for food. It was an idyllic place, and yet there was a tension in the room. Briony felt it in the way the woman watched her as she folded towels. It was as though she was weighing her up.

'I wanted to say thank you,' Briony began, meeting her eye. 'For the projector.' She mimed rolling film, like in a game of Charades.

'*Prego.*' The woman nodded. 'You ... watch it?' She sank onto the kitchen chair opposite, clutching a pillowcase against her chest.

'Yes. It's the Villa Teresa, isn't it?'

'*Si, si.* In the war.'

Briony leaned forward. 'Mariella, why did you want me to see it?'

Mariella shrugged in surprise. 'Why? You are historian. You find out maybe, the people? Who they are?'

'They're British soldiers, definitely.'

'*Si*, but their names, who they are. You can find out.' Mariella appeared so eager, but why, why?

'This is obviously important to you, Mariella. Where did the film come from?'

That wariness again. 'Somebody give it to me,' she mumbled. She would not meet Briony's gaze.

Briony, puzzled, tried once more. 'Who?' she asked gently. 'And why?' but the questions silenced Mariella altogether. She held the pillowcase tightly, her face as expressionless as a smooth brown nut.

'May I?' Briony murmured, getting up to fill her glass from the tap. The drops of cold water splashing on her skin steadied her. She tried again. 'Mariella, where did the film come from?'

'The Villa Teresa,' Mariella said finally. She laid the pillowcase on the table and neatened the folds. 'My father find it there long time ago. When he was a boy.' Now she'd decided to speak her words came out in a rush. 'He die last year and these things he leave. I don't know what to do with them.'

'What things?' Briony felt a prickle of interest. She couldn't forget the face of that soldier in the film, weary, but cheerful, despite all that he must be going through. She remembered her grandfather had been like that, a steady man who been happy to live for the present and rarely spoke of the past or the future.

'I will show you.' Mariella left the kitchen and Briony heard her light tread on the stairs. After a couple of minutes she returned with a rectangular tin like an old-fashioned sandwich box. She flipped open the lid and took out a fat folded manila envelope that was soft and furry with age. She handed it to Briony, who turned the package over hopefully, but nothing was written on the front. She looked to Mariella for guidance.

'Open,' Mariella invited.

Briony untucked the worn flap, peeped inside and carefully withdrew a thick pile of old letters tied together with a length of frayed blue ribbon. Mariella sat down again, folded her arms and watched her with an expectant air.

The knot would not undo and it took Briony a while to ease the ribbon off the bundle. The envelope on the top was crumpled, as though someone had once forced it out, examined it and tucked it back under the ribbon again without much care. The ribbon suddenly split and the letters flew out over the table, twenty or thirty of them, maybe more. She herded them together, hoping the order was right, picked one up off the top and studied it, then another.

The letters were all addressed to a Private Paul Hartmann in the same educated English hand; elegant italic, a woman's probably. Briony studied the addresses but they'd mostly been sent via the British Forces Post Office, so she couldn't tell where Hartmann had been when he received them. Some envelopes were scrawled over in blue crayon, clearly forwarded from place to place. There were several letters without envelopes, including one that must have been folded and refolded so many times it was falling apart. She put that down and selected another. Wafer-thin paper crackled in her hand. The writing on it was fairly easy to make out. *Flint Cottage*, the writer had headed the page. *1st September 1940.*

'Read it,' Mariella bade her, so she read it aloud in halting tones, sometimes having to go back to convey the sense properly. *Dear Paul*, it began.

I promised to write to you again very soon and apologize that this is the first opportunity that I've had, I've been so busy with the garden. We're picking soft fruit, do you remember all those raspberries we planted at Flint Cottage? Well, there's a good crop, mercifully, and Mrs Allman and I have been kept busy with pies and bottling for weeks, what with damsons, now the pears and the blackberries, and the Bramleys not far behind. It's a nuisance that there's so little sugar to be had.

Now I'm rambling and I haven't asked you how you are. Did the last parcel from your mother arrive, with the soap and the blue jersey? I'm glad you're not near London at present, given the news. If you do get moved let us know, won't you. We think about you a great deal and try to imagine what you're doing. You're keeping your spirits up, I hope?

Diane is in Dundee still and we hear from her occasionally. Mummy is taking First Aid classes along with Mrs Richards! We are all keeping bright considering. Your mother is well and seems to like the library books I choose for her. We miss you like anything at Westbury Hall. All is well there, though we've hardly seen a blink of the Kellings. Ma and Pa, I mean. Diane's seen Robyn in Dundee. I will try to write again soon.

Yours,
Sarah

It was a well-judged letter, warm and deliberately cheerful, but a little distant, Briony thought when she'd finished. A letter between friends. September 1940. The Allies hadn't arrived in

Italy until 1943, of course, so Hartmann must have received it when he was elsewhere. It struck her that this meant he might have carried it around with him for several years. It must have been special to him.

Briony looked up to see Mariella's eyes upon her, calm dark pools, but with a touch of trouble. 'Please take them,' Mariella said. 'Maybe you find her family and give them.'

'Maybe.' Briony frowned. 'I wonder who Paul Hartmann was.' There was something about the voice of the letter she'd read, its vitality, and the lightness of the handwriting, that stirred her interest. She could almost imagine the writer sitting by a window with a view of an autumn garden, the air smelling of bonfire smoke, as her hand flew over the page.

'Please.' Mariella was pleading. 'The film, these letters, they do not belong to us. You take them.'

'But Mariella, if your father took them from the villa without permission, perhaps I shouldn't have them. They don't belong to either of us.'

To Briony's surprise, Mariella drew herself up proudly, her dark eyes glinting. There was no sign of anxiety now in the stern line of her mouth, the firmness of her hands clutching the table edge. 'Some people say he steal them, but I tell you the Villa Teresa belongs to my family,' she said.

'Oh,' Briony said in surprise.

'What happened in the war was important to my father. The young people, they say it was so long ago. What does anyone care now?'

'I care,' Briony said quietly.

'Yes, so I tell you a little. The Villa Teresa belonged to the father of my grandfather, you understand?'

'Your great-grandfather.'

'Yes. But he die in the war and then my grandfather and the

cousin of my grandfather both say the villa belongs to them. So, for many years they fight about it, until there is no more money to pay *l'avvocato.*'

'The lawyer?'

'*Si*. And then my grandfather die, some say of sadness. For many years, we do not know what will happen.'

'But no one lives there now?'

'No. The villa is falling down. No good.' Mariella smoothed her hair and sighed. Then with the same quick movements that she used to fold linen, she straightened the pile of letters, pushed them back into the big envelope and shut them in the tin. 'Take, take,' she said, pushing the tin towards Briony.

It was apparently impossible to refuse and part of Briony didn't want to. Whoever Sarah, the letter-writer, turned out to be – an acquaintance of her grandfather or otherwise – Briony was curious.

'I can try to find her family, I suppose. If not, maybe I should give them to an archive? Museum,' she explained hastily, seeing Mariella frown.

'Yes, museum.'

She took the box. When she thanked Mariella, she was surprised when the woman embraced her warmly. Only as she made her way down the hillside did it occur to her that Mariella had not properly answered her questions, but instead raised new ones.

'So the Villa Teresa was occupied by Allied troops during the invasion of Italy, but when the time came to give it back to its owners, Mariella's great-grandfather had died and the family argued about who should inherit it,' Briony explained to Luke and Aruna later that afternoon. She was sitting at the pool's edge, her stripy sundress drawn up over her knees, swirling her feet in the water. 'And the case has lain unresolved for years and years, the old people are all dead and no one knows what's happening.' The dolphin mosaic on the bottom of the pool wriggled and bucked.

'The bureaucracy. Unbelievable!' Luke's teeth flashed in a sardonic grin. 'It could only happen here.' He was sitting on a sunlounger, a paperback splayed face down on his stomach. His body had already turned a pale gold in the sun.

'That still doesn't explain why Mariella gave us the film.' Aruna, in her white bikini, gleamed darker than ever. She was sitting awkwardly on the sunbed next to Luke's, examining a nasty blister on the side of her foot. 'Damn these shoes,' she muttered, wriggling her toes. 'Bri, chuck me the suncream, will you?'

'It's not fair,' Briony grumbled, obliging. 'All I get is this boiled lobster look.'

'You are a delicate English rose,' Aruna agreed with a grin. Her sparkling nose jewel brought out the brilliance of her sharp brown eyes and a coiled snake tattoo on her ankle emphasized the delicacy of her bone structure.

Briony smiled back with fondness. Aruna was so slender and perfect it was no surprise that everyone fell for her. Luke was a case in point. Briony had been with Aruna when the couple had first met and she still remembered the besotted expression on his face the instant he set eyes on her friend.

'You're both gorgeous,' Luke sighed. 'Now go on with the story, Briony.'

'Mariella's family think of the villa as theirs and her father had taken the film and the letters away without asking anyone and she didn't know what else to do with them.'

'It all sounds a bit odd to me,' Aruna said, arranging her towel on the sunbed. 'So you've got some film of your grandfather and a few old letters and she's got the stuff off her conscience.' She reached for her Ray-Bans and lay down to cream her stomach.

Luke sat up, peering at Briony over his sunglasses. 'Do we know anything about this woman who sent the letters? You said her name was Sarah.'

'I've only read a couple, so no. She lived in Norfolk, I think, somewhere called Westbury.'

'You know Norfolk, Luke,' Aruna murmured sleepily.

'I don't. It's my parents who have moved there, not me. We can certainly look Westbury up on the internet next time we get a signal. I'll tell you what, though.' Luke took off his glasses and fixed Briony with narrowed eyes. 'The villa. How about a spot of trespassing when it's cooler?'

'That's a great idea.'

'Aruna?'

'If it isn't too much of a slog,' Aruna groaned.

'Try wearing some proper shoes for a change,' Luke's voice was gentle.

'Oh shut up,' she murmured.

'Should we ask the others?' Briony said tentatively.

'They don't like walking, haven't you noticed?' Aruna said with a laugh. She rolled over. 'Here, will you put some cream on my back, Luke? Pretty please?'

Five

Mike and Zara didn't want a walk, so towards evening it was only the three of them who set out. The light breeze in the lane brought the trees to life and in their shadow the air was deliciously cool. They were hot and tired, though, once they'd scaled the hillside and reached the rutted lane that led to the villa. Worse, despite her better shoes, Aruna was hobbling from her blister. She sank down on the grass verge to inspect it and Briony observed the tenderness with which Luke crouched to wipe the dust from her heel and stick on a plaster he took from his pocket.

'You carry them around with you!' Briony was impressed.

He held out his hands to show old scratches and scars. 'Occupational hazard,' he said, 'even with gloves.'

Luke ran his own business in South London, designing and planting city gardens. Briony still teased Aruna about the way they'd first met. 'Your knight in faded denim,' she'd say with a chuckle. 'Rescuing the beautiful maiden's moggy.'

Purrkins, Aruna's beloved blue Burmese, was supposed to be an indoor cat, but sometimes made a break for it. On this

occasion he'd been missing for two days and Briony was helping
search for him. Luke's van was parked outside a house three
doors down and Briony nipped along to ask if he'd seen a big,
fluffy, blue-eyed cat. He hadn't, but he'd heard mewing from
the house next door where someone said the inhabitants were
away. Purrkins, it turned out, had become stuck behind a one-
way cat flap. Luke simply clambered over the garden fence and
let him out. Aruna was so grateful that she immediately asked
him to join them for supper. Briony, seeing which way things
were going, murmured an excuse.

She liked Luke more than most of Aruna's previous boy-
friends, who had tended to be either stylish media types who
ran a mile after meeting Aruna's very traditional parents, or,
during phases when Aruna was trying to please her mother and
father, conventional professional men with whom she quickly
grew bored.

At first Briony imagined that given her own world of books
and ideas she and Luke would have little in common except
Aruna, but not a bit of it. Luke was well read. He simply came
at everything from a different angle, which was refreshing. And
he was so easy to talk to that the three of them got on famously.
Still, sometimes she felt a bit of a gooseberry.

Aruna slipped on her shoe again and stood up. 'Come on,
let's go find this place,' she snapped. It was clear she was still
in discomfort. Luke put his arm round her slim waist to help
her along.

When they reached the old gates, Luke was as charmed as a
boy by the overgrown garden. 'Did you find a way in?' he asked
Briony as he peered between the rusted palings.

'No, I didn't like to try,' she said, but Luke was already off
exploring. In one direction the wall skirted the edge of a deep
drop, so she followed him to the left where it disappeared into

a tangle of trees. These initially defeated their attempts to break through, then Briony found a place where she could duck inside and squeeze along a path winding between tree trunks until it reached a crumbling section of the wall. Propped up there she saw the remains of an old ladder.

'Hey, over here!' she called, and after some crashing around Luke emerged from the greenery.

'Aruna's sitting this one out,' he said, brushing twigs from his hair. 'Blimey, who's been here then?'

'No idea. Is she OK?'

'Think so, just wants a rest. You're lighter, do you want to go first? I'll hold the ladder.'

Briony tested each rung before putting her weight on it, then scrambled onto the wall and looked down the other side.

'More jungle,' she called back. 'Oh, and a ladder down.' The top rung of this one was sound, but the next snapped and with a cry she half slipped, half tumbled the rest of the way, scraping her hands, before landing in a bush.

'Briony?' Luke's voice was muffled.

'Still alive, just!' She inspected her palms and was picking out the splinters when Luke lowered himself safely beside her.

'Let's see,' he commanded.

'No, I'm fine, honestly.'

'If you're sure,' he said, looking about. He helped her up, then began to move away through the green light under the trees. She tagged along, thinking how extraordinary it was, like swimming through a submarine forest. She could even hear running water.

'Hey,' came Luke's voice ahead. 'Come and see.'

She found him investigating a narrow channel where silvery water gushed over pebbles. Sinking down, she plunged her smarting hands into the ice-cold flow with a sigh of pleasure.

'It's come out of the rock somewhere,' he muttered, craning
to see, but the foliage was too dense.

She rose, shaking her hands dry. 'Come on. The house'll be
this way.' She stepped over the stream and pushed on through
the branches until suddenly she came up against the wall of an
outhouse. Like a tomb, darkness leaped from its gaping doorway, and she recoiled from a foul stink of decay. Her feet found
an old path, which passed a tumbledown shed held together
with ivy, its rotted roof bright with moss. Her trainer kicked
against something hard that clanked and she paused to discover a rusted engine. Left perhaps by the British soldiers, she
thought, her pulse quickening, then, 'Eeurgh,' she said.

'What?' Luke was close behind.

'Got oil on my shoe. Oh, what's this?'

A stubby tree trunk fallen sideways turned out to be an old
fountain. Briony ripped at the greenery and revealed a cherubic
face with a hole instead of a mouth. Luke peeled off more ivy
and exposed a stone wing.

'One of the four winds, don't you think? Hey,' he glanced
about, 'maybe this whole area . . . Yes, look at that wall. This was
once a pool with the fountain in the middle. And a tiled border
round it, and over there, pillars, like that one.'

'With a ball on top. How typically Italian.'

'So sad it's come to this.'

'Do you suppose it happened in the war?' Briony wondered.

'Dunno. Could be the years of neglect.'

Quietly they surveyed the ruined glory around them before
stumbling on.

Then, suddenly, the mass of the house loomed up before
them. They were on a ruined concourse in front of the elegant villa familiar to them from the filmstrip, but the change
wrought by time was terrible. Its shutters were hanging off, its

broken windows stood open to the weather, the white-painted frontage was blistered and crumbling. There were signs of past beauty, though, in the graceful lines of the roof and the rusted iron latticework of the upstairs balconies.

Briony said, 'I feel bad that Aruna's missing this.'

'Me, too, but let's look inside now we've got here.'

They picked their way across a mess of shattered roof tiles and flakes of plaster to peer in through a window like a gaping mouth. The spacious room beyond was full of rubbish, broken chairs, twisted pieces of machinery, rotten beams, all thickly coated with dirt. The walls were blotched with damp and fungus, but on the far one was fixed a noticeboard still bearing a few scraps of paper. Bleached of whatever had been printed on them, Briony guessed; it was difficult to tell at this distance. She felt a low thrum of excitement seeing this sign of army occupation. Grandpa had been here. The idea was extraordinary.

A thought occurred to her. 'The place can't have been like this when Mariella's dad found the film reels. They'd have been ruined.'

'I expect he took them quite soon after the army left. Come on, let's look for a way in.'

Initially they had no luck. The main doors had rotted in their frames and would not shift, despite Luke's attempts, but on rounding the right-hand side of the house they found a narrow entrance, with what must once have been a door, lying warped amid the debris inside.

They peered into the gloom. 'Scullery, do you think?' Luke said. A huge stone sink stood under the back window. Daylight glowed from a doorway opposite that must lead further into the house.

'Is it safe to go in?' Briony's voice echoed.

'Probably not.' Their eyes met. He shrugged.

She stepped inside, brushing past cobwebs as she meandered round the cool, dark room then through the far doorway into a bright kitchen with a rusted range and an old bread oven. Sunshine falling through latticed panes patched the tiled floor. It would have become hot in here, she thought, but the scents of baking and delicious sauces must have been wonderful, and from the windows there would have been a view of fruit trees and terracotta pots of herbs ... She was so caught up in this vision she didn't notice where she was going. Her knee bumped against an ancient cupboard. Its door flew open and she screamed as a family of rodents shot out.

'Briony?'

'It's OK,' she gasped as Luke's alarmed face appeared. 'Mice!' He rolled his eyes.

'It was the shock,' she said crossly. 'Oh, that's pretty.' He was holding a patterned teacup.

'It's such a shame, isn't it?' he said, placing the cup on the range and looking about dolefully. 'This place must once have been idyllic. A garden villa up in the hills. What do you think – Mariella's family's summer residence?'

'Rather than a farmhouse? She didn't explain.'

A long time ago, people had been happy living here. It had that atmosphere. She'd felt it a moment ago, but when she glanced at the window now, she saw it was cracked and filthy and that where she'd dreamed herbs and fruit trees was actually tangled jungle which almost reached the house. Something that could be the remains of an old truck lay just visible under a blanket of creeper. She shivered, imagining how the soldiers might have treated the place, wondering what brutal things had happened here.

'Briony?' She jumped. Luke's muffled voice came from

further into the house. She turned to see that he'd opened another door. She followed and found herself in the front hall, where bits of wooden banister hung down from a ruined staircase. 'Hey.' Luke's figure filled the doorway to a room at the front. 'You must see this.'

It was the room with the noticeboard that they'd glimpsed from outside. The clatter of wings announced a fleeing pigeon. It cocked its head at them from a high beam. Broken tiles crunched under their feet and patches of bare earth were slippery with damp and bird droppings.

The flakes of paper on the rotted board were held to it only by rust or habit. 'A map once, I think,' she murmured, seeing the ghost of a pattern, and for a moment was aware of Luke's presence close by, the warm, salty scent of him.

'What were they doing here?' Luke was murmuring, gazing round the room. 'These soldiers, in the middle of nowhere?'

'The Allies invaded mainland Italy in September 1943,' she told him. 'This would have been roughly on the route north after Naples.'

'But why would they have come up here to this villa?'

'I don't know. Maybe it was a good lookout place before all the trees grew up. You would be able to see down to Tuana.' It was then they both heard a distant humming. 'Hey, is that a car?'

They listened. 'It's some way away,' Luke said. 'Whatever, we ought to go and rescue poor Aruna.'

Briony nodded.

He took one more glance about, then as he turned, his foot slid on a tile, which struck something that clinked. He prodded at a lump of mortar with his toe, then bent and picked out a small, oblong tin that had been hidden underneath. It was light in weight and rusted shut, but when Briony shook it gently, she heard a rustle from inside.

'Let's take it with us,' he said.

'Do you think we ought?'

'Yeah. Come on. I'm worried about that car.'

But by the time they'd left the house the engine noise was fading.

When they reached the lane beyond the gates, there was Aruna sitting on the rock exactly where they'd left her, her pointed face furious.

'You've been nearly an hour. What the hell have you been up to?'

'It wasn't that long, Ru. How's your blister?' Luke murmured, stooping to see, but she drew her foot away in a sharp, rude movement. He looked dismayed.

'We're sorry,' Briony cut in, trying to help. 'It's my fault, I kept wanting to see more. It's an amazing place, I wish you'd come. The gardens must once have been beautiful. And the house ...'

Her friend shrugged without speaking. Luke stood up slowly and folded his arms, contemplating Aruna, one eyebrow cocked.

'And what's that?' Aruna said finally, nodding towards the tin in Briony's hand.

'Just something we found.'

'What's in it?'

'Have you got a key?' Luke asked. Aruna had and the women watched him work away at the lid of the tin. Eventually, he levered up one corner, bent it back and squinted inside. 'Here,' he said, passing it to Briony, who took it from him. She tipped a heap of dry, tawny shavings out into her palm, rubbed and sniffed its faint remaining pungence.

'Tobacco, is that all?' Aruna said, disgusted.

Briony didn't answer. She knew that dusty fragrance. It brought her grandfather instantly to mind, his voice soft and husky like hers, the feel of his big hand in her child-sized one. The memory was so strong that for a moment she was overtaken by grief and longing.

She stared at the dust in her hand. The film, the letters, the scent of her grandfather's pipe. Everything was drawing her back in time. What had her grandfather been doing here in wartime Italy? Who were Paul and Sarah? What had once happened in this remote valley?

Six

Briony hoped the trip into Tuana would answer some of her questions. Again, it was just the three of them, she, Luke and Aruna, and they'd come because Luke had cracked a tooth on an olive stone, but had managed to get an emergency appointment with a dentist in the town. The sun was high in the sky by the time they dropped Luke, so after buying some supplies and poking about in a gift shop, Briony and Aruna had fallen gratefully into chairs at a pavement café with an aspect across the main square. Icy lemonade revived them, though not to the extent of encouraging anything energetic.

'Is the church open? The guidebook said there are wall paintings.' Briony counted coins onto the table and nodded towards the sand-coloured Romanesque hulk that dominated the small paved square.

'I'm too hot to even stand.' With sunglasses, carmine lips and a gauzy scarf over her hair, Aruna looked like a film star travelling incognito and was drawing curious stares.

'It'll be cool inside,' Briony coaxed. 'And we have to see a bit of the town or there's no point us all having come.'

'Do we? That's a difference between you and me. I'd be quite happy to collapse here till Luke's ready. Have you finished with this?' Without waiting for an answer she swallowed the last of Briony's lemonade and grinned lazily at her. They'd been friends for so many years that they knew each other intimately. They'd shared a student flat and later a house together in London before getting places of their own. Aruna had been generous, drawing Briony into her huge circle of friends. She could be lazy about housework and had always been a great borrower of everything from shampoo to books, less good about returning them. Still, Briony had never really minded.

'The church, come on, Aruna.'

'OK, you bully.' They collected up their bags and returned the waiter's flirtatious '*Ciao*' then drifted off across the square, Aruna still complaining about the heat.

It was open, and Briony was right. The shadowy interior of the building provided blissful relief from the fierce sun and she was surprised they were the only ones taking advantage of it. Aruna pulled off her scarf, pushed her sunglasses into her hair and dumped herself down on a chair in the nave from which to view her surroundings. Briony was more methodical, following the perimeter to study the statuary and the memorial slabs on the whitewashed walls. She came across the famed frescoes in a side chapel. They were a pair of simple scenes of saints standing amid flowers and trees, the colours still thrillingly bright after many centuries. She pondered the rapturous faces and tried to imagine how treasured the pictures must have been in their time by ordinary people, not for any financial value, but as visual aids to worship and prayer.

She was turning to go when a beautiful memorial slab on the wall near the altar lured her across. It was an oval of white marble etched with trails of gold-leaf flowers. The name on it was *Antonio Mei* and when she calculated the dates it touched her heart that he'd only been fifteen when he died. 1944, it had been.

She walked away with a feeling of melancholy and went to sit beside Aruna. 'Have you got the guidebook?' she whispered, her voice echoing in the space.

Aruna felt in her backpack. Briony flicked to the entry about the church and held the guide between them.

'I love the translation.'

'It's great,' Aruna said. 'This bit, for instance: *"A shell in 1943 destroyed part of the south aisle, but it has since been most happily restored."* Isn't that a lovely phrase?'

They glanced along the right side of the church, but there was indeed no sign now of the bomb damage. Briony drew the book towards her. Her eye had snagged on the name Antonio Mei. She read on, quickly. Fifteen-year-old Antonio had lied about his age and tried to join the army. Later, he'd been killed in an accident and his grieving family had raised the money for the memorial.

She was brooding on this tragic story when a sudden sound made her look up. An elderly priest had entered the church through a door near the altar. He nodded at the two women and set about preparations for a service, so, after a minute, they got up, thanked him and left.

Outside, they sat on the steps in the shadow of a tree, taking turns to sip from Briony's bottle of sparkling water. Briony studied the pictures in the guidebook. There was a town hall, apparently, but no mention of a museum.

'So, Briony,' Aruna interrupted. 'Are you being "most happily restored" by this holiday?'

A bolt of panic shot through her. She waited and it passed. 'In some ways, yes.' She gave a short laugh. 'It will take more than a couple of weeks to sort me out.'

Aruna surveyed her sternly and Briony, used to her friend trying to organize her life, rushed on. 'Sorry, I don't mean to sound rude. It's so lovely of you to have invited me here, but . . .'

'I know, it's all been a bit tense, hasn't it. Mike's a total ass. Why do girls as sweet as Zara end up with such men?'

'That's one of the world's eternal questions.'

'I bet you feel a right spare part.' She shot Briony a glance full of sympathy.

'Not really. You know me, Aruna, happy to wander off on my own. And Mike's not that bad.' He had been helpful over the film, at least. 'You and Luke have been brilliant. Really, Luke's been incredibly nice, given that he hardly knows me.'

'He likes you, Bri, so it's not difficult.'

Briony was pleased to hear this. 'You've picked a good one there!'

'I have, haven't I.' Aruna beamed at her and confided, 'I think he may be, you know, The One. I hope so, anyway. Even Mum and Dad like him and you remember how difficult they are to please.'

'I wondered if that was the way things were going!' Briony said. She felt happiness for her friend, but had to confess that a teeny part of her felt forlorn. Would this be how it would continue to be as she grew older, her remaining single friends pairing off?

Aruna touched her arm. 'Oh, Briony, I wish there was someone for you, I honestly do.'

'Don't worry. I don't. It's like my dear old dad says, if something's meant to happen . . .'

'You should make it happen. Give fate a nudge. What about that dating site Louisa swears by? She says it's brilliant.'

'Brilliant for Louisa, yes. She's tougher than me.' She tried not to sound sarcastic, but while their outgoing friend Louisa thrived on the excitement of meeting men she'd only previously talked to online, Briony was appalled at some of her stories. And the very idea of advertising herself in that horribly public way made her feel cold with horror. The possibilities for rejection seemed endless.

'Is there really no one at the college you like, Bri?'

She thought about it. There were several men who were the right age and, so far as she knew, single, but one was probably gay, and the only one she fancied of the others wasn't interested, she could tell. She shook her head and mumbled, 'Not really. And if it went wrong, I'd still have to go on working with them.'

'You're looking at the downside all the time. I think you should try online.'

Briony didn't have time to respond before Aruna's phone burst into a jaunty pop tune. Luke was calling to say his tooth was fixed and that he would meet them by the car in a few minutes.

'What will you do the rest of the summer?' Aruna murmured, as they set off. 'Some of us have to go straight back to work, of course, but you academics . . .'

'Same here, actually.' Briony sighed. 'I'm teaching on summer schools for two weeks – you know, for visiting students – and then I've got the rewrites of my book to do. The new publisher is brilliant, but, blimey, it's more difficult writing for a non-academic audience than I thought. My editor's come up with so many suggestions. Anyway, once I've tackled that, I might take a week or two off.'

'Sounds good. What will you do?'

'I don't know.' She paused. 'Actually I do. I'd really like to see what I can find out about Grandpa and what he was up to here. Maybe I'll try to trace the woman who wrote those letters.'

'Sarah, you mean?'

'Yes.' She'd given the matter some thought. It wasn't simply Sarah, it was the whole new vista of the past that fascinated her. There was the spell of the ruined villa and its garden, the grainy images on the film of the man she was sure was her grandfather, Mariella's story, all these were mixed up together somehow and she was curious about how and why.

'Great idea. And, Briony, I know we shouldn't be talking shop while we're on holiday, but I can't let a good chance go by. If there's some amazing story in it you will let me know? It's exactly the sort of programme I could interest the commissioning board in.'

'I suppose so.' Briony sighed. Once, before her horrible television experience, she'd have been pleased at Aruna's suggestion. She'd worked at the same college since doing her PhD there and had reached a plateau regarding promotion. She supposed her new publisher would expect more of the kind of media exposure that had been so disastrous for her. After her ordeal by Twitter the thought was terrifying.

When she mentioned her plans to Luke, sitting in the back of the car as he navigated the tight winding roads back to their holiday villa, she was touched when he said, 'You know you said Sarah lived in Westbury? Well, I googled it when I was waiting in the surgery. Westbury is not far at all from my parents in Norfolk. I'm sure if I asked nicely they'd have you to stay. They love having visitors. Dad misses London gossip.'

'I'll bear that in mind, Luke, thanks.' She'd rather be somewhere on her own than staying with strangers and having to be on time for meals, but it was sweet of him to offer. 'I can't go anywhere for a while, though. There's too much I need to do in London.'

This last bit was true, but she spoke wistfully. She could already feel the pull of the Norfolk past.

Seven

'I hope it's to your taste,' Briony said, handing over the brace of bottles she'd brought from Italy. 'It's the local stuff.'

'It looks very pukka to me,' her father replied, his eyes lighting up as he examined the labels. 'We like a good Italian red. Come on through. Lavender will be back from yoga in a few minutes.'

Briony's father, Martin, had spent all his life in the Surrey market town of Birchmere. This was where his parents had settled after the war. In the 1950s and 60s his father had taken the 7.30 train up to London every morning to his job at the Ministry of Defence, arriving home again in time for supper at six-thirty. In 1968, eighteen and ready to leave school, Martin replied to an advertisement in the *Birchmere Chronicle* for a trainee reporter. His eager demeanour and an excellent reference from his headmaster managed to deflect attention from his predicted unexceptional exam results and won him the job. Soon he was painstakingly typing up stories about stolen bicycles, lost dogs and petty vandalism. It was a year after his training finished that his breakthrough came. He happened to be studying the price of engagement rings in the window of the local jeweller's on the very afternoon that it was raided by a masked gang. His dramatic account of the hold-up and the gang's getaway made the front page and was syndicated several times, and after that he never looked back. That and the pay rise he received gave him the courage to propose to his girlfriend Jean, the woman who was to be Briony's mother. Martin remained loyal to the newspaper all his working life – until eventually it broke faith with him.

By 2006, when the brave little *Chronicle*, like many local newspapers, experienced declining circulation and was bought up by a national media conglomerate, he'd reached the dizzy heights of Managing Editor, in charge of the schedules. He loved this post, which gave him responsibility, but not too much, and when the new owners shed fifty per cent of the *Chronicle*'s workforce, the loss of his job nearly broke his heart. His second wife, Lavender, Briony's stepmother, was still a few years off retirement as a school secretary, so what with his pension there was enough money coming in and he discovered a new interest: photography.

Briony entered the living room of her childhood home with the usual mixed memories of pleasure and irritation. The house was a comfortable mock-Tudor semi, a few minutes' walk from the picturesque old town centre with its tree-edged pond and its market cross. When her mother had been alive it had been a cheerfully messy family home in which her brother's half-constructed model planes had battled for space with her mother's houseplants, stacks of her father's vinyl records and her own books and sheets of flute music.

Now it was tidy and dust-free, the records replaced by CDs neatly arranged in alphabetical order on the shelves and Lavender's tapestry cushion covers of cats adorning every chair.

Their real-life cat, an elderly tabby, lay stretched out on the sofa, its ears twitching as it hunted birds in its dreams. Briony smiled at it fondly as she placed her bag on her father's desk, and brushed accidentally against his computer mouse. The screen flickered into life at a photograph of a place she recognized.

It was a beautiful shot of what seemed more like a fairy pool with silver birch trees round it than the muddy town pond. She bent to examine it. 'Is that the mere?' she said, incredulous.

'Right first time.' Her father was a stocky man, his habitual pose being hands in pockets, chest out, conveying a sense of bonhomie. But now, at nearly seventy, he had a definite paunch, though his smiling blue eyes behind their spectacles still twinkled with boyish enjoyment

'It's not a documentary photograph, though, is it, Dad? The mere is OK, but not this pretty. You've touched it up, haven't you?'

'Maybe just a tad. It's art, Briony, that's what you have to remember. People can't bear too much reality these days.' He laughed. 'Now who said that?'

'T. S. Eliot, I think.. Well, you've certainly transformed it.' She'd have preferred the realistic version with all its associations of her childhood. Feeding the ducks with her mother; Jimmy Sanderson throwing her lunchbox in the water when she was twelve; both memories made her sad for different reasons.

'I'm starting to receive quite a few orders for this sort of thing,' her father continued with satisfaction. 'There's an art gallery opened up near the church that already sells my cards, and I reckon they'll take some framed enlargements if I play the manager right. Look.' He tapped the keyboard a couple of times and pictures of other local scenes slid across the screen. The mediaeval parish church, the Georgian high street, the oldest pub. All had been bathed in the same unnaturally warm light to give the impression of being olde-worlde.

'They're great, Dad,' she said and they grinned at one another. He had always been a glass half-full man, absorbing himself in each new interest as it came along, resilient, never dwelling on disappointment for very long. There were times, though, when that hadn't been helpful, but she dismissed the thought.

'Can I show you something of mine?' she asked. 'I was given it in Italy.'

She pulled up another chair, logged into an internet account and found the digital version of Mariella's filmstrip which a pal in the college archive had created for her. It took a couple of goes to open it on her father's curmudgeonly system, but then it worked. Together they watched the jerky clip of film begin and she felt quite emotional with him here beside her. How her father would react, she couldn't guess. It was very moving to see someone from your past on film, more so than simply a photograph because you were seeing them come to life, breathing, gesturing, maybe hearing their voice.

'Look,' she said, freezing the film. 'Watch this man here.' Her father took her place at the desk, adjusted his glasses and inspected the screen as she let the film move on.

She heard his sharp intake of breath. 'Well, I'm blowed,' he murmured, then, 'Play that bit again, can you?' She replayed the scene a couple of times, froze it again when the man's face was clearest, and her father sat back in his chair, staring. 'It's extraordinary,' he said finally, removing his spectacles, studying again that smiling face from so long ago.

'Do you think it's Grandpa Andrews, Dad?'

'It's definitely how I imagine he would have appeared at that age. And doesn't he look like Will? I did tell you Grandpa

Andrews said he'd been in Tuana. What is this building, did you say? And what about the other men, do we know who they are?'

'I don't, no. The place is the Villa Teresa, a mile or so from Tuana, up on the hillside.' She told him briefly about the ruined house and garden.

'Well, it must be him then. It's remarkable. He would have been there in forty-three or forty-four, I suppose; he never talked much about it. I asked him once if he would do an interview for the paper for an anniversary, but he wasn't keen, not keen at all, so I backed down.'

'Do you have anything belonging to him from the war, Dad? Photos or letters or anything?'

'I believe your granny threw away a lot of things after he died. Your mother was a bit upset, I remember. There may be a shoebox of stuff stashed away somewhere, but ... now is it on the wardrobe or in the loft? Surely you've seen it before, though?'

'I don't think you've ever mentioned it.'

'We'll have a look after lunch. Ah good, here's Lavender.'

Through the window they watched a car roll onto the drive and a petite, curvy, energetic woman with a dandelion puff of silvery-blonde hair climb out. She was wearing a tracksuit and manoeuvring a huge organizer bag. This, Briony knew, would be full of things pertaining to all the different aspects of her stepmother's busy life, from shopping lists for the elderly ladies she visited, to a pair of yoga socks, her latest book-club paperback and her phone, loaded with photographs of her grandchildren and step-grandchildren. Lavender waved and Briony was concerned to see her face was a little thinner. Perhaps it was simply that her stepmother hadn't put on make-up for yoga.

She came straight in and gave Briony a hug. 'How lovely to see you. I'll nip up and change, then we can have lunch. Martin, love, will you put the oven on at one-eighty?' Her voice trailed down as she climbed the stairs. 'And offer Briony some Prosecco. Just the elderflower for me.'

Martin went about his duties with every appearance of contentment. Briony followed him into the big sunny kitchen noticing all the new little touches since she'd last visited: a glass worktop protector with rabbits round the edge, a rubber-spiked doormat by the back door, a pretty china dish for the shepherd's pie that her dad fetched from the fridge.

She felt a wave of affection for Lavender, who loved to buy new things for the house. Briony and Will hadn't always felt warmly about her. After their mother's death their father had adopted the stiff-upper-lip approach to grief, leaving it to his own mother to manage his teenage children after school and during holidays. He had kept Jean's mother, Granny Andrews, at a distance, which probably hurt her deeply, though after her death he confessed to Briony that he hadn't been able to bear her terrible sadness in addition to their own. Briony's memories of her were fond. Granny was a calm, wise person with smiling eyes, but after losing her husband and her grown-up daughter in quick succession something seemed to break in her.

For years, Briony's father wouldn't consider the idea of dating again and then, when he did, the relationships didn't last long. It was therefore a shock to Briony and Will when, in their early twenties, Lavender walked confidently into their lives.

'Briony, there's someone I'd like you to meet.' Briony had almost dropped the phone in surprise at what followed: the revelation that her father was in love.

At least – probably prompted by Lavender – he had tactfully

arranged introductions to take place at a neutral venue, a carvery pub on the outskirts of Birchmere. She and Will had sat opposite the new couple and, as she took in Martin's fondness for Lavender, she'd felt overwhelmed by grief all over again. Their father couldn't keep his eyes, or indeed his hands, off this woman. Lavender had been slim back then, a lively, friendly, large-eyed woman who hardly stopped talking. After the meal they went back to the house for coffee and Briony found it painful to see Lavender fetching mugs, a tray, teaspoons, out of all the right cupboards as though she lived there already.

She was divorced from her husband, she told them. She showed them a snap of her daughter, a pretty girl of their own age in a nurse's uniform and with her mother's extraordinary wiry hair.

'I'm sure her ex couldn't get a word in edgeways,' Briony said cattily to Will later when he dropped her off at her student house in South London.

'Do you suppose Dad used to look at Mum like that?' Will wondered. 'It won't last, surely. It can't. She's not like Mum at all.'

'She's already put some of her clothes in Mum's wardrobe,' Briony warned. She'd retreated upstairs to shed a quiet tear and hadn't thought it at all shameful to spy. After all, to protect Dad she had to know what they were up against. Time passed, though, and it became clear that Lavender wasn't a manipulative gold-digger or an obsessive bunny-boiler. She was simply a thoroughly nice middle-aged woman who had fallen in love with a man as lonely as herself.

Now, years later, when Briony looked back, she blushed to think how selfish she and Will had been. They had their lives before them. Will was already going out with the girl who would become his wife. It had been mean of them to resent Dad finding happiness again. At the same time, their feelings had been understandable. She now knew from dealing with her students how self-absorbed and vulnerable twenty-year-olds could be. Dad finding someone new would naturally have brought back feelings of loss. She and Will had struggled with the belief that he was betraying their mother.

In time, as they loosened their ties with home, they came to appreciate Lavender, if not to love her. Briony was privately amused at her stepmother's enthusiasms and the way that she'd domesticated her father. Saucers for coffee mugs, boxes of fruit teas, magnets bearing coy little sayings clamping the grandkids' drawings to the fridge, all these were so unlike Martin Wood's previous environment that Briony was amazed at his acceptance of it.

As they ate their lunch at the sleek table in the glass extension that had transformed the gloomy old kitchen, Lavender asked about Briony's holiday and spoke with eagerness about their own forthcoming one – in a Greek island paradise with creative writing classes, outdoor yoga for her and photography for Martin.

'That sounds fun, Dad,' Briony said, catching her father's eye.

'I just do what I'm told these days,' Martin grumbled.

'Martin, you agreed it would be good for both of us!'

'If you're happy, I'm happy,' Briony's father said, beaming as he collected up the dirty plates, and Briony could see that he meant it. He was perfectly satisfied with his life. She felt a prickle of envy.

She glanced around the kitchen. There was nothing much of the past here. No photographs of her mother. Everything was new, from the knives and forks on the table to the landscaped garden beyond the French windows. Sadness and disappointment had been wiped from this house as though they had never been. She supposed she ought to admire her father and stepmother for this, but she couldn't quite. It felt as though her own past had been expunged, too.

Still, it was worth it to ask: 'Dad, about Grandpa's things.'

'Ah, yes. Lavender, where did you put Jean's father's bits and bobs?'

'The drawer under the bed in the guest room,' she said after a second's thought.

The guest room was actually Briony's old bedroom, though it had been redecorated twice since she left home, just as Will's room had been appropriated as Lavender's sewing room.

After the meal was over and the kitchen restored to a pristine state, Briony followed her father upstairs. She stared around at the flowery bower that her bedroom had become and wondered at the fact that she still slept in it occasionally without realizing that Grandpa's things had been underneath her all the time. She'd peeped in the drawer before, but had only seen spare duvets and pillows. Now when she pulled it out from the bed and pushed aside a duvet, she saw with a stab of tenderness that she'd missed hidden treasures: four framed photographs of her mother stacked neatly together, her parents' wedding album, a box with 'Jean's schoolbooks' written on it.

For a couple of years after their mother's death little that had been hers was removed from the house. It was Granny Andrews who had insisted on sorting through her clothes with the help of Jean's closest friend from school. Her few nice pieces of jewellery were put aside for Briony, though the pearl necklace and the gold dress watch were not the sort of things she'd wear. Instead she secreted away for herself the things that reminded her of her mum – a phial of Chanel No. 19, a lipstick, half spent, some of her favourite novels, a black velvet choker she'd worn on evenings out.

Because of a difficult housing market, Martin and Lavender, when they got together, decided not to move, and Lavender tactfully disposed of much else during the early years of their marriage. Occasionally her father had given Briony something of Jean's – a pretty majolica vase bought on holiday, a framed handbag mirror with shells stuck round it that she'd made for Mum at primary school. She'd grown mature enough to recognize that the house must properly become Lavender's, but she always felt there would be this wedge between her and her step-mother. Now, seeing these photographs of her mother buried away, and the box of papers, by rights hers and Will's – not that Will ever showed any interest in such things – made her feel the sharp edge of it digging in.

'Try in the corner there,' her father said over her shoulder and she moved the wedding album to reveal the corner of a green, lidded shoebox, pale with age. She pulled it out.

'I'll leave you to look at it on your own, shall I?' Her father smiled. 'You don't want me getting in the way.'

'You are never in the way, Dad,' she said, 'but thanks.'

Briony cradled the box and sat on the bed with it, eased off the rubber band that held it and lifted the lid. Inside was a jumble of photographs and news cuttings. There was a small flat blue box, too, which when she lifted it out proved to contain several medals. She laid it on the duvet and picked up a photograph from the top of the pile. It was a studio portrait of her grandfather as a young man of, what, thirty, good-looking with deep-set, laughing eyes, short dark hair smoothed back. Odd to think he'd be a hundred now if he had lived. She only had the haziest memories of him now; he'd died nearly thirty years ago.

A wedding photograph, just the two of them, Granny in a neat suit, though she carried flowers. Grandpa and Granny had met in London at the end of the war, so the story went. Her grandmother had shared her sandwich with him on a park bench and they'd got talking. A whirlwind romance that had lasted a lifetime, she dying broken-hearted a few years after her daughter. It was strange, Briony thought, looking at their young faces, Granny's radiant, Grandpa's proud, and remembering that she was already much older now than they'd been then.

From further down the pile she found herself holding a sepia-coloured postcard of camels and pyramids. She turned it over, but it was blank. Further into the box were several letters, and, at last, another photograph, this time of several soldiers lounging in front of an army truck. The building in the background she saw was none other than the Villa Teresa and her heart leaped. This was what she'd been searching for. She recognized one of the soldiers from the film footage – a tall, athletic, dark-haired lad with a serious expression. This time when she flipped it over, she was rewarded. *Ivor Richards, Harry Andrews, Paul Hartmann*, someone, possibly her grandfather, had scrawled in a triangle to match the position of the figures. The serious-faced young man must be the Paul Hartmann of the letters. She'd found him.

Riffling through the dry papers in the box, she came to a small whitish envelope on which was written only a name: *Sarah Bailey*, she read in surprise. What on earth was it doing here? She lifted the flap easily, withdrew a sheet of paper and pinched it open.

Sarah, she read. *Sorry for the rush, but Harry's promised to get this message to you. I'm back in Blighty and wondered if you'd received a letter I sent you a few days ago. I'm staying at the —. All my love, Paul.*

The name of wherever he was staying was smudged and illegible. But the word 'love', that intrigued her.

Why had Harry Andrews kept a letter that clearly wasn't his? Had he not been able to deliver it?

Eight

December 1938

Sarah kept a protective hand on the shoebox beside her as she stared out of the train window at the wintry Norfolk countryside. White-laced trees bordered fields where hazy sunshine dazzled off a cloak of snow. A flock of starlings swirled up like cinders into the sky, imbuing her spirits with a mixture of joy and melancholy. Joy because she was returning to the countryside she'd loved since a child, melancholy because the innocent happiness of those times was now lost to her. Her lips trembled at the reminder that her father would never see the English countryside again. She glanced at her mother, sitting opposite, but Mrs Bailey was not noticing the passing landscape, so absorbed was she in her book.

The train gave a long, mournful wail and began to slow as their station slid into view. Sarah nudged Diane, who'd been dozing against her shoulder since Ipswich.

'Are we here? Thank goodness.' Her sister gave a dainty yawn, stretched like a cat, then craned to check her appearance in the foxed mirror on the carriage partition. The nap had not refreshed her, Sarah thought, watching her adjust the angle of her hat and smooth her fur collar. There were dark shadows beneath Diane's eyes that face powder failed to disguise. Their mother looked the same. Months of grief, preparations for departure from India and the stormy sea voyage had taken a toll on all three of them.

'I don't know what we shall do if there's no one to meet us.' Belinda Bailey's upright figure registered regal disapproval as she slipped a soft leather marker between pages and stowed book and spectacles into her bag.

'I'm sure the Richards' maid will have passed on the message, Mummy. She sounded very efficient.'

'I suppose we could ask someone at the station to summon a taxi.'

'Mummy, I'm sure it'll be all right.' It was unusual for Mrs Bailey to fuss like this, a rare sign of nerves.

The train's brakes squealed as it juddered to a halt. A rubicund gentleman in plus-fours, who'd got on at Stowmarket, assisted them with their luggage. Sarah, clutching her precious box under one arm, managed a case with the other, while their mother carried the hatbox and Diane was left with only a handbag.

'Always a pleasure to help the ladies!' The gentleman beamed from the door when they thanked him. The whistle blew and the train edged into motion.

By the time they turned their attention to the piles of cases, a young man had magically appeared. He was smartly dressed, with a neatly wrapped striped scarf. His smooth blond hair was cut in military fashion, and his moustache did not quite disguise a certain tightness around his perfectly moulded lips.

'The Baileys, I presume?' His voice was louder than necessary, and he touched his hat as if in salute. His chestnut eyes surveyed them with hesitation.

'That's right,' Sarah's mother said haughtily. 'And who, may I . . . ?'

'Aunt Belinda, I'm Ivor.'

'Ivor, dear, of course,' she said more warmly, shaking his hand. 'You must excuse me, it's so long since I've seen you.' She introduced the girls to him. Sarah felt the grip of his hand, and his eyes held hers in a way she found pleasantly disturbing. To Diane, who glanced at him shyly, he merely nodded.

Their mother was speaking again. 'The last time we saw you, heavens, it must have been . . .'

'I was twelve apparently. I'm afraid I don't remember it, though I wish I did.' He gave a gallant smile. There was a tension in him, Sarah realized. He thought before he spoke, as though he was watching himself, which intrigued her.

'Oh, but I do remember you.' Her mother's bright voice grated. 'It was the autumn I brought the girls home, because you were starting school, Sarah – you were eleven, weren't you? – and Diane was nine. I believe you had recently started at Downingham, Ivor. Your school uniform was crisp and new, and you told me very confidently that your ambition was to follow your father into the regiment.'

'Did I really? What a precocious little oik I must have been.'

Mrs Bailey gave one of her rippling laughs that Sarah hated, the one she reserved for impressionable men. 'On the contrary, I found your directness refreshing. And, after all, that is exactly what you've done. Your mother wrote that you're already a lieutenant. Congratulations.'

'Thank you.' Before he turned to look for a porter, Sarah saw that Ivor Richards was blushing.

There had been plenty of young men of his type out in India susceptible to Mrs Bailey's charm, boys far from the stern eye of their mothers and starved of female company. Junior officers eager to make their mark, but clearly carrying around with them a burden of unhappiness, usually to do with parental expectation. Sarah wondered whether this was the case here. She and Diane didn't know the Richards family well, but they'd always known about them. Major Richards had been a close friend of her father's from military training days before the Great War. The injuries he'd sustained in that terrible conflict had ended his army career and now the family lived in a house on an estate on the Norfolk–Suffolk border, where the Major was Estate Manager.

'I left the motor right outside.' Ivor led the women to the station exit, leaving the porter to manage the luggage. 'Shall I carry that box for you, Miss Bailey?'

'No thanks, it needs to be kept in a certain position,' Sarah replied. 'Which regiment are you, Lieutenant?'

'The Norfolks, like my governor. Your father, too. I was sorry to hear about his death. But please, it's Ivor. May I call you Sarah?'

'Yes, of course.'

This time the smile was spontaneous. 'Good. Here we are.'

His vehicle was an old shooting brake that looked as though it usually carried muddy spaniels. Mrs Bailey eyed it with distaste.

'It seemed sensible to bring this, given the luggage,' Ivor said by way of apology. He dusted off the front passenger seat and held the door while Mrs Bailey somewhat gingerly got in. He helped the porter cram the boot with cases and soon they were off, driving with caution down the icy roads, the girls hanging onto the straps in the back, an over-efficient heater scorching their shins.

'How far is it?' Diane asked above the hum of the engine.

'Fifteen minutes away,' Ivor called back.

'It's only three or four miles,' Sarah told her. 'Do you not remember?'

'Obviously not,' Diane hissed. 'I haven't seen the Richards for years, have I?' Their boarding school had released her at sixteen as she had demonstrated so little interest in her studies, and she'd returned to India on the boat with Sarah, who had just finished sixth form. It was envisaged that the girls could train as typists in Bombay if they wanted something to do, but otherwise they could keep their mother company until such a time as they found husbands. Anyway, they knew it would only be a few years before Colonel Bailey retired and they might all return to England together.

It had been Diane who had found him, one blazing hot Sunday in July.

As the final preparations were underway for her twenty-first birthday party, Diane had stumbled in from the garden, chalk-faced with shock and babbling to Sarah and her mother to be quick. She had come across her father lying senseless on the path, the glass of gin he'd been drinking smashed on the gravel. He had suffered a massive heart attack and although the doctor arrived smartly, nothing could be done.

'Mother is meeting us at Flint Cottage,' Ivor was explaining to Mrs Bailey. 'There's a man cutting the holly bush in front. Not exactly the weather for it, but your tenants had let it run riot. We could barely reach the door.'

'It's good of your parents to arrange matters,' Mrs Bailey said, clutching at the door handle as the car slid on a tight corner. 'It was impossible for us to organize anything from India . . .'

'They were glad to,' Ivor said with warmth. 'It was the least any of us could do in such sad circumstances. I'm afraid, though, that because the Watsons only vacated the place last week they left things in a pretty poor state. It's been something of a rush getting it habitable for you.'

'Your mother said that in her letter. I suppose we should have given the Watsons more notice.'

'You couldn't help that, given the situation.'

'No. Once we reached London it felt important to be in before Christmas.'

Sarah half listened to this conversation and wondered, not for the first time, where the poor Watsons with their young children would be spending the festive season. Really, their mother did get such ideas in her head that simply couldn't be shifted. Sarah would have readily endured Christmas at Aunt Susan's in Wimbledon, though she had to admit that her mother and Colonel Bailey's spinster sister had never been close.

Her attention was caught by the sight of an old man in a cloak digging a sheep from a snowdrift. His dog, a streak of black, was making little rushes to gather the rest of the flock. Clouds hung low, swollen with snow. It was like a Christmas-card scene. How many years had she longed for a traditional English Christmas with her family, instead of being in India or with Diane at Aunt Susan's, but now it was here it would be a sad one. At least they would be dressed for it, thanks to their recent raid on Aquascutum's.

'Westbury Hall on the left,' Ivor Richards announced, waving a gloved hand as they passed a high-arched gateway with a statue of a great dog on top. Through it, the briefest glimpse of a snowy drive up a slope to a house topped by Tudor chimneys and then it was gone.

A minute or two further on, the car slid to a halt next to a long flint stone wall. Ivor climbed out, plodded round and opened the door for Mrs Bailey, then set about unloading suitcases from the boot.

The women emerged more slowly and stood together at the low gate, gazing at the square lines of the Victorian detached house that would be their new home.

'Looks pretty,' Diane tried, uncertainly. They both glanced at their mother for a reaction, but she said nothing. Instead she swung open the gate and, with Sarah holding her arm, started carefully up the path, which, though swept clear of snow, was still icy. Diane followed, complaining about the cold.

The holly Ivor had mentioned marred the frontage, but the house seemed larger than Sarah had expected. Two storeys, she saw, and gabled windows in the roof suggested attics. It lay amid a generous plot of garden bordered by great sheltering trees and studded with the white-shrouded hulks of bushes. What treasures the snow concealed, she must wait for the thaw to discover. She shivered in a sharp gust of wind and held the precious box closer.

As they neared the mare's nest of holly that blocked their path, the brisk snap of shears could be heard and the bright berried branches shuddered.

Mrs Bailey spoke and the snapping ceased.

'Sorry, ladies,' a soft male voice cried. 'Wait a moment, please. I'll make you a way past.' A cloth-capped, clean-shaven face became visible above the branches, then when his bulky form appeared, Sarah gained an impression of bright eyes in an intelligent face.

'What a job,' Sarah said politely as he steered them safely round the obstacle.

The man smiled as he returned to his task. 'It was much worse an hour ago, I assure you. I'll be finished soon.'

Sarah asked, 'Mummy, shouldn't we ask him to save some branches for Christmas?' and when Mrs Bailey agreed, she asked the young man, 'Would you, please? The berries are splendid.'

'Of course. I was going to propose it anyway. I will leave some in the conservatory, if you like.' His smile made his grey-blue eyes twinkle. They were almond-shaped, in a pale face that contrasted sharply with what she could see of his dark hair. He spoke perfect English, but pronounced the words softly, almost tenderly.

'I say, Hartmann.' Ivor's rough tones ripped the air. 'Take these in, will you.' The young gardener flinched at the rudeness, but he propped up his shears without complaint and went to lug the cases.

A handsome bosomy woman in a country tweed suit appeared in the porch. 'Belinda, darling, you're here!' she squealed, spreading her arms out to Mrs Bailey in welcome.

'Oh, Margo!' It had been many months since Sarah had last seen her mother spark into life. She watched, unexpectedly moved, as Mrs Bailey rushed into the other woman's embrace. The two friends clung to one another, Belinda Bailey's thin, powdered cheek pressed to Margo Richards' plump, sun-browned one. Belinda's eyes squeezed shut, her face crumpled with grief. Aunt Margo, Ivor's mother, was someone Sarah barely remembered, but she knew the two wives had formed as close a bond as their husbands, sustained by infrequent meetings and the exchange of letters over the years. Seeing them together now, Sarah at last understood why her mother wanted to retreat here to the deep Norfolk countryside rather than rent a house in London. After the strains of her marriage and the sudden disorientation of widowhood, Belinda Bailey needed a place of safety.

'I told you the place wouldn't be ready, darling,' Aunt Margo scolded as they gazed round inside, dismayed to see the wretched state in which their tenants had left the house. 'I wish you'd agreed to stay with us.'

'Perhaps we should have done,' Mrs Bailey sighed, 'but we're here now, so we'll have to make the best of it.' Oh, her mother's obstinacy.

It had been Major Richards who, when the girls had returned to India after their schooling, had telegraphed Colonel Bailey to say that Flint Cottage had come up for sale and who, under Colonel Bailey's subsequent instructions, had organized its purchase. Colonel and Mrs Bailey wanted somewhere in England to retire to eventually, and in the meantime they would let it out. Furniture, curtains and carpets belonging to the previous owner had been included in the sale, but nobody had realized before the Watsons' departure how dingy the decoration had been.

Sarah saw that every room bore the marks of a vigorous family of children and animals. The Watsons – Mr Watson a writer of detective novels – had had four boys as well as several dogs. The wallpaper was marked by grubby hands and the wheels of toy cars, and most of the doors showed evidence of scrabbling claws. One of the sofas in the drawing room had collapsed on one side and splashes on the wooden floor near the writing desk suggested that a bottle of Royal Blue ink had been dropped on it from a height.

All these things Aunt Margo pointed out as they toured the house, Ivor having been despatched to buy some urgent supplies. Their mother appeared annoyed rather than cast down, however, but Diane's expression was dismal. 'I didn't think it would be as bad as this,' she whispered, shocked by the mould on the bathroom ceiling, but Sarah wasn't listening. She was already beginning to see the house's possibilities.

She liked the large and light-filled rooms. The walls were thick enough to imagine it snug once they got fires burning in the grates. She left the others admiring a view of the church from a bedroom window and returned downstairs to explore on her own. One door off the hall had revealed a gloomy formal dining room. The kitchen and a good-sized scullery she had found more cheerful, but the room she had liked best was a sitting room at the back, which she went into now. Its windows looked out onto a snow-covered terrace with a lawn beyond. Something else, though, had roused her curiosity: through a French door a conservatory had been built onto the side of the house.

Sarah listened to the voices and footsteps overhead, before trying the handle. The door was locked, but a heavy iron key on a nearby shelf fitted and turned easily enough. The door swung away and she stepped down into the grey light of a stoutly built wooden garden room with a snow-covered glass roof and windows all round. A grapevine spread like a delta up the wall of the house, its branches clutching the beams over-head. Doors either end led into the garden. Despite its cloak of snow, or perhaps because of it, the room felt less icy than she'd expected. Yes, she thought, this might be the place. For the moment, anyway.

She slipped back into the house and from the hall collected her shoebox and returned with it to the conservatory, where she set it on a potting shelf and addressed her attention to the string, unpicking the knots impatiently. Then she eased open the lid and lifted the layer of straw beneath. Thank heavens. The row of tiny plants inside were undamaged in their pots and, when she prodded with a finger, the earth felt damp still from this morning's drenching. She bent and sniffed the exotic smell: India in a box. She'd guarded these cuttings safely on their long voyage across the sea. They were flowers from their garden in Kashmir, her father's favourites. She had no idea if they would survive here in English earth, but she was determined to try. She transferred the pots to a narrow stone trough under the vine and was still considering whether this would be the best place for them, when Diane's heart-shaped face appeared around the door, its expression impatient.

'There you are, Saire. Come and choose a bedroom. It's the one with the washbasin I like, but I shan't care if you want it.'

Diane's tone indicated that she would very much care and Sarah, knowing Diane would have to have her way but not really minding, rose to follow her, taking a lingering look back at the long-suffering plants in their new home.

As she prepared for bed that night, in the bedroom with its view of the church tower through the trees, she saw that the snow was coming down once more in thick, tumbling flakes. It fell on and off for days, burying the sleeping garden, overlaying the newly cleared path. It covered the village of Westbury, its old stone church, the mediaeval bridge over the frozen stream. It coated the handsome statue of the Great Dane on the gateway of Westbury Hall and piped the chimneys and crenellations of the manor house itself. Across the whole of Norfolk it fell, on towers and steeples, on fields and woods and the mysterious Broads, on desolate marshes and the icy North Sea. Under the snow everything lay silent, holding its breath, perhaps, for what was to come.

Nine

On Christmas morning, Sarah woke to find her bed bathed in an eerie light. She rose, shivering, pushed aside the curtains and rubbed at the window to look out. It seemed that a cloud had descended on them in the night, for all she could see was dense fog from which fluffs of snow floated against the glass. She whisked in and out of the bathroom and dressed warmly, choosing her thickest woollen skirt and jersey, then pulled her dressing gown on over the top for good measure and padded downstairs in her slippers. There she found the new maid, Ruby, hunched over the range, measuring oats into a pan for porridge. Next to it a kettle was sighing into life.

'Merry Christmas, Miss Sarah. Proper white one, isn't it?' Long-lashed eyes sparkled out of a pinched face that put Sarah in mind of a malnourished kitten. Little Ruby was fifteen, the eldest daughter of the Martin family who populated one of the estate cottages at the other end of the village. The girl had been glad to leave off helping her mother look after her numerous brothers and sisters in order to work for the Baileys, but she wasn't used to sleeping alone.

'Happy Christmas to you, too, Ruby. I hope you were warmer last night?'

'Them extra blankets and the hot brick worked a marvel, Miss Sarah. I shouldn't have got out of bed at all this morning, 'cept I were desperate for the privy.'

'Yes, indeed. Don't worry, I'll make myself tea. I can see you're busy.'

Sarah carried her cup through to the drawing room, where Ruby had already opened the curtains and lit a fire. There she stood sipping her tea, warming herself by the crackling wood and staring dreamily out of the window. The blizzard seemed to be easing. The room wasn't exactly cosy, but it was getting that way.

She had decorated the downstairs rooms with the bright holly that the gardener had left. Hartmann, as the Richards family referred to him, had visited every day since the Baileys had moved in, to clear fresh snow from the path and fix a window that wouldn't shut. Yesterday, unasked, he had arrived humming a German carol and bearing a slender fir tree in a pot, which now occupied a corner of the room, decorated with candles that the new cook, Mrs Allman, had discovered in a cupboard. Next year they'd have proper glass baubles, the Bailey women agreed, but for now Sarah felt a deep thrill at the simplicity of this country Christmas with the snow and the intriguing little pile of gifts bought in London, carefully wrapped, under the tree, and the anticipation of a candlelit church with a wooden nativity scene, to which today a carved swaddled Christ Child would be added.

In India, Christmas had never felt real to her. The colours and the climate were all wrong. But at least – and here she was pierced by the memory – there had been Daddy.

It was nearly eight o'clock now, so she carried a tray of tea upstairs for Mother and Diane. Diane had to be called twice to wake and drink it. Later, Ruby served porridge and toast in the dining room, which was freezing, for all the heat from the fire there went straight up the chimney. As the snow came down outside, they worried about the depth of it, for it was banked up almost to the level of the window.

'At least we won't have to go to church,' Diane said, cutting her toast into dainty pieces. 'Bung over the marmalade, Saire.'

'We still ought to make the effort,' their mother said. 'If we could convey a message to the Richards, they would surely send someone to clear the path.'

'Mother, it's Christmas morning.' Sarah sometimes found her nearest and dearest appalling. 'We can't ask people to leave their families.'

'Then I simply don't know how we'll manage to go up there for luncheon.' They were due to spend the day with the Richards. Mrs Allman had departed the day before to stay with her sister in Ipswich and Ruby would go home to her family once she'd completed her morning tasks.

After breakfast Sarah helped Ruby clear the table, leaving the bowls to soak in the sink for Ruby's return that evening, then joined the others in the drawing room where the fire was dancing merrily. Diane had lit the candles on the tree and was gathering up the pile of presents from under it.

'I think, perhaps, the snow might be stopping,' Sarah said brightly, peering out of the window, and, indeed, the fog was lightening and the flakes coming down more sparsely. 'And, look, someone's come.'

She watched eagerly as a bulky figure clutching a shovel emerged from the misty lane like a yeti from a storm. Its gloved hands pawed at the garden gate and when this didn't budge, it simply lifted one leg and stepped clumsily over the top. Then, brandishing the shovel in a gesture of greeting, the creature waded up the path.

'It's Mr Hartmann. Thank heavens, we're saved,' Sarah said, wresting open the window. 'Hello,' she called out into the dead air, her breath billowing. 'Happy Christmas. It's jolly good to see you.'

'And Happy Christmas to all of you.' His eyes sparkled though his words were muffled by his scarf. 'I thought you might need digging out.'

'We certainly should, or we won't get our Christmas dinner.'

He laughed and sank his spade into the snow. 'I'm building up an appetite for mine.'

'Sarah, do close the window or we'll perish,' her mother snapped behind her.

'In a moment, Mummy.' She called, 'I'll make you some tea, Mr Hartmann. Would you like a drop of brandy in it?'

'That sounds wonderful. I'll clear by the front door first, so you can bring it out to me.'

'Give me a moment,' she said and refastened the window, shivering.

'I knew they'd send someone,' her mother said, drawing her chair nearer the fire.

'I suppose this means we must go to church now,' Diane grumbled.

'I'll see to Mr Hartmann's tea,' Sarah sighed, and went out to the kitchen where she found Ruby gobbling chocolates from a garish box that Cook had given her all to herself.

The morning service was poorly attended – of the Richards family there was no sign – and the wooden pews were almost as cold as the stone pillars, but Sarah enjoyed singing the traditional carols and the vicar's voice had a quiet musicality that whispered round the ancient walls. She felt part of a worship that had been going on in this place for hundreds of years. Cut off in this little village by the snow, it was difficult to believe that there was any world beyond Westbury. Never had their old life in India seemed further away.

The Reverend Tomms was as round as the sound of his name, a short man whose moon face was wreathed in smiles. He shook hands very firmly with each of the Baileys and welcomed them to the parish. Outside, the girls couldn't help giggling at the memory of his rubber boots peeping out from beneath his cassock. *How rare it is that we hear Diane laugh,* Sarah observed, brushing at the light snow falling on her face.

At Flint Cottage the path was clear, and the only trace of Hartmann, his empty mug in the porch. Ruby had gone, too, but the house felt invitingly warm. Over coffee, the women opened their gifts to one another. Mrs Bailey unwrapped an engagement calendar from Diane, and an evening stole of dove grey which Sarah had seen in Harrods and had spent a large part of her monthly allowance on. She loved giving presents, really thinking about what people would best like. She'd found a pair of soft kidskin gloves for her sister there, too, which Diane exclaimed over, pulling them on immediately and testing their suppleness. Their mother gave them gold necklaces that had once belonged to Colonel Bailey's mother, embroidered evening bags and some money for treats.

When she unwrapped her gift from Diane, Sarah was amazed at the rightness of it. The chunky dark green book, with its title embossed in gold, read, *The Culture of Vegetables and Flowers*. She sampled the pages eagerly. 'Amaryllis,' she said. 'Oh, asparagus, I must try that now we're in Norfolk.'

'Do you like the book?' Diane wasn't used to such an enthusiastic response to her presents.

'I love it, thank you,' Sarah said. 'It's so clever of you to have found it.'

'I couldn't think what to get you, then I saw it in the window of Bumpus's while you were searching for Mummy in Liberty. It looks just the thing for this garden, doesn't it?'

'Just the thing, and you're a dear. While I read it I'll dream of spring and the things we'll grow.'

Diane gave one of her faded little smiles that were as much as she could ever manage. 'I don't know what I'll do till then,' she said in a small, wan voice. She fingered the new evening bag in her lap with her gloved hands.

'Oh nonsense,' said her mother. 'We'll find you other young people. I'm sure Ivor Richards will make some introductions.'

'Winter will be fun, Di. Perhaps there'll be skating on the stream, that's what Ruby says anyway. We'll borrow some skates from somewhere. And our boxes will be arriving soon. Think how we can make this house lovely with all our things.'

'Won't that be strange,' Diane said in a bitter voice. 'They'll remind us of India and Daddy. I don't think I'll be able to bear it.' And for a moment they were silent, hearing only the snap of the fire and the distant cooing of wood pigeons in the trees.

Ten

It was a small party that gathered later that morning at the Richards' handsome, white-painted Georgian cottage. Sited in woods at the edge of the Westbury Hall estate, the Baileys reached it by walking along a sheltered footpath leading off the main drive to the old manor house itself. Including Major Richards' elderly widowed mother, an austerely dressed lefto-ver from the Victorian era with a face set in permanent distaste at the modern one, seven souls sat down to a splendid luncheon of roast goose and all the trimmings.

It was the first time the Baileys had met Major Richards since arriving in Westbury, and Sarah's youthful memory of him as an unsmiling, highly strung military type of strong opinions but few words proved to be an accurate one. She was able to observe him closely during luncheon because she'd been seated next to his place at the head of the table. Powerfully built, he clearly liked his food. He took plenty of everything from the dishes presented by their long-suffering maid. No, she could never manage to call him Uncle Hector.

'Amen and tuck in,' he said after rushing the brief grace, and

Sarah was all too aware of him working his way through his meal, sorting and turning the different components as he loaded his fork then chewed each mouthful noisily. At the draining of each replenishment of claret in his glass his face grew more flushed, and oily strands of greying hair began to fall over his forehead.

For a while the conversation was desultory as everybody tucked in.

'How much leave do you have for Christmas?' Mrs Bailey, who was sitting opposite Sarah, asked Ivor, who sat between the girls.

Ivor swallowed his mouthful and looked eager. 'I'm to report back tomorrow evening.'

Major Richards cleared his throat and Sarah noted the wary way that Ivor glanced at him before continuing. 'There's a big exercise planned, Father, but with luck I should get away again at New Year.'

'Does anything amusing happen in Westbury at New Year?' Sarah asked and Diane looked up with interest. She'd no more than picked at the fatty slices of meat on her plate, Sarah noted.

'The Kellings are in London unfortunately,' Aunt Margo remarked with a sigh. 'They usually throw such a splendid party for the hunt on Boxing Day.'

Sir Henry and Lady Kelling had chosen to stay in their Belgravia residence this Christmas. Their daughter, the Hon. Robyn, had come out in society earlier in the year, and Lady Kelling, it was always said, preferred London society to anything Westbury had to offer. This, Aunt Margo had already told the Baileys. She was very interested in the Kellings' lives. Too interested, Belinda Bailey used to say snidely after reading any letter from Aunt Margo, but Sarah's father would put in mildly that the interest was natural. The Kellings lived in Westbury Hall and were, after all, Major Richards' employers.

'I was going to say,' Ivor chipped in. 'The Bulldocks are putting on a do. Perhaps I could snaffle an invitation. If you girls should like to go, of course.'

'The *Bulldocks*,' Major Richards sneered as he jabbed a roast potato, but he failed to add anything to explain this comment.

'Jennifer Bulldock is a very nice girl,' Mrs Richards ventured.

'Of whom do we speak, may I enquire?' asked the Major's mother, rook-eyed and with one hand cupping her ear.

'The Bulldock children, Mother.'

'Oh, the *Bulldocks*.'

'If you *will* go,' Major Richards addressed his son, 'find out, will you, what the old man's up to now.'

'Yes, Father.'

'What is the matter with the Bulldocks?' Sarah's mother asked. 'Should the girls be going to this party?'

'Of course they should, darling,' Aunt Margo said. 'Don't take any notice. They'll have a marvellous time.' She rang a small bell and the maid bustled in to clear the plates.

Sarah hated Major Richards' offhand manner with his son, as though Ivor were a dog to be kept on a tight leash. She reminded herself of the trials the older man faced and tried to feel charitable. It had been a matter of revulsion to her as a young child that Major Richards had lost his right foot to a hidden mine during the last days of the Great War. Now she was older she saw how the artificial replacement gave him discomfort, for he used a stick and the lines of pain etched into his face made him appear a decade older than his fifty-two years. And the wound had been more than physical. Soldiering had been his profession, her mother had once explained, but when he'd eventually left hospital in 1919 he'd found himself on the scrapheap as far as the Army was concerned, on civvy street with a small pension, a wife and a young son to support, and competing with thousands of others for the handful of jobs available that were suited to his station. After two years of bitter disappointment, the colonel of his old regiment wrote out of the blue advising him to apply to Sir Henry Kelling, whose estate manager was retiring and to whom Colonel Battersby had mentioned Richards' name. The family had moved into Westbury Cottage and had lived there ever since; Major Richards being competent at his job as far as anyone knew.

Everyone *oohed* and *aahed* as the maid bore in the Christmas pudding, the brandy aflame with blue light. When they had each eaten a portion and old Mrs Richards had recovered from choking on the hidden sixpence in hers, someone remarked on how early it was growing dark outside.

'It's snowing again,' Diane noticed with alarm. 'What will happen if we get stuck here?'

'You'll all have to sleep on the floor,' Ivor said, eyes twinkling. 'And we'll have cold goose for days and days and burn the furniture for firewood.'

'Oh really, Ivor,' Mrs Richards said, seeing Diane's alarm.

'What nonsense did the boy say?' the old lady cut in.

'Nothing, Mother.'

'It's so kind of you, Hector, to have sent your Mr Hartmann to dig us out this morning,' Mrs Bailey said to get the conversation rolling again.

'We didn't send him exactly, Belinda. Ivor would have gone, of course, but then Hartmann called by to say he would.'

'Really? Well, it was very thoughtful of everyone. Hartmann's been very efficient. He's your gardener, did you say?'

'He's under-gardener for the estate,' Major Richards said, cracking open a walnut. 'He lives with his mother in a little lodge up near the hall.'

'He seems, well, a cut above the usual. And that accent. Is it German?'

'He's a Hun, yes, or half a one. That's his father's side. His mother is English, though you wouldn't guess it. He was born and raised in Germany, but he and his mother arrived a year ago. Something rather unpleasant happened to Herr Hartmann.' Here Major Richards drew a finger across his throat. 'Fell foul of those Gestapo chaps, or so we gather. Anyway, Lady Kelling is some relation of Mrs Hartmann's and Sir Henry made them welcome, gave the boy work. Hartmann seems pleasant enough, but I'd be careful what you say near him.'

'Be careful?' Sarah wondered. 'Of what?'

'If we go to war he'll be the enemy, won't he?'

'Oh, surely not. Anyway, do you think we will go to war?'

'Farmers like Bulldock and his ilk would say not. You were still in India, of course, but you could almost touch the sense of relief round here when Chamberlain pulled us back from the brink. I'm the last one to want us to go through war with Germany again, mind you, but this Hitler cove, I don't trust him an inch.'

'Mr Hitler, did you say? The man has no breeding,' old Mrs Richards barked. 'What are things coming to?'

Everyone was silent, in respect for what Major Richards had endured, Sarah imagined, or perhaps it was fear of what might be to come. Surely, though, it was unthinkable that Europe should go to war again. They had fought the war to end all wars such a short time ago and nobody would seriously contemplate a repeat of it.

'War would be different this time,' Ivor Richards said, his quiet words distinct enough in the silence even for old Mrs Richards to hear. 'We've seen it in Spain. Cities bombed and set aflame. Women and children killed. And the Germans, those

tanks they've got, remarkable machines, whole, terrifying divi-
sions of them—'

'Ivor, stop it, dear. It's Christmas Day. I won't have talk of it.
You'll frighten the girls.'

'Sorry, Mother, you're quite right, of course. It's talk about
Hartmann that started all this.'

He doesn't like him, Sarah thought, surprised. She sat quietly
and sipped her glass of cognac. Hartmann was dangerous,
but not in the way Ivor meant. It was the animosity his name
roused. But whatever it was Sir Henry Kelling saw in Paul
Hartmann, she saw too. His parentage was irrelevant. She liked
him for his kindness to them.

The snowfall did not last long and the woods seen from the
drawing room where they'd retired for coffee were bathed in a
rosy light. 'I'd rather like a walk,' Sarah suggested, but only Ivor
offered to join her. They muffled themselves up to the eyes in
coats, scarves and gloves and set forth into a dream landscape,
following the path up towards the hall, because Sarah said she'd
like to see the place.

'It's so wonderful out here,' she said, laughing with pleasure
as the snow crunched under their boots.

'I've always loved snow. It's like having a holiday. No one
has to do anything except survive it.' Ivor's voice had a wistful
catch that made her glance at him, but he was concentrating on
staying upright.

'Who are the Bulldocks?'

'Oh, the *Bulldocks*.' His sudden laugh caused birds to fly
up in panic, scattering snow from the trees. 'They're an
old Norfolk farming family. My grandmother fell out with
old man Bulldock's mother years ago and my father thinks
Bulldock's a lily-livered Nazi-lover. Part of the happy band of

Hitler-appeasers in Norfolk, of whom there are more than one or two. Mr Mosley's Blackshirts have been seen round here, you know.'

'They sound appalling. I suppose none of this will stop Diane being able to go dancing?'

'Good lord no. We'd not speak to half our neighbours if we took that attitude. I say, your sister's a damned pretty girl, but I've yet to see her smile.'

'I wish you wouldn't swear. Mummy wouldn't like it.' For a moment Sarah walked ahead, feeling unaccountably disturbed. Actually she didn't care sixpence about him swearing, she had said it simply to shut him up.

'Sorry, I didn't mean ...'

She turned. 'Listen, Diane's had a worse time than any of us,' she said sharply. 'I don't want to talk behind her back, but please remember that.'

'I said I'm sorry.' His brow creased with anxiety and she relented.

'No, it's I who should apologize. I spoke too harshly. Forgive me.'

'Of course.' He gave her a sorrowful smile. 'I sometimes say the wrong thing, but I don't mean to.' Now she felt a rush of sympathy for him, glimpsing a sensitive nature, and laid her hand briefly on his arm to reassure him.

They trudged on for a while up the steep hill, breathing heavily with the effort, then the woods came to an end, and suddenly there before them, a few hundred yards away, was Westbury Hall. They stopped to rest and Sarah stared at gracious lines of its old ochre brick walls, the crenellations and turrets crested with drifts of snow, the diamond-paned windows overhung by icicles.

'Lovely pile, isn't it?' Ivor remarked.

'Elizabethan?' she asked as they set off towards it.

'That sort of whatnot. As Mother said, the family are in London much of the time. Money's tight. Can't afford to run a full staff, Dad reckons. If there's another war, well, you can understand why the Kellings, the Bulldocks and their ilk are resisting it so loudly.'

'Sir Henry Kelling, too?'

'He's not as bad as some of the others,' Ivor admitted. 'But another war would put paid to his sort, that's what Father thinks.'

'Don't you think the danger is past? That Germany has all it wants now?'

'I don't know.' Ivor spoke as though weighing his words. 'Surely they're not foolish enough, but the stories you hear of the strength of their forces tell otherwise. We can only hope. What do they want, that's what I'd like to know. And what could we do against them? Sometimes I think the Bulldocks of this world are right and we should stay out of it, but then . . .'

'We have obligations.'

'Yes, we do, and we cannot cut ourselves off from our sworn allies.'

They were close to the house now so that it towered over them, and their boots met gravel under the snow. Sarah, on tiptoe, clutched a sill to look in through a window, and was put out to find the curtains were drawn. Instead Ivor led her under an arch into a courtyard at the side of the house, then on through a snowbound garden, where they passed the muffled shapes of bushes, statues, a simple fountain. Two sides were lined with poplar trees, but along the far edge ran a high brick wall of the same ochre hues as the house and into one end of this was set a studded wooden door. It was closed and banked up with snow.

'The kitchen garden's through there,' Ivor explained, 'and beyond that the cottage where the Hartmanns live. I say, we should start back, don't you think?'

A doleful twilight brooded over the snow, and Ivor turned to go, but Sarah was reluctant. The thought of the walled garden beyond the door was intriguing. She longed to see it, but Ivor was already ahead. As she hurried after him, the thought of a warm fire and Christmas cake rose in her mind. She'd return here and see the gardens properly in the spring, she promised herself. Hopefully with an invitation, for today it felt they were trespassing.

They arrived back at Westbury Cottage in cheerful spirits only to be puzzled by their reception.

'Goodness, dears, how bright-eyed and bushy-tailed we look,' was Aunt Margo's greeting as they entered the stuffy drawing room. And everyone stared at them in amusement, which Sarah found unnerving.

There had been something unreal about the whole day, she reflected that evening, the alien light on the snow, the sense of desertion at Westbury Hall. She'd longed for the delightful Christmases of her childhood, for although there had been icicles, candles and a leaping fire in the grate today, and rich marzipan fruit cake, it was marred by bereavement and rumours of war. The innocence of those far-off days of her childhood was gone for ever.

Eleven

Jennifer Bulldock, who opened the farmhouse door on New Year's Eve, was a tall girl, but awkwardly coltish rather than gracefully willowy.

'Oh goody, Ivor, you're just in time for Blind Man's Buff.' Her hearty voice competed with the yapping of the small terrier dog which she was trying to collar.

'Maybe once I've got a drink inside me,' Ivor laughed. 'Jen, this is Miss Sarah Bailey and her sister Diane.'

'Wonderful to meet you both. Do come in. Whoops, don't mind Chester, he gets overexcited.' The dog was making angry rushes at the newcomers, but Jennifer was finally able to nab him and bundle him into the arms of a maid who bore him away.

'You're very kind to have us,' Sarah said, liking this girl immensely. She possessed an air of good humour and took their hats and coats without any fuss before ushering them into a large cheerful drawing room where a scene of chaos greeted them. The furniture had been pushed to the walls and a dozen young people were crowding around a burly ginger-head in an ill-fitting dark suit. His blindfold, a ladies' polka-dotted scarf, pushed his fringe up into a spiky halo.

'He's all yours, Harry!' somebody shouted.

Harry, a muscular, smiley young man with dark, healthy good looks, seized the blindfolded boy by the shoulders and turned him till he was dizzy. Everyone drew back as the victim staggered free and the girls squealed as he barged about, trying to catch one of them.

Sarah enjoyed the game from the sidelines, feeling too old for this buffoonery, but she couldn't help laughing when Diane was caught and took her turn, though the girl appeared terrified as Harry tied the scarf over her eyes. Then her heart went out to her sister, for she looked so utterly lost as he released her and she stumbled about until the lad himself took pity and allowed himself to be caught.

'She's rather a sport, your sister,' Ivor remarked, appearing beside her with two glasses of steaming mulled wine.

'She's always liked parties.' It was true. Something about being in a crowd appealed to Diane. Perhaps other people helped take her mind off herself. Sarah remembered with sudden pain how it had been too late to cancel Diane's party on that awful summer afternoon. The guests arrived only to turn away at the sad news of Colonel Bailey's illness, but Diane had begged them to stay. Sarah had discovered this about grief, that she kept being reminded of her father at the most unlikely moments.

'Are you all right?' Ivor said. His sincere brown eyes examined her anxiously and she was touched by how attentive he was being.

'Yes, yes, of course.'

'We'd better not stand here or Harry will get us for sure. Watch out!'

*

They ducked Harry's lurching figure and Sarah followed Ivor out through the hall and into the candlelit dining room where a large bony woman with a look of Jennifer and wearing spectacles on a gold chain was ordering the finishing touches to a supper table groaning with dishes and fussing at the terrified maid about the number of chairs around the wall.

'Ivor, dear, it isn't ready yet,' she snapped by way of greeting.

'I'm sorry, Mrs Bulldock. I simply wanted to introduce Sarah Bailey.'

The woman fixed a glare upon Sarah, who felt a little shiver pass through her as though she was being judged and found acceptable. The lines on Mrs Bulldock's forehead betrayed her as a worrier. 'So you're the elder Bailey girl then? Such bad luck about your father. I gather he didn't leave your mother much to live on? It's a lesson to us all.'

'I'm not sure who you've heard that from, but Daddy looked after us very well.' Sarah could hardly manage to be polite, she was so irritated by this stranger who seemed to know so much about them and felt free to comment.

'How are you finding the cottage? Those tenants you had were a poor sort, I'll say. The boys ran wild.'

'They weren't too bad,' Ivor put in, eyeing the sausage rolls hungrily. 'Their father was the artistic sort, that's all.'

'With morals to match, I suppose. The wife must have been shy, she always slipped away if one tried to speak to her. Still, Sarah, I hope you'll be happy here. I'll pay your mother a visit soon, tell her, I expect she'd be glad of the company. And I need someone sensible on the summer fete committee. Lady Kelling's our chairman, you know, but she's in London most of the time so she leaves these things to me. I'm sure your mother will fit the bill. Mary, don't leave the butter near the candles, you silly child.'

The thought of her mother agreeing to help on a committee

was so unlikely that Sarah had to stifle a laugh. Mrs Bailey had always avoided the duties of an officer's wife as far as she could, apart from the entertaining, for she enjoyed basking in male attention.

Finally everyone was called through for supper. Sarah noticed that Diane was flushed and giggling and her eyes were unnaturally bright. Was it, she wondered, the effect of the high jinks or of the contents of the empty wine glass in her hand? Oh, what did it matter, for the moment her sister appeared happy.

Jennifer, she saw, became anxious in her mother's presence. Mrs Bulldock criticized the perfectly reasonable-sized portion of Jubilee chicken her daughter was helping herself to, which made Jennifer drop some on the lace cloth as she jerked the spoon back towards the dish.

Ivor, apparently popular and at ease in this company, introduced Sarah to several of his friends, the sons and daughters of gentleman farmers for the most part, with whom he'd grown up and mixed with during holidays from school. The cheerful, handsome lad, Harry, was one of them. Despite his earlier boisterousness he proved perfectly presentable company, easy to talk to and with a good word for everyone. He popped a sausage roll into his mouth and fixed her with an amiable, round-eyed gaze. 'I say, what do you plan to do with yourselves now you're here?'

'We don't know at the moment,' she replied, accepting a dish of trifle Ivor brought her and aware of him hovering at her elbow. 'We're still settling in.'

'I hope you don't find it very remote here. Though I suppose coming from India you're rather used to remoteness.'

'Yes, we were out in the sticks there, but the thing is we were always among people.' Too many people sometimes, though she didn't tell Harry this. Though the bungalow in Kashmir had been spacious and set in large gardens, she had rarely had the privilege of feeling alone. Lonely, yes. One could feel lonely in a crowd, but the pleasure of one's own company and the time to pursue one's own interests, not only was that rare, but it was looked upon with suspicion. To survive as a member of the colonial force in the country, the thing to do was to stick together, to keep up the appearance of being civilized. There was unease with loners or the eccentric.

After supper Jennifer set up the gramophone and there was dancing and much horseplay and laughter. Diane was steered about the floor by Harry, who held her slight frame carefully as they quickstepped, as though she might easily be crushed. Ivor danced with Sarah several times, which she thought gallant of him. There was only a few inches difference in their heights and he was a good dancer, on which she complimented him.

'Is it one of things new officers learn at Sandhurst?'

He smiled down at her. 'There is certainly a good social side to be had there.'

She found he was different here, in company, than during that time on Christmas Day when they'd walked together in the snow. He seemed happier, more relaxed, sure of himself. The other Ivor, the one she saw when they'd been alone, she wasn't sure she'd liked as much, but there was something that made her sorry for him. His father was hard on him; maybe he didn't mean to be, but he was. Ivor wore the weight of his father's expectations, perhaps that was what made him highly strung.

Some of the guests were staying overnight, but since it hadn't snowed again Ivor drove Sarah and Diane home slowly through the wintry darkness. In the porch of Flint Cottage the lamp had been left burning, making the house appear golden and welcoming.

*

Sarah was lying sleepless in the grey snow light of her room, the laughter and the music still playing in her head when the latch clicked, the door cracked open and Diane's pale face appeared.

'Nothing's wrong,' she whispered, slipping into the room. 'I can't sleep, is all. Too cold.'

Sarah made room for her shivering body. 'Oh, your feet,' she breathed through her teeth, 'they're like blocks of ice.'

'My hot stone was hardly warm.'

'Mine is still. Here, that's it.'

They hugged each other till Diane's shuddering ceased. Despite the familiarity of the scent of her hair and skin, Diane felt to Sarah like a foreign little creature, unknown, unknowable, her slender limbs as finely wrought as a bird's wings, her cropped hair soft as down against Sarah's cheek.

'I feel a bit icky,' she said, using their old childhood word.

'You're not going to be sick, though, are you?'

'I don't think so. Did you like it tonight?'

Sarah sighed. 'Yes, of course. Did you?'

She felt Diane nod. 'It was fun. I don't think it was for you, though.'

'Why do you say that?'

Diane rolled over to face her so that her troubled eyes filled Sarah's vision.

'I could tell.'

'You're wrong, I was perfectly happy. I liked Jennifer.'

'Yes, she was all right. The salt of the earth, that's what Daddy would have called her. Oh I do miss Daddy.' A little sob.

'I know. So do I. Diane, is it all right for you here? Norfolk, I mean.'

'Of course. Why shouldn't it be?'

'I don't know. It's so different from what you're used to. Maybe you're wondering what you want to do here.'

Diane rolled away and Sarah heard her swallow, then whisper, 'But I never have, Sarah. Never have known what I want to do. What I'm for. And I'm different from you because I don't care. I don't feel things like you and Mummy. There's just a deadness. Is there something wrong with me, Saire?'

Diane turned her head and their eyes locked in the hazy light. Sarah felt such a rush of shock and sadness at this revelation that she couldn't think of a thing to say. Instead she reached and pulled her sister close and pressed her lips gently against her forehead. Diane snuggled against her and they simply lay there. Soon Sarah felt her sister's body go limp and her breathing deepen as she fell into sleep.

No sleep for her. Diane's words troubled her and she thought again how unknowable her sister was. It was touching that she had come to her in the night like this, an unexpected gift. She got cramp with one arm pinned under Diane's chest, but when she tried to move, her sister groaned. She'd wait before trying again.

The picture came to her again, as it had many times since Daddy's death, of Diane's face that day as she'd rushed in from the garden. The shocked whiteness, her shallow breaths, the muttered words that didn't make sense. 'I didn't ... I didn't mean ...' Didn't mean what? When she asked her weeks later, Diane appeared to have forgotten, for her hands flew to her face. 'It was so dreadful. I should have helped him, not left him lying there.'

'There was nothing else you could have done, dear. You are guilty of nothing, don't you see?' Diane simply stared at her with pleading eyes. There were no tears. If Diane cried for her father she did so alone and unseen. Sarah sometimes wondered whether Diane had been marked by something, the earlier trag-edy that had struck their family. The thought was too painful and she brushed it away.

'It's all right, darling, it's all right,' she whispered to her sleeping sister. 'You're safe here. I'll look after you. I'll always look after you.'

Twelve

The enormous board mounted next to the great whitewashed gateway took Briony by surprise. She drove up an asphalt road towards some promising-looking chimney tops gleaming in the late afternoon sun and slowed down in wonderment. Spread before her was a perfect Elizabethan manor house, the brick-work cleaned up and mended. As she neared a gravel turning circle in front, she noticed a car park discreetly screened by hedges to the left, an elegant metal bicycle rack, unused, television aerials on the roof.

The great wooden front door bore a brass plate with 'Reception' engraved on it. Briony lifted an iron latch, the door creaked open and she found herself in a gloomy, high-ceilinged hall of panelled dark wood. Nestled in the elbow of the sturdy wooden staircase was a glass-sided lift. To the far left a great fireplace yawned. To the right was a sleek mahogany desk behind which a glossy young woman was tapping a laptop keyboard with purple-nailed fingers. Her neat black ponytail bobbed as she rose, smiling. 'Hello. Can I help you?' She reached for a sales brochure from a stack on the desk, but put it down again when Briony said, 'I'm looking for Westbury Lodge. Was it you I spoke to on the phone? Kemi Matthews?'

'Oh, you're . . . Briony Wood? Lovely to meet you. Yes, I'm Kemi.'

She opened a cupboard on the wall behind her, and selected one of the sets of keys that hung there. 'Take the narrow drive past the house that way' – she gestured – 'follow it round and you'll see the cottage to your right, past the long wall. All the instructions are in a file on the kitchen table. Everything's ready, but if there is anything I can help you with do give me a call. Take care now.'

Driving down between the right-hand side of the house and a long high brick wall, Briony eventually found a Victorian cottage set in a sunny spot. She stared at the house in delight. It was two-storeyed, built of ochre brick, dark with age. Pointed, white-edged gables sheltered hatched windows and a shallow porch. It was like the gingerbread house out of Hansel and Gretel. What an enchanting place to stay in for a fortnight.

The email had arrived two weeks after her return from Italy. Luke's Dad, Roger, sounded a bit of a character: 'A lady in my wife's book club knows of a cottage in the grounds of an old manor house a few miles hence, where her apparently rather charming daughter works. The last tenant has recently quitted the cottage and the owner wants to give it a lick of paint before re-letting, but as this isn't a priority it appears you can stay there for a bit, if you don't mind a bit of dust (and no doubt a few ghosts!).'

Now, Briony walked the short, flower-bordered path to the stout oak front door. Inside, a compact hallway gave way to a chintzy sitting room to the left, a thankfully modern kitchen to the back and, at the right-hand side of the narrow staircase, a door which opened into a small dining room, rather crowded with a glass-fronted dresser, matching table and chairs and a heavy sideboard; gloomy remnants of a more formal age that valued best glass and dinner services as signs of status. Still, the table would be a good place for her to lay out her papers, and a wifi hub winked from a corner.

The house felt so recently inhabited, with cleaning materials, spice jars and new celebrity gossip magazines stacked on shelves, that she fancied she was intruding. Mounting the stairs, she found two small bedrooms, the double bed in the bigger one made up ready for her arrival. The bathroom needed updating, for the wallpaper bubbled in places and her nose wrinkled at a lingering smell of damp. At least there was a shower over the worn bath. She'd seen worse, she decided, remembering the grubby shared bathroom in the overcrowded house where she'd dossed once with Aruna as a student in London.

After she'd hauled her case up to the bedroom she paused to look out of the window. It was high enough here to see over the long brick wall into a garden beyond, but she was disappointed not to see any burgeoning flower beds, only a dozen neat geometric shapes of cropped grass divided from one another by gravel paths. It was like a tiny park with a bench or two. On one sat an elderly man, wrapped in a coat and trilby hat despite the warmth of the day. He was sitting, lost in thought, walking stick in hand. It was too far away to see the expression on his face, but he seemed peaceful enough. It was a sunny place to sit.

It must be the old kitchen garden, the walls providing protection for the plants from the elements, Briony thought as she returned to the car to fetch the rest of her luggage. Hadn't there been something about it in Sarah Bailey's letters? Whoever Sarah had been, Briony would be walking in her footsteps. As she carried in the canvas tote bag containing Sarah's letters and her grandfather's box, she experienced the strange sense that the past was here all around, if only she could reach out and draw back the veil.

Thirteen

March 1939

A wild wind blew in from the north, 'straight from Siberia', as Mrs Allman the cook remarked, but Sarah stepped out into the garden of Flint Cottage with optimism, seduced by the sunlight on the grass and the puffs of cloud dashing across a sky of boundless blue. Only for the cold to cut right through her, forcing her back inside to fetch a thicker coat. Even then her enthusiasm to start work on the vegetable bed quickly waned and she retreated to the shelter of the potting shed.

Here it was gloomy and draughty, but smelled comfortingly of earth and creosote. A rummage on the shelves brought forth riches; a few garden tools, boxes, potting compost and some envelopes of seeds. After several trips from the shed with pots and compost she established herself in the sun-warmed conservatory and was as happy as the proverbial Larry for the rest of the morning, sowing lettuces and summer flowers, dreaming of deep blue spikes of delphiniums and the delicate scent of sweet peas that she remembered from working in the headmistress' garden at school.

Remarkably, her little *Hibiscus syriacus* plants from India had survived the severe winter, but she pondered the wisdom of planting them outside yet. The blooms had been a delicate pink with a dark red heart in India and she hoped they would be here, though the soil was different. She knew exactly where she wanted them, right in front of the cottage, but maybe she should consult Mr Hartmann about the matter.

The thought must have summoned him, for shortly after luncheon he appeared, knocking softly on the frosted glass door of the conservatory. For a moment Sarah imagined this man in jacket and collared shirt to be Ivor, but he was taller and burlier than Ivor. Anyway, he couldn't be. Ivor had returned to Aldershot. She wasn't sure whether she was relieved or disappointed. Her feelings about Ivor were complicated.

'Come in,' she called, glad to have Mr Hartmann to talk to about her work. Her mother and sister had no interest in the messy business of gardening, appreciating only the beauty of the results.

'Hello. My goodness, you've been busy.'

He smiled to see her pots and trays and agreed with her about her hibiscus cuttings, that they should be kept inside for the moment and planted outside once the frosts had gone. His manner was as usual polite and encouraging, which gave her confidence.

'Here's me rattling on,' she said. 'Did you call for something in particular?'

'Yes. I'm on my way to Cockley Market to have some tools sharpened,' he explained in his soft accent, 'and wondered if you wanted me to take any of yours.'

'Oh, I do,' she said, getting up. 'That's so kind. There are some shears I found in the shed that are probably blunt and a pruning saw ... I'll fetch them, shall I?' She started to pull on her coat, then paused, her mind working. 'I say, would you mind if I came with you, Mr Hartmann? I'd like to choose a really good pair of secateurs.'

'Of course. If you promise not to call me Mr Hartmann. My name's Paul.'

'*Pol.*' She repeated it as he had pronounced it. 'And I'm Sarah.'

He'd borrowed the shooting brake and proved a more cautious driver than Ivor as they set off down twisting lanes where primroses bloomed and the hedges foamed white with blackthorn blossom.

'It's lovely, isn't it, your countryside here?' he remarked. 'So flat, the wide skies, it reminds me of home. And when you grow things, well, I think you come to love the land that gives them life.'

'Yes, that may be true,' she said, thinking of their garden in India. 'Someone, Mrs Richards, was it, said you were from Hamburg.'

'Yes. And I read Botany at the university, where my father taught, but after … after what happened … I was not able to continue my studies.'

'I'm afraid … I don't know about what happened. Though please, I won't be offended if you don't wish to speak about it.'

'I don't mind. It helps me keep him alive to me. Quite simply, my father protested against discrimination once too often at the university. One of his colleagues betrayed him. Maybe more than one, who knows. Anyway, he was arrested and later, well … it is enough to say that he did not survive. Listen, none of you here really understands how bad it is in Germany. Landowners like Sir Henry, they dream of past glories. Of course they do not want war. Nobody should want war, but it'll be the only way to stop it all. Turn down that heater, please, if it's burning you.'

'No, no, it's fine.' Sarah considered what it must be like to be betrayed, like Herr Hartmann, by your own countrymen, your colleagues. It could never happen here, that would be incomprehensible, the very idea of it. She felt uncomfortable all the same. What if Paul was right? Maybe their way of life, their freedoms, could only be preserved by war against Hitler and all he stood for. Suddenly, she felt ashamed for not understanding.

They passed the rest of the journey in relative silence, Paul lost in his thoughts, for when she glanced at him he was frowning, his eyes on the road. She folded her hands on her lap and watched a flock of birds follow a horse-drawn plough, trees swaying in the wind. It was all so beautiful that it was hard not to be happy. She knew she had a great capacity for happiness, which made her feel even guiltier about Diane.

Cockley Market wasn't busy and they were able to park right outside the ironmonger's. Inside, Sarah breathed in the comfortable smells of leather, oil and animal feed. She chose and paid for her secateurs, then sat on a stool while Paul Hartmann conducted his business with the knife grinder. The old man who served him breathed strenuously and she noticed his scarred hands. When he spoke to Paul, his mouth twisted with bitterness. She understood at once that it was Paul's accent that disturbed him. The man was likely to have seen active service in the last war, she decided, but still rage boiled in her. An old war was hardly the younger man's fault, was it? Why did some people react with so little intelligence, like a dog that had been kicked once, which damned all humankind. She felt she should apologize for the knife-grinder's attitude, though Paul would surely know that not all Englishmen were like him.

When he was ready to go, it was the desire to make some public gesture that made Sarah say in the knife-grinder's hearing, 'Paul, would you mind if we had tea somewhere. I'm feeling a little headachy,' as though they were good friends, at ease together. Which they would be, she decided. So what if he was only a gardener? He was far better educated than she was. They had so much to talk about, too. For a moment the face of her late father flashed through her mind. They both grieved, but Paul's loss was so different that she felt humbled. It was impossible to compare the two.

The cosy teashop they found, with its panelled walls, had probably once been the parlour of a house. They established themselves at a table in the bay window, where between the gingham curtains they watched a man chase his hat down the street. A shy young waitress came to write down their order.

'I'm sorry about the man in Askey's,' Sarah said, when the girl had gone. 'He was awfully rude.'

'Ach,' Paul said with a shrug. 'It was worse at home. Here they cannot get you thrown in prison if they do not like you.'

'I feel ashamed.'

His eyes found hers and he smiled. 'You have nothing to be ashamed of. Your family has shown me and my mother nothing but kindness.'

In truth, Sarah thought as the maid carefully laid out the tea things, her mother and sister had been too absorbed in their own lives to notice the gardener much. During the sunny February, Paul had visited Flint Cottage several times to clear the worst of the brambles and trim the shrubs at the front, but it had been Sarah who had paid him. He had protested, but she insisted. 'Your mother is not at all well,' she reminded him. He had let slip that she was prone to bronchitis and her nerves were in shreds. 'You must need to pay the doctor.'

In a moment of enthusiasm she made a sponge cake once and walked with it up to the Hartmanns' cottage herself. *Such a pretty place*, she thought as she waited, but nobody answered her knock so she left the tin on the doorstep with a note. A few days later the empty tin was returned with a letter of thanks penned in shaky italics and the promise of an invitation for the Baileys to call 'in the spring when I'm sure I'll feel much better'.

'How is your mother?' she asked now.

'Better than she was, thank you,' Paul replied. 'She has always had a delicate constitution.' Although there was no one else in the room, he lowered his voice. 'She nearly died having me, you know, and my parents were told by the hospital to have no more children, which is why I have no brothers or sisters. Herr Klein, the consultant who treated her, was Jewish, and he left Germany with his family for America two years ago. My parents' friendship with him was used as another black mark in the case against my father.'

The tea was ready to pour now, strong, hot and restorative. Sarah closed her eyes briefly as the warmth flowed through her. Teacakes arrived, scented with cinnamon and dripping with butter. How homely it all was. She could almost push away thoughts of the events that Paul described.

It was in the car home in the gathering dusk that he spoke more about his father. He did not look at her, but spoke as though to himself, remembering, his voice stumbling with grief and anger over the worst parts of his narrative.

Klaus Hartmann had been a lecturer in biology at the university for twenty years. His name had more than once been mentioned for preferment, but then he'd added his name to a letter protesting against the exclusion of Jewish students and found his path to promotion was blocked. His response was a heartfelt resistance to the regime's interference in higher education. He declined invitations to join conferences organized by the government; he continued to teach any student who wished to learn, no matter what their background. Paul and his mother did not know exactly which activity it was that had triggered the Gestapo's visit to their modest house in the Rotherbaum quarter early one morning in November 1937 and Klaus' subsequent arrest and incarceration. There was to be a trial, the charge: treason, but it kept being postponed, due to 'the illness' of the defendant. Frau Hartmann and Paul were admitted to the prison hospital to see him, and were shocked to see the bruised, emaciated figure lying barely conscious in the bed. Only his eyes spoke to them and they were full of pain and fear. Klaus clutched his wife's hand as though he'd never let her go and she broke out sobbing. 'What have they done to you?' It was only a few days later that his lawyer came to the house with the news they'd dreaded. Klaus Hartmann was dead, the official reason given that he'd been shot during an attempt to escape.

'We know that's not true,' the lawyer said heavily. 'You saw him. How would a man in his condition be able to escape? He was beaten, you saw that for yourselves. Frau Hartmann, I beg you, take Paul and leave Germany. There's no future for either of you here and it will become dangerous to be English if there's war. It is best if you go home.'

'Home! My mother's parents were dead and she had lived in Germany since she was eighteen, when she'd been sent to live with a German couple to learn the language. Lady Kelling's mother was my mother's cousin,' Paul went on, 'and in the end she wrote to them. The Kellings have been kind to have us.'

'I'm glad.' In fact, Sarah thought he had spoken stiffly when he mentioned the Kellings and wondered if they had not treated this little German branch of the family in distress with as much kindness as they might. However, she'd still not met Sir Henry and Lady Kelling, so maybe it was too early to form such an opinion.

Instead she said, 'Do you intend to continue being a gardener?'

He slowed the car to let some schoolchildren cross. When they set off again, he answered her. 'My plan eventually is to finish my doctorate. There's a botanist with my specialism at Cambridge University I might write to, to see if he'd be my supervisor, but I need to save some money first. We were able to bring nothing out of Germany . . .'

'I'm so sorry,' she said, 'I expect you would worry about leaving your mother, too.'

'That's it exactly. You understand.' He glanced at her and smiled. 'It's been dreadful for her losing my father and she grieves deeply for him. Maybe when it's warmer she will start to feel a little stronger, and if I move to Cambridge perhaps she would come too. At the moment, though, the arrangement here suits her and she won't think of going anywhere else.'

He sighed, and Sarah saw how much the situation frustrated him. At twenty-six, a year older than he was, she knew a little of how he felt, that life and youth and the possibility of a future were ebbing away. Her parents' generation had lost so much in war. Would it soon be the children's turn?

Fourteen

All Saints' Westbury was as different from the church in Tuana as it was possible to be. Where the latter had been bleached by the glaring Mediterranean sun, this grey stone hulk with its stubby tower stood hunched up against the cold wind on a graveyard mound that grew wild with grasses and flowers.

Inside, out of the wind, it felt much warmer and the sun falling through the windows cast colourful patterns over the flagstones. Briony was wrapped in quietness as she wandered about, breathing in the musty scents of aged wood and leather and stroking the carved ends of the ancient pews. Halfway down a side aisle she came to a console table and opened a slim calf-bound volume that was lying there. The creamy pages whispered of the past as she read the beautifully hand-written names of the dead of two world wars from the parish, frowning as she tried to recognize any. It was a shock to come across her grandfather's name, *Harry Andrews*, but then she saw the date of death was 1916. Perhaps this had been a young uncle who'd died of wounds during the Battle of the Somme. No name from the Second World War entries leaped out at her. No Hartmann, no Andrews or Bailey. She'd almost come to the end when she heard a sudden snore and nearly jumped out of her skin.

The sound came from a choir stall where an elderly man with sparse white hair dozed, a newspaper open on his lap. He was so still that, but for the rise and fall of his chest, he might be taken for a painted wooden carving. There was something familiar about him.

He must have sensed her watching, for his eyes fluttered open and when he saw her he straightened and gave her a smile that shook his wrinkles. 'Bless you, my dear. I must apologize.' His hand groped for the stick leaning against the seat beside him and she realized: this was the old man she'd seen sitting in the walled garden on the day she arrived.

'There's no need. It's a good place for a nap,' she said, taking a concerned step towards him as he rose unsteadily. He wore a clerical collar, she saw, though he was surely too ancient to be vicar here.

'Don't worry, I'm quite all right. Simply a little stiff. I see you've been examining our memorial register.'

'Yes, I hope you don't mind. I'm Briony Wood and I've recently discovered that my grandfather's family came from Westbury. My grandfather moved to Surrey after the war, which is where I'm from. I'm trying to find out a little about him.'

'You'll only find the names of the war dead there, of course. Who was your grandfather?'

'His name was Harry Andrews. Not the one in the book who died in 1916. Grandpa was born in 1915. And died in 1988. I tried looking him up on the internet,' Briony went on, seeing his interest, 'and found he was in the Norfolk Regiment. I think he joined up in 1939 or soon after, anyway, and I know he served in Italy.'

'Andrews, yes, that's a name I recognize.' The old man stopped to clear his throat. 'Though I haven't actually met any living ones here. This was never my parish, you see. They don't let you retire in the place where you've been vicar. They think you might cause trouble with the new regime, I suppose.' His faded blue eyes glinted with humour.

'I didn't know that. Have you lived in Westbury long?'

'Fifteen years, it must be. My final parish before I retired was near Ipswich. Westbury has an interesting history, you know. One of Charles the Second's mistresses is said to have been born at the Hall. But Andrews, Andrews. Let's try the graveyard record.' Briony followed as he shambled over to a table near the door where, with quivering hands, he opened a plastic folder lying there. 'I drew this up for the rector soon after I arrived. It might offer some names that are familiar'

He fumbled past the typed pages and from a pouch at the back slid out what turned out to be a meticulous hand-drawn plan of the graveyard with *Revd George Symmonds, 2002* written in tiny letters at the bottom. 'That's you?' she asked when he showed it to her and he nodded with a modest smile.

'The list is alphabetical by surname, then you cross-check the grave reference on the plan '

Briony pulled the folder towards her and began to read the columns of names. 'There are lots of Kellings and Foggs round here, aren't there? But not many Andrews.' Then she saw with sudden surprise. 'Oh, there's a Hartmann. Here. Barbara Hartmann. I've seen some letters to a Paul Hartmann.' There was no Paul listed, though.

'I'd forgotten about her, poor lady. From the state of her grave I fear everyone has. Except God, of course, and I suppose that's the most important thing. Would you like to go out and look? I don't remember mention of any Paul, though.'

Barbara Hartmann's grave was in a secluded corner, shaded by an overhanging tree that scattered tiny shell-like blossom. The engraving on the stone slab was weather-worn, but Briony could make out most of the detail. *Barbara Ann Hartmann* was the lady's full name. Then a date, *1940*, and, below that, a reference to a husband.

'Klaus Hartmann,' George Symmonds said, peering through his spectacles. 'According to the documents, he's not buried anywhere in this churchyard.'

'Maybe they were Paul's parents.'

'Tell me about this Paul.'

'I was given some letters which were written to him during the war by a woman called Sarah. I think her other name was Bailey. She lived at Flint Cottage. Do you know a Flint Cottage?'

'I do, yes. It's further up to the left, on the other side of the road. A couple with a young family moved in recently. Nice people. He's a GP and she's a consultant something at the hospital.'

'They probably won't know about Sarah if they're new.'

'No, I suppose not. Do you live near here?'

She explained that she was staying at Westbury Lodge.

He nodded. 'I drive up that way sometimes. Pastoral visits, you know.'

'Then it must have been you I saw. Sitting in the walled garden a couple of days ago.'

'I confess it was! I love it there. It has a particular atmosphere which I find very conducive to thought. Though I find the line between meditation and sleep to be a fine one these days.' His eyes twinkled.

While Mr Symmonds picked the moss from Barbara Hartmann's memorial stone, Briony wandered round the graveyard, examining the inscriptions. The centre was dominated by a large, plain catafalque fenced round with black iron palings. 'That's the Kelling family tomb,' the old man called, seeing her interest. 'What a monster, eh?'

The Andrews graves were scattered about. She bent to read the stones. *Hannah, Elizabeth, Percival* – the names and dates meant nothing to her, but she enjoyed a pleasant sense of connection to these possible shadowy ancestors. Despite the brisk east wind this was a beautiful place to end up, she thought, with its dancing trees and the dreaming stones.

Thanking George Symmonds, Briony walked slowly back up the lane towards the Hall. On the way, she passed a large cottage with a garden behind a flint wall. A small oblong concrete plaque set in the wall, which she hadn't noticed on the way down, read *Flint Cottage*. So this was where Sarah Bailey had lived. She stopped and listened to the sounds of children playing somewhere behind the house. Then a young spaniel appeared at the gate and yapped at her, so she set off once more. She'd call in another time.

Walking under the gateway with its Great Dane statue, she heard a car turn in behind her and glanced back. It was a silver saloon with an expensive-sounding engine and when she stood to one side to let it pass, the driver stopped and lowered his window. The man was a few years older than her, with dark, unshaven looks, a little tousled, but his crisp navy jacket was as sleek as his car.

'Morning. I hope you don't mind me asking,' he said, in a well-spoken voice that while polite was used to being obeyed. 'You have business here, do you? It's simply that this park is private.'

'It's all right, I'm staying close by.'

'Oh, I see. My apologies then. We've had problems lately with tourists treating the place as a picnic spot and leaving litter.'

'I've rented Westbury Lodge. I promise not to drop any litter.'

'Ah. Now I'm embarrassed.' He flashed a friendly smile, showing even white teeth. 'In that case, hop in, let me give you a lift up the hill.'

'It's all right, thanks,' she said, folding her arms in mock umbrage. 'I was brought up not to get into strangers' cars. Anyway, I'm enjoying the walk.'

His forehead crinkled and then he decided she was teasing and grinned again. 'Sure, though I'm perfectly safe. Nice to meet you, anyway.' She watched him drive away, but instead of going to the Hall, as he'd implied was his intention, he took a left turn, hooted his horn and waved at her, before the car was swallowed up by a thick grove of trees.

'That'll be Greg Richards, my boss.' Kemi in reception at the Hall was dressed in a deep blue skirt suit today, striking against her raven hair and sparkling dark brown eyes. 'He's usually only down at weekends now the building work's done.'

'Does he stay here?'

'In the Hall? No. He has a house in the wood down there.'

That seemed to be the extent of Kemi's knowledge about the man, or what she was prepared to say about him, anyway, but the thought of his attractive, good-humoured face, his dark hair and shadowy beard, stayed with Briony for the rest of the day.

It came almost as no surprise, therefore, when the following afternoon she answered a knock on her door to find him waiting on the path. He wasn't as tall as she expected, was her initial impression.

'Hi. We met briefly yesterday. Greg Richards. I hope I'm not disturbing you.' His smile was as charming as she remembered.

She looked at him and then down at the cellophane-wrapped bunch of flowers he'd taken out from behind his back.

'What are these for?' she asked, taking them from him with a frown. They were pretty, bright gerbera and gypsophila, *what was its other name, baby's breath*? But she wasn't used to getting flowers and found herself questioning the motives behind these.

'You must have thought me rude yesterday,' Greg said. 'I'm sorry, I didn't mean to be. This is by way of amends.' He appeared sincere in his penitence.

'Thank you. You shouldn't have worried,' she said, softening. 'I wasn't offended really. Having strangers leaving rubbish on your property must be horrible and I don't blame you for challenging me.' She smiled. 'Come in for a moment. I was sitting in the garden, having failed to muster the energy to do some work. I'm Briony, by the way. Briony Wood.'

She led him through to the back of the cottage where a small pear-shaped lawn was edged by flower borders. Hollyhocks and foxgloves grew up against a wooden fence.

'All very English country garden,' he remarked, looking round. 'Nice. I haven't been out here since our tenant left. Kemi deals with everything.'

'Pretty, isn't it? I've been trying my hand at some weeding, but I'm not very good at telling which the good plants are.'

'Hmm, well, don't ask me, I don't know either. I wish I did. I'd like to develop the gardens here. Put the place on the map a bit. Haven't quite decided what yet. It's difficult as I'm up in the City all week.'

'So Kemi said. I'm a Londoner, too, an academic, though.'

'Oh, so you're Professor Wood.'

'Just Doctor, so far.'

'What subject?'

'History. At Duke's College. I specialize in the Second World War, but a great deal of my time is spent teaching students. While I'm here I'm going over the draft of a book I'm writing,' she said, and changed the subject because she didn't feel like pouring out all the details to a stranger on a lovely warm Sunday afternoon. 'It's just the place to do it,' she went on quickly. 'I've fallen in love with the Hall. Do you own the whole estate? Kemi said you were her boss, but I didn't think what that meant.'

'I am the owner, yes.'

'Has it been your family home? It must have quite a history.'

'I haven't owned it long. It came onto the market several years ago. It belonged to the Kelling family for centuries, but they ran out of money.'

So he was simply a property developer making a buck. That was a shame, she'd hoped he'd be more involved than that.

'I do care about the old place, though,' he said, smiling, as though he'd read her thoughts. 'There's a family connection. My great-grandfather, one Hector Richards, was the estate manager here between the wars. I live in his house.'

Briony found herself warming to Greg now. He was being very friendly, she thought. There was no sign of his bossiness of yesterday.

'That's wonderful. Apparently I have connections round here, too. My grandfather's name was Harry Andrews?'

He shook his head. 'I don't know any Andrews. So is that why you chose to come here? A little foray into family history?'

'Sort of,' she said. There was a sharpness about his question that made her guarded. 'Mainly, I want to get this writing done and it's difficult to concentrate in London in summer.'

'Yeah, kind of enervating, isn't it? And if you go out, every-where is full of tourists. I'll tell you what, though, I'm seeing my old dad tomorrow. He lives out on the coast at Blakeney. Bit of a sailor, my dad. I'll ask him if he knows of any Andrews.'

'Thanks, that would be brilliant.'

After she'd shown him out, Briony arranged his flowers in a vase and placed it on the kitchen windowsill. It pleased her that she would see them every time she entered the room.

She made a mug of tea and, with a deep breath, went into the dining room, where she'd set up a working space in the window looking out at the front. She sat down, brought up her manu-script on her laptop and began to scroll down until the editor's first comment appeared. *Evidence?* it said.

A movement outside made her glance up to see an old, very stooped lady walk slowly past the house tugging an equally ancient pug dog on a lead. For a moment she watched their ago-nizing progress, the dog swaying like a barrel on its stiff little legs, then she addressed herself again to the screen in front of her.

The Auxiliary Territorial Service was by far the biggest of the wom-en's services, she read in her introduction, *and had its origins in the First World War.* She supposed it was a bit vague. She moved the cursor to the beginning of the sentence and inserted: *Totalling 200,000 by 1945.*

She worked solidly for an hour and a half, stopping fre-quently to consult one or other of the books and paperwork she'd brought with her or to find a reference online, but when she stopped to remove her reading glasses and rub her tired eyes she saw she had addressed only the comments in the first three-quarters of the introduction. Beyond the window the slanting sun was making shadows of the trees across the lane. She felt hungry.

In the kitchen she filled a roll with ham and salad, arranged it with a slab of carrot cake on a plate, made another mug of tea and carried the whole lot outside. She went to the front this time, and through the door into the walled garden, picking the bench where she'd seen the old man.

It was a calm, sunny place, sheltered from the breeze. From the few gnarled fruit trees espaliered against the crumbling walls and the patches of lawn, it was possible to imagine how the layout might once have been in the glory days of the hall. *When had it stopped being a proper garden*? she wondered as she licked the icing off the cake. Years and years ago, she supposed. She drank her tea, then sat for a while with her eyes half closed, enjoying the peace of the evening, trying to be in the moment as her counsellor had advised. Beyond the walls a gentle breeze ruffled the tresses of the poplar trees, where pigeons warbled. Near her bench a fat bee zigzagged low over the daisies. For a moment she thought she heard footsteps on the gravel path, but when she looked there was no one. *I'm going barmy*, she told herself, and stood up briskly, brushing the crumbs from her lap.

Back inside, she tidied the kitchen and checked her phone for messages. Aruna had posted a happy selfie on Facebook of herself and Luke on Brighton Beach, which she smiled at, but it made her feel lonely and restless. Perhaps she'd made a mistake coming here on her own. In the twilight gloom the place took on the mantle of another age. It was something about the cramped rooms, the pungency of old wood and old fabric, of lingering smoke from long-ago wood fires. She switched on a table lamp which cast the living room in a cosy glow, so she settled herself on the sofa with a mint tea and the tin containing Sarah's letters and laid them out on the coffee table before her, trying to ensure they were in date order. Her eyes widened as she read the address on a white envelope she hadn't noticed before. 'Paul

Hartmann, esq., Westbury Lodge, Westbury'. For a moment her mind couldn't function for surprise. Paul Hartmann had lived here in this very cottage where she was staying! She looked about her. The stone fireplace, that was surely the original, but the heavy chintz sofa and armchair, how old were they? Still, the view from the window must be much the same, and she could imagine Paul walking across the lane to the walled garden every day to work, as another of Sarah's letters had intimated.

Inside the envelope were several short notes of only a few lines each. None was properly dated. The first one she unfolded made her smile.

Tuesday

Dear Mr Hartmann,

I trust this finds you well. My mother would be glad if you would call at your convenience to advise us on a tree that is worrying her. She fears a dead branch will fall on our heads. I hope you don't mind this intrusion on your time. It will at any rate be nice to see you. My regards to your mother.

Yours sincerely,

Sarah Bailey

Another note asked him if he'd mind buying her some raspberry canes on his visit to Askey's on Saturday. How very touching, Briony thought, that Paul had kept a scribbled note from Sarah on a matter as small and inconsequential as this.

The next one she examined was neatly written and far more considered. The light spirit of the first notes was missing entirely. *Dear Paul*, it began.

Thank you for your letter. I was glad to have your explanation as I was worried that I'd offended you this afternoon, and I had no intention of doing that. The truth is that I worry I will never find what I'm to do with my life if I don't take this opportunity now. I am quite sure that your time will come ...

As she read on, she began to understand something of what had drawn Sarah and Paul together. They were both keen gardeners, both fatherless, but it was more than that. They were both restless souls whose futures were hampered by a strong sense of family duty.

Fifteen

March 1939

Warm sunshine and little tugs of breeze accompanied Sarah on her walk up to the walled garden one morning. The boxes from India were arriving later in the week and Mrs Bailey had brought in decorators to repair the damage the Watson family had wreaked on Flint Cottage. What with the noise and the stink of paint, Sarah couldn't bear to be in the house. There was plenty to do in the garden at this time of year, but Mrs Bailey was out of sorts with the upheaval and took every opportunity to interrupt and send Sarah off on some errand. Diane had gone to Norwich with Aunt Margo in search of dress material, so Sarah thought she would satisfy her curiosity and see properly the garden where Paul worked, for she had only seen it in its wintry state. She took a box of home-made biscuits for his mother and set off with them in a basket that also contained a cutting from a plant she was hoping he would identify, her new secateurs in case there was anything she could help with while she was up there and an envelope that had arrived in the post for her the day before.

The wooden door in the wall stood ajar and she paused to

run a hand over the bright green moss growing on the pitted surface of the ancient brick. Then she slipped inside, only to stop short at the top of a flight of steps.

An extraordinary feeling came over her. It was as if she was passing from one world into another. The kitchen garden where she found herself was large enough for the needs of a manor house, but small enough to feel intimate, safe. There was no one there, but there were signs of activity, a spade dug into the freshly turned earth of a flower bed, several trays of seedlings on the path nearby. A clattering sound and she glanced up as a door in the opposite wall flew open and Paul entered, carrying a coil of hose on his shoulder and in one hand a heavy pail of water. For a moment he didn't see her, so intent was he on his work, and she watched him shrug off the hose, sink one end in the bucket and test the handpump affixed to the other end. Then he sensed her presence. She brightened at his pleasure on seeing her and laughed as he doffed his cap and the water ran over his boots.

'Don't let me stop you getting on,' she called. 'I only came to take a look.' She descended the steps and set her basket down. 'What are you planting? Lettuces?'

'Dozens of them,' Paul wiped his face with the back of his forearm. 'They'll be ready to eat when the Kellings return for the summer.'

'I'll give you a hand if you like.'

'No, no. Let me have a little break and I'll show you round. These fruit trees are pretty, no, such delicate blossom?'

He spoke with knowledge and enthusiasm as they circum-navigated the garden and she duly admired the peach trees, their spread branches pinned to the south wall, and followed him into a lean-to greenhouse where a grapevine like the one at Flint Cottage grew in a latticed shape above their heads. Here, seedlings flourished in trays and pots on all surfaces and last year's strawberry plants, safe from the frost but pale-leaved, waited in a corner to be replanted.

Outside once more, he showed her beds where the air was fragrant with herbs, flower beds pungent with manure. 'These trenches are for the asters. Over here will be mixed annuals for the house. And sweet peas should come up over there by the dwarf plums. Lady Kelling very much likes sweet peas.'

Paul had explained before that the head gardener who supervised him was muttering about retirement, and that apart from himself as under-gardener there was only a boy from the village called Sam who was being trained. But the gardens were not extensive and the family rarely in residence outside the summer months, though a box of fruit and vegetables in season was sent up to their London residence on the train twice a week. Major Richards supervised other estate workers to manage the woodland.

'It's a lovely place, this garden. It feels so quiet and safe. And very old. What's this rose?' Sarah was examining a plant that rambled over the wall above the flower beds.

'It grows beautiful cream flowers with pink edges, but I don't know what it's called. I think you have them at Flint Cottage, too. Perhaps they're a local speciality.' Paul smiled and returned to his lettuces, spraying the ones he'd planted with the handpump.

'Oh, I forgot,' Sarah said and went to forage in her basket. 'I bought these biscuits for your mother – and for you of course.'

'Thank you! Best to leave them by the steps there, then I won't squash them by accident.'

She laid down the box, then more hesitantly picked up the envelope. 'There's a letter I want to show you later. I'd like to ask your advice.'

'My advice? I'd be honoured. I'll finish planting first or the old man will wonder what I've been doing this morning.'

'I'll help, really. I like this kind of planting, the rhythm of it.'

'If you insist, then thank you.'

While she pulled on her gloves, he fetched a bit of old carpet for her to kneel on. She set about making deft holes with her forefinger, into which she dropped the delicate plants, and gently pressed the earth round them.

When they'd finished, Paul doused the lines of plants with more water, then tucked his gloves under his arm and took the letter she handed him.

'What is Radley?' he said, looking up from his reading, eyes puzzled.

'It's a college in Kent for women gardeners.'

'Ah.'

'They say they might be able to offer me a place for the autumn. I wrote to them a week ago, but I didn't expect to hear back so soon.'

'You seem uncertain.'

'Yes. I mean it sounds possible that I could start there. It's a shock. My letter was . . . speculative, I suppose. I would have to find the fees, but Mummy gave me some money to remember Daddy by. It's simply . . . it would mean leaving her and Diane.'

'And you don't want to do that.'

'I do want to study. I need something to occupy me, you see, and I love the idea of designing gardens. Of course, I haven't a clue about the techniques, so this would enable me to get started.'

She stopped, seeing that his attention had shifted, and turned, following his gaze. In the doorway to the garden a man had appeared, an older man who stood stiffly and leaned on a stick. It was Major Richards. He touched his hat to Sarah and glanced quickly around, his shrewd eyes taking in the half-dug beds, the wheelbarrow, the array of tools lying on a tarpaulin on the path. 'Keeping busy, are we, Hartmann?' he said. 'I'm sure Lady Kelling wouldn't like to think time was being wasted.'

'I'm very aware of that, Major.' Paul passed the letter back to Sarah and slowly, very slowly, grasped the handle of the spade and tugged it from the earth.

'Good afternoon, Sarah. Your mother is well, I hope?'

'Very well, thank you.'

He nodded, and shooting Paul one final admonishing glare, he turned awkwardly and went on his way.

'I cannot advise you, Miss Bailey,' Paul murmured, setting both hands on the spade. 'It is a decision for you alone.'

He sank the spade into a patch of hard earth and with it plunged Sarah's spirits. There was a remoteness about his expression that confused her, made her wonder whether he was a different person to the one she'd imagined. Was it merely anger at Major Richards' interference?

'I know it's my decision. It's simply there isn't anyone else I can ask. I used to speak to Daddy about these things.'

'Then you must make your own judgement. It is your life.'

'Yes, of course.' She spoke unhappily. There was no point asking Mummy or Diane. Mummy would think she was mad and Diane would be upset. She folded the letter up and slid it back inside the envelope.

Sarah had read about horticultural colleges in a gardening magazine and written to Radley, which she'd liked the sound of, to find out more. The letter offering her an interview for a place had jolted her out of her dreaming. The thought that she really could pursue a career was both invigorating and alarming. She would need all her strength to leave her mother and Diane. She could imagine the conversations, Diane's pleading eyes, her mother's cold silence and her own guilt for putting her needs above her family's. What would her father say if he was looking down on them? The thought gave her heart, because in fact she believed he'd have been sympathetic to her. 'That's my Molly,' he'd always said in response to her success – Molly was his pet name for her. He'd been puffed out with pride by her final school results. Tears pricked her eyes at the memory and she blinked fiercely.

Paul had begun to turn over the earth in the bed. Everything about his posture spoke of unhappiness. She snatched up the basket, but then her eye fell on the box of biscuits.

'Is your mother in?' she asked him. 'Perhaps I could take these to her.'

He paused in his work and forced a smile. 'She is. That is kind of you, I'm sure she would appreciate it.'

Mrs Hartmann took a long time to come to the front door and she opened it with hesitation, timid dark eyes in a pale oval face peering at Sarah, but when Sarah introduced herself and showed the box, she drew the door wide. 'How nice of you. Come in for a moment, please.' She had a low, gentle speaking voice.

'I'm sorry, the house isn't tidy. I wasn't expecting anyone.' Her glance darted from the shabby hallstand to the threadbare rug, her anxiety obvious. She was a small, slight woman dressed in navy, a colour which Sarah thought aged her. The effort of speaking made her cough and her whole body tensed up with the exertion.

Sarah surveyed her with pity, imagining what she must have gone through with the loss of her husband and her home. The experience had broken her health. 'I won't stay,' she assured Mrs Hartmann. 'Your son said it would be all right to call. I baked the biscuits this morning, so they're quite fresh. I hope you like ginger.'

For the first time a sparkle came to Mrs Hartmann's eyes. 'I love it. I have happy memories of making gingerbread as a child with my mother,' she said, taking the box and opening the lid. The sudden spicy smell filled the air. She smiled as she breathed it in and Sarah saw that she'd been pretty once in a frail, dainty way.

'It's a favourite of mine, too.' *I'll bring her flowers next time*, she thought, watching Mrs Hartmann place the box on the hallstand. *Daffodils, they'll brighten this house.* They hadn't been able to take many possessions away with them from Germany, she remembered Paul telling her, and again she felt a rush of pity.

Mrs Hartmann's troubled eyes rested on her now. 'Your family has been so kind, we are so grateful.'

'Not at all. We were sorry to hear of all your trouble. We hadn't known before what things were like in Germany.'

A shadow passed across Mrs Hartmann's delicate features, causing Sarah to wish that she'd held her tongue. 'That is the problem. No one here really believes it.' She stopped for a moment to cough.

'I think a great many people have their suspicions,' Sarah ventured, 'but nobody wants war.'

Mrs Hartmann batted the excuse away. 'This country is asleep. I have met people here, some our closest neighbours, who say England should stay out of Europe's business. They think that things can go on here as they always have done, that Germany does not want to go to war with us so why should we? But I tell you, Herr Hitler is not a man to trust on any account. Think of Kristallnacht. Oswald Mosley's bullying is almost nothing to that. There is great evil moving in Germany. It'll engulf us all if it is not checked.'

This sounded so dramatic, almost biblical, that Sarah could not think what to say. She knew about last November's events, the vicious attacks on Jews in German cities. She knew, too, Mr Churchill's view, that Hitler could not be trusted. Yet, whatever the level of violence in Germany, could it be that a whole nation was infected by evil? Surely this was an exaggeration.

When she left soon afterwards, her mind was troubled. Paul's sudden coldness to her and his mother's dire predictions had upset her deeply.

At home in the early evening Sarah heard the letter box rattle and shortly afterwards Ruby brought a letter to her in the drawing room where they'd all settled after dinner. 'Miss Sarah Bailey' was written in thick black ink in a hand she did not recognize. But before she could open it, Diane switched on the wireless and her hand stilled on the envelope. She listened with horror to the news, the first they'd heard today. *'German troops have marched into Czechoslovakia.'* Sarah knew what this meant. Hitler had lied at Munich. He wasn't interested simply in a Greater Germany, he had grand imperial plans. And if Czechoslovakia wasn't safe, then Poland wasn't either. *Mrs Hartmann is right*, her thoughts ran. The news ended and Mrs Bailey turned off the wireless.

'Why's everyone so serious?' Diane looked wildly from her mother to her sister, worried by their silence. 'It's all so far away, what does it have to do with us?'

'We don't know yet,' Mrs Bailey said calmly, extracting a cigarette from the case in her bag, but her hand trembled as she held the lighter.

Sarah opened the letter without interest and smoothed out the single sheet inside. *Dear Miss Bailey*, it began. Reading seemed an effort, but she sighed and started again.

Dear Miss Bailey,

My mother has asked me to convey once again her thanks for the biscuits. Your kindness to her means a great deal in these difficult times.

I wish also to convey my apologies for I must have appeared rude to you this afternoon. When you asked my opinion about your future career, I was, most selfishly, reflecting upon my own prospects. You ask my advice and I say go, apply for this course. It will not help your family for you to be held back, frustrated, unable to exercise your talents. I wish I could tell myself the same thing, but my mother would be completely alone if I left her now and I must wait.

My regards to you and your family,
Paul Hartmann

How nice of him, she was touched. She thrust the letter into the pocket of her cardigan, determined to reply to him that evening. He had been too courteous, it occurred to her, to mention Major Richards' interference, though that had clearly annoyed him at the time. His advice was sound. She would apply to the college as he suggested, though perhaps not immediately. She needed to speak to her mother first, and tonight's bulletin made it more difficult to plan for the future.

Sixteen

Briony finished the little notes from Sarah, imagining Paul reading them here in this house and smiling at her cheerful asides. His mother surely had to be the Barbara whose grave she'd found, and it seemed she'd married a German man, so Paul would have been German, too, or at least half German, if Barbara was English. That wouldn't have been easy in wartime, and she wondered how he had ended up serving in the British Army.

She picked up the next envelope from the pile and tried to extract the letter inside, but at some point it must have become damp, and she saw she couldn't pull it out without tearing it. She inspected the next one, to find the same thing had happened. Perhaps if she held it in steam from the kettle ... It was too dark to do anything about it now, though, so she tied the bundle together, put it back in the tin and went upstairs to read in bed.

After she'd switched off the light she lay in the darkness thinking. It might make sense for her to type fair copies of the letters as she read them. It would mean that reading them would take longer, but they'd be easier to refer back to that way. As she fell into a drowse she was sure she could hear the whisper of a woman's voice in her mind and fancied it to be Sarah's.

The museum was in a castle on a mound with a view over Norwich and Briony stood out on the concourse for a while the following day, a sharp wind lifting her hair, looking out across the gleaming glass and metal shapes of shops and offices below, with the stone towers of churches rising here and there among them. In the misty distance, dark canopies of trees girded the city, a sign of where the countryside began.

A church bell nearby began to chime the hour and when it finished, another answered. Eleven o'clock, the morning was flying by. Briony walked briskly through the castle entrance into a high-ceilinged hallway that was bathed in watery light. At the reception desk, she pulled out her purse to buy a ticket.

In the busy labyrinth of the museum, she dawdled first in a room full of stuffed zoo animals whose glass eyes glinted at her, then wandered through another full of birds before mounting a flight of wooden stairs to the gallery above. Here she found what she had been searching for, glass cases of objects representing the museum's military collection. She inspected trays of medals with rainbow-coloured ribbons, cheery postcards sent home by soldiers and examples of uniforms. Here and there hung faded flags, proud symbols of old glory. A display board featured a mosaic of photographs of straight-backed soldiers from the Second World War, all trimmed moustaches and grave expressions. She examined them carefully but recognized no one.

She wasn't certain what she had hoped to find; names, she supposed, evidence of her grandfather, more precise details of what his battalion had been doing in Italy. Anything else would be a bonus. But there wasn't much useful except context. She read a great deal about the Norfolks' action in France in 1940, about the retreat from Dunkirk in little boats, about the soldiers who'd been taken prisoner and marched to Germany. There had been the terrible massacre of a hundred soldiers from the 2nd Battalion ordered by a German commander at a place called, by some awful irony, Le Paradis. Later, battalions of local infantry had been dispatched to Singapore, many men ending up as prisoners of the Japanese and enduring desperate hardship. Some never returned. Those that did never fully recovered. All these stories of bravery, loss and endurance abroad were intensely moving, but there was no mention of Italy.

Briony went downstairs to ask at the information desk. 'Many other documents are in the Norfolk Record Office,' the woman there told her and explained where County Hall was, a mile or so distant. She'd best make an appointment, apparently.

When she returned to Westbury Hall and was about to turn the car down the lane to the cottage, Briony had seen a van parked in the turning circle by the house. The name on the side, in writing looped with flowers, was 'City Gardenscapes'. That was Luke's. She'd swung her car in next to it, killed the engine and opened the door. Instantly she'd heard their voices.

'What are you doing here?' she cried. 'I thought you were in Brighton.'

'Brighton was yesterday,' Aruna said with a sigh. 'Don't you ever look at your phone? We texted this morning to say we were coming.'

'The battery's run out, I'm sorry.'

'You are hopeless.'

'Aruna has a couple of days off and I'm between jobs, so we came down last night to stay with the parents.' Luke sounded as ever more reasonable. 'We thought we'd pop over to see you on the off chance. We had lunch at The Dragon, then walked round the village.'

'How lovely. Come and see where I'm staying. Hop in, you can leave your van here.'

Luke climbed in next to her.

'What's the pub like then?' she asked. It seemed that he and Aruna were getting to know the place better than she did. So much for peace and privacy.

'Great food and a lovely orchard garden,' Aruna said from the back seat. 'Very pleasant. Oh, this guy came over when we were getting out of the van just now.'

'He wanted to know what we were doing,' Luke added as Briony reversed the car. 'We told him we'd come to see you and, hey presto, he was sweetness and light! He says he'll call round and see you as he's got some news. Greg somebody, the name was. Ring any bells?'

'Yes. Greg Richards. He's OK.'

'Is there something you wish to tell us, Bri?' Aruna said in a suggestive voice.

'No, there isn't,' Briony replied crossly as she drove up the lane to the cottage. 'He was going to ask his dad something for me, that's all.'

'How are you getting on with your search?' Luke asked.

'Not very fast,' she replied, 'but you'll never guess, Paul Hartmann probably lived in my cottage.' They were approaching it now. She parked the car and, when they got out, smiled at their pleasure in Westbury Lodge.

'It's like a gingerbread house, isn't it?' Aruna said, digging her phone out of her pocket. 'The pointed windows, I love them. And the ochre brick. Turn round, you two. Let me stand between you. There, now say cheese!'

'Or gingerbread!' Briony laughed as she posed, then went to wrest open the front door.

She sniffed at the now familiar musty smell in the house and hurried to throw open the windows and put the kettle on.

There was a more cheerful atmosphere in the house with Luke and Aruna there, she thought as she gathered mugs from the cupboard. She was aware of Aruna busily looking into every room and coming back with comments on everything from the flock wallpaper to the careworn furniture.

'Aruna, don't, it's rude,' Luke pleaded, exasperated, but Briony merely laughed.

'Don't worry, it's only a rented place. If you said that about my flat it would be different.'

'But you've got good taste so I wouldn't,' Aruna said. 'Even though you insist on having "old stuff" everywhere.' She mimed quote marks in the air.

After they'd finished their tea Briony smiled at them. 'There's somewhere interesting I'd like to show you both; Luke, in particular.'

She led them outside. 'It's really special,' she said, pushing open the stout wooden door.

'An old walled garden,' Luke breathed when they entered. 'Such a shame it's no longer in use.'

'Maybe you can imagine how it was. Sarah talks about it in her letters.'

Briony watched him saunter about, amused by his obvious pleasure. He stopped from time to time to inspect a twisted old tree, its branches still wired to the wall, or some metal struts in the brick that marked where a shed or greenhouse must have been. Then he stood, arms folded, as he gazed across the expanse of grass, lost in thought. It was wonderful to see his reaction. An idea set root in her mind.

Aruna hardly noticed the place. She had sat down on the bench to consult her phone, then walked around, gazing at the screen from time to time and frowning. 'I can't get a signal,' she called to Briony.

'That's funny. It works in the cottage,' Briony replied. She endured her friend coming to take a selfie of them both, though, with the chimneys of the hall growing out of their heads as an amusing background.

Drawn by their laughter, Luke drifted towards them. 'This place is great,' he told Briony, with a delighted smile.

'I thought you'd like it,' Briony said. 'I—'

'It would have been the kitchen garden, right?' Aruna butted in.

'Yes, in the house's heyday,' Luke said. 'There's an interest in them again now. Lots are being restored.'

'For reasons of heritage, I suppose,' Briony murmured.

'Yes, but I reckon it's also our current interest in where food comes from. It's wonderful to think that a garden like this might have supplied everything from artichokes to the downiest peaches, though things had their season, of course. We've become too used to anything being available in supermarkets all the time.'

'Yes, Easter eggs at New Year and mince pies at Hallowe'en,' Briony said with a laugh.

'That's simply the way commerce works now,' Luke said with a frown. 'There always has to be a build-up to the next big festival.'

That was true, Briony thought. She worried about people's loss of connection to the natural world, to the changing seasons. The reasons for the old religious festivals were being forgotten, how Candlemas in January had filled the deep dark days with light, why a good harvest was an occasion for thankfulness, why the self-denial of Lent had helped a pre-industrial population through the last bit of winter when stocks of food had run right down. 'We live such artificial lives now,' she sighed.

'You should do a programme about it, Aruna,' Luke said.

'Maybe, but I'd need an angle,' Aruna mused. Briony knew how competitive it was to get new radio programmes commissioned. Aruna's bosses liked edgy, unusual subjects fronted by high-profile presenters; programmes, it went without saying, that were also cheap to make.

'There'd be plenty about that sort of thing in the radio archives, wouldn't there?' His voice trailed off. He was examining the small hard apples on an old tree nearby, lines of dark red already spreading across their pale green peel. 'I'm no expert,' he said, 'but I think these are quite an unusual variety.' He stepped back and contemplated the tree with his familiar arms crossed pose. 'Have you found out much about this place?' he asked, and when Briony shook her head, 'What about asking the girl Ru and I spoke to at the Hall earlier?'

'You met Kemi? She's lovely, but she seems to know more about selling flats than history. Perhaps I'm doing her down. We can try asking, but I haven't had much luck so far.'

Kemi was there as usual, but she had been taking a middle aged couple around the show flat and so they had to wait a few minutes until the pair had finished their questions and left. Then Kemi smiled at the new arrivals somewhat warily. She was nervous of Briony with her difficult questions.

'Luke and Aruna, friends of mine. Kemi, we were wondering about the old walled garden. Do you have any information on it?'

'Let me think. There is a little bit in here,' Kemi said, picking up one of the glossy prospectuses on her desk and flicking through the stiff bright pages. She came to the one she wanted and passed the open brochure to Briony, who read aloud from a paragraph headed *Heritage*.

'*Westbury Hall was owned by the Kelling family, knights of the shire, for three hundred and fifty years. After the death of Sir Henry Kelling in 1952, the baronetcy died out, but the Hall passed to his second cousin, Unwin Clare, and, on his death in 2014, was sold to Greenacre Holdings who have converted the house into luxury flats that are sympathetic to the original design of this magnificent Grade II listed property. Westbury Hall retains the benefit of large, landscaped gardens, which include the site of the old Walled or Kitchen Garden, a pre-war plan of which is owned by Mrs Clare and may be viewed by arrangement.*'

'Why was the house sold to Greenacre?' Luke wanted to know.

'I believe that the Clares couldn't afford to run it or something,' Kemi said.

'Couldn't pay the inheritance tax, I suppose,' Luke muttered. 'It's a shame that we're not really in Norfolk long enough to try to see Mrs Clare. Does she live far away?'

'No, not far.' For some reason Kemi's eyes were full of amusement.

'In the village maybe?' Briony prompted.

'She lives here at Westbury Hall,' Kemi said, laughing. 'Her apartment is along the corridor.'

'Here?' Briony's jaw dropped in surprise. The former owner had been here all the time?

'Yes! Would you like me to ask her if it's convenient to see you now?'

Seventeen

Only a few minutes later they were admitted to a large sunny living room looking out onto the back garden of the hall, and when Briony shook hands with Mrs Clare she recognized her at once as the stooped old lady with the pug she'd seen walking past her window. The dog had risen with effort from its basket under the window, waddled over and was now issuing croaky yaps at the visitors from the shelter of its mistress' skirts.

'You would like to see the plan of the garden, I gather? It's all right, Lulu, they're friends, friends, I tell you. Go back to your bed.' She spoke gently as though the pug were a toddler, and back in its basket it sat glaring and snorting at these foreign invaders.

'Are you sure it's convenient?' Briony asked politely. 'We didn't expect to be able to see you so quickly.'

'It's really no trouble.' Mrs Clare must be at least ninety, Briony realized. Probably once tall, she was now frail and shrunken. Her sparse silvery-grey hair was arranged into flattering curls around her face. Her eyes, the palest of watery blues, were sunk into hollows in an oval face as wrinkled and careworn as her dog's, and yet those eyes were guileless, dreamy, and there was something about her of the girl she must once have been. It was there in the delicacy of her bone structure, the lightness of her movements.

Mrs Clare drew her visitors across to a framed chart hanging in a shadowed part of the room and fumbled at the cord of a light set above it. 'It's pen-and-ink and watercolour, you know, and one must be careful of sun damage,' she explained.

'And this is the walled garden?' Luke asked, leaning in to examine the picture.

'As it was in 1910, we think. Before the Great War, certainly.'

'This is amazing,' Briony whispered as she and Aruna gathered close to Luke to look.

It was a hand-drawn plan of the garden whose overall shape Briony recognized, delineated by its wall. The growing area was divided into four main sections, labelled variously as flowers, vegetables and fruit bushes in tiny, but readable calligraphy. There was a greenhouse against the south-facing wall, where Briony remembered seeing the metal struts, and an octagonal herb garden lined with low box hedging in the centre of the garden. A key drawn in the left-hand corner of the page referenced some of the different crops.

'Gooseberries,' Aruna said, 'I've never eaten them.'

'Really?' Briony wasn't sure whether to be surprised. 'My granny grew them. They're sharp, need loads of sugar. Look, damsons. Granny had plum trees, too.'

'There used to be a splendid grapevine in the greenhouse,' Mrs Clare said beside them, 'and the grapes were delicious. I've no idea what type, but they really had a wonderful purple glow.'

'You must have lived here a long time then. Well, of course you did, with your husband ...' Briony coloured at her clumsiness.

'Mrs Clare didn't seem offended. 'Longer even than that. I was born here. Unwin was my father's second cousin, though we didn't meet until we were both grown up.'

'Oh, and your father was ...' *When were they talking about?* Briony was even more confused.

'Sir Henry Kelling, of course. I was born Robyn Kelling and I was the last of the direct line, but because I was a girl I couldn't inherit Westbury Hall and so it passed to Unwin. Sir Henry's father and Unwin's father were first cousins, you see.'

Briony was amazed. This lady was a Kelling! She couldn't stop herself wondering whether the marriage was one of love or convenience, but of course she couldn't ask. She felt Robyn Clare's clear-eyed gaze upon her, as though she could read her thoughts. Something else occurred to her, too, which was that Unwin Clare's surname would surely have been Kelling, too, if one followed the male line, but that seemed nosey to ask on first acquaintance, as well. 'It must have been a relief that you didn't lose your home,' she settled for finally.

'It was. I grew up here between the wars,' Mrs Clare continued. 'Did the girl on the desk not explain anything at all? I was born in 1921. I'm ninety-five this year, you know.'

What age did a woman have to reach before she began to be proud of it? Briony wondered, as she and Luke made noises of congratulation. Aruna, however, had lost interest in the conversation and instead crossed the room to where a display of photographs were set out on a console table.

'Are these your family, Mrs Clare?' she asked brightly.

'The one on the right is my son Lewis,' Mrs Clare said, with new warmth in her voice. 'He and his wife live in London. I find it strange to have a child who's an old-age pensioner!'

They moved over to inspect the photographs. 'This one's my dear Unwin with Digby, taken some years ago, but it's a favourite of mine.' A mild-looking country squire in his seventies, wearing a Barbour jacket, held a scruffy terrier that peered out through a curtain of rough hair.

'And this one?' Aruna reached toward a large old black and white print in a dilapidated frame, propped against the wall.

'Careful with that. Here, let me.'

Mrs Clare lifted the frame with both hands and Briony craned to study the group of figures lined up in sombre rows before what was clearly the frontage of Westbury Hall. The women sat on chairs, the men standing behind, all except for a distinguished-looking gentleman with a handsome moustache, who occupied the chair at the centre next to a lady with a disdainful expression, wearing a neat, elegant hat at a fashionable angle.

'My ma and pa, Sir Henry and Lady Kelling,' Mrs Clare said, quietly.

'And that's you?' A much younger version of Lady Kelling sat next to her mother in the picture, her expression startled as a fawn's.

'You are clever. Yes, that's me. I always hated being photographed.'

'Who were all these other people?' Briony continued. 'I mean, I know they must be staff.'

'That's Mrs Thurston, the cook,' Mrs Clare murmured, 'and Jarey, the butler, he was a sweetie. I don't remember everyone's name.' There was a housekeeper, several maids, a terrified waif of a kitchen girl, seven or eight men and boys, two with smart jackets and short hair trained into side partings identifiable as house servants, and four more muscular outdoor types of varying ages including a callow lad Mrs Clare said was Sam, the apprentice gardener.

Sitting next to the young Robyn was a slight, middle-aged woman with a pinched expression, simply dressed in a close-fitting dark dress. Who was she? Briony asked, since the old lady didn't mention her.

'She was a relative of my mother's who came over from Germany in the late thirties, after her husband died. I can't say I often saw her because we were away in London so much. Cousin Barbara, that's it. Her family name was, goodness, it was something German-sounding.'

Briony looked up in amazement. 'Was it Hartmann?'

'That's right. How did you know that?'

'I saw her grave in the churchyard. And did she have a son, Paul?'

'Yes! He had a kind smile, I remember that. Did you say you were staying in the Lodge? That's where they both lived—'

'May I see? Is she this one?' Aruna interrupted and leaned in to gaze at Barbara Hartmann's face.

Briony stared, too, and was struck by how sad the woman appeared to be. 'Which one is Paul, then?' She began to examine the faces of the men again.

'I don't think he's there, is he? No. I wonder in fact if it wasn't he who took the picture.'

'Oh.' Briony felt a rush of disappointment.

'It was a sudden whim of my father's to have the photograph taken, one morning shortly before war was declared. I think he had some presentiment that things would change, and he desperately wanted them to stay the same. It was a horrible summer, I do remember that. The waiting, the certainty that something awful was about to befall us. After the war they said horrid things about my father, that he'd been a Hitler lover, but he wasn't, he simply desperately wanted English life to continue as he thought it always had been. He hated the idea of the old order with its old values being lost. He knew it might mean the end of Westbury Hall.'

'But the Hall is still here,' Luke said gently. 'What would he have thought of it now?'

'He'd have hated it,' Mrs Clare said.

A silence fell over the room.

The old lady turned to gaze out of the window, gripping the sill with one frail hand. Outside it was raining and the scent of wet foliage reached them.

Briony wondered at how strange it must be to see your childhood home bought by developers and so utterly transformed. How could Robyn Clare bear to live here still?

Again, as though she was in tune with Briony's thoughts, the old lady spoke. 'I never wanted to live anywhere else. If I'd married anyone but Unwin I'd have had to leave Westbury Hall, so I've always been very thankful at the way things turned out. This apartment used to be our drawing room and when I saw how nicely they'd converted it I had to have it. My son thinks I'm ridiculous, he wanted me to go and live with them, but I could never have borne a Barbican flat. All that concrete. No, I belong here. I plan to end my days quietly with Lulu. If I go first, then Lewis promises to adopt Lulu, so I'm not worried on that score.'

'I can understand your feelings,' Luke said gently. 'I felt dismal when my parents sold my childhood house in South London and moved to Norfolk. Sometimes I have to drive past the old place and I hate the things the new people have done to it. Shutters instead of curtains, ugly dormer windows, that sort of thing. It doesn't look as though it wants me any more.'

'You should never go back, I keep telling you, Luke,' Aruna said waspishly. 'Oops, Mrs Clare, that sounds rude, but I'm quite different from you and Luke. I couldn't wait to leave the house where I was brought up.'

'Why was that, may I ask?'

'I felt trapped there, and my town was a place you'd want to get away from if you had any ambition. I go back to see Mum and Dad of course, but everyone's exactly the same. My sister even married her boyfriend who lived down the road. Her two kids will go to the same school as we all did, I expect.'

'I understand your point of view. What about you, dear?' Mrs Clare asked Briony. 'Do you revisit your childhood home?'

'My father still lives there with my stepmother,' Briony said hesitantly. 'Maybe if I hadn't lost my mum when I was fourteen I'd want to go back more often.' She felt a lump in her throat, could never get used to the way grief could strike you afresh even after years and years. She added hastily, 'We probably ought to leave you in peace, Mrs Clare.'

'Yes, thank you for showing us the picture.' Luke gave Mrs Clare one of his best smiles.

'Not at all. We like to see young people, don't we, Lulu?' The dog licked its chops and began to pant, gazing adoringly at its mistress. It wasn't a very lovable-looking animal, but still, Briony hoped that dog and mistress would not ever have to live long without one another.

'Do come and see me again if you have a spare moment while you're here,' the old lady said to Briony. 'Though I'm afraid I talk about the past a great deal.'

'That's exactly what interests me,' Briony replied. 'I'd love to.'

'Penny for 'em,' Luke observed as they made their way back to the cottage.

'What?'

'I saw your face when Mrs Clare mentioned the name Hartmann.'

'It's astonishing, isn't it, to think that she knew Paul, even slightly. I should have asked her more about him.'

'So you'll go back to see her?' Aruna asked, sounding disbelieving.

'Of course.' She bit her lip. 'And I didn't ask if she knew my grandfather.'

'You should definitely go back,' Luke said.

Aruna said little for the rest of the visit and Briony wondered what was wrong. Perhaps she was simply tired. Never mind, she'd loved having them both today. The three of them got on so well, with Luke always the mollifier, so easy to have around to offset Aruna's spikiness. Yes, the couple were a good balance for one another. She was happy for Aruna to have found someone special.

Later, when they left, she walked up to the van to wave them off.

'We're in Norfolk for a couple more days,' Luke told her, after giving her a hug. 'Mum said to ask you over to a meal. Would tomorrow evening suit?'

'That's so nice of her. I'd love to, thanks.'

'Great! I'm texting you the address now. It's fairly easy to find. There!'

As Briony watched the van disappear through the great arched gate, a nameless melancholy washed over her. Usually she felt perfectly reconciled to her own company, but as she walked back to the cottage alone, wrapping her fleece tightly against the cool of the evening, she knew it to be loneliness. Perhaps it came from thinking about her mum.

Once upon a time her family had been a close little unit, loving, supportive. Both sets of grandparents lived nearby and she remembered seeing a lot of them when she was small, though Grandad Wood, her father's father, had died when Briony was five or six.

Grandpa Andrews, her mother's father, she remembered because he'd been so busy and active in his retirement, either up and repairing something in the house or garden, or out and about with the Rotary Club or the Ramblers. He was a sociable soul, but when he came home he liked Granny to be there, calm, reassuring, the heart of the house, sewing, or entertaining friends to tea. If she was out he'd be like an abandoned dog, ears pricked, listening for her to come home.

The Woods were a family who were always arguing about small things, but rarely discussed the large ones. Neither Briony nor her brother rebelled, so far as she could remember. Each of them had their own passions. Birchmere wasn't far from Gatwick airport and her brother, two years her junior, had always been fascinated by the planes whose noise infuriated everyone else. He would always rush out to spot Concorde on its evening flight and badgered their father constantly to take him to air shows. He and Briony had little in common with one another apart from family ties, and just as it was natural for him to have become an engineer with British Airways, so it was for her to follow her obsession with the past. She loved to lose herself in a world when flight had been no more than a fantasy for humans. And with their father constantly working long shifts at the paper it was their mother who had held them all together, encouraging their separate interests. During the months of her illness they all felt helpless, unable to communicate with one another. When she died, a silence fell between them all. Was this why she was alone now, Briony had asked Grace, her counsellor; because aloneness felt natural to her? Or was the seed of it from somewhere even further back? Grace hadn't been able to tell her.

Eighteen

June 1939

Sarah hacked ferociously at the stump of ivy, then dug the fork under it again, trying to loosen the roots, but it would not shift.

'Damn you,' she told it, wiping her brow with the back of her hand.

'Having problems?' a voice called. She looked up, shading her eyes against the sun to see a man in uniform striding across the lawn. It was Ivor.

'Good morning, nice to see you back.' She had heard he was home on leave. 'It's a battle to the death here, but one I'm determined to win!' She gave the stump a kick.

'Let me try.' He took the fork out of her hand and she watched him sink it into the soil, far deeper than she'd been able, and brace himself against the roots. The ivy gave creaks of protest but did not budge.

'Wait a minute.' Expression grim, he flung his jacket over a chair, rolled up his sleeves and returned to the job. He dug out the network of smaller roots, and this time, when he plunged the fork in under the stump, it broke away suddenly with a series of snaps and groans. 'That's settled him.' He mopped his brow, his eyes bright with triumph.

'Thanks,' she said, seizing the stump and dragging it free. 'Alas, poor Yorick.' She held it aloft in imitation of a skull, before tossing it into the wheelbarrow. When Ivor laughed, she thought, *Mummy's wrong about me, I'm not in the least stand-offish.*

After a cool spring, the first week of June had been sunny and warm, not comfortable for this kind of exertion, but following a difficult conversation with her mother that morning, Sarah had needed to take out her frustration on something and the recalcitrant ivy, a gnarled great-grandfather of creepers, whose leaves encompassed the whole rear wall of the house, had seemed a suitable adversary.

She'd first broken the news to Mrs Bailey about applying for gardening college back in April, and the reaction had been exactly as she'd feared; that she was needed here in Norfolk with her mother and sister and it was extremely selfish for her to think about doing anything else.

Diane's reaction depressed her even more. Her sister looked so pitiful that it twisted Sarah's heart. Still, though, Sarah wouldn't change her mind. She wrote back to the college, expressing interest in a place, and a fortnight later was invited to Kent for interview.

She had liked the principal very much. Miss Agatha Trot was a trim, handsome woman in her prime, who had travelled widely in her younger days, hunting for new plants in South and Central America, which had given her a ready host of stories to tell. When a letter offering a definite place arrived a day or two later, Sarah's first instinct was to accept immediately and enclose a cheque for the deposit. But doubts quickly began to set in. *If there were to be a war.* Those were the words that entered any conversation now about the future. It was difficult for anyone to make plans. In the end she had sent a holding letter in reply.

This morning's argument had followed the arrival of another letter from the college administrator enquiring whether Miss Bailey intended to take up her place, and if so, would she please supply the deposit as requested.

'You'll be wasting your money,' Mrs Bailey snapped, 'but I suppose you must do what you choose. You usually do.' This was particularly unfair; Sarah felt stung.

There had followed a moment's silence, during which Mrs Bailey read a note that had arrived from Margo Richards. 'Apparently Ivor is returning today for a visit,' she said, over her spectacles. 'I expect he'll call. You know, Sarah, he does seem very interested in you. I can't think why, you're always so stand-offish with him.'

'I am not!' She was particularly surprised as she found it easy to be friendly to him. She felt sorry for Ivor because of the weight of his father's expectations on him and he was good company, always interested in what she was doing. In turn, she found his views on politics thoughtful and well-informed. However, her mother's pointed comment confirmed something that she'd privately been beginning to wonder herself. He hadn't been home very much at all recently, but when he had he'd made a point of coming to Flint Cottage almost immediately.

On this occasion it was telling that he hadn't even taken the time to change out of his service dress.

'You shouldn't be doing this heavy work,' he said, reclaiming his jacket and hooking it over his shoulder. 'Mind you, the garden's looking splendid. Do you have any help? I'm sure we could send Hartmann down.'

'Jim Holt who does the vicar's garden comes in once a week. I wouldn't bother Mr Hartmann. He has enough to do.'

Did she imagine the satisfaction with which Ivor nodded? Because of her mother's remark she found herself watching him with new eyes, and wondering about her own reaction to him. She was aware of his glowing demeanour, the brightness of his gaze.

'How is Aldershot?'

'Chaotic. We're training the new recruits we've been sent. Pretty raw, most of them.'

'One of Mrs Allman's nephews in Ipswich has signed up. Her sister's very concerned.'

'Tell her not to be. There's no sign of anything happening at the moment.'

'No, but it's hard not to fear that something might.'

Ivor's tone had been light, but the way he avoided her eye betrayed his underlying fear. Sarah, who made a point of reading a daily paper and listening to the news, knew about the increase in defence spending and the plans for a Women's Land Army to improve food yields. Slowly but surely the country was creaking into war mode. And yet ordinary life was going on as usual. Mrs Allman said that her sister had told her about a German hockey team that had visited and played in Ipswich recently, and what did Mrs Bailey think of that? A week ago, at Whitsun, Sarah and Diane, taking the train to Norwich, had found the station platform packed with excited families heading for the coast. A bank holiday was a bank holiday, after all, and why shouldn't the children have donkey rides and ice cream?

A knocking sound. She and Ivor looked up to see Diane, struggling to open the conservatory door, which was swollen by damp and always caught. Ivor marched over and tugged it open and Diane emerged in her dainty, fawnlike manner, her blue eyes huge and anxious. 'How lovely to see you, Ivor,' she said gravely and held out her hand. He shook it carefully and asked how she was keeping.

'Very well, thank you,' she replied, but her eyes darted to Sarah now, reproachful.

'You've heard my sister's news, I expect,' she asked him, a sharpness in her voice.

'No, what news is this?' He turned enquiringly to Sarah.

'Oh really,' Sarah murmured. Diane should have left it to her to explain in her own time.

'She's leaving us,' Diane said, her chin jutting.

'I'm not going anywhere quite yet, Ivor. It's simply that I might be going away to study.' She explained about Radley. 'I want to do something with my life, be useful and, as you know, I love growing things.'

'I see. Has Hartmann put you up to this?'

'No, of course not. Why would he?'

'Simply what my father said. That he'd seen you together.' Ivor's eyes glittered.

'Well, it wasn't anything to do with Mr Hartmann. It was my own idea.'

'I don't think she should go, Ivor, do you?' Diane said 'Oh, I wish you wouldn't, Sarah. I would be so lonely.'

'Diane.' Sarah warned. 'Don't embarrass poor Ivor. And you wouldn't be lonely. You have plenty of friends. Jennifer Bulldock's always inviting you to things.'

She couldn't rid herself of a sense that everyone was lining up against her: her mother, Diane, Paul Hartmann and now Ivor, too, for he was regarding her with lips pressed together. *I may not go if there's a war.* She'd have said that to Ivor, but not with Diane there. She and her mother had an unspoken agreement not to speak about politics in front of Diane, knowing how she hated it.

She worried about Radley all that day, then come evening she wrote the letter accepting the place and enclosing a cheque. Only after she had dropped the envelope into the box outside the post office did she feel a sense of peace. The decision had been made.

Nineteen

It was July, the House of Lords was in recess for the summer and the Kellings had come home to Westbury. In church the Baileys sat two rows behind the Kelling family pew. They were tall and thin, all three Kellings, Sir Henry with his clever, grave face and salt-and-pepper hair, elegantly dressed Lady Kelling with her striking hawkish looks, and between them their daughter, The Hon. Robyn, a girl of Diane and Jennifer's age, her still, pale face and colourless hair almost ghostly in the grey light. They left smartly after the service, stopping merely to address a few words to the Reverend Tomms and no more than nodding to the Bulldocks, who had gathered eagerly to speak to them outside. Robyn trailed obediently after her parents, trained to do so no doubt by her stern mama.

Watching their car drive away, Mrs Bulldock did her best to make excuses for them, which Sarah saw from the disappointment in her broad face were really to disguise her hurt feelings. 'The poor man really does appear exhausted,' she said to the Baileys. 'Lady Kelling is very worried about him from what I hear. All those late nights discussing the international situation.

It's too bad of the Germans. And Robyn, well, you've seen the girl yourself, very plain, don't you think. It's her second season, poor thing, and there is still no sign of an engagement. Such a pity after all that money and effort. I'm so glad we didn't go down that route for Jennifer.'

Mrs Bulldock appeared completely unaware that a similar comment might be made about Jennifer's single status, or that it was tactless to say these things in front of Mrs Bailey, who had two unmarried daughters, but then the Baileys were getting used to Mrs Bulldock's frequent faux pas.

'Now are you sure, Mrs Bailey, that we can't interest you in our whist drive next Tuesday? It's to raise money for the mission school in Nigeria, well, you heard all about it from Mr Tomms just now. The Stevensons are doing such a marvellous job out there with the heathen, we must do our best to support them.'

'I'm afraid I have a previous engagement on Tuesday,' Sarah's mother lied smoothly as she'd done on so many occasions before, 'but I'll send you a donation.' She'd do as she promised, Sarah knew, smiling to herself, but nothing on God's earth would get Belinda Bailey playing whist with a lot of Westbury matrons.

Given her aloof behaviour at church, the Baileys were surprised to receive an invitation from Lady Kelling for tea at the Hall the following Saturday afternoon. They went, of course, out of courtesy, but also curiosity. Who else would be there? Quite a crowd, it turned out, and the three women were directed through a dark-panelled hall into a sunny drawing room filled with vases of blue and pink sweet peas and out onto the back lawn where tea was arranged on tables under the shade of a marquee.

The Bulldocks were there in force – Sarah heard Jennifer's infectious laugh before she saw her – as were all three of the Richards, as well as members of two or three other local families whom the Baileys hadn't met before. Ivor Richards was absorbed in a game of croquet with Robyn Kelling, Jennifer and Jennifer's elder brother Bob. Harry Andrews was there, the cheerful dark-haired lad Sarah had first met at the Bulldocks' New Year party. She and Diane both liked Harry, who was always part of any Bulldock social occasion. With his open, wide-eyed expression and his friendly air, it was impossible not to warm to him. Sarah noticed that today the presence of Harry's father, a dour thuggish-looking man, seemed to affect his normally good spirits.

'Delighted to meet you at last, Mrs Bailey. And these lovely girls are your daughters? Charmed. You've met my wife, have you?' Sarah liked Sir Henry with his serious, intelligent eyes. 'I gather you were out in India. Very sorry indeed to hear about Colonel Bailey. I knew him only by reputation, of course, but he's spoken of as a heavy loss.'

'Thank you, Sir Henry,' Mrs Bailey murmured.

'I stayed in Bombay for a while when my uncle was out there,' he went on. 'Many years ago now, but I've never forgotten the experience. Tell me, Mrs Bailey, did you and your husband ever come across my cousin ...?' He linked arms with Mrs Bailey and led her away to the tea table, leaving Sarah and Diane at the mercy of his wife Evelyn, Lady Kelling, who from the moment she opened her mouth revealed herself to be a snob of the first order.

'I hope that you're happy in Flint Cottage? I must say we were glad to hear that you were moving in. The Watson family were very amusing, but not quite the right tone for the village.'

'They left the house in the most frightful mess,' Diane put in shyly, keen to make an impression.

'Why doesn't that surprise me at all?'

'We're very happy there, though,' Sarah insisted, feeling a

sudden warmth towards the poor Watsons whom she'd never met but whose memory was being smeared for all the wrong reasons. 'And everyone in Westbury has been so helpful. Mr and Mrs Richards, particularly, and your gardener, Mr Hartmann.'

'Yes, it might have been he who told me you're something of a gardener yourself. You planted some lettuces for us, so sweet of you.'

'Not at all. I enjoy it, but I can't claim to have much skill. I don't know all about the different plants like Mr Hartmann. I gather that he and his mother are relatives of yours. Are they coming this afternoon?'

'No.' Lady Kelling's voice was chilly. 'One doesn't usually invite one's gardener to tea, it would appear odd. And the family connection is extremely distant. Of course, Sir Henry was correct to insist that we help them, given that the lodge was vacant. It came at a most convenient time, what with our previous man retiring. I'm so hoping that there isn't to be a war. It really is a most inconvenient time to have German relatives.'

Sarah could hardly believe her ears. The woman was obsessed with appearances and betrayed little sign of kindness. She remembered what Margo Richards had said, that Lady Kelling had once been plain Evelyn Brown when she'd met the Hon. Henry, as he'd been then, during the first London season after the war. She must have been very beautiful; Sarah could see that beauty still in her fine dark eyes, arched nose and high cheekbones, but Sir Henry, it was said, had long fallen out of love with her. They'd lost a child, apparently, and years of unhappiness and resentment must have killed all the good in her.

She sighed with relief when Lady Kelling swept on to skewer some other victim.

'Come on, let's find some tea,' she said to Diane. Out on the lawn the game of croquet was coming to a noisy conclusion and soon Ivor and Jennifer dashed up the steps laughing to greet them.

'Play with us after tea, girls,' Jennifer begged as they all loaded their plates with sandwiches and cake. 'Ivor's being horrid and won't.'

'I've had enough of you beating me,' Ivor said, selecting a giant piece of Victoria sponge. 'I want to talk to Sarah.'

'Diane, you'll come and play, won't you? Bob's useless, you'll beat him easily.'

'All right,' Diane said, her face lighting up, 'but I'm not much good either, I'm afraid.' Sarah inwardly blessed Jennifer who had that rare gift of making people feel wanted.

After tea, Sarah and Ivor watched the game from the terrace for a while, amused by Bob's showing off and Jennifer's mock anger. Diane hit a clever ball and her eyes rounded with satisfaction as she watched it shoot through a hoop, knocking Jennifer's off course.

'Well done, Diane!' Sarah called out, delighted. Lady Kelling's comments aside, it was a perfect afternoon in this fresh July garden. The lemon cake sprinkled with loaf sugar was delicious, the sun shining through the gushing fountain was beautiful and so was the lovely old house, basking in the sun. Diane looked happy and her mother was enjoying the bright chat of a laughing group of men that included Sir Henry. And Ivor – Sarah glanced at him sitting next to her at the table, smoking and smiling at the croquet game and saw again how good-looking he was, confident today, at ease. She noticed the pleasing line of his jaw, the strength and sensitivity of the hand that held the cigarette, and a warmth stirred deep within her. As though in response he turned his head and met her gaze, and as if it was the most natural thing in the world, his hand found hers and squeezed it gently.

Sarah sat very still, knowing that some understanding had shifted between them without her meaning it to. She wasn't sure what to do now, whether she wanted it. She stared down at her hand lying in his and very gently withdrew it.

As the warmth of the day faded, the tea was cleared away and the tablecloths lifted in a sudden chill breeze. As though at an unseen signal the guests began to depart. 'Goodbye, goodbye.' Lady Kelling seemed delighted to see them go, though Sir Henry was warmer, shaking hands with everyone and wishing them well. The Bailey women and the Richards left together, but Ivor hung back to walk with Sarah. He pointed out to her a narrow lane she hadn't noticed before. It skulked away in the shadow cast by the high wall of the kitchen garden.

'Let's go down this way. There's something I want to show you.'

'Do you think we should?' Sarah looked back at the house, but the front door was closed now and no one seemed to be watching.

'Yes, of course, why not.' She signalled her intentions to her mother, then followed Ivor down the secret lane, along where the wall was green with moss and ferns. Soon they crossed the parkland into an untidy thicket where Sarah needed to step across muddy patches on the footpath. Trees grew up all around and the gloom intensified. Suddenly Ivor stopped. The way ahead was blocked by a snarl of barbed wire. Beyond was an expanse of water overhung by great trees that sheltered it from the wind. Flies played in the air above. Mysterious rays of light danced off its obsidian surface or made rainbows out of rising bubbles.

'This is what you wanted me to see?'

'Yes, it's the old manor stew pond. It's a special place I used to come to when I was younger. Rather atmospheric, I always thought. There are still fish – you'll see one in a moment.' As they watched, a flicker of movement in the middle of the pond rippled its mirror stillness. 'No one else ever comes here. Not even the village boys as far as I know. It's because of the ghost, they say.'

'A haunted pond? Oh really, Ivor.' But her laugh sounded wrong in this place, as though she'd broken some unspoken rule.

'I've never seen anything, but I'm showing you this because it'll help you understand the Kellings. This is where it happened, you see. They had a son, little Henry, their firstborn. He drowned here when he was four or five. Ran away from his nanny, so the story goes. He liked to come and watch the fish. I suppose he leaned too far trying to catch one. Anyway, they were devastated, as you may imagine. The son and heir. So now there's no boy to inherit the title or the estate and it's said they blame each other. Sad, isn't it?'

'Dreadful,' Sarah breathed. 'Simply dreadful.' Up from the depths of her mind a memory came unbidden. A curtain of white toile rising and falling in a draught, and the sound of a woman sobbing and wailing. And suddenly the pressing weight of sadness felt so great that it was hard to keep back tears. She swung away from the pond and Ivor, the panic rising inside. *Why was he doing this? How could he be so cruel?*

'Sarah? Sarah, are you all right?' His hands gripped her shoulders. She pushed them off and, stumbling back to the path, began to hurry away. His voice came from behind, panicky, pleading. 'Sarah, what's wrong?'

She snapped, 'Nothing, Ivor. Nothing. I'll be all right if you let me be.' Her pace quickened into a run.

'But what have I said?' He hurried in her wake.

She spun round to confront his puzzled face. 'Don't you remember?' she hissed. For a moment she wondered with puzzlement if anyone had ever told him, but surely they had. 'Peter. You must know about Peter.'

She saw the horror dawn on Ivor's face. 'Oh God yes, yes. Sarah, I'm sorry, I'd completely forgotten. I shouldn't have ... I didn't mean to ... Sarah!'

Walking faster, fists clenched in anguish, she reached the shadow of the garden wall, turned its corner towards the road and bumped into the all too solid figure of Paul, who was emerging from the kitchen garden, a hoe across one shoulder.

'Whoa! Sarah!' He held her steady. She stood panting, confused, just as Ivor barrelled round the corner. Seeing Sarah with Paul, he pulled up short, his expression of distress darkening to anger.

'Let her go, Hartmann. The situation is perfectly under control.'

'If you say so.' Paul withdrew his hand from Sarah's arm, giving Ivor a shrewd look that belied the mildness of his words. 'Are you all right, Sarah? I'm sorry, I didn't see you coming.'

'I'm completely fine, thank you. Thank you, both of you,' Sarah managed to say with a catch in her voice. 'I really ought to go home now. Ivor, it's been a splendid afternoon, but we'll say goodbye here.'

'Let me walk with you down to the gate.'

'No, I'll find my own way. Really.' All she knew was that she wanted to be by herself. As she set off down the hill, she was aware of the two men staring after her.

Her feet took her home automatically. She certainly didn't notice her surroundings, for her thoughts were too agitated. The fluttering curtain and the woman crying were all she could remember now of the day her little brother died, but the sorrow the memory evoked was deep. She'd managed not to think about it for years and years, but the silent pond, the host of midges hovering over its surface and Ivor's tragic tale had brought back the sadness and bewilderment, of waking in bed and watching the toile curtain billow and sway and hearing the commotion beyond her bedroom door. The baby had simply not woken up that morning. The ayah's wailing had filled the bungalow.

All those years and she did not remember Peter's name being spoken. She did not remember the funeral, and thought perhaps that she didn't attend. Their father had sat her down and, with Diane on his knee, had told them Peter had gone to heaven to be with the angels. For a long while she'd carried the happy image in her mind of her little brother with his dreaming eyes lying smiling in the grass surrounded by tumbling winged cherubs. Perhaps her mother had spoken to her when it happened, but if so she had no memory of it. Once, at school in England she had read *Peter Pan* and to the puzzlement of the other girls had sobbed uncontrollably when she'd reached the scene where Peter returns to the house but finds himself shut out by his mother, who had forgotten him.

How her mother had borne this sadness she did not know. Mrs Bailey's response to life's troubles was essentially a practical one, to lose herself in daily tasks. Admirable, some people thought. Hence she had declined to be an Indian widow, waiting in seclusion in hope of another husband in India – and there was no doubt in Sarah's mind that she'd have found one; she was much admired. Instead, she'd sized up the dangers of the international situation and taken the sensible decision to return with the girls at once to England.

When Sarah reached Flint Cottage it was to find welcome tranquillity, her mother and sister sitting lazily in the garden with Ruby setting the dining room table for supper.

'Where did you disappear to?' Mrs Bailey asked, stubbing out her cigarette.

Sarah dropped her hat onto the table and sank down in an empty chair. 'Oh, just for a walk with Ivor,' she said, suspicious of the glint of interest in her mother's eye.

'My godson has turned out well, I think, and his prospects are good. I daresay many young women would regard him as quite a catch.'

Sarah glanced at her mother with annoyance. 'I expect you're right,' was all she said. She had never confided in her mother on such matters and wasn't going to start now. Beside her, Diane cast her magazine aside with a deep sigh and went indoors.

Ivor Richards. Was she interested in him or was she not, Sarah asked herself as she weeded the rose bed after supper. She breathed in the sweet fragrance of the huge white blooms and considered the matter. He was attractive and she was drawn to him because of that, but aspects of him irritated her. She did not like the way he treated Paul Hartmann – as though the German man were inferior – and she feared that something, his disappointed father's expectations maybe, had wounded his sense of himself.

She wondered sometimes at her cold response to most men. She had had several suitors in India – of course she had, the place was full of red-blooded bachelors desperate for an English bride – but the only man she'd fallen in love with, ten years older than her, a fascinating but cynical type, had not felt as strongly about her. She'd let him make love to her, then bravely brooded over her hurt feelings in secret. Perhaps he'd spoiled her for good.

In the garden, the light was beginning to fade. She batted at a cloud of gnats and looked up to see Diane close by, watching her, a woollen shawl drawn tightly over her slender shoulders.

'Do come in and play bezique, Saire.' Diane loved playing cards and board games.

'In a moment. Why don't you set up the card table?'

'All right. I say, aren't they beautiful, so pure.' Diane reached out a hand and touched a full-blown rose. 'Oh,' she cried, as its petals floated to the earth. 'Did I do that?'

Her voice was so anguished it tore at her sister's heart. 'Don't worry, Diane. It was ready to go, that's all.'

Her sister's sensitivity as usual alarmed Sarah. What would happen when she went away to college? How would Diane survive? A common-sense part of her asserted itself. Of course she'd be all right. Diane had friends – Jennifer and Bob Bulldock and their circle. Still, there was something very childlike about Diane. Her pale, delicate beauty had attracted one or two of the wrong sort in India, bullies or effetes. Her father, as ever her defender, had caused one to be posted a thousand miles away, simply to rid Diane of the man's boorish attentions. Diane was another reason for Mrs Bailey's decision to return to England. At least one knew the kind of families who lived in Norfolk.

'Where did you go with Ivor today?' Diane said. She was looking down at a petal on her palm and running her thumb lightly over its soft hollow.

'He showed me an old path that led to a rather desolate spot, Westbury's old stew pond, you know, where the lords of the manor kept their fish stocks, though they don't use it any more. Don't ever go there, dear. I found it rather creepy.' She decided against telling the story of the drowned Kelling boy. Instead she asked suddenly, 'Di, do you remember anything much about Peter?'

Diane looked up, her eyes troubled, then a serenity came into them. 'Our brother? Not really, no; I was only three, wasn't I? There was something wrong with him. That's why he died, wasn't it?'

'I think he wasn't ... like other babies.'

'He didn't sit up or crawl, did he?'

'No. Poor little chap.' She recalled touching his silky brown hair, the way he stared up at her from his pram as if in silent wonder, and grief twisted deep inside her.

'So I expect it was a good thing that he died really.'

'Oh, Diane! You are ... surprising.' Perhaps Diane was right. That might have been why their parents had appeared to accept his death. She tried to imagine her mother with an older Peter. Adult even. And couldn't. Of course, there were institutions that would have had him. In England, anyway. She didn't know what would have happened in India, didn't like to think about it. There were so many appalling things the people there had to endure.

Diane let the petal fall. 'I'll go and lay out the cards,' she said. 'Don't be long, Saire, will you?' and Sarah watched her walk lightly away through the evening light, puzzled as ever by the changing surfaces of her sister's moods.

'It's only a matter of time.' Early August and once again Ivor was visiting. It was a Saturday afternoon, and he and Sarah were lounging on chairs in the shade, drinking Mrs Allman's excellent lemonade. Diane was over at the Bulldocks' and Mrs Bailey was upstairs helping Ruby deal with a moth infestation in a clothes chest. Ivor had found Sarah picking blackcurrants and assisted until she scolded him for eating too many and it had grown too hot anyway so she decided they had enough for supper and packed it in.

Ivor had been away for nearly a month and as he wasn't much of a letter writer this was the first time they'd really exchanged news for a while.

'Anyone who thinks war can be avoided is deluding themselves. Look at the overtures Hitler's making to Russia. It's obvious that they'll make their move on Poland and then we'll be obliged to honour our promises. Believe me, these rehearsals with blackout curtains and whatnot are only the start of it. It'll be the real thing soon.'

'Jennifer's father is still adamant it won't happen. He thinks Hitler doesn't want to go to war with us at all, that he doesn't view us as an enemy.'

'In which case the Führer's putting up the wrong signals. What was his Graf Zeppelin doing off the coast at Lowestoft? Visiting the beach for the day?'

Sarah laughed, then was sober again. If there were to be war ... she knew she shouldn't think selfishly of her own life, but she wouldn't go away to college. She'd be a land girl, she thought suddenly. That would suit her best. Somewhere near home it would have to be.

When she surfaced from her thoughts it was to see Ivor studying her, a round-eyed expression on his face as though he was working himself up to something.

'What is it, Ivor?' She wondered whether she'd offended him. It was difficult to be natural with him sometimes. She couldn't simply say what came into her head as she had been able to do with her father. Was that the kind of girl she was, the type who would never marry because she was in love with her father? She smiled privately at her own nonsense.

Ivor started to speak, checked himself, then as she watched, fascinated, he blew out his cheeks and resolution came into his face. 'I was thinking, Sarah, simply this. That if there is a war and I have to go away then, well, I'd like to think that I had a girl at home who was waiting for me. And if that girl were you then, well, I don't know, but I'd be the happiest man alive.' The resolution had quite gone and Sarah was struck instead by the naked vulnerability of his expression. His eyes were bright with emotion and his brow crumpled with tension. She didn't want to hurt him, but nor, she realized, did she want what he offered.

'Ivor,' she said, trying to be gentle, 'we're not at war yet and there's no need for any rush. We haven't known each other very long and . . . I don't know that it feels right yet.'

'You haven't been long here in Westbury, no, but we've known of each other all our lives. Our families being so close . . . And my parents approve. In fact they would like it very much.'

'My mother would too,' Sarah conceded with a sigh, 'but we can't always do what our parents want.' Impatience was constricting her chest and shortening her breath.

'Sarah, please, just listen . . .'

'No, Ivor, don't.' She rose with a flounce of her skirt and began to pace the terrace, trying to control the feelings of frustration. Just as she'd been planning to govern her own destiny, duty to family always closed in again, smothering her attempts at independence.

She tired of pacing and returned to her seat, where she drew up her knees and clasped her arms around them. 'I need time,' she said to put him off, but she could hardly bear to look at him, knowing there would be disappointment in his eyes.

War came despite what anyone said. Each day in August the people of Westbury felt it grow inexorably closer. One morning stacks of sandbags appeared outside the village hall. The Bailey household's gas masks hung in the hall like harbingers of doom. Strangers with brisk voices came knocking at all hours of the day, asking impertinent questions about their circumstances, ticking off items on lists. In shops and in bus queues the air was thick with rumour of air raids and spies.

Then came a Sunday in early September when the church was full of grave country faces. Mr Tomms prayed for peace, but when they went home in the beautiful sunshine it was to hear on their wirelesses that Britain was at war with Germany.

Twenty

In the Sandbrooks' garden, the gentle undulating lines of the sleeping goddess drew Briony's touch. The calm face of the reclining sculpture spoke to something deep inside her, loosening her habitual knot of anxiety.

'She makes me feel happy,' she said, turning to its creator. Tina Sandbrook was completely different from Briony's idea of what Luke's mother would be like. She thought she'd be, well, motherly-looking and conventionally dressed and Tina was neither of those things.

'Good, she's supposed to.' Tina Sandbrook's wise blue eyes were like her son's, but otherwise she had the fine-boned appearance of her daughter, Luke's younger sister Cherry, whose laughing face adorned the Sandbrooks' fridge in a series of snapshots with her partner Tristan and their toddler twin sons. Tina was of medium height, light-framed, with shoulder-length hair coloured ash blonde with a streak of pink down one side. Despite her age, her loose cotton vest-top, dirndl skirt and the strappy sandals on her narrow, tanned feet put Briony in mind of a sixties flower child. When she moved, her beads and bangles tinkled pleasantly like wind chimes. There were one or two of those hanging from the eaves of the tiny cottage, Briony noticed as she wandered the maze of paths in the back garden, admiring Tina's small bronze statues, half a dozen different versions of calm, happy womanhood. They were deep in the countryside here. Swifts darted through the early evening air, and in the garden hedgerow where blackberries were ripening a robin was singing his heart out.

Tina stooped to pinch dead blooms from a potted pelargonium. 'It's been so liberating moving here, Briony,' she said. 'I thought I'd miss London and my teaching, but I haven't, not really. I've achieved so much in a short time. It's been good for Roger, too, though he finds it a bit quiet. He was wearing himself out at that school, trying to be someone he wasn't and not getting on at all with the whizzy new headmistress.'

Briony could glimpse Roger Sandbrook with Luke and Aruna through the open French doors of the sitting room, and heard his deep, carefree laugh, so like his son's. Then Luke stepped outside with a bottle of sparkling wine, his face screwed up with concentration as he eased the cork up until it shot out with a pop.

"Tis done well, boy,' his father cried as Luke went back inside. It was interesting how people were shaped by their jobs. No one hearing Roger Sandbrook speak could have any doubt that he had taught English and Drama. A moment later he emerged ceremoniously bearing a tray of crystal flutes filled with winking bubbles of pale gold. Springy hair like Luke's stood up from a similar high forehead, but Roger's was greying and his eyebrows were bushy as one day Luke's would no doubt become. Their personalities were different. Roger was an ebullient man, though a kind one. Luke was more gentle, but just as kind.

Aruna stepped out after them with her own glass. She was quieter than usual, Briony thought, and wondered whether she found Luke's parents overwhelming. They gave every impression of being fond of their son's girlfriend, so this puzzled Briony.

'What are we drinking to?' Luke asked, when everyone had a glass.

'How about wine and women, may we always have a taste for both?'

'The girls won't say that, Dad!'

'Good health and happiness then. It's lovely to have you with us, Briony.'

Briony thanked him, laughing, and drank. The champagne made her feel light as one of the puffs of cloud passing overhead. The evening was so warm and lovely and the garden with Tina's exotic sculptures such an unexpected pleasure that she felt she was filling up with contentment.

'Are you comfortable in your holiday let?' Roger asked. 'I gather it's in the grounds of the old house.'

'That's right. Some people might find it shabby, but it's just right for me. I like a bit of atmosphere.'

'A nice one, I hope?' Tina asked.

'There aren't actual ghosts, I don't think. I occasionally wake up thinking I've heard something, but it's probably the woodworm gnawing away.'

There was laughter at this. 'I think it's like a witch's house,' Aruna said. 'You know, the gingerbread one where Hansel and Gretel picked sweets off it and the witch caught them.'

'Are you a witch, Briony?' Luke said, smiling.

Aruna made a little moue. 'She's as clever as one.'

'Thanks, Aruna!' Briony said, trying to laugh it off, while feeling a bit hurt. 'Don't forget what it meant to call a woman a witch. Next thing you'll be blaming me for the ills of the community, calling for me to be thrown into a pond and, if I float, hanged.'

'Didn't they usually burn witches?' Luke asked gravely.

'Hanging was more usual.'

'Hanging or burning, which would you prefer, Briony?' Roger said, amused.

'This is a horrible conversation and I can't bear to listen.' Tina set her empty glass on the tray and briefly covered her ears. 'I'm going to put supper on the table.'

'Would you like any help?' Briony asked, seeing an opportunity to escape. She rather wanted to get to know Tina a little.

'We'll all come, won't we, Aruna?' Luke said, sliding his arm round Aruna's waist. Aruna relaxed into him and smiled.

'Thank you, everybody, but I'm fine,' Tina said. 'It's mostly carrying things through, so I'll borrow Briony.'

Briony was given oven gloves and charge of a salmon and broccoli tart, all toasted and fragrantly steaming. There were pottery bowls of salad and warm herb bread freshly made by Roger. She loved the inside of the cottage where the walls were stacked floor to ceiling with shelves of odd-sized books or studded with bright abstract paintings, though the men had to duck under the low doorways when they came in for supper. The wide table nearly filled the cosy dining room. The diamond-hatched window looked out onto a sunken lane where the evening sun poured through the restless beech trees, casting ever-changing patterns of flickering shadow.

'Which part of the country do you come from, Briony?' Tina asked after they'd started to eat. 'I mean I know you live in London now, but were you born there?'

'Mmm, this salmon is delicious. No, I was born in Surrey. A place called Birchmere. No one's ever heard of it and nothing ever happens there. My dad's parents grew up there, and my mum's moved there after the war. Apparently Grandpa Andrews was from round here, which is really why I've come. I think Luke may have told you.'

'He did mention the bare bones, didn't you, Luke?'

'I thought you'd like to tell it, Briony,' Luke said.

She explained more fully about the film they'd seen in Italy and the letters that she'd been given.

'I've started making my way through them and typing them up, but it's slow work. They're interesting because they give a sense of life here at the start of the war. Sarah lived in Westbury village with her mother and sister.'

'And who was this man she was writing to?'

'His name was Paul Hartmann. He was employed on the Westbury estate as under-gardener, but the very elderly lady we met yesterday at Westbury Hall said his mother was a distant relative of the family. The really amazing thing is that Paul's mother lived in the cottage where I'm staying, and Paul, too. They were German. Well, Paul's mother was English but she had lived in Germany most of her life.'

'I don't understand about him being German,' Luke said. 'Would he really have been fighting in the British Army in Italy?'

'It wasn't unknown,' Briony told him, 'but it must have been an incredibly difficult decision for people like him. I mean, even if you believed that Nazism had to be destroyed, you'd still be shooting your fellow countrymen.'

Tina was nodding, her face troubled. She was revealing herself as a very empathetic sort of person who took things to heart and Briony warmed to her even more.

'And what did Sarah write to Paul about? Were they lovers, do you think?'

'From Sarah's side, which is all we have, I'd say no, just friends, but I haven't read all the letters yet.'

'What you need are the letters Paul wrote back to her,' Roger said.

Briony nodded, her mouth full. 'If only,' she said eventually, 'but I'm not sure where to start looking. There's nothing in the Record Office in Norwich. I suppose I could trawl the catalogues of the war museum, for instance, but finding surviving family might be my best bet.'

'Well, good luck,' Roger said. 'And with finding your grandfather.'

'Thanks. His name was Harry Andrews.'

'We know an Andrews, don't we?' Tina said to her husband. 'Do we?'

'It's a very common name,' Briony said, apologetic.

'That man we spoke to at the wine-tasting,' Tina continued. 'There's a rather nice farm shop near Westbury, Briony. It has a café and runs events.'

'I remember now. The wine wasn't bad, we bought a mixed case. Was it Jim or Tim Andrews?'

'David,' Tina said promptly. She and Roger stared triumphantly at Briony.

'Thanks,' she said, smiling at their eagerness. 'I suppose there's always the possibility that he's a relation. I wonder how I can find him?'

Twenty-one

When Briony let herself into Westbury Lodge late that evening a thick envelope lay on the mat. It had her name written on it, Miss Briony Wood, in proper fountain pen and had been delivered by hand. She turned it over and slid her finger under the flap. From inside she drew out a printed booklet entitled *Gas Masks and Greengages: Westbury at War* with a postcard clipped to it of the stained glass window in the church. She flipped it over to see it was from the old man who'd shown her Barbara Hartmann's grave.

Dear Miss Wood,

It was a great pleasure to meet you yesterday. After we said goodbye I conducted a little snoop about to see if I could find anything potentially useful to you, and the vicar drew my attention to this publication, written by one of our parishioners some years ago now. I hope that you at least find it an interesting account of the wartime era.

With kind regards,

George R. Symmonds

Briony flicked through the booklet quickly. It offered a
short account of the village and its people in 1939 from the
Kellings up at the Hall to the family who ran the post office.
She scanned the index for mentions of any Andrews or
Hartmanns, but there were none except for a reference to a
Lawrence Andrews who, she read, from summer 1940, when
Britain was most fearful of invasion, had headed up the local
Dads' Army, the Home Guard whose job it was to be alert for
possible enemy attack and to patrol and protect vulnerable
spots in the area such as the railway station and the bridge.
On the opposite page was a grainy photograph and she gazed
at it hard. Captain Andrews had been a broad-shouldered
man in his sixties with a bulbous nose, his stern expression
showing how seriously he took his responsibilities. There
was no family likeness to her grandfather that she could
see, except possibly in the line of the mouth. With a sigh, she
turned the page and her eye fell on a reference to the Bailey
family that she hadn't noticed before. It was in a section
about evacuees. A young boy named Derek Jenkins had been
taken in by the Bailey women at Flint Cottage in September
1939. There was a photograph of half a dozen children who
had arrived at the village school at that time. They looked
miserable and confused, as well they might if they'd been separated from their parents and schoolmates to be sent among
strangers. The name Derek Jenkins sparked something, but
for a while she couldn't remember what.

That evening as she was typing up one of Sarah Bailey's letters an idea came to her and she brought up the Record Office
website. Yes, there it was, a reference in the catalogue. *Derek
Jenkins, evacuee*. It was a tape of an interview. She would make
her appointment and go and listen to it.

*

'*You are Derek Jenkins and you were once an evacuee in Westbury, Norfolk?*' a light, well-bred female voice asked. Briony listened intently in the spacious modern building that housed the Record Office.

'*Yes, that's right.*' Derek's was an old man's voice, high-pitched, tremulous, and he sounded nervous at first. '*Two days before war broke out we were told to be at school early with our luggage, and when we got there they'd laid on buses to take us down to the docks. Well, I hadn't hardly been out of London before, so you can imagine what it was like saying goodbye to my mum. I never hardly seen her cry before, she was always the strong one. As for going on a boat, now that was exciting at first, though some of us was sick, it was a bit choppy out there, which wasn't so nice. No, I didn't feel too good, but my stomach was churning anyway, what with nerves. It was four or five hours round to Great Yarmouth and when we docked there it wasn't a moment too soon so far as I was concerned. They took us off the boat and sent us to a school where we stayed for the night, then it was on to buses again. I remember passing out of the town and seeing all that lovely countryside and thinking what a great adventure it would be if only my mum was there . . .*'

Twenty-two

September 1939

'A boy. We can't take a boy.'

'You'll have to, Mrs Bailey. If you'd come down earlier there were several girls, but other families took them in and this one here is all that's left.'

'If I'd known, I'd never have agreed. I'm not having a boy.'

Sarah, who had just changed out of her gardening clothes, came downstairs to find her mother gazing down horrified at a skinny little lad who looked back at her from the open door with the expression of a cornered rabbit. His mid-brown hair was cut at an angle across his forehead above a pair of bewildered hazel eyes in a pale, freckled face. The sleeves of his jacket were too short, exposing bony wrists. There was a luggage label pinned to his collar and the canvas bag lying at his feet was pitifully small. She wanted to bear him away at once to soothe and feed him, but if her mother had her way he wouldn't get further than the doormat where he stood listening to the harassed balding man he'd come with arguing with the posh lady who wanted to send him on his way.

'Please, M'am,' the official was saying. 'Yours is the only home left on my list.'

The boy's expression of frightened despair was more than Sarah could stand. She took the last few steps down to the hall and, ducking down before him, smiled and asked him his name.

His lips moved, but no sound came.

'May I see your label?' She reached out a gentle hand. It read 'Derek Jenkins', but the rest of the writing was smudged, perhaps by tears.

'And how old are you, Derek?'

A whispered, 'Nine 'alf.'

Sarah was surprised. He appeared younger.

Her mother and the official had stopped arguing to stare down at them. Mrs Bailey's arms were crossed in that pose which Sarah knew from experience brooked no opposition.

Sarah rose to her feet. 'Mummy,' she said fiercely. 'You can't turn him away. Suppose this was me or Diane?'

'But it's not, is it? It's a boy.'

'He's a good boy, I'm sure, aren't you, son? If handled firmly he shouldn't give you any trouble.' The official was sounding desperate.

'I can't look after a boy,' Mrs Bailey whispered to Sarah, her voice pleading. 'Not again.'

Sarah saw with amazement that the fear of noise and naughtiness was not the reason. Her mother was anxious. And she thought she understood. A boy in the house would remind her of the one she'd lost. Peter. But this child's need was greater than her mother's tamped-down grief.

'Will you allow us a moment, please.' She steered her mother into the drawing room, shut the door and leaned against it.

'We have to take him, Mummy, don't you see. We've all got to do things we don't want to do. He is lost without his parents. We cannot be so cruel as to turn him away.'

'I would have had a girl.'

'I know, but we've been given what we've been given. Father would have taken him.' It was a cheap shot, but it worked. Her mother flushed, whether with guilt or anger, Sarah couldn't tell.

'Yes, your father would have. Whatever else he was, your father was a good man.'

There was a silence, then Mrs Bailey tossed her proud head. 'Very well,' she snapped. 'But if it all goes wrong I'm not taking the blame.'

Sarah opened the door and followed her mother out.

'Right,' Mrs Bailey sighed. 'We'll take him.'

'He's a good boy,' the official repeated with obvious relief, and blew his nose. 'Goodbye, son, behave yourself.'

Derek didn't even nod. He looked at his feet and his shoulders shook with silent sobs.

'Come along now,' Sarah said, taking his hand. 'I'll introduce you to our cook, Mrs Allman. She may have a biscuit for you. I expect you're hungry, aren't you?'

Derek was very shy and quiet at first and those deep-set brown eyes troubled the household. He was frightened by the tiger-skin rug with its snarling head on the floor of the drawing room, but to everyone's surprise Mrs Bailey declared that she hated it, too, and rolled it up and gave it to Major Richards, who had always admired it.

Derek felt the pain of separation from his mother, they could all see that, though Nora Jenkins did write every week, short notes on lined paper about how she hoped he wasn't giving any trouble. Once, to the boy's excitement, she came down to visit; a short, stocky woman with a palely pretty face and the same shy manner as her son. She stared round Flint Cottage in delight, and declared to him that he'd fallen on his feet here all right. She was 'a nice woman with sensible values, though common as muck, of course,' Mrs Bailey said to Sarah later, but Derek cried so hard after she left that it was decided that she shouldn't come again. He'd only been with the Baileys for six weeks, though, before she came and fetched him away. Some of the other evacuee children went home, too. After all, there had been no sign of bombardment in London and what had the government been making such a fuss about?

The story didn't stop there, though. At the County Record Office Briony listened to the whole interview and thought how the war must have changed the course of Derek Jenkins' life.

Later that evening at home she felt triumphant when she found Derek's name mentioned in one of Sarah's letters to Paul. It was dated May 1940. The war had been going on for a whole eight or nine months and this letter had been sent to an address in Liverpool. What had Paul been doing up there?

Twenty-three

May 1940

It broke Paul's heart to pull up the flowers in the walled garden, but what else could be done? Lady Kelling and Robyn were still in residence, but Sir Henry was in London much of the time. Although the Hall had been officially earmarked as a military convalescent home, as yet it hadn't been needed. In the meantime, instructions from the local Agriculture Committee were clear. Flowers were a luxury and cabbages and potatoes would win the war. Part of the park was to be turned over to allotments and large swathes of grassland were to be ploughed for arable.

Sarah registered as a land girl in order to be properly paid and went away on a month's training course, learning how to drive a tractor and to plant crops in industrial quantities. Before winter set in, it was with a mixture of sadness and professional pride that with Paul's assistance she carved the first furrow in the lush grass around the manor house and sprinkled seed. When in the spring pale green spears began to push their way up through the rich earth, she felt only triumph. She watched over the growth constantly, looking for evidence of pests or disease, but all was well. 'Beginner's luck,' Major Richards said in his usual dismissive manner.

In the walled garden, once the snow had gone, she and Paul dug up the irises, the border lilies and the lupins, mulched the beds and, as the frosts eased, planted out carrots, cabbages, turnip, beans and potatoes, endless rows of spuds, together with a few precious onions. The fruit trees and bushes were allowed to remain; indeed more were added. Weather allowing, they, the elderly head gardener, when he was well enough, and the apprentice, Sam, worked from dawn till dusk. It was gruelling work. Sam talked on and off about joining the army, but he was still only sixteen, a tall lad whose ambitions were in danger of outgrowing his strength. Paul ordered him to build up his muscles by extra digging, which didn't please him at all.

From early on, Sarah noticed the disdainful expression in the boy's eyes whenever Paul directed him. The usually even-tempered youngster was turning surly.

'I told you to finish digging that bed today. What's wrong with you?'

'I'm goin' as fast as I can.' Then he muttered something.

'What did you say?'

'I din't say nothin'.'

'Get on with it then.' Paul turned back to his task and only Sarah, glancing up from her hoeing, saw the boy's rude gesture and stared him down. She made sure she walked back to the village with him that afternoon when the light began to fail.

'You'll land yourself in trouble, Sam, if anyone else sees you doing things like that. What is the matter with you? And don't say "nothing". There's obviously something.'

'I don't like takin' orders from 'im. It don't seem right. He's the enemy, in't he? That's what my dad say.'

'Sam, he's not the enemy. He's German, yes, but he's on our side. You know what the Gestapo did to his father, don't you?'

Sam shrugged, but his expression was still dark. 'He's still one of 'em, Dad say, when the chips is down.'

Sarah sighed. 'If the authorities are happy, Sam, I'm happy with him, too, so you'll do best to get on with your work. It's not for you to question.'

It was well known locally that as an enemy alien Paul had been summoned before a tribunal, but his circumstances had attracted the lowest security rating and he was free to continue his work. Many local people went along with this, but a certain minority didn't. As a result, Paul had to be careful where he went. He'd never made a habit of visiting the Green Dragon, but now he avoided the pub altogether, for Sam's scowling father might be serving behind the bar.

Sam's behaviour improved a little after this conversation, but come the spring, as first Norway was invaded, then Denmark fell to the Nazis, the mood in the newspapers and on the wireless became more urgent.

It was a warm April day when Sarah and Paul sat together to eat their sandwiches on an old stone bench with a view across the grounds. Twenty yards away Sam lay sprawled on the grass, one arm across his face, apparently asleep. As Sarah pulled off her jumper, she was aware of Paul's presence close beside her, but he merely took a long draught from his water bottle, wiped his forehead with the back of his hand and stared into the middle distance. Then he fumbled a small object from the pocket of his jacket and held it in his long fingers.

'Someone threw this at me yesterday,' he said. It was a stone, about the size and smoothness of a pigeon's egg.

'Paul!' she said, in horror. 'Who?'

'I didn't see. Whoever it was must have been hiding near the river. I went to buy some cigarettes after I'd cleared up here, then I stood on the bridge for a bit having a smoke and a think and suddenly I felt a sharp pain in my shoulder.'

'Are you much hurt?'

'No, it was the shock more than anything.'

'Who would do such a thing? Perhaps it was a child messing about. Or a bird. Sometimes you hear about that, a bird flying carrying something.'

'Why would a bird carry a stone? That's crazy.' He laughed suddenly and soon they were both laughing. Sam raised his head to stare at them, then lay down again.

'I don't belong,' Paul said quietly. 'That's why. There are people who don't want me here. I can never feel at home.' He looked so miserable that it made Sarah angry.

'You mustn't bother about them. They don't matter. They're narrow-minded, petty.'

'And full of fear, maybe, I know.'

'Full of themselves, more like. Their own importance. Your mother isn't being bothered, is she?'

'No. Listen, I haven't told her about this. It would be too upsetting for her.' His voice was hoarse with anger, and really she didn't blame him. He rarely complained, but it didn't take much effort to imagine how it was for him, forced to leave his homeland and to come somewhere where he was resented, where he had not been able to pursue his dreams, where he was expected to be grateful, which he was, she thought, but still. Of course, everyone was making sacrifices now, but to be seen as the enemy when you were trying your best to help, that was hard.

She watched him play with the stone, toss it from hand to hand, then he drew back his arm and threw it away down the hill. Sam leaped to his feet. They all watched it bounce out of sight. The boy looked at her and Paul in surprise.

It hadn't been Sam, she thought, relieved. That would have been too much to deal with.

Behind her, Westbury Hall lay dreaming in the sunshine. Things felt in some ways as they always had done.

The news, however, told differently. One Friday in May when Sarah went to change her books at the library in Cockley Market, she took the time to browse the full range of the week's papers. *Careless Talk Costs Lives*, was one of the headlines. The article asserted that the country was full of aliens who were helping the German war effort. Why had Oslo given up the fight so easily? Because Norway was full of traitors. The same with Denmark. And it was happening here in Britain, too, the paper concluded. There were German spies posing as refugees, that was the size of it. Sarah was puzzled. She supposed there must be some truth in this. The paper wouldn't have printed it otherwise, would it? Paul wasn't a spy, of course, but maybe there were Germans in Britain who were. Why had Denmark and Norway given in so easily? Perhaps they had been infiltrated by secret agents; who was she to say differently?

Paul was worried and restless, she could tell. They went to the cinema that evening to watch a film with Errol Flynn and he spoke little and was watchful of others.

Over the following week the news from the Continent worsened. Belgium, Luxembourg, the Netherlands, all were suffering invasion, and France itself was under threat. Once Nazi forces reached the Channel it would be Britain next, people were saying. Everywhere were signs that the country was being put on high alert.

It was on the morning of Sunday 12 May, when Sarah was waiting for the others to be ready to leave for church, that the flustered figure of Mrs Hartmann could be seen hurrying up the path. Sarah flew to the door to admit her. Barbara Hartmann's coat was unbuttoned, her face crumpled in anguish. 'They've taken Paul, they've taken him,' she managed to whimper between wheezy breaths.

Mrs Bailey, who disliked chaotic behaviour, took charge, ushering Mrs Hartmann into the drawing room and sitting her down with a tot of brandy. Eventually, the woman managed to stammer out her story. An hour ago, two policemen had arrived at Westbury Lodge. They had examined Paul's papers, then waited while he packed an overnight case before escorting him to their car. 'Taken away like a common criminal,' Mrs Hartmann wailed.

The more kindly of the officers had told her not to worry too much.

'Not worry?' she sobbed. 'I don't know where my boy's gone or why.'

Sarah, sitting beside her on the sofa, grasped her fluttering hands. Diane poured tea, her nervous fingers rattling the cups on their saucers. After drinking hers, Mrs Hartmann gained strength. 'Do you think they will hurt him?' she enquired. 'I know this is not Germany but these days . . .'

'I'm certain they won't hurt him,' Mrs Bailey said, unpinning her hat because church was the last thing on anyone's mind now. 'Perhaps Sir Henry would be able to enlighten us, or I expect we'll hear something on the news.'

'Evelyn and Robyn are away in London or I'd have gone to them. You have always been my friends, but I'm sorry to throw myself upon you.'

'There's no need for any dramatic talk. Of course, we'll do what we can,' Mrs Bailey said briskly, 'but until we find out where they've taken your son that is likely to be very little.

I'm sure Major Richards will drive you to the police station in Cockley Market to make enquiries. And if that doesn't work we can ask him to ring up Sir Henry in London.'

From the police, the news and general rumour, a rough picture was assembled. The papers were full of the British Expeditionary Force's entry into Belgium. The round-up of enemy aliens across much of Britain was, for Mr Churchill, a natural step in defence against invasion. It was German and Austrian men who'd been interned. The kinder of the two bobbies visited Mrs Hartmann during the week. Paul would have spent a night in a school at Bury St Edmunds before being moved onward, though to where he did not know. Sir Henry was telephoned and he promised to make enquiries.

It was a full week since the arrest before anyone heard anything more, then Mrs Hartmann and Sarah both received letters from Paul on the same day. Sarah's had been opened and bore the censor's stamp, but she was pleased to see that nothing had been blacked out. The letter was written on cheap notepaper and dated 20 May.

My dear Sarah,

First, please be assured that I am safe and well. I am now in an internment camp near Liverpool, Huyton, it's called. The authorities arrested us all then had nowhere to put us, so in the end they sent me up here! It's an estate of council houses which they haven't finished building yet, and so there are mounds of sand and stacks of bricks everywhere and the houses have no furniture or hot water. I'm sharing a very small house with a dozen other men, mostly older than me, and all as shocked and confused as I am. So we are not in the height of luxury, but it could be much worse. There are two among us who should not be here, they are in a bad condition, a Jewish dentist in his sixties

with heart trouble and a boy of eighteen or nineteen who talks to
himself and makes odd noises. He's plainly off his head, if that's
the right phrase, and I believe it cruel to have put him here. He
cries at night for his mother and keeps the rest of us awake.

Don't worry about me. I am getting enough to eat (just!)
and now we have to wait and see what happens. I've written to
Mutti and would be glad if you would keep your eyes on her.
Tell Sam I don't want to see a single weed in the kitchen garden
when I get back. I hope you are able to find someone else to help
with the planting, it is such a big job.

Kind regards to you and your family. Remember me to your
mother.

Paul

'Will they let him out?' Diane said when Sarah had finished reading the letter aloud. 'Won't they interview each one and only keep the bad eggs?'

'I've no idea. The government must know what they're doing. We have to trust them. That's all we can do.'

'Still it doesn't seem fair. I don't think he's a spy, do you? He wouldn't be a very good one.'

'Of course he isn't, silly.' As usual, Sarah regretted being cross with Diane, because it made her look as though she'd been struck. She told her more gently, 'Anyway, I'm sure Sir Henry will be able to speak to the right people.'

The news was not encouraging. Sir Henry had indeed raised Paul's case with the department concerned at the Home Office, but had been told in rather abrupt tones that, regretfully, nothing could be done. Churchill himself had been instrumental in these internments and, as unhappy as the Home Office was about these assaults on innocent people's liberty, this was wartime and the country's security was paramount.

'There is every indication that your son is safe and well,' Sir Henry had written in a letter to Mrs Hartmann in his quick neat hand. 'I will continue to raise the matter as seems appropriate.'

It was hard to witness the tears in Mrs Hartmann's eyes, to know that Paul had been all she had left and now he'd been taken away too.

Paul's letters continued to arrive from time to time. They were bravely cheerful. The Jewish dentist had been removed to hospital. Paul and his housemates were sleeping on sacks filled with straw, quite comfortable but for the odd flea. Could his mother send him a towel and some lavatory paper? Sarah helped Mrs Hartmann make up a parcel and took it to the post office for her. The following week he sent his thanks. A package with books in it did not reach him and Sarah realized they must be careful or they might get him into trouble.

During the weeks after Paul had gone she missed him enormously. At first she didn't have time to think about it properly because they were so busy at Westbury Hall, coping with his workload as well as their own. Major Richards petitioned the authorities and they were given a short, flabby man in his thirties named Ted Walters to take Paul's place in the garden. Walters was a conchie, which didn't bother Sarah particularly, except that he was not a very noble example, always whining that something was unfair: the effect of manual work on his constitution, the meanness of the judge who'd sent him there when he was used to being an office clerk. Major Richards saw at once that there was no point in putting him in charge of anything, so Sarah found herself responsible for training Walters and keeping him hard at it, which she managed by a mixture of threats and encouragement.

It came to her more gradually that the weight of sadness pressing down on her spirits was not simply grief for her father, uncertainty about the present and fear for the future. It was all those things, but it was also to do with missing Paul. They had worked well together and she felt comfortable with him. Sometimes she would look up from her planting, expecting to see him but it would be Ted with his sour expression, or she'd notice the progress of the Indian *Hibiscus syriacus* in her own garden and take pleasure in writing to Paul about it.

He was often in her thoughts. She had long had a habit of holding in her mind, one by one, the people she loved as she lay in bed waiting for sleep, and Paul very naturally joined that number. She would try to picture his bright eyes in his serious face as he considered their conversation, the near blackness of his short springy hair, the strength and fluidity of his movements as he worked, a certain graceful way he had of taking up his jacket and swinging it over his shoulder, or his skill at whittling animals out of bits of wood with his penknife. Life here without him was dull, colourless. Despite working so hard Sarah did not sleep well, waking in the night, wrestling with worries that crowded her mind.

The news from the Continent grew worse daily. On 15 May, three days after Paul was taken, Holland had surrendered to the Germans. The newspapers were full of rumours that seemed to confirm the rightness of Mr Churchill's round-up of enemy aliens like Paul. The German forces must have known in advance about the movements of the Dutch army and they had compiled a list of officials and Allied sympathizers who were to be 'shot on sight'. Holland, too, the rumours said, had obviously been full of spies. Britain must be vigilant! Brussels fell two days later, then, symbolically, on the old battleground of the Somme, German forces succeeded in splitting the Allied armies in two, leading to the debacle of Dunkirk.

Ruby's father arrived at Flint Cottage one lunchtime and bore the little maid home, weeping. Her elder brother had been reported dead after the ship that had carried him from Dunkirk beach was shelled. Ivor Richards telegraphed his parents to say that he had been rescued and was now safely back at Aldershot. For other families in Norfolk it was to be a terrible time of uncertainly before news trickled through. Beloved sons and fathers and brothers were confirmed dead. Others, it turned out, were prisoners of the Germans, which was a relief – at least they were alive. Of a few there was simply no trace at all. In this tide of grief it seemed trivial to worry about Paul, who after all was apparently alive and well, and so Sarah tried to dampen her concern.

Then came a day in June when two dreadful things happened: Norway finally surrendered to the Germans, and Italy declared war on Britain and France. Not long after came the most doom-laden news of all: the Nazis had occupied Paris. France, Britain's strongest and closest ally, had fallen. Now the British were alone.

On the morning of 4 July, Sarah left for work before the papers came, but when she passed Ted's bicycle propped up against the wall at Westbury Hall a headline on a folded copy of the *Daily Herald* left in the basket caught her eye. She picked up the paper. *Aliens Fight Each Other in Wild Panic*, it said. She read the article in growing horror. A British cruise ship named the *Arandora Star* had been sunk by a German U-boat north-west of Ireland. It had been full of enemy aliens, Germans and Italians, being exported, it was believed, to Canada. Hundreds of them, it appeared, had drowned.

She read on, her skin prickling with horror. The article claimed that the German passengers had punched and kicked their way past the weaker Italians in a chaotic scramble for places in the lifeboats. Words like *mob, brutal, sickening* rose to her eyes. She could hardly take it in. Surely it couldn't be true. Someone like Paul would never have behaved like that. But Paul wouldn't have been on board. *Would he?* The realization spread through her like the freezing waters of the north Atlantic. Internees, it seemed, hadn't simply been shut up in camps in Britain, they were being sent on elsewhere, by ship, at the mercy of the German navy, who wouldn't have had a clue that they were torpedoing their own people. *But surely Paul's mother would have been told if he was being sent away ...* Suppose, though, she hadn't been. Sarah had seen Mrs Hartmann walk past the walled garden the previous afternoon and gone to speak to her. The woman had said nothing about any kind of news from Paul. What should she do – warn her and show her the newspaper, or was she jumping ahead of events and worrying unnecessarily? She must wait, she decided, laying the paper back in the bike basket. If something had happened to Paul then there was nothing any of them could do and they'd hear soon enough.

The days passed and there was no news. She wrote to Paul and briefly mentioned the doomed *Arandora Star*, but there was no reply. It was unbearable living without knowing if he was safe.

At last, two weeks later, a letter came and when Sarah read it her heart lifted. He'd been ill with a fever, it turned out, and was sorry he'd not been able to write before. There was no mention of her letter to him so she wondered if it had got through the censor. He begged her to write back, also to send more supplies. She and Mrs Hartmann hastily packed up a box of food and toiletries. As an afterthought, Sarah plucked some rosemary and lavender from bushes that had survived the great cull of the kitchen garden, wrapped them in greaseproof paper and slipped them in with the milk powder, the socks and the soap, thinking of the pleasure it would give him to smell the scent of his English home.

Home. Even that was to be taken away from him. One hot August day as tiny planes did battle for Britain's fate in the skies above its green and pleasant fields and orchards, Mrs Hartmann climbed onto a rickety chair in her kitchen to reach the last big jar of plum jam from the top cupboard. The weight of it must have surprised her, for she overbalanced, cracking her head on the corner of the sink as she fell to the floor.

It was there that Sarah found her late in the day when she came to deliver some library books, a slight figure like an old rag doll lying in a pool of broken glass and purple fruit, the fallen chair and the open cupboard telling their simple, tragic story.

It was the hardest letter Sarah had ever had to write Paul, to tell him that his mother was dead, harder still that he wasn't allowed to return to Westbury for the funeral. The service was arranged by Lady Kelling and taken by Mr Tomms, and Sarah was touched to see how many people came. Sir Henry was there, she was pleased to see, though Robyn hadn't been able to take leave from the Wrens. The Richards and Mrs Bailey were in attendance, of course, but a surprisingly large number of the villagers came too. Those who had known Mrs Hartmann's story felt sorry for her. The postmistress represented the mood when she said afterwards that she felt it a dreadful shame about Paul being sent away and she hoped the poor lady was at peace. The service was unremittingly English in style, Lady Kelling having been heard to say that there would be no German hymns or organ music at a time of national crisis like this. Afterwards there were refreshments in the village hall.

'Is there anything that you can do to help Paul?' Sarah asked Sir Henry when she was able to speak to him on his own.

'I assure you that I haven't given up,' the man growled, his tone impatient. Perhaps he had been trying and been frustrated. Perhaps he didn't care.

Lady Kelling told her that the cottage would be put in order and closed up for the time being. *She assures us nothing will be taken away*, Sarah wrote to Paul, *so please don't worry on that score.*

It was in a cloud of despondency that she returned to work, knowing that the fragile woman of whom she'd become fond was no longer there to visit, would no longer walk past with a wave and a smile on her slow way down to the village. It made Paul's absence weigh more heavily, knowing she was now the one who cared for him most; more, she believed, than the Kellings seemed to. She didn't think anyone else wrote to him regularly or even kept him in their thoughts and that made it even more important that she kept doing so. He relied on her, she knew; she sensed that in his letters. There was quite a pile building now. Sometimes she would take them out and reread them, and now her eyes sought out tender phrases.

The thought of you keeps me going ... the memory of us working in the walled garden is dear to me ... I picture the garden as it was, and walk round it in my mind, naming the plants. How is it that we do not appreciate peace and beauty enough at the time, but often only value it when it has been taken from us?

The things she, in turn, wrote to him about were ordinary details of everyday life. Her tales about Ted Walters' ineptness were amusing, though it would seriously annoy her at the time whenever the man did something stupid. His latest sin was leaving the gate of the garden open, thus allowing wild deer to wander in during the night to trample the beds and tear bark from the trees. *I read him the riot act about that, I assure you!* she wrote. *I won't be surprised if he doesn't show his face tomorrow. The trouble is, if we lose him, I doubt that we would be given a replacement.*

She was also trying to keep the vegetable patch at Flint Cottage going, she told Paul, and what with that and keeping their own chickens and goats which Mrs Allman fed scraps to and spoke to as though they were her own children, life was very full.

The great news, she wrote in mid-October, *is that Derek, our evacuee, has returned.*

A letter from Nora Jenkins, addressed to Sarah's mother, had arrived two weeks earlier. Mrs Bailey read it and passed it to Sarah. *I'm writing to ask if you'll take our Derek again. The bombing is terrible, if the planes come we get no sleep, and if they don't I still lie awake waiting for them. Derek is so pale and tired, it would ease my mind if he could go to you.*

'I don't see why not,' Mrs Bailey said in a mild tone of voice, which completely surprised Sarah, considering the fuss her mother had made about having him last time. And so Sarah took an afternoon off work to receive him from his mother at the station and help settle him in.

Now ten, the year had made a difference to Derek. Food rations must have helped, because although still thin, he didn't have quite that hollow-eyed look of before and his skin had lost its anaemic pallor. She felt for him as he said goodbye to his mother on the station platform and pretended not to notice how he quivered with repressed emotion as she led him down to the waiting bus.

To Sarah's continued surprise, Mrs Bailey welcomed him warmly and came with them up to his box room and helped put away his few items of clothing in the cupboard and stow his case under the bed. She had even managed to borrow some old toys from the Bulldocks, and when the vicar's youngest boy, a chubby-faced lad named Toby, turned up on the doorstep with a football, Derek went off with him shyly to practise penalties on the patch of wasteland behind the village hall.

'Poor child,' Mrs Bailey said, watching them go down the path together, Toby chattering and Derek tongue-tied. 'We must find him better shoes and, Sarah, *he has no proper underwear!*'

Over the next few days her mother's battleaxe side came to the fore. No one, either shopkeeper or neighbour, was allowed to deny her imperious requests, and Derek was soon dressed as well as any other genteel Norfolk child for his first day at the village school, with a satchel of his own and a pencil case full of crayons. Mrs Bailey herself cut his sandy hair and even the sun contributed, bringing colour to his cheeks.

The nights were worrying at first, for Derek heard the air raid sirens in his dreams and would wake crying. One morning he was found asleep under the kitchen table cuddling his pillow, but gradually a normal sleep pattern resumed. Still, he looked every Monday for the postman and when his mother's letter came would run with it up to his room and remain there quietly until someone went up to find him.

His presence made a difference to the household, giving meaning to the daily routine, and making everyone try harder for 'my little man', as Mrs Allman called him. She took him once on her day off to visit her younger nephew in Ipswich and he returned home excited with tales of the marshes and bearing a bird's egg he'd found. 'Reg said I gotta leave the others or it'd upset the mum,' he declared solemnly when he showed them the speckled white egg and explained how he'd learned to blow out the contents through the holes he'd made at either end. The sad idea of the mother bird losing all her chicks had clearly struck home. He had a sweetness to him, a tenderness, to which Mrs Bailey in particular responded. Sarah watched him at the tea table as he tried to remember to close his mouth when he chewed his bread and couldn't help but think of the little, damaged boy the Baileys had lost in India whom their mother would never mention, but whom, it seemed after all, she carried in her heart.

Twenty-four

Briony was woken by a text arriving from an unknown number. When, tentatively, she clicked on it, she realized that Greg Richards must have picked up her number from the automatic reply message she'd set on her personal email. To that he'd been directed by the similar automatic reply on her college email, an address that was freely available on the college website. She had a moment's panic, cursing herself for how stupid she'd been to leave this trail to her very bedside. It would have been so easy for some internet troll to find her, except thankfully, she comforted herself, they didn't seem interested in her any more. She recovered herself and read Greg's message again, more carefully this time. *In London*, it said, *but coming back Westbury Thursday 7-ish. Drink or dinner? Cheers, Greg.*

She lay back on the pillows and considered for a moment. His face rose in her mind, the classic dark good looks, the easy manner, his lively expression. She could probably stand to have a drink with him, and, if that went well, dinner. Above all, she was curious as to what he might have found out from his father about her family's past. So she texted back to say, *OK, where shall we go? I hear The Dragon is good*.

She contemplated the day's tasks, glancing through the kitchen window at the overcast sky as she ate breakfast. Drive into Cockley Market for supplies and a potter, she decided, and then home for more editing. If the rain held off, perhaps a walk along the river later on. She'd noticed a footpath sign by the bridge. First of all, though, she wrote a note to old Mrs Clare at the Hall, tucked it into an envelope she found in a drawer and dropped it with Kemi on her way out. She was asking when it might be convenient to visit again.

It was market day in town. Two rows of brightly coloured stalls ran down the centre of the long street with its gracious Georgian shops, and Briony enjoyed choosing fruit and vegetables before queuing at the baker's for freshly baked bread, where she listened to the gossip. Then, her shopping bag now heavy, she was waiting for a gap in the traffic to nip over to the butcher's when she spotted Aruna on the other side of the street. Her friend was standing outside an old, whitewashed coaching inn, its sign of a heraldic bear swaying overhead in the breeze.

Briony couldn't see Aruna's face because she stood head down, her sunglasses pushed into her hair, reading something on her phone. She'd just raised her arm to hail her when Aruna stowed her phone in her bag and crossed the road, apparently not seeing Briony at all, and disappearing into a little bistro before Briony had a chance to attract her attention. She must be meeting Luke, Briony decided, and hurried up the pavement thinking she'd surprise them, but when she stared past the golden letters on the smoked glass of the bistro into the gloomy interior, she saw that the hazy figure who had risen from his seat at the back to greet Aruna wasn't Luke. She received the impression of a heavy, powerful man wearing a suit. He looked up and she stepped away, suddenly afraid of being seen, then dithered on the pavement arguing with herself. Aruna was her best friend. She knew her through and through. But something furtive about her behaviour just now suggested she didn't wish to be seen. Finally Briony lost courage and walked slowly on by.

It couldn't have been Aruna, she concluded as she stared into a gift shop window at the garish flowerpots and tea towels within. Lots of women had glossy black hair and that style of sunglasses, a tasselled leather bag swinging from their shoulder. What a silly mistake she might have made, barging in to greet her. Her face grew hot at the thought. She stopped at a newsagent to buy a paper and couldn't resist adding a tub of expensive ice cream from a freezer cabinet to her purchases. She walked slowly back past the bistro on her return to the car, but a party of people had gathered inside the door, blocking her view.

Twenty-five

October 1940

Sarah had finished mending a puncture on an upside-down bicycle late one afternoon when she heard footsteps on the gravel path. She glanced up to see a familiar uniformed figure.

'Ivor, good heavens,' she said, holding out oily hands. 'I didn't know you were coming home.' He took off his cap and crossed the grass to hug her and kiss her cheek.

'I thought I'd surprise you.'

'You certainly did that.' His admiring gaze as ever left her flustered. 'Where have you popped up from?'

'Today, London. Before that, Scotland. I've a week's pass. How are you? You look . . .'

'A mess, I know, but I've looked worse. Straw in my hair and dust in my throat a few weeks back.'

'But it was a good harvest, my pa says. That's marvellous. And what I was going to say was that you look as beautiful as ever.'

'Ivor, you're very flattering, but I'm afraid it's simply not true.' Sarah began to rub the grime off her hands with a rag, ashamed of her callouses and broken nails.

'What needs doing here?' He bent over the machine.

'Don't worry, I've done it. I rode over some barbed wire on a footpath. Stupid, really.'

He flipped the bicycle up onto its wheels and tested the handlebars with his weight. 'You've done a good job.'

'Thank you, kind sir. Don't sound so surprised.' She wheeled it into the shelter of the veranda, then invited him inside for a drink.

'Mummy is over at the Bulldocks. Mrs C. has put on a benefit – something to do with India, so she wasn't allowed to say no. And Diane's in Dundee. She's joined the Wrens, I expect you know.'

'Yes, so I heard from Mother.'

'We were astonished when she told us. I don't think she likes it much. She's a coder, whatever that means. Says the work is tiresome and they haven't received their uniforms yet. Pour yourself a whisky, if you want one. I shan't be long.'

Sarah flew upstairs to the bathroom, where she washed her hands and face. As she changed in her bedroom, she caught her reflection in the wardrobe mirror and was horrified at how Ivor must have seen her. Freckles on her face and arms, a long bramble scratch along her collarbone and sun-bleached hair as frizzy as a furze bush. Still, her eyes were bright enough and it was nice to step into a frock for a change. She attacked the furze bush with a hairbrush and went back downstairs.

Ivor was sitting flicking through the evening paper, but threw it aside when she entered. He handed her a whisky and soda that she didn't want and once again she was aware of his admiring gaze as she sat down beside him and sipped the drink politely.

'I can't offer you much to eat, I'm afraid,' she sighed. 'Nothing nice, that is. Mrs Allman's left us a rather fearful-looking cold collation.'

'It doesn't matter. I'm expected home for supper. My mother's killing the fatted calf. Or the fatted chicken, rather.'

'I don't know where we'd be without the hens and the rabbits. Derek, our evacuee, has a young boy's healthy appetite, though he doesn't like goat's milk. But tell me where you've been and what you've been doing. Nothing too dangerous, I hope?'

'It's been pretty dull actually. But I believe we'll see some action soon.' He explained how since coming home from France he'd been mostly training new recruits. He was full of funny stories about incompetent officers and nervous rookies, but behind the laughter Sarah sensed worry and frustration. Apprehension, too. He avoided saying where his company might be going next, if indeed he knew. Instead they moved on quickly to speak of concerns nearer home.

'Has there been any news of Bob?' The Bulldock boy's company had become separated from the rest of the battalion in France and taken to Germany as prisoners. The family had been reassured to hear from Bob via the Red Cross in July. 'But it's a terrible strain on the family,' Sarah sighed. She stood and fetched the decanter to refresh Ivor's glass.

'Absolutely. Whoa, thank you. I heard about Hartmann, too,' he said in a nonchalant way and her hand froze on the decanter as she set it on the tray. 'A poor show sticking everyone behind bars like that, but you have to see it from Churchill's point of view. It's not worth the risk. I know you're sympathetic to him, Sarah, but England is on its own in all this. The risk of treachery is very real.'

'It's downright cruel,' Sarah insisted. 'Paul Hartmann hates Hitler and everything he stands for.'

'He's still a German, though. A man's natural instinct is to support his homeland, though I accept that Hartmann must feel pulled two ways.'

'Rubbish. There was no need to lock him up. You heard about his poor mother, didn't you?'

'Yes, my ma wrote me,' he said. 'A crying shame.'

'She was only fifty-one. I was surprised, as she seemed much older. I was the one who found her, did your mother say?'

'Yes, that must have been a shock.'

'It was. And it was awful writing to Paul to tell him. I feel so dreadfully for him about it.'

'You poor old thing. Still, you mustn't get yourself in a state.'

'I'm not in a state, Ivor, I'm just concerned. What must it be like for Paul? He's on his own now, and nobody seems able to say what will happen to him.'

'Hartmann will be all right. We're a civilized nation. We don't treat these people badly.'

'No? What about that ship that sank, the *Arandora Star*? It was taking enemy aliens to Canada. Canada! How cruel to separate families like that. And to risk the U-boats.'

She'd started to shake and when she sat down again he took her hands in his. 'Nobody wanted any of them to die, Sarah. Oh, you poor girl, I don't like to see you anxious about these things. I'll tell you what, why don't we go out somewhere tomorrow night. It would take your mind off everything.'

'Not tomorrow, Ivor. I'm too damned tired at present.'

'At the weekend, then. Oh, Sarah, I have missed you. I still feel the same, you know. Have your feelings for me changed one little bit?'

He was close to her now, she felt the warmth of his breath on her cheek and her distress was melting away. How could it be that one was attracted to a man and yet not know if one loved them? And then his lips were on hers, hot, fierce, forcing open her mouth, his tongue exploring, and she slid her arms up round his neck.

'Sarah!' he murmured, his mouth moving to her neck, causing her to shiver with ecstasy, then back to her lips again. He pressed himself against her and his body was hard, urgent, unyielding and then his hand brushed her breast and travelled downwards, pulling at her dress, forcing its way between her thighs.

'No,' she said. 'No.' She fought against him till he let go and they sprang apart panting and gasping.

'I'm so sorry,' he said, the shame clear on his face. 'I'm a brute. But you do it to me, Sarah. I can't get you out of my mind.'

'I shouldn't have let you . . . oh, what's the point. You'd better go, Ivor. The others will be back soon.'

'I'm sorry, darling.' He leaned in and she let him kiss her more chastely on the cheek. Then he snatched up his jacket and backed out of the room, giving her one last lingering look. She heard the front door slam and his footsteps smacking on the path.

She wiped his kiss from her cheek and sank down on the sofa. Her body shaking all over, she fought against threatening sobs. What had she done? She didn't love him, she knew that really. Didn't even like him, hated the casual way he'd spoken about Paul. She knocked back the rest of her whisky and sat staring at the shadows moving on the wall until she was calm. At the creak of the garden gate, she stood up, checked her face in the mirror and went to open the front door to her mother.

Sarah did not see or hear from Ivor at all the following day, and she supposed he must be angry with her. She told herself that she didn't care, but she hated falling out with anyone close to her and it was with a heavy heart that she went about her tasks on the estate.

On the morning of the second day, a silent, bullet-headed man arrived on cue to take away the two pigs they'd been fattening in a wooden sty behind the kitchen garden and although she told herself not to be sentimental Sarah couldn't help having a little weep after they'd been loaded onto his wagon and driven away squealing, more in dismay at being separated from their trough – or so she wanted to believe – than in anticipation of their brutal end. Still, there must be ham and bacon and that was that. She marched determinedly past the desolate pig house, which she couldn't face mucking out while the straw was still warm, and engaged herself with Sam in some industrial-scale cabbage planting to take her mind off her troubles. These, she remonstrated with herself, were not really troubles at all compared with some people's.

At four o'clock as the light was beginning to fade, they both downed tools, and Sam went off home smartly on some pretext that Sarah thought was to do with a girl. She, however, pottered about a while longer in the Kellings' garden behind the hall. There had been signs that builders would be at work on the interior soon doing whatever was required to turn the hall into a rest home for wounded soldiers. She imagined that the invalids would want a pleasant garden to sit in, so she had been trying to keep the weeds down in the flower beds while Sam periodically scythed the lawn.

It was almost an hour later, as she was scraping clean her tools, that she glanced down the hill, then shaded her eyes against the lowering sun to watch a lonely figure hefting a bulky bag trudge up the drive. There was something furtive in his movements – he kept glancing behind him and once or twice broke into a weary trot before falling back again into the plodding walk. Realization crept up on her. It couldn't be. Then their eyes locked and when he raised his hat and waved it at her, Sarah was sure. She dropped the trowel, left the guttering tap and took a step towards him, then another, and soon she was running.

'Paul!' she cried. 'Oh, Paul.' And then, somehow, they were in each other's arms, hugging and laughing with joy. How thin he was, she noticed with concern. She could feel his ribs beneath his threadbare jacket. When they disengaged themselves, she was shocked to see the hollows under his eyes. He might have been ten years older. What had they done to him?

'I called at Flint Cottage just now,' he said, beaming at her, 'but there was only Mrs Allman and a boy.'

'Yes, that's Derek, our evacuee. Oh, Paul, you're home. I can hardly believe it.'

'And you mustn't believe it. I'm not home, Sarah. Only visiting. I should not be here at all.'

'Why?' She didn't understand, then she froze. 'You didn't run away, did you?'

'No, no. I've been formally released from the camp. I'm not sure yet, but I think I have Sir Henry to thank for that.'

'Good old Sir Henry.' She allowed herself to think warmly of him again. 'I wonder how he managed it.'

'Some of us are being released now the danger of invasion has receded. But, Sarah, I am forbidden to come home to Norfolk. Any coastal county. They still fear that we will escape to the Continent, I suppose, or pass messages on to German ships. If I'm seen here ... well.'

'But you came anyway.'

'I wanted to see Mutti. I've just visited the churchyard and saw the wooden marker. She's in a nice place there under the trees, I'm glad.'

'Paul, I'm so sorry.'

'I know. And I wanted to see my friends, you particularly. Sarah, you don't know how much I looked forward to your letters. They helped me so much.'

'They weren't very exciting, I'm afraid.'

'It was the normality of them that kept me going. The sense that you were all there carrying on as usual. Mutti's letters ... ah, I shouldn't complain. I loved to hear from her, but they were full of her unhappiness.'

'She was so worried about you, Paul. But now she is beyond all worry.'

'Yes. I must learn to think like that. And now I'll visit the house. There are some things I need and—'

'I expect you'd like to be by yourself for a while.'

'Yes, you understand, I knew you would.'

'How long will you be here, Paul?' Would she see him again before he left? 'What will you do?'

'An Austrian man I met was released at the same time. He has family in London and says I'm welcome to stay there. It's in Hampstead, near the Heath. I don't know what work I'll do, but it's a start ... *Mein Gott*,' he breathed.

He was staring off at something behind her. When she turned, her breath caught. It was Ivor, trampling across the cropped field towards them, his face, as he drew near, like thunder.

'Hartmann,' he called out. 'What are you doing here?'

Paul said nothing, only waited for Ivor's approach.

'I didn't know they'd let you out.'

'Yes, two days ago. I'm not back to work, I'm afraid, tell your father.'

'You're not supposed to be here. You know the rules as well as I do.'

How did he? Sarah wondered.

Paul took a deep breath. 'Don't worry, I'm only here to collect some clothes and then I'll be gone. There'll be no cause to suspect I'm a traitor, please be sure.'

'I didn't mean ...'

'I think I do know what you meant,' Paul said smoothly,

but two bright spots on his pale cheeks conveyed his anger. His eyes blazed. 'Whatever your reasons, you don't want me here, so I am pleased to assure you that I'll not trouble you long. I am sure you would not deny me the short respite, but don't worry, tomorrow, I will, as you have often told me to, cut along.'

Ivor growled, 'It won't be soon enough as far as I'm concerned.' His expression was fierce at Paul's directness.

'Oh don't, both of you,' Sarah cried in distress.

'You and I must say goodbye, Sarah,' Paul said, taking one of her hands and kissing it in a daring gesture. 'There may not be an opportunity to see you in the morning. I think Captain Richards here will want to be sure I'm gone.'

'Goodbye then, Hartmann.' Ivor spoke quietly, then they watched Paul swing his bag onto his shoulder once more and set off round the corner of the walled garden in the direction of Westbury Lodge.

Sarah surveyed Ivor coolly until his face reddened. 'You've disappointed me, Ivor. I expected better of you. Why are you so hard on him? Are you jealous because he and I are friends?'

'I don't like him being around you, that's all. He's not good enough for you. I can't think your mother would approve. He's German and he's the under-gardener. Or rather, he was.'

'And what about me, in this? I'm a land girl. Paul's better educated than I am. His father was a university lecturer and his mother is related to Lady Kelling. But why do I bother to say all this? All you see him as is a humble gardener.'

'A humble German gardener. Without even the decency to go back and fight for his country.'

'So now you're accusing him of cowardice?'

'Sarah, please, I don't wish to quarrel with you over Hartmann. He's not worth it.'

'Well, he'll be gone tomorrow, so we won't need to quarrel about him. I'm off home, Ivor. I'm tired, dead tired.' Wearily she rescued her trowel and fork from the ground, wiped them dry with a rag and shut them with the other tools in the shed.

Ivor waited for her. 'When will I see you next?'

'At the moment, Ivor, I honestly don't know.' She pulled on her coat, tied her scarf round her hair and mounted her bicycle. Only when she reached the bottom of the drive did she look back at him. Ivor was standing legs apart, hands on hips, watching her with the pride of some mountain chieftain, she thought. *As though he owned her.* Crossly, she turned her face from him and set off in the direction of home.

Her mother was pleased to hear that Paul had been released, but otherwise not more than politely interested. Sarah did not hear from him that evening, though she was alert to any knock on the door or rattle of the letter box. In bed she lay awake for a long time imagining his lonely vigil. The morning brought only the usual post, gathered from the mat by Derek, who bore it proudly to the table before taking his seat. She noticed he was being careful not to slurp his porridge and thereby bring the cold eye of Mrs Bailey upon him, but he relaxed when her critical gaze fell instead upon Sarah.

'What's the matter with you today? You're jumpy and it's getting on my nerves.'

'There's nothing wrong, Mummy, except a headache. I didn't sleep well. Is that really a letter from Diane? What does she say?'

'The food is good, but her stockings are all dying, and she wants her pale-coloured nail varnish. Here, you can read it yourself.' Diane was as poor a letter writer as Ivor, her missives full of requests.

Sarah's mind was in turmoil. Seeing Paul again, yesterday's

conflict with Ivor, both had struck deep at the roots of her happiness. Each of the men was important to her, she recognized that, but each disturbed her in different ways. Ivor, with his fair good looks and definite position in the world, made her body thrill to his touch, but his sense of his manhood could be fragile, as though some fault line ran through his psyche. She was aware of this sensitivity when he was with his father, or with Paul, which was worse, for Paul, despite his greater height and physical strength, was in a weaker position than Ivor was. Yet, for some reason, Ivor could not be generous to him, an exile from his homeland, a landless, lordless man. Was it this lack of status that Ivor despised, as well as Paul being German? Or was it jealousy of a potential rival in love that drove him? She didn't know and wondered whether Ivor did either.

As for how she felt about Paul, she knew she cared for him very much, but something held her back. His vulnerability unsettled her, his lack of confidence in himself. His loyalty, she felt, had been to his mother, and without Mrs Hartmann his ties to his life in England might be loosened. Perhaps this was why he needed Sarah. Well, she would be his steadfast friend. Part of her wanted to put her arms around him and hold him close, but would this be right? Did she, Sarah, need him?

She wished, not for the first time, that her parents' marriage had been happy, that from it she might have learned what to do. Her father had never made her mother content. He had adored her, but she remained aloof. Sometimes she wondered if her mother was capable of deep love. Diane seemed sadly to be the same. *But I am*, she told herself. *If I can't love deeply then I will never marry. I'm perfectly happy to be by myself.*

These thoughts went round and round in her head like howling devils in the depths of the night. This morning, nothing was any clearer to her.

'Perhaps the fresh air will blow the headache away. Goodbye, Mummy. Don't be late for school, Derek.'

The garden's looking sad, so much straggly or dead, Sarah noted, as she wheeled her bicycle to the gate. Well, it matched her mood.

Round each corner on the way to Westbury Hall she expected to meet someone, Paul or Ivor, Ivor or Paul, but she reached the walled garden without even seeing Sam, who was late for the second time that week. She leaned her bicycle against the tool shed and walked along the lane to the Hartmanns' cottage and knocked on the door.

Nobody came. She tried the door but it was locked. He'd gone then, she thought dismally as she returned to the garden and surveyed the day's work. The apple trees were heavy with fruit. It was time to prepare the crates for picking.

At home that evening there was still no word from Ivor and, feeling guilty, Sarah wrote him a letter, saying that she was sorry that they'd quarrelled and suggesting that they meet for tea at the weekend.

Initially, there was no reply. The following day a note arrived. It was cool to the point of formality. He was very sorry, but he was required to leave on Saturday to rejoin his battalion. He accepted her apology and considered the matter closed.

How hurtful and bemusing, she thought angrily, rereading the letter. Despite the coolness, there was pain between the lines. The only concession he granted her was that he would write. Very piously he asked her to pray for his safety. She sat on her bed for a long time after this, trying not to feel hurt. Was he withdrawing from her for good, or simply being cruel and playing with her?

Twenty-six

Her best jeans with the pearl-buttoned ivory shirt, or a pale green cotton dress with flared skirt? Briony surveyed the heap of discarded clothes on the bed and wished she'd brought something smart with her. She was only meeting Greg at The Dragon, but if he was driving straight from London he might still be in his city suit, so it wouldn't do to appear too casual. The dress was badly crumpled, however, and when she put on the shirt and inspected herself in the mirror it showed signs of strain at the bust. Jeans and a loose top it was, then. She pulled them on then hooked silver drops into her ears and fitted strappy sandals on her feet; a modest heel or she would be taller than him, though did that matter? After all, it wasn't a date, was it? As she twisted her hair into its habitual knot and painted on lipstick, she asked herself why, in that case, did she feel so nervous?

The pub down by the old stone bridge was pretty with its hanging baskets and a glimpse of lush back lawn running down to the river. Inside all was old beams and polished brass. Briony followed signs to the bar through a series of tiny rooms opening into one another until she reached a large main lounge. There she saw Greg, thankfully not too formally dressed in navy cords and a soft blue open-necked shirt. He was standing talking to an elfin-looking youth with a bright flame of magenta hair serving behind the bar. She crossed the wooden floor and touched his arm.

'Greg.'

'Briony, hi,' Greg, said, turning, his amiable, handsome face lighting up with pleasure. He kissed her tenderly on both cheeks. 'What'll you have to drink?'

'One of those, please,' she said, pointing to the pint of foaming amber that stood before him, and the red-haired elf obliged. She took a mouthful of creamy beer and felt her nervousness fall away.

'I hope you don't mind,' Greg went on, 'but I've booked us a table for eight o'clock. My lunch was a cocktail sandwich and a very tiny samosa.'

'Not enough for a growing boy,' she laughed. She didn't mind that her plans for an early exit had collapsed. Really this beer was delicious. Evening sunshine sparkled through the diamond-paned windows and the beauties of an English garden beckoned. They carried their drinks out to a small round table under the willows whose branches trailed in the rippling stream.

'You are lucky having a place here,' she sighed. 'It's idyllic.'

'The drive can be a slog, but it's well worth it,' he agreed. 'I was brought up nearby.' He named a village and when she said she hadn't heard of it he laughed, 'No one has. It's about five miles away off the main road going towards Norwich, so I've always thought of round here as home.'

'Didn't you say the house where you live now had been in the family?'

'That's right. My great-grandfather was estate manager at the hall and the house came with the position, so his son, my grandfather, was brought up there.'

'And you, the wealthy scion, have come and taken over the lot. That is a very modern example of the Wheel of Fortune!'

He smiled. 'I suppose you could say that. It's certainly odd to think that a Kelling of Westbury Hall is now a leaseholder of mine. I gather from Kemi that you've met old Mrs Clare.'

'Yes, and I don't believe she thinks of herself as beholden to you in any way.' Briony gave Greg a look of amusement as she raised her glass to her lips.

'No,' he sighed. 'She probably doesn't.' He rubbed his stubbled jaw in a thoughtful manner and the sunlight sparked off a gold ring he wore.

It was true that he must have done well in life to be able to buy the Hall and its park, though high finance was a blur to her. She wondered how wealthy you'd have to be. *What was he – early forties*, she reckoned. His shirt was crisply ironed. Everything about him was neat, well-manicured, but bruised shadows under his shrewd blue eyes, a tautness about his lined forehead, spoke of strain.

His gaze lingered on her and, self-conscious, she tucked a stray lock of hair behind her ear and sat up straighter. 'How did you go about the development at Westbury Hall?' she asked. 'I mean, the whole building project must have been complicated.'

'It was,' he agreed. He talked for some time about planning permission and raising finance, partnerships with a specialist architect and builder, their difficulties in sourcing the correct materials and finding workers with the requisite skills. Problems with damp and wet rot. To her surprise, it fascinated her. The Hall had been dilapidated and failed to attract a buyer to restore it, which is why his proposals had eventually been accepted. The whole thing had taken several years. As he spoke and showed her before-and-after photos on his phone, Briony realized how much the place meant to him, and not simply on a financial level.

'What about your house?' she asked. 'Are you going to keep it as a weekend place?'

'To be honest, I haven't decided. I had been going to move up here with my wife, or ex-wife, I should say. Perhaps start a family. All that stuff. It didn't work out.'

'I see. That's sad.' This must be the reason for his underlying strain.

She waited in case he wished to confide, but he merely drained his glass and looked wistful, as though miles away. Their table was ready. They gathered up their things and moved indoors.

In the gloomy restaurant, candlelight flickered over crystal and silver to create an intimate setting. The waitress brought artisan rolls and tiny patterned roundels of dewy butter; poured white wine, clear and cold.

As they waited for their starter, Greg asked her about her work, the book she'd written, how she thought the changing political situation would affect her college. She did a passable impression of the pompous Head of Department who was obsessed with statistics and the bottom line, which made Greg laugh. She wondered if he often laughed, there was something guarded about the way he broke off and pressed his lips together.

It was with embarrassment that she described what had happened to her earlier in the year, how she'd been hounded on social media. He looked horrified. 'I've no time for that sort of thing,' he said. 'I don't do any of it myself, Twitter and Facebook and stuff.'

'Nor do I now, except Facebook, but I never post anything.'

They were interrupted by the arrival of the first course and for a while ate quietly, she enjoying the tastes of fresh basil and creamy mozzarella delicate upon the palate. She was glad that she hadn't splurged out how deeply the trauma of trial-by-media had affected her, unsure as she was how sympathetic he would be. There was a side of him that seemed very cut and dried. He might be of the 'put up and shut up' school, a way of dealing with problems she often tried herself, but which simply hadn't worked for her this time. Instead, as their fish and chips arrived, she asked what she'd been bursting to all evening.

'What did your father say the other day?'

He gazed at her with eyebrows raised and she stumbled on, 'Sorry, you kindly said you'd ask him if he knew anything about my grandfather.'

'Ah, yes, of course.' She sensed reluctance in him and wondered privately whether he'd wanted to avoid the subject. 'And the other guy, what was the name?'

'Hartmann, Paul Hartmann. What did your dad say?'

'That's the difficulty. He asked about you, who you were, where you'd come from, and of course there wasn't much I could tell him, except that you were a historian and were looking into some family history.'

'And how did he respond?'

'He seemed a bit quiet. I don't think he got on with my grandfather very well, but at the same time he's quite protective of his memory. Even now, though he's been dead for ten years. I knew him, of course, but not well. He didn't give much of himself away. He was a bitter old sod, to tell you the truth. Thought life had been against him for some reason. Anyway, that's as far as I got with Dad.'

Nowhere at all in fact, Briony thought, crestfallen.

'I'm sorry. I can see that you're disappointed.'

'I am a bit, yes. I can't remember how much I told you, but I was given a collection of letters written to Paul Hartmann, who was a gardener at the Hall during the Second World War. The letter writer was a woman called Sarah, who apparently lived in Westbury. Then I found a note to her from Paul in a box of my grandfather's things, and I realized they must all have known one another. So it's important to me to find out about them. It's family, you see. We lost my mother when I was very young and I'm fascinated to know about where we came from. You feel that, too, don't you? Why else would you have bought the old house where your grandfather once lived?'

'I like the idea of being somewhere I could put down roots. That's how I saw it with Lara, anyway. We'd settle here and have kids, who would go to the village school.'

'The country dream in fact?'

'Yes, but then Lara chucked me out.' He spoke bitterly, as he speared his last piece of fish, ate it, laid down his knife and fork and took a gulp of wine from his glass.

Briony finished her own food and waited for him to say more about his ex, one of the usual explanations probably, about a stupid affair or the dying of romantic love. But he didn't and she was puzzled, but also relieved as she never knew what to say in response to these stories, of which one only ever heard one side and that might not be entirely truthful. People wove their own versions of events in order to make sense of themselves, she often supposed. Certainly when studying the great personalities of history she found this to be true. Are the worst lies the ones we tell ourselves?

'I thought at the beginning about living in the Hall itself.' Greg was speaking again. 'But the upkeep would have been ginormous. The cottage is fine for me and, yes, the family link is attractive.'

'And, as you said, you're owner of the whole park this time round!' She spoke laconically.

'There is pleasure in that element,' he said, with a wry smile.

Although his explanations made sense, she had the impression that there was something he was not saying. She and he, descendants of two Westbury families, had never met before and yet they were circling around some big and unknown subject.

'Everything all right for you?' The waitress collected their plates and pointed out a blackboard of specials.

'The desserts aren't bad here,' Greg murmured to Briony. 'I'll go for the apple and blackberry crumble and cream. What about you?'

'Maybe a scoop of ice cream to keep you company. I couldn't possibly manage anything more.'

'Listen,' she said as they waited. 'I don't know if you meant it about wanting to develop the garden, but I have a friend who designs gardens. You met him and his girlfriend the other day, that is, you spoke to them when you passed them on the drive.'

'Yes, I think I remember.'

'His name's Luke, Luke Sandbrook. I don't know if he's got time or anything, but he's up staying with his parents for a few days. I showed him the walled garden and he loved it. He's very good, everyone says so.'

'Perhaps you'd give me his number,' Greg said. 'Some advice at this stage would be useful.'

'OK! I'll tell him, shall I? That you might call.' She was pleased that she might have done Luke a favour.

'Sure. I've no problem with that.'

*

After dessert they had coffee and squabbled over the bill, which the persistent Greg ended up paying. It was dark by the time they emerged from the pub and went to stand for a moment on the bridge, enjoying how the downlights under the eaves picked out the soft creamy walls of the building and sparkled on the flowing water. Briony felt full and sleepy, but when Greg said that given the amount they'd drunk it would be sensible to leave the car in the car park overnight she was content to walk with him through the village and into the soft darkness of the lane that led up past Westbury Hall.

In London she usually found darkness unnerving, a hiding place for muggers, but here it was gentle, calming, magical even, with the restless sound of the wind in the trees and here and there bright eyes in the undergrowth that would shine briefly before vanishing. High above, in gaps in the canopy, bright pinpricks of starlight began to gleam.

They hardly spoke, awed by the darkness perhaps, though she heard Greg's soft breath as they toiled up a slope. And then the tunnel of trees opened out and she sensed rather than saw the black shape of the gateway and, above it, the gleaming white dog and they passed under it into the park. Up ahead a faint glow was all they could see of the hall.

'Isn't it beautiful?' she breathed and in the darkness she felt Greg's hand close over hers, firm and strong, and it felt perfectly natural that they walk, hand in hand. After a while, his arm slipped round her waist and in this manner they drifted slowly up the drive to where it forked, and in one direction lay his house and in the other the hall and her own little lodge. There they stopped and he drew her to him and kissed her face and lips in the darkness, softly at first and then more urgently, his fingers stroking her hair and neck, sending shivers of desire through her. He kissed her again and again until she was dizzy. He sighed and moved to nuzzle her neck, pressed her to him till she felt she was moving in a dream. He whispered her name, but it wasn't her name, and she came to herself and drew back.

'I'm not Lara,' she said, placing her finger on his lips to show she was not angry, but a little hurt.

'I didn't say you were.' She could make out the pale planes of his puzzled face and heard confusion in his voice. He kissed her again and murmured, 'What should we do? Your place or mine?'

There was something wrong, but she couldn't quite grasp it. 'No, Greg,' she said. 'It's been a wonderful evening, thank you. This is lovely, but we hardly know each other.'

'Of course,' he said, drawing back, 'I'm sorry.'

'There's nothing to be sorry for. It's just ...'

'It's too soon. My apologies. I was overwhelmed.'

'I think I must have been, too.' She reached and stroked his face. He took her hand and held it against his lips and bit it gently, but not so it hurt. She laughed.

'To be continued, maybe?'

'Maybe.' She let the word trail.

They said goodbye and Briony walked on up towards the Hall, her heart still racing, her lips swollen with his kisses. The whole episode had upset her. It must have been the close intimacy created by the darkness that had dissolved her natural reserve. She had felt, as Greg said he'd been, overwhelmed, not in control, that was the truth and that was unlike her. A great round moon the colour of old bone was rising over the Hall, illuminating the long brick wall of the kitchen garden to her right and the pale shape of its doorway, which drew her in. And as she stood under its arch looking out across the grassy patches of the sleeping garden, the wide arms of the trees whose fruit swelled in the silence, she knew suddenly and for certain that it hadn't been his ex-wife's name, Lara, that she'd heard Greg whisper, but 'Sarah', which didn't make sense at all.

Robyn Clare. Such a pretty name, and the handwriting was beautiful, too, if shaky with age. Briony had got up late the next morning and found the envelope sticking in the letter box. The invitation to tea had been penned on a piece of good cream card with *Westbury Hall, Norfolk* embossed at the top. Nothing so vulgar as a postcode. Briony wondered whether its vintage was a time when Unwin Clare was alive and Mrs Clare still Lady of the Manor. Perhaps she believed she still was.

It was lovely to receive a handwritten card like this, and so rare now. She placed it on the mantelpiece and thought how much things had changed. Paul and Sarah would have taken great care writing letters, thinking about exactly what the right words might be, reading and rereading the ones they received from each other, considering the right response. People today could communicate in an instant, but that brought its own problems, as she well knew. They could be thoughtless about what they wrote, uncaring of how words can hurt. And it was sad that in the future the electronic generation would probably have no collections of letters to keep and cherish and reread when they were old.

This time when she was admitted to Mrs Clare's ground-floor flat the fat pug simply sniffed at her sandals and withdrew to its basket, plumping itself down with a snort of dismissal and laying its head on its paws. Its mistress was safe, but it obviously intended to keep an eye on the plate of delicious-looking cakes and scones waiting on the coffee table.

From the direction of the kitchen came the sound of activity and soon a portly middle-aged country woman, introduced by Robyn via a 'Bless you, Avril,' came through with a rattling tea trolley. There were proper porcelain cups and saucers accompanied by silver teaspoons with decorated handles, Briony noted with delight. Briony selected a scone from the proffered selection and took a delicate tea plate. Enthroned in the armchair opposite, old Mrs Clare swallowed two pink pills from a foil packet and accepted a generous slice of Victoria sponge.

'We always used to have to eat four triangles of bread and butter before cake in the nursery here,' she said, her eyes twinkling. 'The nice thing about getting old is that you can break all the rules.'

'As long as you do what the doctor says, Mrs Clare,' Avril said as she poured the tea, then smiling at them both, withdrew.

'You said "we" when you mentioned the nursery.' Briony bit into the scone and delicious buttery crumbs melted on her tongue.

'I had an elder brother, but he died in a terrible accident when I was small. There's a pond further along the path past your cottage. That's where he drowned.'

'How awful.'

'It affected my parents very badly, and me, I suppose. I felt I was no use because I wasn't a boy. It's all a long long time ago now. You said in your letter that you'd like to ask me more about your grandfather.'

'And Paul Hartmann,' Briony added.

'Yes, and Paul. I'm afraid I don't have very much more to say. I wasn't here for most of the war. This place became a convalescent home and my parents lived in London most of the time. Daddy worked at the Home Office, you see. And I became a Wren. Mummy liked the Wrens best because they had the nicest uniform. I had a very interesting time and became engaged to a lovely naval officer. Then he was killed in 'forty-three when his ship was torpedoed in the Bay of Biscay. That word *heart-broken*, it means precisely that. George's death took the stuffing out of me for months.'

Briony nodded in sympathy and waited for her to go on. Mrs Clare brushed cake crumbs from her lips and continued.

'Paul's mother, Barbara, died – when was it? – quite early in the war, I think. Mummy was staying at the house in Chelsea and I was visiting her at the time. I didn't come down to the funeral as I had to return to Dundee. Mummy said Paul wasn't there, but I can't remember why.'

'From a letter I've read I think he was in an internment camp when it happened.'

'Ah yes, of course, that would have been it. A letter, you say? What letter is that, may I ask?'

Briony explained about the letters she'd been given, which interested Mrs Clare greatly, but when the name Bailey came up, her wrinkled face clouded.

'You must have known the Baileys if they lived in the village?' Briony asked carefully, seeing that the reminder was not a welcome one.

'I certainly did. Sarah was very pleasant. I liked her. She was our land girl and a good one, too. Her sister Diane I got to know a little because she was a Wren like me, but we weren't close. We were together in Dundee for some months before I was transferred to Portsmouth. She was a strange one. Something had got to her, I'd say. Oh, it's all so long ago. I can't remember what happened now. Their mother, Belinda, was a different kettle of fish. A cold woman, I always thought, brittle, but considered herself very attractive to men.' For a moment, Mrs Clare paused, before plunging on.

'She was my father's mistress for several years, do Sarah's letters say that?'

'No,' Briony was taken aback. 'I haven't read that anywhere.' She was struck by Robyn Clare's bitter tone.

'Well, she was and I could never forgive her for it. It nearly broke my mother. You can imagine the shame if it had come out at the time. I only discovered the affair by accident. I walked in on them once in our house in Belgravia.'

'Your mother knew about it?'

'Oh yes, I'm sure of that. I was away for much of the war, but I came home to London on leave from time to time and I'd wish I hadn't bothered. "Would you ask your father if he's finished with the paper?" my mother would say at breakfast. Or he'd tell me, "Please inform your mother that I'm dining out tonight." They were united only by one thing, which was that the servants shouldn't know they were quarrelling, which was ridiculous as Cook was old and deaf and the daily woman too harassed about her family's survival to care what her employers were up to. It's sad to think of it all now . . .'

Robyn Clare's words drifted away as though she'd forgotten Briony was there. She was staring out across the garden now with a faraway expression, her fingers plucking at a loose thread in the upholstery of her chair.

Briony calculated that Robyn must have been seventeen or eighteen when war broke out. How marked she was still by the troubles of that time, when life had dealt her excitement, yes, but also tragedy and strife.

'They did eventually make it up,' Robyn continued, her tone still melancholy, 'but only when my father became ill and needed Mummy. It wasn't until 1946 that Westbury Hall was returned to us, but Mummy and Daddy stayed in London most of the time. Then Daddy died and Unwin and I took it on. You know the rest of the story.'

Briony nodded. Unwin and Robyn had struggled on over the years to keep the Hall going until with Unwin's death the family had been forced to admit defeat. And now Greg, the grandson of one of their own employees, was in effect, if not in name, lord of Westbury Hall.

Twenty-seven

November 1940

Dear Paul,

 It was a great relief to hear from you and I'm glad to have an address to which to write, but how dreadfully tragic about your Austrian friends. Thank heavens you were out of the house that evening. Such a small thing as a bus that didn't show up, which you probably cursed at the time – but by the grace of God it saved your life. I say by the grace of God, but the bombs are so random it sounds simply like luck. Well, you've had so much bad luck, Paul, that I truly wish that this is the start of a good run. I'm sorry your hostel is so crowded and hope that you find somewhere nicer to live soon. Working with refugees sounds a fine thing for you to be doing, but I'm interested to hear you're thinking about joining the Pioneers. Keep yourself safe, Paul, that's all we ask.

 Here, with the first frosts, there's little to be done at the Hall. I'm sure I smell permanently of eau de manure, especially since it's difficult to dig it in as the ground is hard. Otherwise, it's mostly tidying up. And paperwork, of course. The dark evenings are endless, but the merrier for having young Derek to

*amuse. He's a great one for jigsaw puzzles and I've got into the
habit of reading to him at bedtime. We're trying* The Jungle
Book *because he wanted to know why we called Daddy's old
tiger rug Shere Khan.*

*Diane is well from what we can gather – we had a short
letter from her last week – however, she's been reprimanded for
drinking whisky someone smuggled into a dance. She's seen
Robyn Kelling a few times and says she's quite a different girl
away from her parents, more cheerful and chatty. It's good for
Diane and Robyn to stand on their own feet, one positive thing
at least to come out of this war.*

*Write soon, Paul. You're not alone in the world while I'm
here and remember you have so much to offer.*

Yours truly,

Sarah

Briony finished typing up Sarah's letter, noticing the address,
a Salvation Army hostel in Pimlico, where Paul must have
mixed with all sorts of people after being bombed out. The idea
of the Pioneer Corps piqued her curiosity, and she googled the
name to remind herself what they did. The Corps had a long
history. They were non-combatants who went wherever their
labour was needed to keep a military operation going. During
the war they'd handled stores and ammunition, built camps,
airfields and fortifications, cleared rubble, mended roads, rail-
ways and bridges ... the list went on and on. Briony sat back in
her chair and flexed her aching shoulders as she pondered what
she'd read.

As an enemy alien, Paul would not have been allowed to join
up to fight early in the war, even if he had wanted to. Entering
this corps would have still meant him being prepared to support the destruction of his fellow countrymen. Even so, that

must have been a tough decision for him to make, and not for the first time Briony longed to know his thoughts. He'd have had to be physically strong, but as a gardener he would have been. Despite what the months of internment had done to him. And there would have been training, of course.

She sighed and selected the next letter in the pile. Altogether this had been an interesting afternoon, she reflected. Robyn had remembered Briony's grandfather Harry and that was a breakthrough. Briony could almost hear Robyn's crisp, clear voice speaking:

'A cheerful, happy-go-lucky sort of boy, Harry. He was one of those it was impossible to dislike. I sometimes wondered what happened to him, but we weren't close and I didn't see anyone to ask. Everything was so difficult after the war ended. So many of the young people one knew had scattered. Several of my friends were killed. So Harry moved to Surrey, it seems. Did he have a brother? I can't remember. If so, perhaps the brother took over the farm eventually.'

Briony tapped the end of her pencil against her teeth as she noted Robyn's words. There was much that was puzzling. Not simply about what had happened to Paul Hartmann, but to others. The Baileys for instance. Where had they gone after the war ended? She should have asked Mrs Clare. She leaned forward and reached for the next letter.

Twenty-eight

Early 1941

London wore an air of decrepitude, like a bruised old man in a moth-eaten overcoat. In the welcome warmth of the Lyons Corner House on Oxford Street, Sarah ordered a pot of tea from a waitress. By the misted-up window a motherly-looking woman sat alone in a halo of wintry sunshine reading a letter, dabbing at her nose with a hanky, the toasted teacake before her untouched. At the table next to Sarah a pair of sharp-faced shop girls tucked into fish and chips and discussed a colleague who gave herself airs.

Paul was late, but as she took her first sip of scalding tea and told herself not to worry, Sarah registered that a smart young man in uniform was pushing open the door. It was him and gladness spread through her. His eyes settled on her at once and his face lit up. He removed his cap and she felt the brief cool of his cheek against her warm one before he hung up his coat and sat down opposite her.

'I'm sorry I'm late. Nothing works on time any more,' he said, studying her face as though to notice everything about her. 'This time a crater in the road at Marble Arch meant that the bus went down a side street where we got stuck at a tight corner.' His animated face was lean now, she thought, rather than gaunt, and he held himself straight with a pride she hadn't seen in him before.

'You've arrived, that's the important thing.'

He signalled to the waitress, who brought a second cup and saucer at once and he ordered luncheon for them both, which was shepherd's pie. Sarah noticed a new-found confidence in him, and saw the courtesy with which the waitress addressed him, a man in a British Forces uniform.

The pie, when it came, turned out to be mostly vegetables, but was hot and salty and there was plenty of it. They ate hungrily, Paul talking between mouthfuls. His short period of training was about to begin, he told her. His camp was on the coast – yes, it was all right for him to be on the coast again! – but he wasn't allowed to tell her where. He'd already been set to work, but it was hard, especially outdoors in this cold weather. He spoke softly, so as not to be overheard, and she had to lean in close to hear him.

'At last I'm a part of it all, Sarah. It feels good. And there are others like me in the Corps, good Germans, many are Jewish. We are all exiles from our homeland and we'll work together to free our country from the evil that has overtaken it.'

'Oh, Paul, I'm glad that you've found a way to do your bit.'

'Yes, I can hold my head high now. No longer am I a spare part, a nuisance to be spied on or locked away. This is a good feeling.'

'You look very … Your uniform becomes you,' she said.

'Do you think so? I'm proud of it. This badge on my cap, here, you see what it is?'

She angled the metal pin towards her. 'It's a spade!' She laughed. 'Very suitable for a gardener.'

'A shovel is what they call it, Sarah. There will be plenty of digging, but it may be trenches for soldiers and guns, not spuds.'

'Strange produce indeed,' she said, fingering the sharp edges of the badge. 'At least you won't be fighting like so many Westbury men.'

'What news is there?' Paul asked as he forked up the final crust of mash from his plate and the hovering waitress bore their plates away.

'Nothing really. That's the trouble. Young Sam has joined the army, I think I wrote to you about that. Jennifer Bulldock says she's heard a rumour that Ivor and Harry's battalion are preparing for action, but who knows where. Diane's still in Dundee. Still hasn't set foot on a ship, but is enjoying the attentions of some Dutch naval officers who've arrived. That's put the wind up Mummy all right.'

'Excuse me, but will there be anything else?' the waitress broke in. 'There's a nice bit of sponge pudding with custard.'

When it came it was glutinous and not very sweet, but they ate it without complaint.

'I often think of your mother, Paul. It's sad that the little cottage stands empty. I've been visiting her grave as you asked. There are daffodils coming out in the hedges and I've dug some up and planted them there.'

'Thank you, that's so kind. Is it marked still?'

'With the wooden cross. One day I'll help you choose a proper stone.'

'I cannot believe that she has gone. It is difficult to grieve for her properly. Does that make me a bad son?'

'No. Of course not. You've been separated from her for so long. And it was cruel that you could not attend her funeral.'

'I prefer to remember the happy times. When I was a child

in Hamburg she would dress me in my best suit and take me to the English tea rooms. She said that's what her mother did in London, have tea in a hotel as a treat, so that it made me feel that a part of me was truly English. And here I am in an English restaurant, but it's not like I thought it would be.'

'I must take you to Brown's sometime. Or what about the Ritz!'

'I'd like that.' Again Paul's face lit up with that bright smile and Sarah's heart went out to him. He might have become more confident, but there was still an air of vulnerability about him. She had to remember that he'd lost everything, was having to start again, remake himself. But perhaps she was wrong to pity him. He was a good man, honest, straight and true. There was nothing of the mercurial in his nature, that shadowy depth that made Ivor so attractive to her. Paul was someone to rely on. He would always be her friend.

They pooled their change to pay for the meal, she insisting, he protesting, then nodded their thanks to the waitress. As they walked out, Sarah noticed one of the shop assistants staring and realized with a spread of delicious warmth that it was envy she read in her glance. She did not resist, therefore, when Paul took her arm and tucked it into his own. It felt that it belonged there, safe and secure.

'I must catch a train at four,' he explained. 'I have only a twelve-hour pass.'

'I'll come and see you off if you like,' she said and he smiled his thanks.

'But first I'd like to buy you a present,' he said. 'What would you like?'

'Oh, Paul, I don't need anything. You must keep your money.'

'No, I insist. Something pretty, a scarf, maybe.'

They were near the Charing Cross Road now. 'Perhaps a

book,' Sarah said, pleased with the idea now it had occurred to her. 'A book you think I might like.'

They ducked through the entrance of a tiny second-hand bookshop in St Martin's Court, where an earnest old gentleman with large spectacles sat with his nose in a thick tome amid tottering piles of books, hardly noticing that he had customers. They browsed in silence, each thinking their own thoughts, then Paul pounced on a large, slim volume. 'These are beautiful,' he said, showing her as he turned the pages. It was a collection of botanical drawings. Sarah loved the chalky feel of the paper and the delicate colours of the flowers and fruit, so he distracted the shopkeeper from his reading and paid for the book, which the old man wrapped in brown paper as wrinkled and faded as he was.

On the bus to Paddington, Paul wrote in it and presented it to her. She read what he'd written: *Für meine liebe, Sarah, with my true affection, Paul,* and whispered her thanks, then spent the rest of the journey poring over it, examining the captions until he nudged her gently and said, 'hey' and she looked up to find him smiling tenderly at her. 'I'm still here, you know!' She'd not seen his face so closely before, the dark stubble beneath the smooth skin, the gentle curve of his brows and the sweep of his smoky lashes, and something melted within her.

'Of course you are!' She took his hand in hers and they sat together in companionable silence. Her heart beat in her chest as though to a new rhythm. She didn't want this journey to end and nor, she sensed, did he.

The station concourse echoed with the shriek of whistles, the huff of steam and the slamming of doors, each one like a blow. On the platform, Paul turned to her, took her into his arms and hugged her. 'You will write?' he said into her ear.

'Of course I will. And you, too.'

'As often as I can. Don't forget me, Sarah.'

She held him from her. 'How could I, silly?' and for a second they were frozen, staring into one another's eyes, she astonished at this transition, stirred almost to tears.

'May I?' he whispered, leaning in, and her lips met his in a kiss that was light at first, then more urgent as he crushed her to him. 'Oh, my *liebchen*,' he murmured, 'my darling' and, pressed against his breast, she felt the beat of his heart against her own. He must have sensed she was trying not to cry for he asked, 'What's the matter?'

'It's all too late,' she gulped. 'Because you're going again.'

'But there will be leave. We will see each other.'

'You promise me?'

'I promise.'

Beside them the train doors were closing. 'I must go,' he said, forcing her away and shouldering his knapsack. 'Here, don't forget your book.' He rescued the brown paper parcel from the ground and pushed it into her hand.

'Goodbye.' He kissed her once more, then reached to catch a door before it closed. 'Take care, my Sarah!' he cried, leaning from the open window. She stepped forward and grasped his hand, then the moving train tore them apart.

'Goodbye, goodbye.'

She waited until the train was a puff of black smoke in the distance then turned and walked slowly away in a daze. What had just happened she could not properly gauge. Just that her feelings had performed a volte-face and she realized it was Paul she'd wanted all along, Paul, not Ivor at all. Then came anger, anger at herself for not recognizing this sooner. Now Paul had gone and she did not know when she'd see him again.

*

Two days later young Derek distributed the morning post, which arrived just as he was leaving for school. Seeing Paul's neat hand on the letter he handed her, Sarah slipped upstairs to read it, her fingers shaking with eagerness as she slit open the envelope. She stood at the window where cold lemony sunshine cast diamond shapes across the page. As she read, she heard Paul's voice in her mind, his soft consonants like a caress.

My dearest Sarah, he'd written and her heart gave a flutter of joy.

I hope you will allow me to call you this. It is certainly how I have come to think of you, but because of what happened yesterday I now have the courage to say it. Dearest Sarah. Yes, I've said it again. It sounds very good.

I trust this letter is not unwelcome. Oh, how my hopes have risen and fallen in these few hours since we parted. Do you regret what happened in the moment of our farewell? If you do you must tell me at once. I shall be miserable for a while, but recover and we shall return to being friends. I fear so much that I've damaged our friendship, which is the most valuable thing in my life

Dearest Sarah (there, I cannot stop saying it), I beg you to write to me as soon as you can. I know you will be kind, but you must tell me the truth. I am strong enough to bear it. It would be worse to go on without knowing, or believing in a lie.

Goodnight, my dearest Sarah (ah, the pleasure in writing these words),

Your Paul

Sarah lay down on the bed, reread the letter more slowly, and for a long time smiled unseeingly up at the ceiling as she mulled over its contents. He loved her. But he was far away.

He loved her. She might not see him for weeks. Or months. He loved her. He might be sent somewhere dangerous, he might be killed. He loved her ...

She sat up. He didn't know that she loved him. She must write to him at once. And maybe send him a photograph. There was a recent one she had. Harry had taken it at that afternoon tea party at Westbury Hall in 1939, a day that seemed so long ago now, but was in reality hardly any time at all. It was in a drawer in the writing desk, she was sure it was. She almost flew down the stairs to find it, catching sight of the hands on the sober old grandfather clock as she sped through the hall. She was late for work, well hang work, there were more important things to do today! She found the photograph under an old cigar box of her father's in which she kept Paul's letters. She looked so serious in it, the photo made her smile.

'Sarah, is that you?' Her mother appeared in the doorway to the dining room, an envelope in hand. It was late on a Friday afternoon in the middle of February.

Sarah, who was sorting buttons, stopped still at the queer expression on Mrs Bailey's face.

'It's from Diane. She says she's coming home. Something's wrong. Here, what do you make of it?'

Sarah took the letter from her with a sense of foreboding. It was a bravely written little note, quite unlike Diane's usual desultory, wooden style. Her fingers brushed the smudges on the paper. Were those tears? Did Diane ever cry?

Dearest Mummy

I'm afraid I've done a very silly thing and have been discharged. I'll tell you both why when I get home, but I'm not too cut up about it so don't go worrying that I am. I'm cross at

myself if anything. Don't go telling anyone either. I won't be
able to stand the likes of Aunt Margo and La Bulldock gushing
over me. I've made my own bed and I'm jolly well going to lie
on it. Simply dying to see you and Sarah. Tell Mrs Allman a
lovely Dutch officer has given me half a pound of sugar and
maybe she will make a cake with it. I long for proper sponge
cake, really sweet and buttery and moist. I'll see you tomorrow.
   Tons of love from your bad daughter, Diane.

The following afternoon as the light was fading from the sky,
it was a small, sad-eyed figure that stepped down from the pub-
lican's dray that had brought her from the station. But Diane's
chin lifted bravely and she gave coins to the lad who'd driven
her with the air of a great, but doomed, lady, so that he tipped
his cap to her in due deference and struggled gallantly up the
path with her trunk without being asked.

After he'd gone, Sarah and her mother hugged her, at which
her bright red lips twisted and she burst into weeping such as
they'd never known of her, not even after she'd found her father
dying. They were horrified. Sarah led her into the drawing
room and tried to comfort her, while their mother called to Mrs
Allman to bring them tea right away and to give Derek his meal
in the kitchen when he came in.

The tea revived Diane enough for her to exclaim that she was
glad she was home and that she never wanted to go back, even
if they'd have her, which to Sarah didn't seem likely after her
sister told them what had happened.

Mrs Bailey had been right in one respect – there had been
plenty of parties for Diane. At one impromptu gathering at the
dockyard before Christmas, she'd drunk more gin than was
good for her and had gone stumbling out in search of fresh
air when she'd almost bumped into a distinguished-looking

officer who was passing on the quay and who spoke to her with annoyance, at which point she'd promptly been sick. He had softened enough to assist this Wren in distress by offering his handkerchief and escorting her safely back to her quarters.

When she next encountered him, it was in the high street and when she stopped him to thank him, she was surprised to learn that he was a senior officer on a destroyer that had recently docked. One thing led to another, and before long she became his mistress – *yes of course he was married, Mummy, or it wouldn't be as bad, would it*? Then somehow his wife found out and she had arrived and complained to Diane's commanding officer. The scandal that threatened to engulf the guilty couple could only have one outcome. The officer kept his post. Diane was discharged in disgrace.

There was one crucial strand of this sad but all too common tale that Diane omitted to tell her mother and sister, but she confided in Sarah the next day.

It was a Sunday. Diane came downstairs late to breakfast and refused point blank to attend divine service, so Sarah suggested the two of them go for a walk instead.

They took the footpath beside the river, glad of their rubber boots given the mud from the recent rain. It was wonderful to experience the world coming to life again after the long winter; the birds singing their hearts out, hazel catkins like lamb's tails scattering pollen, coltsfoot and celandine everywhere in splattered dots of yellow. All these things Sarah noticed as though for the first time, unable to keep her mind bursting out into little thoughts of happiness about Paul, promising herself she would write to him about spring in Westbury.

But for now she must concentrate on Diane, who was walking along sadly, seemingly fixed on a scene far away rather than the beauty all around. As they followed the bend of the river, they came upon the sight of a pair of swans treading against the current under the willows and stopped to watch. Diane gave a deep, shuddering sigh and her wan expression moved Sarah to say, 'Oh, Diane, dear, don't take it all to heart so. It must be awful, I know, but you're here safe with us. Do you still love him very much?'

Diane shook her head. 'It might sound better if I had done, but I didn't.' This stunned Sarah, but before she could respond her sister went on. 'He was kind and so grateful. His wife is the most selfish old tartar you can imagine and I made him happy for a while. There, I've shocked you, haven't I, but you know me. I can never do anything right. The other Wrens were complete bitches about it. I'm glad to be done with them.'

'It's good that you're home then. There'll be something else you can do instead.'

Diane turned to her, her blue eyes pools of desperation. 'I have to tell you, Sarah. I'm so sorry, I never meant to hurt you and Mummy, but the situation is not that simple. I . . . I think I'm having his baby. One of the bitches said I must be and I went to the doctor. I don't know how my CO found out about it, but she did. That's why they didn't simply reassign me.'

'Diane, gosh, I'm so . . . sorry.' For a moment Sarah felt numb, then the sight of her sister's distress made sympathy flow and her mind began to work again. 'No wonder you're so upset.' Another thought occurred to her, something ugly and dangerous. 'You haven't tried anything, have you? To . . . get rid of it, I mean.'

'No. I heard of a girl in Dundee who nearly died doing that. I'll have to have the baby and give it away. Sarah, I can't tell Mummy, it'll kill her. You'll have to do it for me.'

'I certainly will not,' Sarah retorted. 'Of course it won't kill her. She'll be jolly cross for a bit, but she'll come round.' She remembered once walking in on a conversation her parents were having in India about one of the junior officers who'd got a local girl into trouble. The boy concerned had wanted to marry her, but that was unthinkable. Mrs Bailey took charge, visiting the Indian girl's parents and arranging for a payment to be made. Sarah had asked her mother about it later. 'Oh, they'd have found some young man for her whose family was glad of the money,' Mrs Bailey had said dismissively. Sarah sometimes thought of this girl and wondered about her fate. At least Diane wouldn't be cast out of the family or ritually killed or any of the other nasty things that she'd heard rumours of in India. Sarah's mind worked quickly. This was something she'd inherited from her mother, the ability to think clearly in a crisis and do the sensible thing. Maybe Diane could be sent away somewhere – to Aunt Susan in London perhaps – and return once the baby was born ... A little niece or nephew; no, it wouldn't do to think about it like that, if she would never get to know it ... Oh, why had Diane been so stupid.

Pull yourself together, she told herself. Right now, her sad, prickly little sister needed love and reassurance and she was ready to give it. 'Come on,' she said, taking Diane's hand and steering her away from the water's edge. 'Wait until after lunch and Mrs Allman goes off. I'll take Derek to look for early frog-spawn and you can tell Mummy then.'

Later, on her return to the house with Derek, who found no frogspawn but had netted a single bewildered minnow now swimming in his pail, Sarah half-expected to see the roof of the house raised several inches, but all appeared calm as usual. She entered with caution, to find it silent. A scribbled note on the console table in the hall informed her that her mother had taken Diane up to Aunt Margo's. Poor Diane, she sighed. The two women would doubtless plot her fate. But in this she was wrong.

'Mummy actually lied to her.' Diane's eyes were full of wild fun later. 'She told Margo that I'm on leave and am going to be transferred somewhere else, that's the story. Mummy's going to write to Aunt Susan this evening and everything will be all right. It's such a relief, Sarah.'

'What about the baby?' Sarah couldn't stop herself saying. 'Aren't you going to be terribly sad to give it away?'

'Possibly, but what else can I do? It's like Mummy says. It's no good crying over spilt milk. What's done is done.'

Sometimes Diane took her sister's breath away. That closed expression had come down across her face. Did her callous remark indicate shallowness or stoicism? The girl was ultimately unknowable.

Twenty-nine

OK to pop by this morning?

Briony replied immediately to Luke's text. *Please do. Working, but will stop for elevenses.*

She motored quickly through two hours' editing, fuelled by pleasant anticipation of Luke and Aruna's arrival. On the dot of eleven she looked up at the sound of crunching gravel to see Luke's tall lithe figure coming down up the path. Of Aruna there was no sign.

Curious, she went to the door. When she admitted Luke the summer breeze came too. He was like a breath of fresh air in her dusty hall, in pressed T-shirt and jeans, his mane of toffee-coloured hair blown about.

'Hi,' he said, hugging her briefly. His eyes crinkled as he smiled, but there was something distracted about him today.

'Are you all right?' she enquired. 'Where's Aruna?'

'Gone back to London. Work commitments. Yeah, I'm great, thanks. You?'

'Fine,' she said hurriedly, wondering why he'd come and if she'd misread his subdued expression. 'Come through, I'll put the kettle on.'

In the kitchen he leaned against a work surface and watched her spoon coffee into mugs.

'I'm sorry not to see Aruna.'

'There was some crisis in her office. I offered to drive her, but she said Mum and Dad would be disappointed if I left early too, so she took the train.'

Briony nodded. It was on the tip of her tongue to mention having seen Aruna in Cockley Market the other morning, but she decided that discretion was probably the best course. Luke probably knew Aruna had met someone there – but suppose he didn't? Aruna was her friend, she'd never make things difficult for her.

'So ... I took the opportunity to come over. I might look round the walled garden later in case Greg Richards gets in touch.'

'Good idea.' Luke had been pleased that Briony had recommended him to Greg.

'Hey, there's another thing. Do you remember Mum mentioned meeting a David Andrews at a wine-tasting?'

'Yes, why?' she said, passing him his coffee and grabbing a packet of chocolate biscuits. 'Let's sit outside.'

She wrenched open the back door and they settled themselves at the table on the patio. It was a glorious morning, with clouds chasing across the sky and the wind rustling the beech trees.

'Typical Mum. She chatted up the guy at the farm shop, who checked his mailing lists and told her where he lives and everything.' Luke consulted his phone. 'Thicket Farm near Westbury. There's a postcode and a landline number.'

'Thicket Farm?' Briony frowned. 'Just a moment.' She licked some chocolate off her fingers and went inside. Under a pile of papers she found the local history booklet the old priest had given her and returned with it, flicking through the pages till she came to the photograph she wanted.

It was the grainy picture of the Home Guard. In a paragraph further down the page came the name Thicket Farm, home of the Andrews family.

'It must be the family farm then,' she said, laying the booklet between them on the table. 'I should have checked it out.'

The man who answered the phone spoke gruffly with a hint of a local accent. 'Harry Andrews, you say? You're his granddaughter?'

'Yes.'

'Wait a second, please.' He put down the receiver and she heard the sound of retreating footsteps, then some distant conversation that she couldn't make out. Finally, his voice came once more. 'I'm sorry to keep you waiting, young lady, but my wife and I are puzzled. Are you sure you mean Harry Andrews of Thicket Farm?'

'I don't know exactly where he lived, but my grandfather was definitely called Harry Andrews and he was from here.'

'You're staying in Westbury?'

'Yes, as I said, at the Hall in one of the cottages.'

'Well, I never. I suppose you'd better come over then. We're here this afternoon if you like.'

'Something's odd,' she called to Luke when she finished on the phone. He was strolling round the cottage garden, inspecting the overgrown borders. She described the hesitancy in the man's voice. 'Do you think I should go?'

'Why not?' he said, surprised. 'I'll come with you if you like. Mum's gagging to know if she's been useful.'

'Of course she has. OK. That's kind.'

*

'This really is the back of beyond.' Briony's satnav had taken them through a labyrinth of narrow lanes between fields of ripening grain before it gave up trying and Luke had to turn to the map. 'It should be the next opening on the right.' They almost drove past the sign *Thicket Farm*, for it was overgrown with ivy. Briony reversed the car and drove slowly up the deep-rutted track towards a scattering of farm buildings half-hidden by the rise of a low hill.

A man of her father's age appeared in the porch of the old flint farmhouse, hands in jeans pockets, watching them park in the muddy yard. The building was run-down, its roof patched by repairs, and the yard was criss-crossed by the tracks of farm vehicles. A pair of ageing corrugated-iron barns loomed at one side. As they got out of the car a young black Labrador pushed past its master to greet them, licking their hands, its tail rotating with joy. The man whistled. 'Flossie, come here,' and it retreated obediently to his side, trotting at his heel as he came to meet them, looking to its master for further instruction.

They shook hands. 'I hope you don't mind that I've brought my friend Luke,' Briony said, all the while sensing a guarded air about this man, who inspected them with curiosity in his steady brown eyes under his flop of grey hair. He was pleasant, with a weathered appearance, his local accent less pronounced now as he welcomed them. He seemed to warm to Luke, who fed him questions about the farm with a charming measure of deference.

'What do you grow?'

'Wheat this year, mostly,' Mr Andrews answered. 'A couple more days of sun, I reckon, and it'll be all systems go with the combines. You've caught me, well, I won't say at a quiet moment, but quieter than it will be in the next few weeks.'

'I'm very grateful to you for seeing us then,' Briony said.

'No, you're all right. It was a bit of a surprise for us, that's all. Come in and meet Alison.'

Briony saw at once when she entered that the farmhouse was Alison Andrews' domain, with rows of house plants on every windowsill, and an old-fashioned wooden kitchen with a crowded dresser. Alison, a curvaceous woman in her late fifties, all bangles and smudged mascara, greeted them in the same guarded fashion as her husband and led them through to a comfortable living room with a big fireplace. The garden door stood open and beyond lay flower beds burgeoning with late summer blooms. 'So pretty,' Briony murmured politely.

'The garden's been lovely this year, but it's getting to the scruffy stage now. Do sit down, won't you. I've got some coffee on the go if that's what you drink.' Alison bustled off to make it and returned a few minutes later with a loaded tray.

'The farm's been in our family five generations,' Mr Andrews was telling Luke.

'Six, if you count us,' his wife put in, handing round the mugs of coffee.

'Six, then, if you must,' he said grumpily, but Briony sensed from Alison's indulgent smile that mild disagreements were simply an enjoyable feature of their relationship rather than an indication of anything wrong. The dog, rolling on its back on a sunny patch of carpet, clearly wasn't bothered.

'Five or six,' Luke said, 'either way it's impressive.'

'Ay.' Mr Andrews gave a grave nod. 'And our daughter's interested in taking it on,' he said with pride. 'It nearly wasn't ours, though. That's why I was surprised to hear from you.'

'We didn't know about you, you see,' Alison said. 'You won't blame us for feeling a bit worried.'

'Worried?' Briony repeated with surprise.

'My dad was the second brother,' Mr Andrews said and it

dawned on her. They obviously thought her arrival indicated some claim on their inheritance.

'So I suppose we need to know you are who you say you are. Harry's granddaughter.'

'I haven't come to take anything away from you,' Briony said.

'There must be some mistake, I reckon,' Mr Andrews was saying carefully. 'Your grandpa must have been a different Harry Andrews. I wasn't born till 1946, so I never met my uncle. He never came home after the war. In the end he was declared dead.'

'Dead?' Briony was bewildered. 'But he wasn't. Why didn't he come home and tell you?'

The Andrews exchanged doubtful glances.

'His name wasn't in the book at the church,' Briony remembered, and explained further. The Andrews didn't know why Harry's name hadn't been mentioned. They rarely went to church, so had never looked.

'Well, there we are,' Mr Andrews said, putting down his coffee, half-drunk. 'We thought Uncle Harry died in the war and now here you are saying you're his granddaughter. We don't know what to say to you, except that the farm is legally ours now.'

'I don't want the farm,' Briony said. 'Honestly. What would I do with it? Luke here will tell you I can't be given a pot plant without killing it.'

'That's true,' Luke said, with a laugh.

'It's not worth anything either,' Mr Andrews said dismally. 'All debts, and it'll be worse once the subsidies go.'

'No, it's yours,' Briony said with feeling. 'I simply want to know what happened. I ... I had no idea that my grandfather had gone missing, only that he'd fought in Italy in the war and presumably come home, met my grandmother in London and decided to settle down near her family. I was given some letters from that time, that's what brought me here. I only heard about you because Luke's parents met you.'

'You said that on the phone,' David Andrews reminded her. 'Artist lady, isn't she? Do you remember, Alison? That evening at the farm shop.'

'Yes, they were nice,' Alison nodded. She covered her husband's hand with her own and they gazed into one another's eyes. Briony realized then how much anxiety she'd caused them. They must have thought that Harry's granddaughter had come to reclaim her inheritance, that they might lose everything. She had no idea what happened in law when someone who'd been thought dead turned out to be alive, and wasn't sure she'd bother to find out. She had no intention of disturbing their lives any further.

As she and Luke drove away from the farm, promising to keep in touch, Briony breathed a sigh of relief. But she was full of questions, and at the bottom of the hill she pulled into a layby and stared out at the golden corn rippling like a lion's back in the breeze.

'What's the matter?' Luke asked softly.

'Sorry, I'm having a wobble.' She covered her face with her hands, suddenly immeasurably tired.

The way he squeezed her shoulder was friendly, sympathetic. She let her hands drop and gave him a wan smile. 'I'm beginning to think I'm going mad. Grandpa let his family believe he was dead – why would he have done that?'

Luke shook his head. 'Perhaps he'd fallen out with them.'

'But even if he had, how cruel. It makes me wonder what will I find out next? I'm almost wishing I'd never been given Paul's letters. They're turning my life upside down.'

'They are, aren't they?'

They were silent for a while, then, sighing, Briony reached for the gearstick and they moved off again, slowly at first.

'It's curious,' Luke said.

'What is?'

'How your grandfather, Paul and Sarah all seem to have been involved in something together. I mean, that note you found in your grandpa's box that he was supposed to pass on to Sarah. Why was he never able to give it to her? Maybe if you find out what happened to any one of the three then you'll solve the whole puzzle.'

She thought about this. 'Yes.' She supposed he was right. 'But how do I do that?'

'I don't know exactly. Is it worth talking to Mrs Clare again? She's the one who knew them all.'

'Robyn? Possibly. I don't know that she likes me asking questions.' Briony was hesitant, remembering the sense she'd had that Robyn was holding back. Was it simply some matter that she wished to remain private, or was she shielding someone? It was impossible to say.

'Just go gently, Briony. Explain it's for your own peace of mind. Tell her about Italy, if you like. About Mariella and how you were given Paul's letters.'

'I promised Mariella that I'd try to find out what happened to the soldiers at the villa, and to Sarah.'

'It is all linked, isn't it?' Luke said carefully. 'Like Aruna said. What was it . . . ?'

Briony waited, looking at him enquiringly and, as she did so, some light dawned in his expression.

'What did she say?' she asked, anxious, but he shook his head.

'Something about unfinished business. She didn't like the Villa Teresa at all. Told me later that while we'd been there, when she was waiting outside, a man arrived in a flash car and spoke to her in Italian. He was pretty angry. She thought he wanted to know what she was doing there and was careful not to say she was waiting for us. She was worried he might have come storming in after us, that he might be violent.'

'She didn't say anything about this to me!' Briony felt surprised and not a little let down. Why hadn't Aruna mentioned any of this?

'Didn't she? I don't know why not. Perhaps she forgot or didn't want to scare you.' There was distance in Luke's tone, as though for an instant he'd forgotten she was there beside him in the car. They came to where the road curved, then the familiar descent through the tunnel of greenery, but as Briony slowed down, searching for the great gateway to appear to their left, the gloomy lane filled with blue light.

'What the . . . ?' Luke said as she braked to allow the ambulance to pass in front of them and under the arch. They watched it speed silently up the drive to the Hall, its light flashing, and stop outside the entrance. By the time Briony had parked, the paramedics had gone in.

She was alarmed. 'Perhaps we can help.'

They hurried across, and Briony tiptoed up the steps of the Hall and peeped into the gloom. There was no one on reception, but from beyond, along the corridor, came sounds of activity. She retreated to where Luke was waiting outside.

'It's Robyn, I think,' she said in a sober tone. She wanted to stay, to find out what had happened.

'We'd better go,' Luke said sternly. 'I'm sure she's being looked after. We don't want to get in the way.'

Just then her attention was drawn by a movement in the darkness within and soft footsteps on the carpet. 'Kemi,' Briony cried, seeing her appear, head bowed, shoulders hunched. 'What's happened? Is Mrs Clare all right?'

When Kemi looked up, her eyes were bright with unshed tears. 'I found her lying on the floor,' she whispered. 'It's like she's had a stroke or something. The dog was barking in a funny way so I got the spare key and . . . They're taking her to hospital. I've got to call her son.'

'Can we do anything?' Briony said, but Kemi shook her head. 'Avril's just come. She's packing a case for her.'

'Briony,' Luke whispered, touching her arm. 'I think we should go.'

Before she could reply there was the sound of commotion from along the corridor, and they stood back as two uniformed paramedics wheeled a stretcher out into the hallway then over the threshold. On it, swathed in blankets, lay the narrow figure of Robyn Clare. Her eyes were open, but clouded with confusion. Briony followed and looked down at her from the top of the steps.

There were a short few seconds while the stretcher was tipped at an angle to fit it into the ambulance and Briony and Mrs Clare locked glances. Alarm leaped into the older lady's eyes and her lips moved in a soundless appeal. Then the stretcher slid forward and the contact was broken. Avril and the suitcase were handed in after and the doors closed tight.

Briony, Luke and Kemi stood forlornly in a line as the ambulance set off down the drive, then Briony insisted on staying while Kemi rang Robyn's son. She was shaking when she finished the call, but told Briony that Lewis Clare was coming down straight away.

From the muffled recesses of the house, a dog began to howl, a ghastly, mournful sound. 'Poor old Lulu,' Briony said. 'I'll take her if you like.'

'If you could for now, that would be great. I suppose I ought to stay here.'

'Will you be all right?' Luke asked her and Briony murmured

that she could come back to Westbury Lodge with them, if she wanted. Kemi was still so young, though she had managed the emergency splendidly.

The girl looked uncertain. 'I'll call my mum. And Greg, to tell him what's happened. I'll be fine. Come on, let's find Lulu.'

Towing the animal, which puffed and snorted, Luke put his arm through Briony's and steered her down the path to the cottage. Her distress was apparent as she fumbled for the key. He took it from her and got them indoors and he bid her sit while he made tea quickly and efficiently. Then he sat down opposite her at the kitchen table, forearms folded, shooting her anxious glances. Lulu gazed up at them from the floor, tongue hanging loose and panting.

'Poor lady,' Briony sighed, circling the rim of the mug with her finger. 'I hope she'll be all right.'

'I'm sure someone will tell us and at least her son will be with her. I think you've done all you can. When does this dog eat, do you think?' A plastic carrier bag containing Lulu's pink bowl and a couple of exotic-looking food sachets lay on the floor.

'She seems hungry now. Are you hungry, Lulu?' Lulu obligingly licked her lips and appeared interested as Briony bustled about, but when she set the food bowl on the floor, Lulu simply sniffed at it and turned her back.

'She's grieving,' Briony said. 'They say dogs always know if their owner is in danger.'

'Probably just overindulged,' Luke smiled. 'She needs a good walk if you ask me. Let's go and look at the walled garden, get her to scamper round a few times.'

'We don't want to kill her off, Luke. A sedate walk might be safer.'

They let the dog off the lead in the garden, but she stayed

close to them, pausing frequently to sniff at perfectly ordinary clumps of grass, then flopping down in a sunny spot from where she watched Luke inspect the fruit trees and write notes in a small black book. Briony sat on the bench nearby and watched him too. He had that enviable ability to lose himself in his work, she thought, seeing him ruffle his hair and tap his pencil on his lower lip as he frowned over some problem. She thought lazily how completely at ease with him she felt. How lucky Aruna was to find him. Perhaps they'd settle down and have children and ask Briony to be godmother. She'd never been a godmother – her brother William and his wife weren't into that sort of thing – and she rather loved the idea of it.

Her thoughts were broken by a growl from Lulu, who hauled herself to standing and yapped, her ears twitching, before trotting towards the doorway next to the cottage where they'd come in. Through it, hands in pockets, strolled the confident figure of Greg. He ignored Lulu sniffing at his shoes, clearly used to her, nodded at Luke across the garden, then turned his attention to Briony, who was walking quickly to greet him.

'You've spoken to Kemi?' she asked, her brow furrowing with concern.

'Yes, half an hour ago. Poor old Robyn.'

'Is there any news?' Seeing her distress, Greg took her hands in a firm grip and she felt again that melting sensation, a warmth that passed right through her.

'I don't believe so. I thought I'd better come and check you're happy with the mutt.' He glanced at Lulu. The pug gave a final discontented snort and sank back down on the grass with a groan.

'She's all right, aren't you, Lulu? I need to find what her routines are, that's all.'

'No idea myself. We'll have to ask Avril, the cleaner. But if you're content to look after her for the time being, then I'm sure everyone will be grateful.'

Briony glanced across at Luke and was surprised to see him staring at them, notebook clutched to his chest, a hesitant expression on his face. Somewhat self-consciously she withdrew her hands from Greg's and took a step back from him. Luke came over to them.

'This is the friend I told you about, Greg. Luke Sandbrook.' The pair exchanged manly handshakes.

'Pleased to meet you,' Greg remarked. 'So, what do you think of the place?'

Luke gazed about him, then smiled at Greg. 'It's wonderful. It has such a lovely atmosphere.'

'Yes, it does. Reckon it has possibilities?'

Briony listened as the men spoke of historical reconstruction, the old plan on Mrs Clare's wall, Greg's commercial ideas of a plant nursery and farm shop.

'The greatest challenge might be irrigation,' Luke told him. 'Whatever the old system was – if there *was* much of one – it might need replacing.'

'That sounds expensive. Still, I'd like to pursue it further. If you'll let me know your rates we can discuss a proper brief.'

'Fine by me,' Luke said, tucking Greg's card into his notebook and pocketing it.

'Good.' Greg stood, hands on hips, chest out, a lord of the manor contemplating his realm. Luke's pose, arms folded, suggested the expert consultant, unfazed. Squaring up to each other, Briony noted, fascinated.

Greg cracked first. 'Well, if you're all right, Briony, I'll ask someone to be in touch about the mutt.'

'Please. And let me know as soon as you hear anything about Mrs Clare.'

'Of course.' He gave her a lingering look and Luke a perfunctory nod, then turned to go, the lowering sun glinting off his hair and his expensive watch. Beside her, Luke audibly breathed out, but he said nothing and Briony was glad.

'Will you do it?' she asked him, meaning the garden.

'I don't see why not. It's a nice job if he's not tricky to deal with. I'll come back another time to take proper measurements.'

'OK. Come on, Lulu. Grub.' She scooped up the dog, who seemed to have given up altogether, and bore her under her arm like a barrel back to the cottage. This time when she set Lulu down in the kitchen she went straight to her bowl.

'Hungry o'clock,' Luke said.

Briony sat down. She felt suddenly exhausted again.

'It's been quite a day, hasn't it?' Luke said, pulling up a chair. 'Are you all right?'

She nodded, comforted by the concern in his eyes, the fact he cared. 'You've been ace today. Thank you.' She wrinkled her nose at him, then glanced down, idly noticing fine hairs on his strong, brown forearms.

'No problem, glad I could help. I hope we hear good news of Mrs Clare soon. At least she was conscious.'

'Yes.' A vision of Robyn's face came to her and she remembered how she'd been struck by her expression. 'Luke,' she said, straightening, 'I've remembered something. It was the way she looked at me as they put her into the ambulance. Did you see?' Luke's eyes widened, but he shook his head. 'It was as though she wanted to tell me something.'

'Really?' he said. 'I thought she just appeared confused.'

'No,' she said, more certain now. 'There was something.' She prodded a teaspoon with her finger absently, wondering what the something could be.

There was silence for a moment, then, to her surprise, Luke reached out and stroked the back of her hand. She felt his calloused fingers circling her slender forearm and froze in shock.

'Don't look so worried,' he said in a teasing voice.

Wordlessly, she looked up at him, taking in his intense expression as he scanned her face. He seemed to be fighting against it, but the passion she read there was unmistakeable. Part of her, the animal part, wanted to respond, but the thought of Aruna arose in her mind and she forced herself to withdraw her arm. Whatever was happening wasn't right. She rose, pushing back her chair, and began to busy herself, washing up mugs, stuffing cutlery noisily into the rack. When she glanced back at Luke he was still sitting at the table, his fingers stroking his chin, wearing a faraway expression. His eyes met hers and, flinching at the look of anger she shot at him, he turned away. He'd thoroughly got the message, she saw.

'I'd best be going,' he said with a studied casualness, and gave her a subdued smile that did not reach his eyes. 'The parents have a family friend over this evening. I promised Mum I'd be there.'

'Duty calls. Lulu, say goodbye to Luke.' Lulu ceased panting and gave a strangled whine.

Though she stood arms crossed in the narrow hallway, keeping her distance, Briony took the trouble to thank him properly. 'You've been great, Luke. I can't think how I'd have managed today without you.'

'*No problemo*. Pleasure as always.' He opened the door and hesitated as though he would speak, then apparently decided against it. 'See you soon, eh? You'll be back in London at the weekend, won't you?'

She nodded. 'And a lot to do on the book before then.'

'Hint taken. I'll be over sometime to look at the walled garden, but I expect you'll be busy.'

'I expect I will.' She smiled at him, sadly. Although he'd probably not meant to, by the work of a moment he'd broken something important between them. Trust.

'Bye!' he said softly, pulled the door to behind him and was gone.

Thirty

October, and at Duke's College the new term was underway. The grand corridors echoed to the sounds of voices in many languages, to bright footsteps and easy laughter as colourfully dressed students poured out of lecture theatres, or lounged in noisy groups on sunny quads and blocked the steps of the colonnades so that Briony had to squeeze past to reach her classes.

She loved this time of the academic year. The returning students were mostly cheerful after the break, full of hope and enthusiasm as they greeted their friends. She took pleasure in helping the homesick freshers and seeing them gain confidence. The only downside was that, what with time spent on teaching, advising individual students, attending departmental meetings and organizing a special project, a conference for the spring, she was now too busy to pursue any research of her own.

She'd only just managed to submit the rewrites of her new book by the mid-September deadline, and was awaiting her editor's response. Goodness knows what questions would then be thrown at her. She'd have to devote evenings and weekends to it until it was done.

She'd had no time to follow up all she'd discovered in the summer about her grandfather. Sarah's letters, all of which she'd read and transcribed now, lay stashed in a drawer in her flat. Her father and stepmother had been away on their Greek island holiday, and there hadn't been an opportunity to discuss with her dad what she'd so far found out about her grandfather.

One Monday evening at half-past six, Briony was still in her office. Outside, darkness was falling and as she reached to pull down the blind, bright white lights snapped on in the rooms of the science building opposite and she stood for a moment, struck by the series of tableaux within, of students in lab coats and latex gloves attending structures like giant marble runs or peering at computer screens.

A shy knock on the door made her start. 'Come in,' she called as she lowered the blind and turned to see the neatly groomed figure of the new assistant in the Department Office. She was clutching a package.

'Hello, Debbie.'

'Sorry to interrupt, Dr Wood, but I'm locking the office now and you didn't collect this.' Debbie held out the package, which Briony took, half-remembering an email about a special delivery. She glanced at it without much interest. It was wrapped in old-fashioned brown paper and held together with thick strips of parcel tape. There was something hard and squarish inside, a book possibly. A small corner of it had pierced the paper.

'Thanks,' she said, dropping it onto a small table already crowded with books and paper. 'I'm afraid I forgot; it's been that sort of day.'

'No problem, Dr Wood. Have a good evening.' Debbie

retreated, closing the door with a respect that Briony knew would wear off after a few weeks.

She shut down her computer. She was meeting Aruna for early supper, having not seen her for ages. The Soho bistro they'd agreed on was only ten minutes' walk. This had made her complacent and she was already late.

As she reached to unhook her jacket from the door, her glance fell on the package. The word *Personal* had been printed on it in laborious black letters. She picked it up. No, not a book, it wasn't heavy enough. She started to pick at the plastic tape, but it was stubbornly unyielding and at that moment her phone pinged so she put down the parcel and fished in her pocket. The text gleamed in the yellow light.

Where are you?

Be there in 10. She switched off the light and opened the door. At the last second her eyes fell on the parcel again. Curious. She snatched it up, pushing it into the depths of her bag.

The bistro was in an old cellar like a smugglers' cave, a series of small, low-ceilinged rooms, poorly lit, and it took Briony a while to find Aruna amid the crowds. Then she rounded a corner to see her friend sitting alone in a secluded booth, a bottle of wine half-drunk in front of her, the paper tablecloth red-ringed from the glass she was holding. The expression on Aruna's face, a mixture of bitterness and distress as she stared at her phone, made Briony hold back, fearing to intrude on a private moment.

She'd only seen Aruna once since Norfolk, and the occasion had been a holiday reunion with Zoe, Mike and Luke. She'd been aware of Luke and Aruna the whole evening, looking for signs that anything had changed between them, but the only awkwardness was her own feeling of guilt, which was, she knew, uncalled for. It wasn't her fault that Luke had nearly stepped over the bounds of friendship, was it, so why should she be feeling this way?

After she'd left Westbury she had dwelled on what had happened – or might have happened if she'd let it – haunted still by the sense of Luke's physical presence, so close to her that she could feel the warm life of him in his breath, the strength and tenderness of his hand on her arm, the concern in his kind blue eyes and, yes, what she surely hadn't imagined, his desire for her.

It wasn't any good, she'd told herself fiercely. She wasn't some naïve teenager. Luke was in a relationship with her best friend and she wasn't going to betray Aruna simply to be Luke's side dish. It had seemed better in the end to try to banish him from her thoughts, to leave the two of them to sort themselves out. It was, of course, a pity that Luke couldn't simply be her friend, but perhaps she'd been too idealistic about that.

Anyway, on the reunion evening, Aruna and Luke seemed fine together, so perhaps she'd misinterpreted the whole episode. In which case she was guilty of something else – fantasizing like some stereotypical dried-up old maid. Either way, she felt unsure and self-conscious with them both, and she hadn't wanted to see either of them for a bit until she felt she could be natural and relax with them again.

Aruna put her phone down. Briony walked out of the shadows.

'Hi. You have hidden yourself away,' she said in as light a voice as she could muster.

'Oh, hi. There wasn't another table.' Aruna jumped up to kiss her, affectionate as ever. She smelled of wine and her favourite flowery perfume, the same as always. Perhaps, thought Briony, she'd imagined that bitter expression. 'It's really busy for a Monday.' No, she decided, Aruna did sound a little sad. She slid onto the bench opposite and Aruna sloshed wine into a second glass and passed it across.

'Cheers. So how are you, Bri? I can't believe it's been so long.'

'I am sorry. My life's been manic.'

'Mine too. Good manic, I hope?'

'You know, the usual. You?'

'So – so. God, I'm tired. I've been away for a couple of nights interviewing homeless people in Glasgow. Not much sleep.' She pushed back her dark hair and sighed. 'And wine on an empty stomach, big mistake.'

'Let's look at the menu then.' Briony handed over one of the laminated cards from its stand on the table and began to study the other, but she was aware of Aruna's phone buzzing and Aruna slavishly peering at the screen.

'Seafood risotto for me,' she said, watching Aruna frown.

'Sorry, this can't wait.' Aruna's finger flew across the screen. Then she laid the phone down, but picked it up when it buzzed again.

After the third time, Briony placed her hand over the phone and drew it out of Aruna's reach.

'Let me have it,' Aruna said with a sigh.

'Only if you put it away.'

'You're such a nag.' She glanced at the screen one last time before pushing the phone into the depths of her handbag. 'There. Let's order.'

They flagged down a young man with a white apron folded round his narrow waist, who listened to their order, then with quick movements delivered a basket of bread, a dish of olive oil with herbs and a handful of cutlery before vanishing again.

Aruna drenched a piece of bread in the oil and ate hungrily. Briony crumbled her piece unhappily, full of concern for her friend.

'How's Luke?' she said, experiencing a stab of tenderness at the name.

'Fine. He's fine,' Aruna said more cheerfully, licking oil from her fingers. 'Though he's been in Norfolk far too much designing that garden. He may be in touch with you, actually. Something about needing to see those letters of yours.'

'Sarah Bailey's?'

'Yes. He told me to tell you. Details of any plants she might have mentioned.'

'Ah. Well, that would be all right.' She was intrigued to hear that the garden project was underway. 'I could email him my transcript. Has he heard anything about Mrs Clare?'

'The old lady? Can't remember. The same, I think. Back at home now and recovering very slowly. You'll have to ask him.' Aruna's lack of interest in the matter was more than apparent.

'You don't like him doing the garden?' Briony asked.

A shrug. 'It's up to him. I wouldn't interfere with his work. But since you ask, no, I don't particularly. I'm having to be away a lot at the moment, too. It's an extra strain on us.'

'He stays with his parents, I suppose. Can't you go, too?'

'If I'm not working, but you know me. I'm not really a country girl. And his parents are very nice, but I'm thirty-eight, for heaven's sake. We shouldn't be spending every weekend with our parents.'

Briony laughed. 'I s'pose not, but his seem laid-back. Didn't your mum give Luke his own room last time?'

'That was so embarrassing. No, his ma and pa don't do that, but the bed there creaks and I always feel guilty if we have a lie-in.'

'Me too, if I go home. My stepmother clears up after me. I daren't leave the top off my toothpaste or my coffee mug unwashed!'

'Thirty-eight! We're like oversized cuckoos, aren't we? D'you think it would be different if we were respectably married with kids?'

Briony thought about it. Her brother and his wife Ally did seem to have a different status when they stayed, but perhaps it was that the grandchildren deflected attention. Her father and Lavender adored Will's two children, and Ally was always so tired she was glad to be relieved of them by her in-laws. Last Christmas she trailed around with a glass of wine and enjoyed being spoiled while it was Briony who helped with the cooking.

'I feel I'm living in a sort of limbo at the moment,' Aruna continued. 'Luke stays at mine most of the time, as you know. It's much more convenient for me than going out to his place, miles from a tube station, and he's got a mate living there now paying the bills, but I haven't got anywhere he can keep all his gardening stuff, so it's difficult long-term. We really need to sell our flats and find somewhere together, and frankly I'd like to get on with it. Mum and Dad keep asking when we're getting married, you know what they're like. And Mum's desperate for me to have children.'

'And you? Would you like them?'

'Sometime, yeah. I suppose I'd like to be sure that I can have them if I wait a year or two. It would be awful to leave it too long and find there's a difficulty.'

She looked wistful now, and Briony felt suddenly sad for Aruna, seeing how much getting settled meant to her.

'What about Luke, does he want kids?'

'I always thought he did, but lately he sounds annoyed if I even bring the topic up. I don't know what to do, Briony.' She tore off another hunk of bread and dipped it in the oil, then simply stared at it.

'Listen, Ru, I'm not a great person to ask, with my poor record, but surely if you love each other and want to be together, then that's the most important thing? The rest will come along behind.'

'I suppose you're right. It's only that lately ... Well, it was Luke I was texting just now. We're supposed to be going to see my parents on Sunday, but now he says he can't go. Can I see if he's got back to me, pretty please? I know it's rude.' Hardly waiting for Briony's answer, Aruna reached into her bag, consulted the phone then slipped it back again. 'Nothing. Oh, never mind ...'

At that moment the slender waiter returned bearing great white dinner plates: steaming buttery rice and fish sprinkled with fresh parsley for Briony, and sizzling cheese-covered cannelloni for Aruna. A couple of twists of black pepper from an oversized mill and an 'Enjoy,' delivered with a mock bow, and he left them to it.

Aruna stared down at her food miserably, then picked up her fork and transferred a blob of cheesy pasta to her mouth. Her expression changed as she realized it was delicious and she began to eat as hungrily as the heat of the food allowed. Briony picked up her fork too and for a while each was lost in her own thoughts.

Briony found she was struggling between natural sympathy for Aruna and a sense of confusion about Luke. What was he up to? Why was he making Aruna so unhappy? She felt simultaneously angry with him and concerned. She'd always thought him absolutely devoted to Aruna and yet his recent behaviour was undermining that view. She glanced at her friend, who appeared cheerful again with food inside her.

'I didn't realize I was so hungry,' Aruna said. Her kohl-lined eyes shone with pleasure as she shared out the last inch of wine from the bottle, of which it had to be said she'd had the greater part. 'I feel much better now.' Briony had always loved this delightful element of the child about her. Aruna's mood would change like the weather in April.

Aruna drained the last drop of wine. 'Another bottle?'

Briony shook her head. 'I've work to do later. Don't let me stop you, though.' There was an awkwardness between them, but Briony couldn't put a finger on why, exactly. After her recent confidences Aruna seemed to have drawn back.

They ordered coffee, and while they were waiting for it, Aruna went to find the loo. When she came back and slipped onto the banquette, she changed tack.

'Did you ever get any further with the research you were doing? Your grandfather and the other soldiers?'

Briony shook her head. 'After Robyn Clare became ill I ran out of people to ask. I wrote to someone who had interviewed Derek, the Baileys' evacuee, in case they had an address for him, but I never heard back. Now I'm too busy.'

'A shame,' Aruna said in a desultory fashion.

'Still want to make a radio programme about it?' Briony smiled and took a sip of her cappuccino. It was creamy but unpleasantly bitter so she tore open a sachet of sugar.

'I don't think so. There's not much of a story, is there?'

'What do you mean?' Grains of sugar scattered over the table.

'You've only got one side of the correspondence. And that man Paul, no one knows what happened to him.'

'I thought you were interested. I'm still finding out, you see.' Aruna was hiding a secret, Briony felt sure. Then she remembered what she needed to ask. 'Aruna, when Luke and I were in the Villa Teresa and you were waiting for us outside, did something happen?'

'Luke told you then. It was nothing important. This big shot in a sports car drove up, just to turn round, I think, but he saw me sitting there and he wanted to know what I was doing. His English was pretty poor, but I could tell he wasn't happy.'

'Did you tell him we were inside?'

She shook her head. 'No. I said I was a tourist and I was resting because I'd hurt my foot.' She chuckled. 'He offered me a lift, like I was going to accept. He started turning the car, then he stopped and pointed towards the house and said it was a bad place. "Bad place," he kept saying.'

'You didn't tell me any of that.'

'Didn't I? I suppose I was cross that you were so long, and then there was all that drama with the stupid tin you found. Oh, Briony, don't frown. Well, what was I supposed to think, you and Luke going off on your own together.'

'Aruna! It wasn't anything like that. We both wanted to see the house, that's all. I'd never had gone if I'd thought you'd be worried.'

'It wasn't just then, was it? What about at Westbury Hall? Luke seems to have become obsessed with the place and that wretched garden.' Briony didn't know whether Aruna meant Luke was interested solely in the place or whether she was hinting something else. She couldn't confront her to ask. She was frightened of ruining their friendship. She chose deliberately to assume it was the place that Aruna meant.

'There's a link between the Villa Teresa and Westbury, that's probably what interests him. The fact of the two gardens, maybe. And Paul and Sarah.'

'Those bloody letters. I wish you'd never been given them. They've stirred everything up.'

'It's to do with my family, Aruna. Nothing you have to worry about.'

'All I know,' Aruna said slowly, 'is that things with Luke have not been the same since our holiday.' The implication, from the accusing look on her pointed face, was that Briony was somehow to blame.

On the way to the tube station Briony's feelings of desolation grew. It was so unfair. She and Aruna had hugged as they parted, but Briony sensed a lack of warmth. Aruna was angry, angry at the situation as much as with her. She wished she could feel angry in return, for the false allegations Aruna hinted at, for the dismissal of what was important to Briony, but instead she felt desperately sad and hurt. Did Aruna think so little of their friendship that she'd lost all trust in Briony without finding out whether Briony really had betrayed her? She touched her card to the ticket barrier and paced the platform before stepping onto a train south, where she slumped down onto a seat amid chattering, laughing people on their way home from evenings out.

I feel old, she thought, *in the face of their energetic youthfulness.*

Aruna had been her friend for fifteen years, the closest she'd had. They were quite unlike, but each in turn made up for the other's differences. Aruna was fun, darting and colourful as a little dragonfly, flitting about with new ideas, finding new ways for them to enjoy life. Briony had been the steady one, comforting Aruna when things went wrong, when she'd been dumped. Aruna had been betrayed by men more than once, deeply hurt. Briony wished, desperately, that she could sort things out between Luke and Aruna, but she didn't know how, only that she must keep away from Luke, possibly from both of them. She'd email Luke the transcripts of the letters, but not encourage further communication.

Her heart felt heavy as she unlocked the front door of her flat and pushed it shut behind her. Her nose wrinkled at a mouldy smell from a basket of washing that she'd pulled out of the machine and forgotten to hang up. A pile of junk mail lay slewed across the hallway. It was one of those nights when home felt very lonely.

She made a mug of green tea and stood sipping it and staring out of the living room window at the row of old houses opposite, where other lives went on. They'd had a street party once, for a royal jubilee. For several days afterwards people had smiled at one another as they passed, said hello, but then life reverted to how it had been before. Or so it was for Briony, who was out so much of the time. Her downstairs neighbours, a middle-aged childless couple, had come up for drinks the previous Christmas, but they lived busy working lives, too, and she rarely saw them.

She finished the tea and, fancying something sweet, remembered a bar of chocolate she'd brought home, but when she padded across to the kitchen and reached into her bag for it, her hand closed instead round the parcel. With a pair of kitchen scissors she began to slice through the parcel tape, cursing its thickness. Inside she found not a fat hardback book, but an old box of similar size and shape. It was a large cigar box made of some light, pale-coloured wood. There was a small cheap envelope taped to it addressed to her and she pulled it off, opened it and leaned on the work surface to read the letter inside.

She reached the end with growing astonishment, and quickly scanned it again.

Dear Dr Wood, it ran, in rounded, feminine handwriting.

You wrote to someone who wrote to my dad, Mr Derek Jenkins, but he is 87 now and his hands are very shaky, so he asked me to write to you for him and send you this box. I didn't know he had them, but he says he got them a long time ago and meant

to give them back, but he never saw her again. He says if you
can find out what happened to Sarah Bailey maybe her family
would want them, but they're no good to him and it would be a
weight off of his mind if you had them.

Yours truly,
Lindsay Sweet (Mrs)

The woman who had interviewed Derek Jenkins, the Baileys'
evacuee, had received Briony's letter after all and passed it on to
him! Briony opened the box and drew a sharp breath, suspecting at once what it was she had.

The box was packed tightly with piles of neatly tied letters,
many still in their envelopes. She slid one from the top of its pile
and read on the front: *Miss S. Bailey, Flint Cottage.* She pulled
the letter out and read the signature at the end. *Paul.* They were
Paul's letters to Sarah and there were dozens of them! But how
did the evacuee come by them?

She hastened with the box over to the sofa and sat down with
it on her lap. Drawing out a pile eagerly, she unpicked the strand
of wool that bound them, took the one on top and unfolded it
from its envelope. The handwriting was in a thick pencil, difficult to read, so she reached for the switch on the table lamp next
to her and shifted into the circle of light.

My Dearest Sarah, it began. Briony's eyebrows shot up.
'Dearest'? The relationship had changed. With growing excitement she began to read the words that followed.

Thirty-one

1941–1942

The North Devon seaside town was embraced by high cliffs, and the window of Paul's hotel room looked out onto the small harbour so that the bright clinks of wind in the rigging attended his falling asleep and his awakening. If he woke in the night he liked to lie and listen, for he found it soothing. When winter storms raged, spray spattered the windows. Paul had never lived by the sea before. He was exhilarated by it, by the waves pounding the hard sand as he ran assault courses on the beach, by swimming in the freezing tidal pools. All this was part of the training. At other times he loved to watch grimy boats unload coal or the morning's catch to the sad cries of the gulls which glided overhead or swooped to squabble over shiny corpses of discarded fish.

The work they were given was gruelling, even by the standards of heavy gardening. Worse, it was boring and frustrating, more so than he'd predicted. It took a while to learn the knack of using the pick and shovel efficiently to dig trenches. Then there was mixing and laying concrete before erecting Nissan huts on the cliffs. The boots they issued him were too big – the joke circulating that they were left over from the Great War turned out to be true – but Paul learned to stuff the toes with newsprint and his callouses eventually hardened over.

His roommate, Wolfgang Horst, quickly became a friend. Horst was Jewish, a fellow countryman four years younger than him who'd been dispatched to a British foster home by his far-sighted parents five years before. He'd attended a Midlands university and spoke fluent English. Horst had often visited Hamburg as a boy, for his grandmother had lived there, and he and Paul sometimes reminisced in a mixture of English and German, though they found it unbearably sad to talk of home. Horst had no idea where his parents were now, or his grandmother. He wrote regularly to his little sister, who was at boarding school in Shrewsbury, and if he was granted leave he went to visit her either there or at the home of the teacher and his wife with whom she stayed during school holidays.

Paul wrote to Sarah every week. He sent her a postcard of the lighthouse, which was an unusual building because it was set into a disused church on the clifftop above the town. There was so much to tell her about daily life and he found the writing came easily to him. *Horst is trying to teach me the violin, but I'm afraid he is wasting his time. The seagulls think I am one of them because of the noise I make.*

He thought of her in quiet moments, trying to keep her face in his mind. He had never been in love before like this. He hadn't met many girls in Hamburg, but at the university there had been a self-possessed young woman named Gisela, with thick fair hair cut into a bob and dancing dark blue eyes. She had let him take her out a few times and for a whole term they sat together in lectures, but then the trouble happened with his father and she started to avoid him. Sometimes Paul had used to wonder whether otherwise it might have gone further. He'd been fascinated by Gisela's determination to succeed, her eager way of turning questions inside out to make one see a problem differently, not to mention her handsome, sturdy figure. She was a talented artist, could draw neat, detailed pictures of flowers and trees. He, on the other hand, knew best how to grow them.

It was Horst who awoke in Paul a love of music, for he'd brought with him his treasured violin, and many evenings he'd rehearse with the camp orchestra. Paul often attended the concerts in the village hall or, on one occasion, in the foyer of a grand hotel out in the countryside.

There were lectures, too, because many in the camp were older men, distinguished professionals in their pre-war lives: lawyers, doctors, university professors, writers. Once, he found himself volunteering to give a talk about growing flowers for cutting, and as he explained how spikes of gladioli, though unfashionable, were invaluable as they remained fresh in a vase for several days, he felt his love of growing things flood back. If he'd had with him some of the botanical slides he'd collected in Hamburg then he'd have delivered a more academic lecture about the wonder of plants, but he had neither the resources nor the time to research or to produce his own drawings.

Six weeks passed, two months. Christmas had not been a religious festival for the large Jewish element of the camp, but was nevertheless celebrated by a performance of *Cinderella*. Come January, work was hampered by the freezing winter weather, but eventually, in early February, Paul and Horst's company was told they were sufficiently prepared to be sent on their first mission.

'Clearing rubble, so the corporal says. I want to go and fight,' Horst said fiercely as he wrapped his precious photograph of his parents in newspaper and fitted it into his haversack.

'I do, too,' Paul said from the window. He'd miss this view. 'Maybe one day they will trust us enough. At least in the meantime we'll be doing something to help, and London will feel more like the centre of things.' And, he hoped, he'd be able to see more of Sarah. That would a great advantage.

Three weeks later, Paul felt less optimistic as he wheeled his heavy barrow along the plank towards the truck and began to shovel its contents into the dumper. The dust this raised set him off on another coughing fit, but he carried on, trying to ignore the cough, just as he tried to ignore the boneshaking pounding of Horst's pneumatic drill. Thankfully, after he threw in the last shovelful, the corporal shouted for a break and he hurried to join the queue for hot drinks at the nearby van.

It felt as though they'd been here for ever. The work involved clearing rubble from the bombed areas around the docks; grim work, 'stone-breaking' as Horst called it, 'old-fashioned hard labour for convicts', but he spoke with a flash of humour. After all, as Paul remembered Sarah saying, most people in this war were having to do what they didn't want. Their lives had been interrupted. Nobody dared speak about the future. Getting through the present was all they could do. He thought about this as he drank the thin hot soup a woman had served him and cupped his palm protectively round his cigarette. In order to fight for freedom, everyone was having temporarily to give it up, that's how he should see it. There was no choice. It was so frustrating, though, to be stuck here shovelling concrete when the fighting was elsewhere.

The corporal shouted for them to return to work. Paul seized a sledgehammer and clambered back over the hills of shattered concrete, plasterboard, twisted girders and brick that he'd been mining, sinking some of his frustrations into the blow he delivered to a ruined flight of steps.

Paul had been astonished when they'd first arrived in what Corporal Brady told them had once been a street of houses. Most of them had been obliterated and the road was cracked and cratered. Only a few jagged elevations remained, reaching up defiantly, the shapes of windows and electric wires hanging like torn tendons, indicating their identities. God knows what it had been like for the rescue teams in the immediate aftermath of the bombs. He didn't like to think about that. It was bad enough now, turning over a girder to find the pieces of a little girl's doll, an engagement diary or a photograph in a smashed frame, precious belongings of the people who'd once lived there. Anything deemed valuable in any way was handed in, though whether its owner would be found alive to reclaim it was a different matter.

He'd heard that another team had uncovered something more gruesome the week before when they'd lifted up a broken dining table, but his lot had found nothing like that, though they knew to be prepared.

As Paul worked, a sharp wind blew up, stirring the dust and muffling the others' voices. What with the mist, the sullen sky overhead and the deadened sound, he was disoriented and reminded for a strange moment of that fierce winter in Norfolk, the Christmas when the Baileys had arrived in Westbury. How the snow had changed everything, making the world alien and forbidding. The moment passed, but as he filled a basket with the crumbling lumps he'd split he was left with the lingering memory of Sarah.

He had a day's leave starting this evening and he'd be meeting her at Liverpool Street train station. Usually if she came to the city she'd stay with her aunt, but tonight would be different. The thought of seeing her gave him renewed energy and he began to dig again almost cheerfully, suddenly not minding the cutting wind or the dust or the pain in his left forefinger where he'd wrenched it on a loop of wire the day before.

Paul's heart filled with love and desire as he saw Sarah in the dim, evening glow of the station, alighting from the train, smart in a soft felt hat and belted coat, purposeful in her movements as she turned to help down an elegant old lady with her suitcase and summoned a porter to her. Then she spotted Paul and hurried towards him, her face open and alive. They clung together briefly and the warm, solid reality of her, her flowery scent, the sparkle of her kind eyes, made everything feel all right. They looked one another up and down and laughed.

'Still the same Sarah?' he teased. It was what he always asked.

'Same as ever.' Her habitual answer.

'And I too.' His anxiety was quelled, but not the thrill of nervous excitement.

He took her small case from her and waited while she located her ticket. 'The journey was fine,' she said in answer to his question as they walked together to the barrier. 'That lady you saw me helping got on at Ipswich. She's off to meet the man her parents wouldn't let her marry forty years ago! She hasn't seen him all that time, just think of that! It's the war, you see. It brings people together as well as driving them apart.'

Paul smiled at her cheerfulness, but saw she was on edge, too. He steered her to the station café where, they agreed, they would sit in the warm fug to drink tea and discuss their plans for the evening. Inside it was so full, the windows had misted up. It smelled of frying and wet wool. Someone was leaving and they pounced on the table. Paul watched her bright face as she enquired of the waitress about cake, and with his eyes he traced the strong lines of her features, the pale shine of her wavy, shoulder-length hair, her wide-spaced gaze. It was impossible to see her without being assured of her honesty and reliability. She was his lodestone in a world in which he had lost his bearings. When she removed her gloves he captured her hands, touched to see that they were as calloused as his. He stroked her fingers tenderly.

'You work too hard.'

'So do you,' she laughed. 'You look so strong now. Stronger than ever, I mean.'

'The work is not so bad.' He'd decided not to complain. Their short time together mustn't be wasted. 'You look so well, a healthy colour. Tell me, how are your mother and sister?'

'Oh, they send their regards.'

'Even Diane?'

'Of course.'

He laughed. It was a joke between them that Diane didn't approve of him. Sarah insisted that this was nonsense. Paul suspected that she was wrong and she knew it.

'How is she, Diane?' he asked in a low voice, but at that moment the waitress arrived with a tray and began to lay out a piping hot teapot, cups and saucers and a plate of rather small and unappealing rock buns.

When she'd gone, Sarah said, 'Let's not talk about her now. Where are we going this evening?'

'There's a good little Italian place I know near Soho Square. I thought we could dine there. Then, well, I hope it'll be all right, a friend gave me the name of a hotel in Kensington. The proprietress is a good sort, he says, very discreet.'

'Oh, Paul.' Sarah's face was ashen. 'You didn't say anything to your pal about me?'

'No, of course not! I said it wasn't for me, that another friend wanted to know. Did you bring ... ?'

She nodded, then dipped her left hand into her handbag. When she brought it out a plain gold band gleamed on her fourth finger. Seeing it there, he felt emotion rise in him, pride, yes, and a deep joy. Their eyes met, complicit.

'Does your mother think you're staying with your Aunt Susan?'

'She didn't ask. I don't think she'd care at the moment, Paul.'

'Every mother cares about her daughter.'

'I think mine has given up on me. Last time we spoke about you she told me I was old enough to make my own mistakes.'

His eyes narrowed. 'What did she mean by that?'

'I think she understands that I won't love anybody else. Ivor Richards was her last hope for me to do the conventional thing. The war has changed everything, she knows that. She's more concerned about ... well, Diane goes about in her own little world at the moment. She's recovered from ... you know, but she is so thin and so dull and quiet.'

'I'm sorry,' he said, peering up at her over his cup as he sipped his tea.

Sarah stirred hers thoughtfully.

'I know I said we shouldn't talk about my family, but everything seems to come back to them. I don't seem to be able not to, Paul.'

'Never mind.' His cup clinked as he set it in the saucer, a lump of sadness swelling in his throat. 'I wish I could forget mine, too.'

'I'm sorry, that was insensitive of me. But you wouldn't want to forget your parents, would you, not really.'

'No, of course not. Sarah, do you believe you will see your father again? And your little brother? I can't bear the thought that I won't ... see my parents, I mean. One of the men in my unit says that while you can remember them they're still with you, but it's that that brings the pain, isn't it? Remembering.'

'Yes, but it's that which makes us higher than the animals, Paul. We can remember those we've lost and anticipate seeing them again. It's like the seasons. After winter comes spring. It's what gives our lives meaning.'

'But what if there is no point to any of it and this world is all there is?'

'Then we only have death and despair and I will not accept that. Paul, look at me.' He raised his eyes to her face, saw the gravity in her eyes and it held him steady. 'You must feel very alone, but you have me and you have a task to do. We can't know what will happen, but we must trust that ... we will endure.'

He reached and gripped her hand, feeling the ring on her finger, hard and warm. And once again he felt the strength in her pass into him and it calmed him.

'You are so *wunderbar, mein Liebchen*,' he whispered, leaning in towards her. And in the same hushed tones, 'Are you finishing your rock cake or may I have it?'

'I'm eating it myself, thank you,' she said, with a toss of her head, and he laughed and reached and dabbed up a crumb before she could stop him.

'*Signore, signora*, please, this way.'

The restaurant in Old Compton Street was charmingly eccentric, with a Union Jack hanging prominently above the bar and cheap prints of famous Italian landmarks on the walls. The very delightful moustachioed proprietor admitted them with a flourish and waved them into a cosy room full of tables laid with gingham cloths and candles stuck in Chianti bottles. It was early yet and there were only a few other diners. Paul and Sarah were briskly relieved of their coats and their luggage and ushered to a tiny table in the window. Candles were lit, menus thrust into their hands, aperitifs brought and orders for food taken.

'For the wine, I have something verrry special. Verrry romantic. No, no, the price is reasonable.' The man waved the matter of money away as though it were nothing.

When he'd left them, Sarah leaned forward to whisper, 'This is lovely. How clever of you.'

'It's very bohemian, I hope that is all right.'

'Very much all right. Listen!' Strange accents floated out from the kitchen, laughter, and above it all a snatch of opera in a hearty tenor voice. The smell of smoky hot oil mixed with herbs wafted through the air. 'Do you think they're doing it on purpose?' Sarah's eyes were full of fun.

'I expect so. We could be in Italy!' Paul said, smiling.

'It's probably nicer to be here than Italy at present, don't you think? With that nasty little Mussolini man in charge.'

A waiter arrived bearing plates, and the food was good, too, vegetable soup served with the freshest bread Paul had tasted for ages. The *menù del giorno* was a rich stew described as *alla romana*, then for dessert there was some sort of creamy 'shape' that was several miles away from the insipid powdered egg version served up in the mess.

Paul laughed as Sarah's eyes narrowed with pleasure at the taste. The dusty bottle of red wine the proprietor had decanted proved to be extremely decent, too, sweet and heady. He hoped he had enough money to pay for it.

They talked about Westbury. 'There's another land girl now,' Sarah told him. 'Rita. She's only nineteen, very sweet, but she's from the East End and doesn't know one end of a cow from the other. I had to explain to her which was the bull.'

'That could be dangerous for her. But I didn't know there were cows now as well as the pigs.'

'Yes, didn't I write? Only a dozen. They're dairy cattle. It was Major Richards' idea. Harry Andrews' father is helping us with them.'

'Is there any news of Harry?' Paul had liked what he'd seen of Harry. A good sort with none of what the English called 'side'.

'He's with the regiment roaming the Scottish Highlands, I believe. Training new bugs. I don't think he's seen action since Dunkirk. Not from what his father says. I say, Ivor is in the same company; yes, I'm sure of it.'

'I wish that I was with them,' Paul growled, spooning up the last sweet scrapes of dessert before pouring more wine. 'This really is very good.'

Sarah nodded, taking a sip from her glass. 'And I'm glad you're not with them, Paul. I couldn't bear it if you were sent into danger.'

'I know, my love, but I cannot help what I feel. Useless, a lesser man. I have written to the adjutant, you know, but all I received was an acknowledgement of my letter. It wasn't even signed by him.'

'Write again if you must, Paul. Though I wish you wouldn't.'

'I will. Do you think it would help if I wrote to Sir Henry too, asking him to provide a reference?'

'I'm sure it couldn't do any harm. Though if there are rules in place that debar you from fighting I don't see how they would be able to accept you even with his support.' Sarah spoke bitterly, as though such a rule was her last hope.

'I am half-English, remember. It might make the difference.'

'After all that you've gone through you say that?'

'Yes, I know it hasn't so far, but I am sure it was Sir Henry who put in a word for my release from internment and his word may carry weight in this, too. And if my letter to the regiment is eloquent enough.'

'Let's not talk about it any more,' she cried, with distress. 'I know it's important to you, but I can't bear it tonight.'

He reached for her hands and held them in both of his, kissed her fingers. 'I'm sorry,' he whispered. 'I'm being selfish, I know, but I'm so tired of being second class. And I want to be a man worthy of you, Sarah.'

'Fiddlesticks,' she whispered. 'I don't care about all that.'

'Well, I do.' Paul signalled for the bill and was relieved to see how reasonable it was, even the wine. In gratitude he left a large tip.

Outside, as they picked their way through the jostling crowds in the moonless darkness, Sarah walked ahead, Paul stumbling clumsily behind. She was angry with him, he knew, but he also knew that there was nothing he could do about it. He was who he was and was determined on his course. He sensed, too, that she understood and she was principally angry with the situation, with the whole war, if you like.

After a few minutes they arrived at the Underground and Sarah fell back and took his arm. 'I'm sorry,' she whispered. He hugged her and she buried her face in his neck and for a moment there was only the two of them, swaying gently in their own private dance. For a sweet moment, the bustling world around them fell away.

The hotel was in a shabby white stucco terrace behind South Kensington station. The street was dark and silent and only the shaded beam from Paul's torch prevented them tumbling into a large hole in the pavement outside. Still, when they entered, the hallway was bathed in a cheerful glow and a vase of artificial flowers on the desk represented an attempt at a welcome. A bell summoned an ageing, vampishly dressed woman from a door at the back. As she presented the register for Paul to sign, she studied them with a benevolent expression. Then she reached for one of the keys hanging on a varnished rack behind her that had *Welcome* in several languages painted across the top. Next to it was a framed list of house rules, which he saw included the scrawled addition: *If there's no hot water, there is no hot water.* This failed to dent Paul's feeling of happiness. His nerves vibrated with energy like the strings of Horst's violin.

'Third floor, dearies,' the woman said, fondling her carmine bead necklace. 'Breakfast is at seven, but,' her smile was kind, 'tell you what, if you're a little late down I'll save you some.'

'Thank you, ma'am,' Paul mumbled in embarrassment. Up several flights of stairs they went, then he wrested open a door at the top, and they found themselves in a small chilly room with a sturdy-looking double bed, a chest of drawers with a jug and bowl on it, painted with flowers, and a matching chamber pot under the bed. The ceiling light didn't work, but the bedside light did and cast a cosy yellow glow.

'I'm sorry it's so ordinary,' Paul said, taking her in his arms. 'I wish we had something more glamorous than this.'

'It's lovely, really.' Sarah kissed him and smoothed the worried lines from his brow. He helped her off with her coat and it joined his on a hanger that clattered on the back of the door, then they sat together on the edge of the bed, knees touching, and he took her hand. After a moment he leaned over and found her lips with his and she stroked the soft skin of his cheek. He kissed her again, more deeply this time, and she kissed him back and he wrapped her tightly in her arms and drew her down onto the pillows. In the glow of the lamp her eyes gleamed hungrily for him and he felt for the buttons of her cardigan.

'How does this work?' he murmured, struggling with the belt of her skirt and she showed him, then helped him with the top button of her blouse.

She shivered in her underwear and he tucked her tenderly between the sheets before undressing himself. She watched, her eyes on the strength and sheen of the muscles of his chest and arms.

'How did you do that?' she whispered, nodding at the angry bruise running down his thigh.

'It's nothing.' It was from a piece of falling masonry; he hardly felt it now. He went and lay beside her in his drawers under the bedclothes, one arm cradling her head. For a time, neither of them moved. They felt the beats of one another's hearts, the warm smoothness of skin against skin, then gently he began to stroke her breast through her petticoat, eased the straps from her shoulders. Sarah sat up and lifted the shift over her head, making her hair crackle with static, but then she hesitated, crumpling the garment protectively across her caged breasts, and from the way she looked at him he knew she had something important to say, something she'd been dreading, but which she would not shirk from, not if there was to be complete honesty and openness between them. He waited, heart thudding.

'Paul, I've been thinking how to say this.' She paused. 'It's not my first time.'

He tensed, the hurt rising in his throat. Gently he disengaged himself and lay apart from her, the back of his arm resting on his forehead. He didn't know what he'd expected, but not this. He sensed her rolling over, then she lifted his arm to see the expression in his eyes, must have read his pain and uncertainty.

She snuggled down again next to him and lay staring at the ceiling as he was. There was a large patch of discolouration there, suggesting there had been a leak in the roof. He wondered if the water had dripped down through the mattress and to the floor beneath and tried to think what to say. He struggled to understand why what she'd said mattered, but eventually he did. He must make his own confession.

He turned his head to look at her and whispered, 'I'm sorry, I should have imagined. We're not so very young, there's so much about you I don't know. Please, don't think I'm judging you, I only need to accommodate myself. It is mine, you see. My first time.'

She was silent and when he turned to her he saw her eyes were shining with unshed tears and his heart melted. What did it matter, after all? What she had done was long before he'd met her and now, seeing her sad, he felt confident again that he could make her happy. He smiled, and bent to kiss the tears away, then her arms were round his neck and they both laughed with the joy of each other. Gently he kissed her neck and his hand explored the soft fullness of her breasts. After that her body guided him in what to do.

Bright spring sunshine glowed through a gap in the blackout curtains by the time the lovers awoke. After they had visited the freezing bathroom down the landing and dressed, they went downstairs to find that their vampish landlady was as good as her word and brought them a rasher of bacon each and a mound of hot toast, which they devoured hungrily, trying not to giggle about her sentimental glances. She must really have taken a shine to them, for she agreed to look after their luggage while they spent much of the day visiting the Kensington museums and walking in the park, exhilarated by the blustery wind.

The time was all the more precious because it was about to come to an end.

'This has been the most wonderful twenty-four hours of my life,' Paul told Sarah as they strolled back to the hotel, her arm tucked in his.

She smiled up at him. 'And mine,' she said simply. It had taken time for him to realize that she did not express her feelings as easily as he, but he loved her for it. He loved everything about her: her neat, lithe figure, the way she wore her hat tipped back, ready to face the world, the generosity in her smile. He felt so proud to be walking with her on his arm and was dreading the moment of parting.

'Goodbye,' she said simply when she saw him onto his bus. His last view of her was as a brave, upright figure, her gloved hand raised in a wave, becoming smaller and smaller until a bend in the road hid her from sight.

Thirty-two

June 1942

Suez, a busy, dusty port at the top right corner of the map of
Egypt on the ops room bulkhead. Because of the Axis domina-
tion of the Mediterranean, Paul's convoy had had to slip down
one side of Africa and up the other to reach it, a voyage lasting
nearly eight hot and tedious weeks. They'd docked on several
occasions for supplies and each time Paul had been glad to
stretch his legs and see new places. He'd found himself in mar-
kets vibrant with colourfully dressed natives and chattering
monkeys that swung down from palm trees to steal ripe fruit
from angry stallholders. In Cape Town, Table Mountain had
been obscured by mist, and he'd had to rescue one of his cabin
mates, found huddled dead drunk outside a brothel, his wallet
gone. And now here he was at his destination, and as they all
crowded on deck waiting for the order to disembark, he felt a
mixture of excitement and disappointment.

Paul had had his wish. He was on the high seas. And now,
finally, they were in Egypt, that was the excitement, but what
he could see did not accord with his mental expectations of the
country. There was plenty of sand, indeed, but it was grey and

stony, and the buildings were greyish, too, and functional in appearance.

'Where are the pyramids then and the crocodiles?' the chap next to him, Bob Black, known as Blackie, was asking, which was a more simply put version of what Paul was thinking.

He smiled. 'At least there are camels, look.' The beasts in question, three of them, were kneeling in the shade of a scrubby tree at the roadside below, and were also greyish, weary, patient beasts. Their drivers squatted beside them in the dust, playing a game of dice to pass the time. Further along the road, the late morning sun glinted off a long line of army trucks, waiting to ferry the troops onward.

The heat was already unbearable on the ship by the time the gangplank was fitted firmly into place. As the men began to swarm downwards, whispers spread back like wildfire. 'Tobruk has fallen, yes, Tobruk. We surrendered to the Jerries.' Paul digested this worrying news with a thrill of shock. Tobruk, everybody knew, was a key strategic port on Libya's Mediterranean coast, right next to its border with Egypt. It had been besieged for months and bravely held by the Allies, but now ...

'That's it, I suppose,' pyramid-loving Blackie declared cheerfully. 'They'll be sending us right over to defend the road to Cairo. Cannon fodder, lads, that's us.'

'If that's what we're here to do then we'll have to do it,' Paul murmured. This was what he'd wanted, wasn't it, what he was trained for, to see action, to fight for his adopted country against the people in power who had killed his father. In a way, he was lucky to be here, he told himself, remembering how it had happened.

The second letter that he'd sent the adjutant more than a year ago now had initially not been answered. He'd written then to

Sir Henry at the House of Lords, asking if it were possible to meet with him. He was surprised to receive a handwritten note from the man himself, inviting him to dinner one night in March at his club in St James's.

The patrician figure of Sir Henry who rose from the leather seat in the bar to greet him was thinner and more worn than Paul remembered, but his grip when they shook hands was as firm as ever and his smile lit up his wise and wary eyes. 'Ah, Hartmann, glad you could make it. Don't suppose there's much let up for you lads at the moment.'

For after a two-month lull the bombers had returned. Over the previous week thousands of incendiary bombs had been dropped over London and Paul's company of Pioneers were scrambled to help with immediate clearance after the rescue teams had finished. It was dangerous, distressing work and there seemed no end to it. It was never long after darkness had fallen and they'd returned to barracks after a hard day that the sirens were in full cry for the next onslaught. Paul would lie awake in the crowded public shelter tensing at each explosion, astonished that so many of the people around him had fallen quickly back into the routine with their thermoses of hot soup, their blankets and their knitting. It was the frightened eyes of the children that got to him. It wasn't right that little kids should go through this, he thought, and his mind wandered to Hamburg, where he fervently hoped the same thing wasn't happening to German children.

'What'll you have?' Sir Henry asked. 'They manage a pretty decent Martini here. Shame there's no ice, but you can't have everything.'

The Martini was indeed sustaining and Paul began to relax a little. He asked after Lady Kelling and Robyn and was briskly told they were both quite well.

Over dinner, which included an actual pork chop and a range of spring vegetables, Sir Henry listened sympathetically to Paul's request.

'I should think they need good sports like you,' he agreed, tapping salt onto the rim of his plate. 'And your knowledge of the lingo could be invaluable. I can't make any promises of course, but I'll put in a word with the colonel.'

'That's very good of you, sir.'

'Not at all. I'm sorry you've had such a thin time of it, especially during the, er, emergency last year, but my hands were tied on that front, you do understand?'

'Perfectly, sir.' The reminder of his internment was a painful one, but Paul no longer felt it so keenly.

'That's settled then. Now, do you have any news of that Richards boy? I gather his father—'

But whatever Sir Henry had been going to say about the Richards family was lost to the baying of the sirens and almost immediately there was a great whoosh and an explosion that cracked the front windows and made the building shake. Several pictures fell off the wall and the lights flashed, then went out.

Although the evening ended in chaos, Sir Henry did not forget their conversation. A month passed and Paul had started to lose hope when a letter arrived from the regiment. The style was formal, distant even, but friendly platitudes were not what he was looking for. He was to report to the barracks in Aldershot the following week. It was with great excitement that he showed it to his friend Horst in the room they shared with two others.

'You lucky swine,' Horst said gloomily, lighting a cigarette. 'It won't be the same without you here.'

'You know what they say, the English: "Be careful what you wish for." Who knows what will happen to either of us.'

'I will most probably die of boredom here. Still, I wish you luck.' They shook hands and turned it into a mock wrestle. Paul would sorely miss Horst. He'd been the best friend he'd made since he'd arrived in Britain – apart from Sarah, of course.

As he edged forward on the crowded deck, Paul reached into his top pocket, brought forth his wallet and slipped out a photograph of Sarah. It was a formal portrait from before the war, a spare of one taken for some official document or other, and slightly creased. He'd come to like it because although in it Sarah wasn't smiling, there was a hint of a smile there, as though she found some private thought amusing. He preferred it to another she'd given him in which Ivor's face could be seen in the background. Paul sighed and tucked it away, returning the wallet to his pocket. His last encounter with Sarah, two months ago, had been heart-rending for both of them. They'd stayed at the vampish Mrs Bert's again and when the time came for them to part they clung together as though they feared never to meet again. The letter he'd written on the ship would have travelled in the military bag home from Cape Town and – assuming it made it to Britain at all – it might be ages before it reached her and even longer before officialdom tracked him down in Egypt with a reply. But enough, now he was nearly at the top of the gangplank and all thoughts of home receded.

On the dockside, a perspiring sergeant waved irritably at a fly and rustled through the pages on his clipboard.

'Hartmann, you said? D Company. Follow the others over there, will you?'

Paul joined the men piling onto the lorries. Even under cover, with everyone squeezed so close together on the plank seats, it was stifling. Someone handed in a water container and they filled their bottles and splashed each other's faces, laughing, though in truth the reality of the climate was starting to sink in. Engines roared into life in a cloud of petrol fumes and one by one the lorries began to lurch forward, leaving the ships and the grey-white quayside buildings, the patient camels and the scrubby hillside behind. Through the half-open rear of Paul's vehicle a hot breeze wafted that failed to freshen and soon it brought with it a gagging stink of sewage as they passed through the slums of Suez.

It was a relief to rattle out onto a desert road and along the banks of a lake of startling blue, but then that too was behind them and they entered a sandy landscape that seemed to stretch on for ever with no relieving feature. Grit swirled into the truck and got into everyone's eyes and throats, so they fastened the tarpaulin across the back opening and the lorries juddered on in sweltering semi-darkness for what seemed to be hours. The other men, none of whom Paul knew well, swapped quiet banter, but he sensed their underlying sense of dread. The news about Tobruk had subdued them. A remark about them keeping the local gravediggers busy was met with silence and they only perked up when the truck slowed and street sounds of what must surely be Cairo reached their ears. They rolled up the tarpaulin and gazed out eagerly upon a new world. They saw men in long white jellabas and flapping slippers, mangy dogs that all seemed to Paul varieties of one dog lying prostrate in the shade or madly barking at traffic. They passed huts built out of sand, bright-coloured rugs hanging in the sun, intriguing glimpses of dark interiors, doorways before which small, dark-eyed children crouched in the dust drawing pictures with sticks. The smell was an unspeakable mixture of exhaust fumes, cooking oil and manure, with an exotic top note of incense.

Soon the streets broadened out and the buildings, in a variety of styles, grew higher, wider and more opulent, sprouting little balconies and canopies. From some hung flags, sometimes the Union Jack, which drew cheers from the soldiers. The truck stopped and started, flung its occupants about at sharp corners, but finally it swung between a pair of large gates, rattled across an expanse of bare ground and drew up outside a great, ornate portico. Here they climbed out, tired and blinking, hauling their kit, under the cruel sun.

Once inside they passed through warm, echoing gloom then out the other side into the brightness of a large, sandy square lined with trees. This was bordered by two long, three-storeyed buildings on either side, decorated with rounded arches. The fourth side of the square was edged by the silvery-grey Nile where, like a stage set, white triangular sails of feluccas slid past a vista of palm trees and misty old buildings. This must once have been a beautiful spot, Paul thought, an old palace, perhaps.

More trucks arrived and disgorged soldiers until a couple of hundred men milled about the square with their belongings, perspiring in the heat. Then an irritable sergeant-major with a sunburned face and forearms, brandishing another list, marched out and began to dispatch the newcomers to various parts of the buildings. 'Some of you will have to kip on the balconies,' he told Paul's little group. 'We're full to overflowing.'

'Hartmann!' a familiar voice roared and Paul turned to be blinded by the sun. Shading his eyes, the dazzle morphed into the figure of a handsome, confident, khaki-clad officer standing squarely several yards away. Paul caught a glimpse of his face as the man stepped forward and he realized with a shock who it was.

'Richards!'

'Captain Richards to you, Hartmann. I suppose you'd imagine yourself the last person I expected to see thousands of miles from home, but you'd be wrong. They gave me advance warning, you might say.'

'Did they? Sir.' This was his old adversary, but Paul was thrown by the new relationship. Richards was the officer here and he, Paul, only a private. And Richards was clearly enjoying the fact.

'Yes, you're in our company here. Major Goodall is in charge, you'll meet him shortly. I'm his second in command.' He mopped his forehead with a handkerchief and consulted a sheet of paper. 'And do you know a man called, let's see, Robert Black? His name's on the list, but it's not been checked off.'

'He was here a moment ago.' Paul looked about, but he couldn't see Blackie among the men lugging their kit tiredly towards their designated sleeping quarters. He wiped beads of sweat from his forehead and forced himself to stay focused on Richards.

'Right.' He made a mark on his list. 'You'd better get on, then. Nothing much to tell you boys at the moment. They say it's chaos out there on the front line. We're simply awaiting instructions.'

'Yes. We heard about Tobruk. Do you think we've still a chance, sir?'

'Of course. We mustn't have any talk like that now.'

'No, sorry. Sir.'

Richards was studying him now, as though playing with him. 'How did you do it, eh, Hartmann? You must have pulled the wool over someone's eyes to get here.'

'Not at all, sir. I wrote to the adjutant several times and Sir Henry kindly provided a reference.'

'Did he now? Well, I have to say I was concerned when I heard. I'll be keeping my eye on you, remember, will you?'

'You don't have to do that, sir.'

'Oh, but I do. There may be hand-to-hand fighting. Don't come whingeing to me about killing your own countrymen.'

'I am here because I want to fight the evil that has taken over my homeland, sir. I won't be asking for any favours.'

'We'll see. And if I hear of you doing anything, anything at all, that affects morale, well, I'll do what I need to, understand?'

'Yes, sir, but you won't.' Every word felt ground out of him. He watched Captain Richards stroll away importantly in the direction of where he supposed the officers' mess to be, and he hated him.

His dormitory stank of some noxious chemical that made his eyes water and since all the beds had been claimed he unrolled his sleeping bag on a shaded balcony where at least the smell wasn't as bad, and lay down, soon slipping into an exhausted doze. When he awoke, the light was dim, but although the fierceness of the sun was gone, the air was still hot and treacly and his head ached. He stumbled inside to find some of the men still sleeping. A small, black-haired soldier by the name of Walters was sitting on his bed, tongue sticking out, laboriously writing a letter. 'The message is we have the evening off,' he told Paul, who nodded and asked the way to a bathroom.

Once he'd washed and tidied himself and found some water to drink, Paul felt better and went off to explore the barracks, eventually finding a clerk who furnished him with money and plenty of advice, some of it unwanted. Since there was no sign of Blackie or the others he'd grown friendly with he went out into the streets alone, determined to see round the city while he could. He signed out using his full name, Private Paul Nicholas Hartmann.

The adjustments to his name had been part of the conditions of acceptance into the regiment. If he was taken prisoner, he could be shot as a traitor if discovered to be German. He'd spent the last year practising a British accent, and if his fellows ever asked, he emphasized that his mother was English and they'd escaped the Nazis. He never spoke of his father or his childhood in Germany. It was partly self-preservation, but he still found the subject too painful for public airing.

It amazed him to see Allied troops of varying nationalities everywhere on the streets, enjoying an evening out. The clerk had warned him off the smart hotels, which were officers only, but he didn't want such places anyway. He wished only to see the souks and the gardens and the architecture in peace, then find somewhere respectable for a quiet drink and something decent to eat.

Eventually he hailed a taxi, a broken coughing vehicle that dropped him near the packed terrace of Shepheard's Hotel with its wicker tables and chairs. He wandered the pleasant fringes of the Ezbekieh Gardens for a while, enjoying the clamour of the birds and the sight of children playing. Afterwards, he visited a British club he had heard about and ate water buffalo steak, egg and chips, washed down with a pint of beer. He was surprised at how hungry he was.

It was dark when Paul came out of the club and the street lights shone with a soft blue light – no one here bothered to keep blackout. So it was that as he passed an archway which presented the vista of a garden with trees studded with coloured lights, he paused, thinking how pretty it was. English voices and the sound of laughter came from within, but a powerfully built Egyptian standing guard with arms folded stared at him in warning, so he prepared to move on.

It was at that moment that the archway darkened as the figures of two officers emerged, wreathed in the smoke from their cigars and reeking not unpleasantly of whisky.

'Good Lord,' one said, seeing Paul. 'I know you from home, don't I? Ivor Richards said your name was on the list.'

Despite the gloom, Paul recognized the friendly open face. It was sunburned, a little older, but there was no mistaking Harry

Andrews. They shook hands warmly, Harry eagerly talking. 'I'd heard from Jennifer that you'd joined up. I had a letter from her just last week, you know. She's in the ATS.'

'How is she?'

'Rather enjoying being away from her mother.'

Paul laughed politely, remembering Sarah saying how infuriating Mrs Bulldock could be with her organizing and her tactless remarks.

'I must say,' Harry went on, 'I'm surprised we're here at all. Our company was kicking its heels in Aldershot back in March and all of a sudden they told us to pack our kit. There was to be an embarkation and they needed us to make up the numbers. Two days later we were steaming down the Channel.'

'We were simply in the wrong place at the wrong time.' The other man, a lieutenant, like Harry, who'd been quietly listening, had a reserved but amiable way of speaking.

'Charles Keegan, this is Paul Hartmann. He's in my platoon.'

'Am I, sir?' Paul said. 'I didn't know that.' He wasn't displeased.

In the conversation that followed they discovered they were all staying at the same barracks. 'Would you like to share our taxi? No, not at all.' It was getting late and Charles didn't seem to mind so Paul gladly agreed. A taxi was duly hailed and they all climbed in, Charles kindly offering to take the seat in front so that Paul and Harry could talk.

'You've come at a particularly bad time. It's been hell out there in the desert. We're only back to regroup. Once they've repaired enough lorries we'll be off to the front again. Shouldn't be long now, a day or two they reckon.'

'So the fall of Tobruk doesn't mean the end?'

'Far from it. We'll give the Jerries a run for their money yet.'

'That hasn't stopped people packing up and leaving Cairo,' Charles said from the front.

'He means foreign civilians. Half of them are off to Alexandria. There's a real old panic on.'

'I haven't seen any signs of that,' Paul said, genuinely puzzled. 'The locals don't seem worried. They'd fight for us, wouldn't they, if it came to it? After all we've done for them?'

Harry laughed. 'That's not how they see it. Most of them would like us out of here. Their king is one of them. They'd have the German and Italian flags whipped up the poles in no time. Wouldn't you?' he addressed the driver, who merely waved a dismissive hand. 'He doesn't understand. But it won't come to it,' he continued cheerfully. 'You wait and see.'

It was this heroic English cheerfulness that always surprised Paul. At first, when he'd joined up he'd thought it was an act, then he'd decided that they believed in it and tried adopting it himself. It didn't stop him feeling frightened underneath, but it helped him keep going.

After the taxi dropped them, Charles wished Paul and Harry goodnight in the lobby, leaving them to talk.

'It's good to see someone else from Westbury. Jennifer's an excellent letter writer, but not all the post makes it through – and there are things she can't say, of course. How is morale? What does the country think about what we're doing out here?'

'I haven't been back to Westbury much. For a long time I wasn't allowed to, the rules of my release, and now with the Kellings gone, my only connection there is Sarah.'

'Sarah Bailey? I didn't know you two were friends. Jennifer says she's worked miracles at the Hall.'

'She does work very hard, poor thing.' There must have been something about the tone of his voice, a softness, perhaps, that Harry, who was a good reader of emotions, picked up on.

'So that's the size and shape of it. Sarah, eh? Jennifer didn't tell me about that.'

'I imagine that she doesn't know. It's a not a big secret, but I don't think Sarah speaks about it in Westbury. Not everyone would understand.' He didn't like to say that Mrs Bailey was not altogether happy that Sarah was seeing him, although she'd not tried to prevent it. He was not a little hurt by this and by the fact that Sarah had not allowed the relationship to be known about, though he understood. Westbury had known him as the German gardener who'd been interned.

'Listen, old man.' Harry looked about at the soldiers passing through, signalled a greeting to one or two, then drew Paul to one side, where their conversation couldn't easily be overheard. 'I need to warn you.'

Paul felt a weariness, sensing what Harry was about to say. He approved of Harry, and trusted him, though he hardly knew him. He was straightforward and liked most people and wasn't bothered if they didn't like him back, though most did. His men would follow him because they trusted him, but he lacked, Paul guessed, a natural authority over them. Perhaps that was why he hadn't seen promotion.

'I shouldn't mention Sarah to Richards, if I were you. It might add to your difficulties with him.'

'I already know what he thinks of me,' Paul said, trying not to sound bitter. 'Thanks for the tip though.'

'Major Goodall's a fair sort. The men like him.'

Again, Paul took his point. Ivor Richards was only the second-in-command. He resolved at that moment to stay out of Richards' way as much as possible.

When, the following evening, he found a quiet few minutes to begin a letter to Sarah, Paul wasn't sure whether to mention the matter, but in the end found it impossible not to. *You'll understand that it's not unexpected that I should come across them here, but that we should all three be in the same company was a surprise. I know that*

Richards is a friend of your family, but you understand my difficulties
with him. He will always be watching me, and that is an extra strain.

It was dawn, two days after Paul's arrival at the barracks, when
the unit assembled in the parade ground ready to travel out into
the desert. The army lorries were lined up nose to tail by the
river, silvery silhouettes against a pearly veil of mist, through
which glowed the great lemon disc of the rising sun. When Paul
drew close he realized with concern how dented and worn the
vehicles were, their famous Desert Rat logos almost erased. By
the time the men had piled in and the supply truck was loaded,
the mist had dispersed and the sun was beginning to blaze. One
by one, engines fired into life, the lorries lurched forward and
moved out of the gates into the awakening streets.

Despite the squash of men and possessions, Paul was thankful that they were actually on their way. The previous forty-eight
hours had been onerous, a relentless round of packing kit,
square-bashing on the parade ground and rifle training. The
evenings had been free, but he'd felt too liverish to roam the
streets much, and last night he'd felt the purging effects of some
falafel he'd bought at a market stall.

'What, are they them pyramids?' Blackie cried suddenly,
and they craned their necks to look, exclaiming at how rough-
hewn they were close up, and what a dirty sandy colour, not
the smooth gold that they'd imagined. There was much hilarity
when they spied the Sphinx with its poor snubbed face. Paul
guessed their next letters home would be full of it all. Some of
those with him, he'd discovered, had never been outside their
home county before the war, let alone beyond Britain's shores.
He felt a sudden sharp comradeship with them out here, all
undoubtedly fearful of what they would endure, but determined
to do whatever they had to with cheerful heroism.

The road bent north, or so he surmised from the direction of the sun, and after a couple of hours low white buildings began to appear on either side, harbingers of a city that rolled out towards a blue horizon. The city was Alexandria and the blue the Mediterranean. Though they quickly swung away from the buildings, the blue grew nearer and more glorious, and soon they were travelling alongside a wide stretch of beach and the cool breeze that blew set up a longing in them. At lunchtime the lorries bumped off the road to circle an oasis and the soldiers undressed as they ran, shouting ecstatically, leaving their clothes on the beach as they splashed into the cool water and cavorted in the waves. Paul struck out far from the shore and when he turned to look back, treading water, he was filled with an intense pleasure in the world and the beauties of the desert. He loved the sense of being accepted by these men and being a part of their endeavours.

It was to be a long time before he felt such joy again.

After tea and bully-beef sandwiches came the call to move on and, sticky with salt and sweat, the men scrambled back into the lorries. The sun had passed its full height and begun to descend. The long heat of the afternoon bore down. There was less energy for talking now and they had to hold on to their seats for the tarmac was full of potholes. From time to time they passed ominous signs of battle, twisted bits of metal on the side of the road, the wreck of a lorry or the burnt-out fuselage of a plane. A group of sappers who were fixing the road stepped back, waving their shovels and cheering as the lorries roared past with horns blaring.

Eventually, they left the tarmac behind and bumped out across the sand, following markers the engineers had left to show a safe route. The light deepened in colour towards sunset and still the desert rolled under the wheels. Everyone was heartily sick of the vast, grey expanses of sand with, apart from the abandoned rubbish of warfare, its featureless landscape.

He must have slept, because when Paul opened his eyes next it was dark, though he could make out, by the weak, shrouded headlamps, the solid shapes of tents. They had arrived at the camp.

'Keep your head down, for Chrissake.' Paul obeyed Harry Andrews' harsh whisper. 'Where's Stuffy?'

'Over here, sir.' Private Stephen Duffy's eyes gleamed in the darkness. There was no moon. Only the ancient stars stared down.

'You and Hartmann, do a recce while we keep an eye on this little lot over here.' Paul lowered himself carefully from his position as lookout, clutching his rifle. 'Watch your backs now, will you, and don't make a sound.'

'Right you are, sir,' Duffy whispered.

Paul rose silently on his haunches and followed Duffy along below the line of the ridge. He dreaded kicking any stones that might start a scree and advertise their presence to the German patrol they'd glimpsed a few moments before. How it had happened, he didn't know, but his platoon had become separated from the rest of the company. One minute they were there, the next, they'd vanished without a shot fired. Now they were in danger of being surrounded, unless Harry Andrews' idea was the right one, that this was a lone German patrol and not part of a bigger unit. They reached a break in the ridge and Paul sensed Duffy, ahead, sink down to negotiate their way round to the other side. Then Duffy froze and he froze, too. The seconds passed. 'What's happening?' he started to say, but Duffy's elbow jabbed him into silence.

Very faintly now he could hear soft sounds, breathing, the

scuffle and scrape of boots on grit. Paul felt a chill shoot through him and his heart began to pound in his chest so loudly that he was sure others must hear it. How far away was this man, and was there only him or others? The scuffling was close now. He felt Duffy tense and his hand closed over his rifle. Then the man was upon them. Duffy leaped, Paul heard a whimper and a grunt as the bayonet went in. The man's body hit him as he rolled past them, the life gurgling out of his lungs. It was the first time it had happened so close. He sensed the warmth of the man, the vain struggle against death, the terrible silence, then his mind snapped back alert, his hearing acute, listening out. There was another sound, someone trying to retreat silently, he thought, but Duffy was in action again, stabbing the air, and Paul followed, colliding with solid muscle and bone, a big man this time. He jabbed upwards and felt the blade slide in. The man gasped '*Nein!*' and clutched at Paul's weapon. Paul felt the full weight of him falling forward, the stink of hot sweat and blood and something else, fear. He lay there struggling uselessly beneath the dead man until Duffy pulled the body off him.

At that moment, further away, shots cracked the silence. Cries of pain went up and shouted instruction, then came a flare of light, an explosion, and sand rained down. 'There's a dozen of 'em there, did you see?' Duffy whispered. 'We must go back.' He gripped Paul's arm and dragged him away. Paul tripped over one of the bodies as he stumbled back the way they'd come to join the others.

Dim in the darkness they saw them, several hunched figures shooting from the top of the ridge, Andrews caught in silhouette tossing a grenade. Another explosion, more cries of grief. A German voice barked an order. *Retreat*. Paul and Duffy threw themselves beside their mates, rising and falling to shoot. A soft thud and Paul glanced to see someone along the line jerk forwards, collapse like a drunk, but he couldn't see who. He raised his rifle, peeped over the top, sensed rather than saw the bulks of several figures scrambling away down the escarpment. He fired in their general direction then ducked again. Beside him, Duffy fired too, and then there was no more shooting. They listened, but all they could hear were fading footsteps and, close by, the grunts of one of their comrades abandoned and in pain.

A glimmer of light behind. 'Briggsy, you poor old blighter.' Duffy's voice came cracked and shrill and Paul glanced down to see him bent over the ragdoll figure of Joe Briggs. Joe looked even slighter in death than he'd been in life and a lump came into Paul's throat.

Andrews had appeared beside Paul and shone a torch down over the ridge, its shaded beam describing an arc of horror. There were corpses, Paul saw, six or seven, and a man curled up like a foetus, shaking in agony. He was the one making the awful sounds.

'Let's go down,' Andrews said softly. 'See if there's anything we can do. Briggsy's beyond help, I'm afraid.'

'There are more of them out there,' Paul remembered suddenly. 'I mean there's another patrol. When their officer told them to fall back, he said they should find the others, I heard him.'

'Damn.' Andrews killed the torch and was silent for a moment. Then, in the far distance, it was as though a firework display started up, cracks and explosions, sparks, then a plume of flame.

'Do you think that's the rest of our lot?'

'Who can tell? They're certainly having a party.'

Without a word, Andrews led the way down the escarpment, pistol in hand, Paul following with the torch. The wounded man tensed, tried to inch away. 'Shh, we have come to help you,' Andrews said, checking him quickly for weapons.

Paul started to speak to him softly in German. He was about

Paul's own age, a compact, muscular young man, his face distorted with pain. Ahead, another explosion lit up the sky. The blood over the clutching hands gleamed like metal.

'Tell him we have to move him.'

Paul translated and asked him his name.

'Hans.'

'All right, Hans.' He and Andrews each slid an arm under a shoulder and with much groaning and cursing they managed to drag him up to the others. There Andrews sent half a dozen of the men on various duties, while the remainder of the platoon crowded round their captive, and Paul, kneeling beside him, sensed their hostility. He ignored them and gently continued to reassure the young man as he applied pressure to the wound in an attempt to stop the bleeding. Someone pushed a phial into his hand. Morphine. He felt for a fleshy part of the boy's arm and jabbed the needle in.

'What do we do with him now?' Duffy asked, but nobody knew. They were marooned, and somewhere out in the darkness this man's pals were undoubtedly searching for them.

Paul bound up Hans' wound, but still the blood seeped through. He gave him sips of water from his own bottle and tried to keep him conscious by speaking to him in whispers. Hans mumbled that he had a brother, who was also in the army, but he didn't know where.

First one, then the other of the patrols returned. They'd found no one. Water and biscuits were passed around, then the patrols dispatched again. Hans was quieter now, he found speaking more difficult. Paul soaked a handkerchief and mopped the sweat from the man's brow. He could see Hans' face more clearly, the gleam of his teeth as he shifted in discomfort. Gazing around, it seemed that the stars were fading and the sky was lightening. Dawn was on its way. The light grew stronger. Paul could see insects moving in the clumps of coarse desert grass. Ahead, all was quiet, but a great cloud of smoke hung over the horizon where the front line must be. He glanced down. The boy was more peaceful now. He seemed to be sleeping, though from time to time his mouth twisted and he whimpered.

It had been the longest night Paul could remember, worse even than after they'd taken his father. He had killed a man, but this rite of passage had not made him feel braver or more grown-up. It had simply happened, been the next thing he'd had to do, without thinking. And here he was trying to save the life of another who, for all he knew, he'd been responsible for wounding in the first place. He didn't feel good about this either. It was so random, pointless, he thought. Why should one die and another live?

His thoughts were broken as he became aware of a low, continuous rumble. He was wondering where it came from when one of the others, Pounder, that was his name, leaped up, in his reckless, terrier-like eagerness, shading his eyes to look east, behind them, into the glare of the rising sun. 'Lorries,' he said in excitement. 'They're ours, lads. We're saved.'

'Get down, you fool,' Andrews snarled and Pounder obeyed, but heads were snapping round to make out what was moving in the dusty distance. Soon it was clear. A convoy of trucks was advancing along the marked-out track. Oblivious to possible danger, the men rose and waved their hats at them until they slewed to a stop in the sand hundreds of yards away. An officer jumped out and began to jog towards them.

'We'll get you to a doctor soon,' Paul told Hans, but the young man slept on, twitching and gasping in his dreams. When Paul inspected the bandage on the wound, he was shocked to see that the bloody mess was crawling with tiny glistening flies.

Thirty-three

Briony woke to daylight filtering through the curtains, confused by the fleeing coat-tails of a dream full of shouting and gunfire. The alarm hadn't gone off. Had she actually set it? She threw off the duvet, causing a sigh and crackle of paper, and sat up, breathing a curse at the sound of something solid hitting the floor, the cigar box. It lay open on its end, its contents spilling across the boards. She seized her travel clock and blinked at it until the hands on its face came into focus. Half-past seven Relief. Was today Wednesday? Yes. No teaching until eleven. She lay back on the pillows, trying to recall whether there was anything she'd be late for. Nothing, she decided. She sighed as she slid out of bed, gathered Paul's letters together and shoved them back into the box. She must have fallen asleep reading them. The result was they'd taken over her dreams.

As she showered, she mulled over what she'd read. Paul had had his first brush with the enemy. He'd killed one of his own countrymen, then saved the life of another. He'd mentioned in a later letter that the man had been sent to a field hospital and survived, presumably to be sent to a POW camp when he'd recovered. Paul's commanding officer, Major Goodall, had summoned Paul and asked him for a full account of events, had commended him for his 'smart work', which Paul had mentioned to Sarah with amusement rather than pride. *He said he was 'glad to have a chap who could speak German in the ranks',* but that *our Captain Richards looked none too pleased at this.* Briony was surprised that all this detail had passed the censor.

Subsequent letters had been written over the following year. She must remind herself of the significant dates in the Egyptian campaign, she mused as she turned off the shower and reached blindly for her towel. The high commands of both German and British forces had changed over that long dangerous summer of 1942. After she'd dressed, she pulled down a book from the shelves that lined her small living room and turned to a chronology. Tobruk had fallen on 21 June. That was when Paul Hartmann's ship had docked at Suez. A few days later his company had joined the bedraggled remnants of the Eighth Army, defending the Egyptian frontier. By 30 June, the Germans under Field-Marshal Rommel had beaten them back to the little border town of El Alamein, and many of the foreign populace of Cairo and Alexandria fled in panic. How close defeat had been for the Allies. It was therefore an extraordinary turnaround that as October segued into November, the Eighth, finding new heart under the command of Lieutenant-General Bernard Montgomery, routed the Germans at the third battle of El Alamein and over the following months, beat Rommel back across Libya and into Tunisia. The Egyptian campaign was finally won.

'Ah, Briony. I'd begun to think you weren't honouring us with your presence today. A word, when you're ready, if you wouldn't mind.'

'Of course. Give me a moment.'

Briony had been unlocking her office at ten o'clock when Professor Gordon Platt, the Head of Department, appeared in the doorway of his, across the corridor. She shoved her bag into her desk drawer, took off her coat and tried to ignore her coffee craving as she hurried over to hear what He-who-must-be-obeyed wanted.

Platt's office was at least twice the size of hers, with a giant antique desk before which was arranged a selection of uncomfortable high-backed chairs. The long Victorian sash windows looked out over the courtyard, where there was usually something of interest going on. During the last protests against fees, students had erected billboards on the grass that featured a cartoon of the then Minister for Higher Education in rather a vulgar pose. Gordon Platt had kept his blinds down all day. In retaliation someone had thrown raw eggs at his window, to which his response, very stupidly, was to call the police. Consequently, his rating with the student body of the college stood at an all-time low.

He was a tall, rangy man in his late fifties, with thinning hair that might once have been an enchanting curly blond, but which was now greying, scanty on top and too long over the ears. He had a penchant for wearing bright-coloured corduroy trousers. Sometimes they were brick-red, on other occasions mustard. On days of important college meetings they would be a more sober maroon or navy. Today was a mustard day and his olive socks didn't quite go, Briony noticed as he came round the desk and shut the door behind her.

'Now,' he said, sitting down again in his comfortable chair. He looked over his bifocals at her with that ruthless, searching manner that had got him where he was today. 'I need to talk to you about our engagement programme. The Vice-Chancellor thinks the department needs to be doing more to reach out to the public, but frankly I don't have the time, so I'd like you to step up to the plate.'

Briony stared at him in bemusement, the thought of the work this might entail rushing through her mind like a giant wave. Talks to schools, conferences, lectures, exhibitions for the public. Essential these days to justify universities' existence. Although other members of staff and graduate students would be actually delivering them, being the organizer on top of all the other things for which she was responsible would take up a great deal of time. Time she didn't have. She gave a sharp intake of breath to steady herself.

'I see that you've put in a bid for promotion,' Platt went on, rocking back in his chair, his hands linked behind his head, giving himself the appearance of a large, malevolent insect. 'I'm not sure that you'll get it, mind, it's quite a step up for someone like you, but taking this task on will improve your chances.'

Great. He'd delivered a double blow. Not only did he belittle her ambitions, but he'd made it plain that refusal of his request now would do her no good at all.

'As you know, Gordon, I've already got a huge amount to do. Can I think about it?' She nearly reminded him how she hadn't been well the term before, but bit her lip, realizing it wouldn't help her status in his eyes. To a man with no imagination who had never suffered from depression or anxiety, people who did were practically basket cases. Of course, he wouldn't have expressed it like that, he knew the jargon, but at meetings she had sensed his unease about the subject of well-being.

'Of course, take all the time you like,' Platt said affably, 'but I need your decision by Monday.' He smiled benignly at her and picked up a file from his in-tray, thus signalling that the conversation was over.

*

By five o'clock, Briony was mentally and emotionally exhausted, but also furious, with Platt, but also herself. This, she recognized, as she glanced at her watch, wondering what had happened to the student who hadn't turned up, was a good thing. Anger could be a positive emotion, her counsellor had once suggested. It could encourage her to take control of a situation rather than allow it to defeat her.

The student obviously wasn't coming. Wonderful, she could go home on time. Deliberately ignoring a sheaf of papers waiting to be marked, Briony locked her office and sneaked out.

At home she kicked off her shoes, poured herself a glass of white wine and went to run a bath. This evening would be for herself, she sighed, as she lowered herself into the hot scented water and closed her eyes. Supper, read more of Paul's letters, watch TV. She wouldn't worry about the wretched Platt. A phrase her dad's father used to say floated into her mind. 'Sufficient unto the day is the evil thereof,' and she smiled as she remembered asking him what it meant. 'Live for the moment and don't worry about the future.'

Her eyes snapped open. Luke, she was supposed to email Luke about Sarah's letters. On the one hand she wanted to, on the other she didn't quite know whether she was stirring something up by contacting him. *Really*, she told herself as she got out of the bath, *pull yourself together*. They were both grown-ups and contacting him with information he needed for his work was hardly unreasonable.

She had his email address, so after she'd eaten her supper she quickly wrote to him, hoping he was well and asking him what it was he specifically wanted to know. Then her phone rang and picking it up she felt a little shock as she saw the caller's name. She swiped the screen.

'Luke? Hello.'

'Hi. I got your email and thought I'd give you a call.' Was she imagining that his voice in her ear sounded tentative, not his usual light confident self? Her heart went out to him and in her agitation she got up from the sofa and went over to the window, looked down onto the night-time street below. There was a black and white cat walking along the top of a fence.

'It's good to hear from you,' she said softly. 'How are you?'

'Fine. How about you? Have I got you at a bad time?'

'No, no, I was watching telly, but nothing important. Anyway, what about things at Westbury Hall? Is the garden project going OK?'

'Yes, it's been going well. I've nearly finished drawing up the plans, then I have to cost them. I need a few more details about some of the plants, though. Kemi managed to borrow the picture of the garden from Mrs Clare's flat, but it doesn't go into enough detail.'

They talked for a while about the specifics. Had Sarah mentioned the location of particular plants in her early letters, Luke wanted to know, before the garden had been turned over to wartime farming? Briony didn't remember.

'I think it's best if I simply send you the relevant transcripts,' she said, 'but there's something I must tell you. You're not going to believe it, but I've found the other half of the correspondence. Paul's letters to Sarah, I mean.'

Below, the cat had settled itself on a fence post, its tail twitching as it stared at something down on the ground. A mouse, maybe, Briony thought, craning to see.

'*Have* you?'

'Isn't it amazing?' She described how she had come by them. 'I've started reading them. Nothing useful about the garden so far, but, Luke, they're full of his wartime experiences. He was in Egypt. At El Alamein!'

'I take it he survived?' Luke laughed. 'Stupid question, I suppose. Unless you've found a letter that says *I'm dying, this is my last will and testament.*'

'I haven't,' she said stiffly, thinking he was making light of her discovery.

'You're still very involved in it all, aren't you?' he said. 'It's more than academic, then.'

'Yes, of course it is. It's about my family. Paul quite often mentions my grandfather, Harry. And Ivor Richards. They were all there in the same infantry company together, which is not as much a coincidence as it sounds, since it was a Norfolk regiment. Though quite what they were doing there I don't know, as on the whole, Norfolk Battalions weren't sent to Egypt.'

'I didn't mean to sound flippant. You know ...' Briony sensed Luke searching for the right words. 'It took a bit of courage for me to ring. I didn't know whether you'd want to hear from me.'

She felt such a flood of feeling that it was hard to say, 'Oh, why?' with coolness.

'I may be paranoid, but you seem to have been avoiding me lately.'

Outside, the cat pounced on whatever it had been stalking. A mouse or a shrew? Briony got a horrible glimpse of the creature hanging from its jaws.

'Luke,' she said, after a moment, trying out her strongest tone. 'Of course I haven't.'

'Right.' His voice was strained. 'Scrub that then. Don't worry.'

'I saw Aruna last night. But of course you probably know that.'

'Yes, she said it was the first time for ages and that it had been good to see you.'

'It was lovely to see her, but she seemed unhappy, Luke. I know it's not my business, but she *is* my best friend.'

'Do you think I don't get that, Briony?'

'All right, it really isn't my business.' She could sense Luke's anger.

'OK. Well, if you'd email me over those transcripts I'd be grateful. The job is taking longer than I'm being paid for. And I'd like to get that guy Greg off my back.' Again, that bitter tone. She chose to ignore it.

'How is Greg? Oh, and poor Mrs Clare.'

'Mrs Clare is back in Westbury Hall with a carer in attendance and improving. Her son gave permission for me to borrow that plan. Which reminds me, Kemi asked after you.'

'Oh, she's so nice, Kemi. Say hi from me. I'll send the stuff over in a moment.'

Briony ended the call and stared out of the window for a long time, watching with distaste as the cat played with its prey, going over the conversation in her mind. Luke was troubled about something, sounded deeply unhappy in fact. He seemed cross with her, too, and she didn't know what she'd done to deserve that. What a mess everything was at the moment. A car drew up outside the house opposite and the cat ran off as a young couple unloaded a baby in a car seat. They were smiling and laughing. The lamplight fell on the face of the sleeping infant, round and chubby with tight black curls. So cute. They looked so content, the little family, caught in the golden aura of the street lamp, that Briony felt suddenly terribly alone.

Thirty-four

'What should I do, Sophie? If I say no he'll spike my promotion, but if I say yes I'll be so overwhelmed by work I won't be able to function.'

Briony was sitting in the office of one of her colleagues, surrounded by posters of illuminated manuscripts with marginalia of fabulous beasts. Sophie was a mediaevalist, Swedish, in her early thirties, with short, clipped fair hair streaked with purple. Her seated pose, upright, long legs in skinny jeans crossed at the knee, suited her forthright, don't-mess-with me manner. She was the department's union rep, so a natural person to go to, but Briony, who hated being confrontational, had really gone to her for friendly, not formal, advice.

'He has no right, Briony.' Sophie jabbed the air with a blue-nailed finger. 'You don't have to take the work on and there would be trouble if he tried to interfere with the promotion board proceedings. Still, he is on it and his word counts. You do want him on your side.'

'So I should say yes?'

'You should say no. Be tough and he'll respect you. That's

the type of man he is. So much of this place runs on people's goodwill, that's the trouble. And he exploits that. But there are rules, and if necessary the union will back you up.'

'I don't want to involve the union at the moment. I worry about appearing a troublemaker.'

'That is a typical female response,' Sophie said with a sigh. 'I like making trouble.' Her eyes sparkled and Briony laughed. It was good to feel that someone was on her side. All too often in this place staff crept about doing what they were told. Once she'd jokingly said to Sophie that she was surprised that the Head of Department had agreed to the appointment of some-one like her with such trenchant views. Sophie's response was direct: 'I was the best candidate for the post. You have to believe in yourself, Briony, and others will believe in you too.'

'You're lucky having such self-confidence,' she sighed now.

She stood to go and Sophie bounced up and gave her a hug. 'So, think about it over the weekend, eh? Then blaze in on Monday and tell him your decision. Remember, it's your life.'

'You're right.' Briony's eye fell on one of the posters. 'That griffin – it is a griffin, isn't it? – looks like someone we both know.' Sophie stared at it and they both burst out laughing. It was the mustard-coloured legs of the creature and the curly bits of feather on its head.

As she walked back to her own office she saw that she had a missed call. Greg Richards. She sat for a while at her desk wondering what he might want, then shrugged, her curiosity getting the better of her reluctance. She touched the screen of the phone to ring him back.

The little mews tucked away in the maze of streets north of Sloane Square was deserted when Briony walked down it early the following evening, the only noise being the flapping of a giant piece of polythene broken loose from the scaffolding that enveloped one of the houses. The builder's board shining in the streetlight read *Judd Holdings Basement Solutions*. Not fun to live next door to, she told herself, examining the numbers on the doors she passed. Number Five, however, was several yards beyond the building work, with a neat two-storey Georgian frontage and a pair of olive trees in tubs standing sentinel at the entrance. Briony pressed the brass doorbell and smoothed her hair while she waited.

The door flew open and there was Greg in T-shirt, jeans and loafers. 'Briony, come in out of the cold, honey,' and she found herself sucked into a warm, dimly lit hallway redolent with the savoury smell of cooking. She could hear the tinkle of piano music. He kissed her on both cheeks and she gave up her coat and handed over the wine she'd brought.

'I don't know if it's any good – the man in the shop picked it.'

He squinted at the label, said he was sure it would be lovely and ushered her into a large, knocked-through living room with two black, grey and sable velvet sofas festooned with furry zebra-striped cushions. The far wall was lined with chunky bookshelves in a light-coloured wood. Ceiling lights like abstract sculptures in glass and metal twinkled above her head.

'It's like the Tardis,' she exclaimed. The modernity of the inside was such a contrast to the exterior of the house. 'Gorgeous, of course, but I'd never have guessed all this lay beyond your Regency front door.' When she slipped off her shoes, the hardwood floor was deliciously warm beneath her feet.

'It's a listed building, of course,' he said. 'But my predecessor did most of the work inside. God knows how she got it past the planning department. Now what can I get you to drink?'

While he was out in the kitchen fetching white wine,

Briony surveyed the contents of the shelves, several of which were set wide-spaced for the outsize art books and his vinyl collection. Rows of hardbacks mostly had titles like *Nietzsche and Leadership* and *The Zen of Globalism*, but there was an impressive line of recent celebrity sporting biographies, too. She was concluding sadly that there was nothing here that she would want to read when Greg returned with a bottle in an ice bucket and a couple of glass goblets. She sat down rather self-consciously on one of the velvety sofas. It was squashy, but very comfortable.

'It's good of you to come,' he said as they clinked glasses and he settled on a sofa opposite, one arm along the back of it. Although his pose was a study in relaxation, she sensed a coiled-up energy and tension in the firm line of his lips. 'I'll be straight with you, Briony. As I told you on the phone, your friend Luke mentioned in an email that you'd found another set of letters, from this guy Paul, and ... well, I'd better explain my interest. Did you bring them with you, by the way?'

'Yes, they're in my bag.' Briony felt a bit annoyed with Luke for telling Greg about them, but recognized he'd done so in all innocence, thinking they might offer further information about the garden.

Greg was eyeing the bag which she'd left by the door of the room.

He leaned forward and, setting his goblet on the table, stared across at her. 'I would like to know what's in them. It's my father I'm thinking about. He's elderly, you see, and he worries about these things.'

'What would he be worried about?'

'That there's something detrimental in them about his father – my grandfather that is – Ivor. I'm not sure what it is exactly, he won't say. It all started when I told him about you that time you came to stay at Westbury Lodge. It seemed to upset him.'

'I didn't mean to upset anyone.' Briony's nerves were on edge. She thought of the farmer, David Andrews, and his wife Alison, how her visit had disturbed them, too.

'I'm not saying that you did. Tell me about the letters, though, Briony. Do they mention my grandfather?'

'They do, yes. I'm not sure how much background you know?'

'Only that Paul was a German who worked on the estate as a gardener and there was some animosity between the two of them.'

'Yes, that's more or less it. They both fancied the same woman – that was Sarah – but it was more than that. Your grandfather disliked him because he thought he couldn't trust him, saw him as the enemy. Then they ended up in the army together in Egypt.'

'Perhaps I should flick through them, then, just to reassure my dad.' Greg's voice was very mild and reasonable and Briony didn't know why a feeling of reluctance came over her. She had to force herself to stand up and fetch her bag. She brought out the cigar box, thinking how light and inconsequential it was. When she opened it, she saw that in her rush last night she'd not put everything back tidily. 'Apologies,' she said, 'it's a bit of a jumble.'

'No worries. I'll sort them out.' They were standing very close together now, so close she could smell his expensive cologne. She glanced up into the friendly, wide-spaced eyes, then down at the box in her hand.

'Let's have a look,' he said and he came and sat down close beside her on her sofa and took the first letter from the pile. She watched him open it and frown at the difficult handwriting.

Greg listened carefully as she read it out to him, tapping the table with the side of his finger. 'I see,' he said, somewhat mysteriously. 'And what about this one?'

The next he picked out was so plainly a love letter that Briony felt self-conscious reading it aloud to this man who sat so close. She did so quickly and folded it away. 'There are several in that vein,' she told him.

'He has a way with words, this Paul,' Greg said in a caressing voice that made her feel uncomfortable and she felt herself shrink away from him on the sofa, wishing now that she hadn't come.

Greg smiled, his eyes glinting. 'Nothing about my grandfather so far.'

'There's mention of him later in some of the ones sent from Egypt, but I still have one or two to read. I had to stop last night because I had work to do.' Why did she feel so on edge?

'What do they say?' His voice had a harsher tone this time. Suddenly she wanted very much to go home. She closed the box and started to stand up. 'Briony, please. I tell you what, perhaps I can keep them, ask my PA to photocopy them in the morning and courier them back to you?'

'No, I don't feel I can do that,' she whispered.

He stood up too. 'Why not? You can trust me with them, can't you?' He looked so pleading and she couldn't say what it was that troubled her.

'I'll finish reading them and type them up. That's what I did with Sarah's letters.'

'Ah yes, Luke sent me the transcript.'

'He did?' That was annoying of Luke, but then he wasn't to know.

'Yes. In respect of the garden, of course. The letters were extremely interesting. There's not much about old Ivor, but there is a bit where Sarah tells Paul she thinks my grandfather really has a bit of a thing for her. So you're right.'

'She talks about it several times.'

'It's what my dad thought, too.'

'Perhaps I ought to meet your father sometime and swap information.'

'I don't think in his current frame of mind that he'd want that.' Again, that whisper of danger.

Briony took up the cigar box and fitted the elastic band round it. 'In that case, we'll have to talk once I've made the transcript. I'm sure I'll be able to reassure him. It's no crime, after all, for two men to have disliked or distrusted one another.'

'No, you're quite right. I can't think why he's so worked up about the matter.'

She drew her bag towards her and fitted the box inside, then stood and turned to face him. 'Please don't worry, Greg. I'm not trying to make anyone unhappy, just to find out some things about my own family. '

'What if you dig up something you'd rather lay forgotten, Briony? Have you thought of that?' Although he smiled, she sensed seriousness behind his words.

'What do you mean?'

Greg only shook his head. 'Shall I call you a taxi?'

'I'll be fine on the tube,' she insisted.

He led the way into the hall where he paused. 'I haven't shown you the rest of the house, have I? Leave your bag there and I'll give you a quick tour.'

It seemed churlish not to agree and she followed him through first into a beautifully lit modern kitchen where his supper was cooling, then up softly carpeted stairs, and in and out of several opulently furnished rooms. The house was lovely but somehow it left her cold. It was a place he stayed, like a hotel. Everything was new and clean and sparkling, but when she glimpsed inside the open door of a walk-in wardrobe there were only two shirts hanging in it. She used the bathroom and was delighted by the soft fluffy towels, perfectly folded, but it seemed profane to dry her hands on one.

When she finally picked up her bag to go, he drew her to him and kissed her mouth. Her skin prickled and warmth shot through her and it was with some effort that she pushed him gently away. She brushed off his offer to walk her to the tube station and set off through the chilly night alone, pulling her scarf snugly round her neck.

As she walked through the crisp evening, fallen leaves rustling under her feet, she felt glad to put distance between herself and Greg. She couldn't work him out. There was a fascinating, charismatic aspect to him, and yet at the same time she couldn't read him. Did he treat all women as he did her, or was there genuinely some spark unique to the two of them? She fancied she could smell his cologne still and walked even faster, trying to throw off her confusion, training her mind instead to go over the events of the evening. His interest in the letters troubled her. She remembered that Luke had shown him her transcript of Sarah's letters to Paul. A lump came into her throat for it felt like a betrayal, though it was her fault for not apprising Luke of her doubts about Greg.

At least she'd hadn't left Greg the letters this evening, she thought, as she entered the tube station and passed through the ticket barriers. Warm air from the tunnels sucked her down the steps to the bright platform. Safe in a seat on the busy train, her hands closed round the box in her bag. Yes, she still had the letters.

*

It was after nine when she closed her front door behind her. In the kitchen she unpacked the milk, bread and a plastic box of sushi she'd stopped to buy, then crouched to delve in her bag for an article she'd printed off, intending to read at the table as she ate. It proved elusive, but when she pulled out the cigar box to facilitate her search, she knew immediately by its lightness that something was wrong. She rolled off the elastic band and opened the lid. The box was empty.

The shock sent her sliding to the floor, where she sat with her mouth open trying to assemble her thoughts. Greg. The bastard. All that schmoozing and showing her round his *pied-à-terre* and he must have seized an opportunity – while she was in the bathroom, probably – to take the letters. She couldn't believe that he'd stoop that low. Though she sensed it would do no good, she hastily emptied the bag, but the letters weren't there.

Her hands were trembling as she fished her phone out of her pocket, so she had to try twice before she found his number, but ended up speaking to his voicemail. 'I never believed you'd do a thing as contemptuous as that. I was right not to trust you. I expect those letters back first thing in the morning or I'll contact the police.'

She hardly noticed the food she ate, she felt so angry and distressed. She held the phone, but the screen stared back at her blank, silent. With a huge effort of will she texted Luke, telling him what had happened and warning him not to give Greg any more information about Sarah and Paul.

Then she made herself mint tea and sat nursing it and thinking, its fresh smell a comfort, going over and over what had happened. What mattered to Greg so much that he had to have those letters? His grandfather did not come across well in them, arrogant, bigoted maybe to modern eyes, but Sarah, in her letters, also portrayed him with fondness. She hadn't read all of Paul's yet – a pile of marking had interrupted – and at the thought a shaft of misery pierced her. He, Greg, would read them first. It felt like a violation. Spurred by anger, she picked up the phone to ring him again, but there was still no answer. She began to pace the flat, like a caged animal, her agitation growing, but short of jumping in the car and racing back to Greg's she didn't know what to do. She had visions of herself banging on his door and shouting and rousing the neighbours and felt hot and cold with embarrassment at the thought.

Briony slumped down at her desk, intending to look through her emails, keeping her phone by her in case. She'd sat here last night, she remembered, reading those damned essays. The cigar box had been here, too, she'd been reading Paul's letters there previously. There were the books she'd dumped from her bag before she'd set off for work. Then she'd snatched up the box, slid the elastic band over it and slipped it in to show Greg. Her eye fell on something, a tiny corner of buff paper peeping out from under the pile of books. It piqued her interest. She nudged the books aside, and the paper revealed itself as an envelope with a loop of familiar black writing on it. She saw to her joy a small haphazard pile of old letters. Paul's letters. She must have left them there, the ones she hadn't read. Eagerly she grabbed them up, half a dozen of them. 'Thank you!' she whispered to whomever might be listening, Paul's ghost perhaps, or Sarah's, smiling in the darkness. The thought enchanted her as she switched on the desk light and opened the first letter. She was quickly absorbed, her eyes widening as she read.

Thirty-five

Sicily, July 1943

My very dear Sarah, I'm sorry it's been so long since I've been able to write . . .

Paul's fear and nausea fought for dominance in the hot, cramped interior of the landing craft, buffeted by wind and waves, juddering from the shells exploding all around. The stink of leather and cordite and rank sweat was overpowering. Next to him in the near-darkness a young lad was rubbing a coin and muttering 'Oh God, oh Jesus,' over and over, until a gruff voice told him to 'Stow it.'

The floor of the craft bumped and scraped on sand and then jolted to a sudden halt, throwing the men forward. As they righted themselves, complaining, metal shrieked against metal, the door was lowered and Paul gulped in fresh air. A gargoyle face looked in, grinned and called, 'Out you get, lads!'

Paul's fingers, sweaty with fear, slid on his rifle as he stood up. It was time.

He stepped out gasping into thigh-deep, chilly brine, remembering in time to raise the gun clear as he dashed with the others to the wide beach. Moonlight, a canopy of stars, then the quiet sky flashed white and a great distant rumble shook the ground. Bullets cracked and the man ahead of him slumped onto the wet sand, a dark stain spreading like a halo. 'Leave him, Hartmann. Get up the beach,' the sergeant's voice barked from behind and Paul staggered onward, tripping over abandoned kitbags and lumps of metal, blasts of sand scouring his face as he ran half-blind to the line of dunes ahead.

Writhing black smoke and flashes of fire. A thud and an ear-splitting crack, and a wall of hot air flew at him, knocking him off his feet. For a brief moment he stared up at the uncaring stars, wondering if this was it, then he felt a meaty hand grip his collar, hauling him to his knees. 'No sleeping on duty,' the sergeant's voice rasped in his ear and he blundered forward again, though every instinct shrieked at him to go back. He faltered, glancing round at the big man goading them on. To see a startling backdrop: great black shapes of ships on a jet-dark sea, the ships that had brought him here, their guns flashing fire, hurling shells over his head at an enemy he hadn't yet seen. Above it all, a silvery barrage balloon was drifting free, its appearance strange, but calm and stately. It gave him courage to go on.

Soon he was plunging through soft cold sand, fearing a hidden mine or a loop of barbed wire at every step, though it seemed that the sappers had done their job. He passed the cruciform carcass of a fighter plane – one of their own, he noticed, briefly wondering about the fate of its crew. A new sound started up ahead, the mechanical repeat of machine gun fire, striking sparks up into the night, then came a roar as a tank overtook them on the brow of a dune to his right and swept onwards inland, its turret spitting bullets. They followed its tracks in the compacted sand, until they reached a lodgement the commando parties had established.

And suddenly Paul saw how close they were to the enemy. On a hillock the other side of a dip in the dunes nestled a concrete pillbox. Here and there on the crest of the hillock he could make out swarthy faces beneath bowl helmets, heard the Italians' cries of dismay as the tank mounted the escarpment and did its deadly work. He recoiled at an explosion, raised his rifle, aimed at one of the faces and pulled the trigger. The face disappeared, but another rose to take its place. Returning bullets struck sand up in his face. Paul ducked, put out a hand to steady himself and was shocked to encounter an arm. Whoever it was he was dead and in the light of a flare he saw the man's face. 'Blackie!' he gasped. The mild, steady man he'd fought beside in Egypt and Tunisia. Taken by a bullet between the eyes. Paul tasted bitterness. Blackie had a wife, two children at home. The thought stirred him into hot anger. He half rose and fired indiscriminately at the enemy's dune, then stopped, aware that they weren't shooting back. Instead, above their position poked a stick, a rag of white tied to it, fluttering in a sign of surrender.

'Cease fire!' someone shouted, and as a localized silence fell a dozen frightened Italian soldiers appeared over the top of the dune with hands raised and stumbled down into the dip. Paul saw Harry reach them first and obeyed his summons. Some of the platoon was directed into the enemy trench to collect up discarded weapons: Paul was set to tying the prisoners' wrists. He was surprised by their sheepish air of relief, by the unpleasant coarseness of their battledress as he searched them for grenades. Then Harry ordered two corporals to lead them back onto the beach, where they'd be transferred onto a ship. Further along the dunes similar scenes were being played out. 'Hoorah for King George,' he heard one Italian call out and the man's fellows gave a thin cheer.

'Cowards!' the sergeant hissed.

'Why won't they fight?' Paul asked Harry, but Harry shook his head. As Paul's spirits lightened, he heard Major Goodall cry, 'Don't think for a moment that this is the last of them.'

And on they forged, weaving their way from dune to hillock, using flares to light their path until they left the sand behind and entered a scrubby hinterland. Ahead were a suggestion of trees and the lumpy black shapes of farm buildings.

A grove of stunted olives, then rows of vines, grapes glistening amid the rustling leaves, a stink of manure, then the rough stones of a wall under Paul's hand. The muffled barking of a dog started up. As they crossed the farmyard they heard the scrape of a door and a gruff voice shouted a challenge. A distant shell lit up the sky, revealing for a moment the burly figure of a gnarled old man brandishing a shotgun. A popping sound and the gun clattered to the ground as the man stumbled and sank down against the wall of his house, his palms clamped to his face. It was Ivor who stepped forward, lowered his smoking pistol, and Paul remembered something he'd once heard him say: 'Shoot first, think afterwards. At least that way you're alive.' Ivor prodded at the farmer with his boot, but the man was dead meat. From its confinement nearby the dog continued its furious barking.

Ivor and Harry summoned Paul and he followed obediently as they stepped over the body and slipped inside the house. They checked the few simple rooms by the flame of Harry's lighter, but instead of enemy soldiers they found only the old man's wife cowering in the marital bed. When she saw them she knew at once her husband was dead and wept, bringing down a stream of curses on them.

'Tie her up,' Ivor said roughly, but when Harry glanced at him in disbelief he changed his mind. 'Leave her be then. She has no way to summon help.' They left the house and joined a party to search the outbuildings. There was no livestock. When they opened the barn door a desperate sheepdog kept them at bay until Ivor shot it, but all it seemed to be guarding was a mangy donkey and a rickety painted cart.

The moon had begun to sink in the sky as they moved on, following several tanks carving tracks across a field of tender plants. Paul knew they must soon turn east, their mission being to secure the port. The Italian defence had been weak, but where were the Germans, that was what they were all wondering. He suspected it wouldn't be long before they found out.

As they tramped along in the greying darkness they sensed the massive presence of Mount Etna in the distance, its summit reaching higher than most of them believed possible, blocking out the stars. A familiar, pungent scent arose all around. A picture of the walled garden flashed into Paul's mind, a sense of Sarah and safety. After a moment he realized what the smell was – the woody scent of thyme.

'Get down.' Harry's low voice came to him on the hot, dense air.

Paul sank silently into a crouch, peering between gleaming vine leaves into the silvery darkness. There! Was that a man or a shadow? He raised his rifle, but to shoot was to give away their position. He had to be sure. The leaves sighed in a warm breath of wind then fell still. No one.

He watched Harry scamper to the shelter of a heap of rocks, so he rose and followed with the others. From the safety of this new position he could see the low wall of a farmyard and, *there*! Was that a movement at the other side, a glint of metal? His hand fumbled behind for the pocket of his kitbag and closed round a grenade. A signal from Harry and he bit out the pin and tossed the ball in a great arc, ducked and held his breath, praying that it wasn't the farmer come out to take a piss.

The explosion momentarily deafened him, the blast shaking the ground. Then screams, and a boy's voice crying for his mother before the Germans' machine gun burst into life and a fireball lit up the vineyard in a sudden nightmarish glare. There were at least a dozen of them, he saw as he rose to lob his next grenade. Another burst of sound and light and the machine gun abruptly ceased. Instead, from somewhere behind and to their right, their own gun started up. There were shouts of panic from the farmyard, then a repeated command. He glanced at Harry for instruction, but Harry was sitting with his back against the rock, one hand clutched to his jaw.

'Are you hurt?'

Harry did not reply, did not appear to hear him.

Paul reached out and pulled away the hand, expecting the worst, but there was no bloody wound and Harry simply looked up at him in surprise.

'Are you all right, sir?'

Harry snapped back into life. 'Of course I am,' he said, staggering to his feet.

'Shall we move in on them now? They're retreating. I heard someone give the order.'

'Yes, at once. Onto them, lads.' The platoon surged forward shooting flame into the darkness, but when there came no returning fire they scrambled one by one over the wall. To find a ghastly scene: a mess of bodies and twisted metal illuminated by a burning straw bale which a fat farmer with a flamboyant moustache was valiantly trying to extinguish. Seeing British soldiers, he dropped his pail and raised his hands. The soldiers ignored him. Most rushed through in pursuit of their prey, but others stopped to collect up weapons. Paul remained to speak to a burly German soldier lying groaning, his leg beneath the knee a shattered mess of blood and bone.

'Our doctors are coming. They will help you.' He spoke to the man in his own language.

'*Was?*' the man grunted, his face twisted with disgust. '*Du bist Deutscher?*' and when Paul didn't answer, drew painful breath and spat at him.

'*Ja*, and your fellows ran and left you,' Paul said, wiping the spume from his face as the man's angry gaze bored into him. It was not the first such occasion and he could never help a rush of shame. But nor did he avoid these situations, because since Egypt, when he'd first rescued a wounded German, he'd felt it to be something he should do. It made no rational sense, of course, first to try to kill a man and then to comfort him, but they were still his countrymen and he felt he owed them something.

'Hartmann!' Ivor's warning voice. He spun to see the wounded German prising a pistol from the dead hand of an officer spread-eagled nearby.

'*Für Hamburg,*' the man cried. A shot and a scream as the pistol skittered across the stony ground. Paul stared at Ivor's smoking gun, then at the German cradling what remained of his hand. His thoughts struggled for dominance. One kind of enemy had saved him from another, but the wounded German now had bloody stumps instead of fingers. Nausea rose in his gorge.

He nodded thanks to Ivor, then crouched and reached in his kitbag for his precious syringe. 'A doctor will help you,' he said again as he plunged the needle into the man's thigh and watched the agony leach from the exhausted face. He was an older man, Paul saw with pity, possibly a labourer of some kind in civilian life. Even if he survived, what would be left for him after his leg was amputated and his hand maybe, too?

'Let's get out of here,' Ivor muttered and, stepping over the bodies, they followed after the rest of their company.

*

The moon had set and they bivouacked in cold darkness behind a sheltering line of poplar trees. Paul lay listening to the whispering of the leaves as he waited for sleep to come. He'd become so worn down over the last two weeks that oblivion usually took him instantly, but tonight every time his eyelids closed, some thought or imagined sound would wrench him back to consciousness. There had been no let-up. After they'd overcome the first Italian defence they'd marched east up the dusty coastal highway under the blaze of the July sun. They'd taken the bridge at the port of Siracusa after a fierce battle in which reinforcements parachuted in had been massacred because of a series of stupid planning errors, a terrible memory that angered everybody still.

Taking Siracusa itself was easier. They had been amazed by the ready surrender of thousands of Italian soldiers, many singing cheerfully as they were led away to ships, clearly believing that their troubles were over. Paul did not wish that he was one of them; there was too much work for him to do. Instead he wrote to Sarah, describing his exotic surroundings, the big-wheeled carts painted with the faces of film stars or holy images, and how he'd helped rip down the posters and banners with Fascist slogans that covered the town's public buildings.

Then it was time to march on to Augusta in their filthy battledress, their feet slipping with sweat in their boots, stopping sometimes to revive themselves on grapes growing in roadside vineyards or to barter cigarettes for oranges while brightly coloured birds and butterflies darted against a scorching cobalt sky.

Augusta with its whitewashed houses and pretty tiled roofs surrendered quickly, then that town too was behind them, but between the triangular vastness of Mount Etna and the coast they walked into trouble. The plain narrowed into a strip and there, finally, a German division was waiting for them. Soon Paul became habituated to a ravaged landscape strewn with the bodies of soldiers, the blackened ruins of warplanes; grew practised at diving for cover from falling shells.

As their advance slowed, the word came back. General Montgomery in frustration was dividing his army. Half were to march inland to forge a route round the great volcano. It felt a loss to watch them go, but everyone knew it to be a race against time to reach Messina at the eastern tip of Sicily and to cut off a German retreat to the Italian mainland. Now Paul's company, amid the thousands of soldiers of the Eighth Army who remained, continued forward along the coastal strip, trying to push the Germans back. It was unforgiving territory, dotted with stone farmhouses, irrigation ditches and hiding places where the enemy's anti-tank weapons might lurk to devastating effect. Every yard, every inch, had to be fought for and the casualties were legion.

Despite their bravery, the practised cockiness and the graveyard humour, Paul was noticing the different ways the stress of conflict was wearing them all down, whittling away any softness, or lightness. Even the youngest of them now looked much older than their years. It wasn't simply the dirt etched into the grooves of their sunbaked faces, the scars of battle raking and roughening their skin, the weight of their tiredness, it was the loss of innocence registered in the hardness of their gaze. They'd seen horrors such as they'd never imagined from their childhood comics of heroism and derring-do. They'd seen dear friends cut down by random shards of shrapnel, or by careless bullets from their own side. They'd seen the corpses of little children and had had to avert their eyes and move on. They could see no reason behind any of these things, it was simply bad luck.

There was something else Paul was wrestling with, too. It was what the wounded German labourer had cried about Hamburg. Paul had asked the Major to find out what it meant.

Though he'd tried to put the incident behind him, the angry contempt on the German's face sometimes rose in his mind. He realized now why he hadn't recoiled from it, indeed, had felt a degree of sympathy. Contempt, he felt, was what he deserved, but not by reason of his origins. All he had seen and been made to do in this war had defiled and tarnished him. All right, he'd been merciful, had eased the man's pain, but then he'd left him, had hardly noticed the bodies of the others at that farmhouse, the men and boys who would never go home.

It had been the next day that Major Goodall had broken the news to him. The RAF had recently conducted a bombing raid on Hamburg, so thorough and so brutal, it had effectively flattened Paul's home city. 'Our payment for Coventry,' the Major had said grimly. 'That's how we're to see it. I'm sorry, old man, but that's how it is.'

Thirty-six

Briony had left her office door ajar mid-morning as a sign that she was open to see students, but the shuffling and giggling starting up outside didn't sound like nervous undergraduates coming to discuss their essays. There came a knock and she watched in astonishment as the door was shoved wide and a vast arrangement of pink, blue and white flowers advanced into the room in a crackle of cellophane. The giant bouquet was carried by Les from the post room, and behind followed Debbie, who bore a packet smothered with special delivery stickers and a large grin on her face.

'Flipping Norah,' was all Briony could say.

'Where shall I put them?' Les groaned. 'On the desk?'

Briony delved for the florist's envelope, which she found on a prong amid some roses, and read the card inside. Then she dropped it in the bin.

'Take them away,' she told Les in her steeliest voice, but she held out her hand for the package from Debbie.

'Yer jokin', aincha?' Les' cropped head poked up over some lilies, his eyes black pools of disbelief, his habitual gum-chewing stilled by surprise.

'I don't want them, sorry. Give them to someone else, Les. Chuck them. I don't care which.'

'Really?' Les' eyes lit up with possibilities, and with difficulty he backed out of the room with his prize.

'Is everything OK?' Debbie looked concerned.

'Absolutely fine,' Briony said through gritted teeth. 'I'm not a fan of the person who sent them, that's all.'

Debbie's eyes widened. She withdrew, respectfully closing the door. Briony hesitated a moment, then scrutinized the padded bag in her hands before tearing it open. As she imagined, it contained the letters that Greg had stolen from her the night before. She glanced through them quickly, judging that as far as she could tell they were all there, then pinched open the sheet of fresh cartridge paper that accompanied them.

Briony. A million apologies, but here they are, safely returned as promised. I'm looking forward to reading the photocopies and will be back in touch. I hope that you will forgive me. The flowers are but a small gesture of my immense shame. Yours in friendship, Greg.

'Shame. Friendship,' she hissed, scrumpling his letter into a ball. Having second thoughts, she smoothed it out and pushed it back in the padded bag with Paul's letters in case she ever needed the evidence. At least he didn't have copies of the entire collection, she thought with satisfaction as she stowed the package in her bag to take home.

She glanced at her watch and saw it was time for the appointment she'd made with Gordon Platt. She'd been feeling trepidation, but now Greg had made her angry. She steamed out, head high, hardly noticing several passers-by fall back as she marched across the corridor to Platt's office. This was not the anxious wreck who'd been tried by Twitter. This was a Briony none of them had seen before.

'Gordon, I'm sorry, but I must say no to the engagement opportunity.'

She stood squarely before him and Platt, who had been lounging in his seat, now sat up and appeared mildly annoyed. 'Come on, Briony, you know we need to pull together here. We're all overworked. Someone's got to do it.'

'Yes, but not me this time. It isn't fair that I should. I'm supposed to have one day a week for research. I don't know when I've last taken that. I've worked weekends most of this term.'

'Very common. I do myself.'

'I'm not going to start naming names, but there are several members of staff I can think of with lighter loads who you could ask. Why not try?'

Platt raised his palms and said, 'I think we need to calm down a little.'

'I am perfectly calm, I assure you.'

He rose from his chair and she saw that his cords were a sober navy today. Some important meeting, she supposed, as she watched him pace the room. Finally, he turned his head with the air of a sinister parrot and said in a petulant tone, 'If that's your answer, then I'll find someone else, but don't expect ...'

His voice died away and he waved a hand, dismissing her.

'Don't expect what?' she asked, remaining exactly where she was. 'I assure you I'll be working as hard as ever, and I hope to be rewarded for that when my case for promotion is heard.'

'I wouldn't dream of suggesting otherwise,' he said mildly,

'but I'm not the only person on the promotions committee you need to convince. Well, I'll say no more.' Then, more to himself than to her, 'Perhaps Colin has some spare capacity. I wonder.'

She left the room, closing the door quietly with a smile. Colin Crawley, the department's last-ditch Marxist, often managed to wriggle out of administrative duties. Like Macavity the cat, when you wanted him he was never there. Privately, she wished Platt luck, while feeling light-headed with triumph at her small victory. She tried to banish the thought that though she'd won this battle the dust clouds heralding the enemy troops could be seen on the horizon. The promotions committee was the week after next.

Thirty-seven

October 1943 was wearing its way to November and Paul could not remember when he'd last lain in a proper bed. Before Italy, before Sicily? Not since they'd left Egypt, he calculated, so over three months ago. This particular morning, thuds of shellfire had torn him from a sleep that left him unrefreshed, but though he struggled from his tent with protesting limbs, his rifle already in his hands, he realized that the noise came from far away and reveille hadn't yet sounded so he'd sunk back inside again.

Gunfire again, nearer this time, and now the thin strains of the bugle and groaning and cursing men surfaced from their tents like the dead from their graves on Judgement Day, reacquainting themselves with their exhausted bodies, testing their weight on stiff legs, apparently astonished to find that they still lived and moved. Some limped off in the direction of the latrines, others to queue at the mobile kitchens for breakfast.

Passing the officers' tents, Paul spied Harry's recumbent form through an open flap. On his way back from breakfast he bent and nudged him, watching him for signs of fever as he fought his way to consciousness. Harry rolled up to sitting and sipped at the mug of water Paul handed him, then splashed some on his face so that rivulets of dirt ran down it. He drained the mug, returned it to Paul with a silent nod of thanks and accepted a bully-beef sandwich with a gloomy expression. Paul left him to come to terms with the day.

It would be the same as the one before, he supposed as he repacked his haversack, which would be the same as the one before that, playing cat and mouse with German patrols in these mountains north of Naples with the fate of being shot or blown up by booby traps all too real options.

Over the last week a wintry chill had set in to make the persistent rain more miserable. All conversation seemed to be about the weather. They remembered the relentless heat of the summer months with nostalgia, for while they'd become dug in, chipping away uselessly at the German defences, floods and merciless bombardment had turned the mountainous terrain, once tree-covered and fecund, to liquid mud and the charming farmhouses to blackened ruins.

Paul read exhaustion on the faces of the men that he passed on his way to roll call. After they'd triumphantly entered Messina back on 17 August only to find the Germans had escaped, his company had crossed over the narrow strait to mainland Italy on 3 September. Then came the Italian surrender to the Allies five days later, and they'd formed part of a light force dispatched up the coast to meet the Americans, who'd made landfall at Salerno and repulsed the Germans there after a bloody and costly battle. The Allies had liberated Naples on 1 October, and when he'd entered the city the following day Paul had been shocked by the wanton destruction wreaked by the departing enemy, and the suffering of its people, the drawn faces of the children, the hunger in their mothers' eyes.

The suffering was telling on them all now. They were being tested to their full extent. Three days ago Paul had seen another private in his company, Smithy, go under, refusing point blank to join a patrol on mine-clearance duty. Smithy had actually shaken with fear and, worse, he had cried, actually cried, this big, solid chap who at home would have been out in the fields bringing in the cows, a steady sort whom everyone had taken for one of the reliable ones, obeying orders under fire. Now his nerves were shot. Paul had witnessed Ivor Richards' rage as he argued with him uselessly, then in frustration taunted the man and struck him with his rifle butt. It was the officer in charge who intervened. He'd sent Smithy to the medical tent, but Richards had not even been admonished. Not that Paul knew of, anyway.

Paul was worried about Harry. He had been ill with malaria, picked up in Sicily. He'd recently suffered another bout of fever, but was now dosed up and on the mend. It wasn't simply his illness that disturbed Paul, though, it was the change that he saw in the man. Sometimes Harry's hands shook, and if his gaze fell on Paul, he had a pleading expression. Ivor was keeping a close eye on Harry, too, Paul noticed that, but instead of sympathy his expression showed contempt.

The ground reverberated as their guns pounded the enemy's mountain hideouts and then they were off climbing the slopes with the tenacity of goats if not their fleetness, for they had to stop frequently to test the ground for mines. Ahead of him, Clarkson, a grocer's son from Middlesbrough, stumbled and an explosion cut off his cry. Paul averted his eyes as they passed what was left of him. *Watch the path,* he told himself, breathing stertorously, *watch.* Gunfire rattled overhead. Something struck a finger of his left hand, numbing it, but by the time he allowed himself to notice the pain and investigated, the tip beneath the nail was swollen and purple. He could still use his gun so he supposed there was no need to get it taped up.

The sight of an enemy helmet above, then a shell burst nearby made his heart leap. He raised his rifle and shot in the direction of the helmet, hopelessly, before drawing back into the shadow of a rock. Some way ahead up the winding goat path, he could see several others, Briggs and Fielding, it looked like, scampering after Ivor. They'd overrun the enemy outpost to approach it from above. He ducked and held his hands over his ears as the grenades exploded, peeped out to see a German officer loping past. Paul felled him with a single shot, then peered down the hill wondering what had happened to Harry. He'd been behind him only a moment before.

Heart in mouth, Paul set off back down the slope, scuttling from rock to tree, taking care where he put his feet. It wasn't long before he found Harry. It was near, very near, where they'd lost Clarkson. Harry was sitting on the ground with his arms around his knees, his shoulders shaking. He'd been sick, Paul saw, his own stomach turning. 'Harry,' he said, dropping all formality. 'What's the matter, man? You can't stay here.'

Harry did not even acknowledge him, but continued to sob soundlessly. Paul put out a hand, felt the man tremble. It must be the fever. 'Harry, don't worry, I'll help you. I'll just signal to Richards if I can. Then we'll go back down. Get you to the doctor.'

It would be dangerous, he knew, moving slowly in this terrain with a sick man, an open target for the Germans above, but he couldn't just leave Harry here. When he scanned the slope above him, he saw that the mist was coming down. There was no sign of the others. He made his decision and hoped it would be the right one. Certainly no other acceptable course presented itself.

Harry was reluctant to move at first and Paul realized for the first time something shocking to him. Harry, cheerful, steady Harry, was scared. No, worse than that, he'd gone to pieces. Paul coaxed him, spoke to him in a reassuring voice then, when neither approach made any difference, explained to him sternly what they were going to do. Harry assented with a nod. They set out, Paul covering Harry's back, keeping to the shelter of rocks and gullies as they descended the hillside.

Passing poor Clarkson was a difficult moment. Harry's eyes squeezed shut and his limbs gave out so that Paul had to hold him up and drag him by the corpse. Shots from further up suggested a sniper, but the mist was merciful, drawing a curtain to shield them from his view. Soon it began to rain again, heavily, so the path ran with mud and their progress became a matter of sliding and falling. By the time another patrol picked them up near the bottom they were bruised and exhausted.

On arrival back at camp Paul delivered Harry to the hospital hut – an old barn – and went to report what had happened, careful to stick to Harry's fever symptoms. He was unsure how the adjutant would respond to the problem of Harry's nerves or whether Harry would thank him for mentioning it.

It was with some trepidation that he returned to the hospital later in the day to enquire after Harry, only to be surprised by the news that he had been discharged. Paul eventually found him sitting wrapped in a blanket on a crate under one of the stores shelters, smoking a cigarette and staring out miserably at the rain.

He greeted Paul with a nod and a raised eyebrow, but not his usual friendly smile.

'This is a good place to sit,' Paul said, ducking in from the rain. 'How are you?'

'A little better. I must thank you for rescuing me up there.'

'That's fine. I asked for you at the meat house just now, but you must be doing well for here you are.'

'They gave me the usual bread pills and cut me loose. Told me they needed the bed. I say, you haven't mentioned anything to anyone, have you?' Harry's face was anxious. 'About how I was ... up there.'

'Of course not. We all get in a funk sometimes, don't we?'

'But you all get on with it. I don't know how I can go on, Hartmann. I was lucky it was you today. Tomorrow it might be the Major or, worse,' he said darkly, 'Richards. You wouldn't have thought it of him, would you?'

'His treatment of Smithy, you mean. May I?' Paul drew up an empty orange box and sat on it. He chose his words carefully, knowing that the Westbury officers were supposedly friends and he was an outsider. 'If the Major won't help you, and it seems unlikely, then go further up. The adjutant who interviewed Smithy sent him back to Naples on guard duty. That's what I heard.'

Harry nodded, a faint look of relief crossing his good-natured face. He drew deeply on his cigarette. 'Do you think of home much, Hartmann? Good old Westbury, our life there – no, I suppose you don't.'

'I think of the people.' Paul banished the thought of his own home city, Hamburg, the desolate and blackened version that inhabited his dreams, and tried instead to think of a garden surrounded by a wall, a peaceful place. And sitting on the steps would be Sarah. He studied his bruised finger, thinking that he'd lose the nail. It didn't matter in the greater scheme of things.

'So do I. The Bulldocks. Good old Jennifer. I wonder where her poor brother is now. You know, if we ever make it back home I'm going to ask Jennifer to marry me. She's a grand girl. I've always been fond of her.'

'That's something to live for then,' Paul said, amused. He was surprised, never having heard Harry mention her in this way before, but from the little he'd seen of the Bulldocks it occurred to him that Harry and Jennifer would make a good go of it together. Both sensible, straightforward sorts. But there were more urgent things to deal with. 'Speak to the adjutant,' he begged.

Harry must have done just that, because the following day he was kept back on mess duties while the rest of the company were sent off once more with the aim of dislodging a German gun turret. Then disaster hit. The path they'd followed the day before had been set overnight with a huge booby-trap bomb, which exploded, killing the Major and two of the men. As the others picked themselves up, ammunition fell on them like malevolent hail, killing half a dozen more and gravely wounding others. Richards survived with a grazed shoulder, and managed to order a staged retreat, but without the Major they were leaderless and mourned the loss of their comrades. The company would have to be broken up, they were told, and men and officers reassigned. For all of them this news was a terrible blow.

It was odd how they were sent back to Tuana, Paul thought. Their company had passed through the valley a week back, pursuing a unit of German infantry through the small town after destroying their hillside redoubt, searching the town hall and the outlying farm buildings to round up the last of them. Paul had liked the place, even in the rain, and felt sorry for the mothers and children cowering in their houses and the old women who scuttled out wailing for their damaged church as the soldiers left.

'You're to establish a garrison there,' the adjutant explained, tapping his map with his pencil. 'It's on the supply route from Naples. You'll have some Jerry prisoners to keep an eye on, from time to time, on their way through. That's where you come in, Hartmann. We'll need someone who speaks the lingo. We're making you a corporal. Congratulations.'

'Thank you, sir.' Paul felt nothing. As they filed out, he was aware that Ivor lagged behind.

'We did our best here, sir,' he could hear Ivor's voice, reasonable but with a touch of the plaintive. 'I'm sorry you're disappointed, but . . .'

'Not disappointed at all, Captain. It's simply that this job's come up. Someone needs to do it and you are the lucky ones. I'd be glad about it if I were you. Getting out of this hellhole. That'll be all.'

A moment later, Ivor pushed past Paul, his expression as thunderous as the lowering sky.

Thirty-eight

A little past midnight, the vibration of her phone tugged her from a deep sleep.

'Is that Briony?' It was a voice she faintly recognized.

'Mmm. Who is this?' She fumbled for the lamp switch.

'I am sorry to ring so late. It's Gita, Aruna's mother, you remember?'

'Yes, yes, of course. Gita.' She sat up, suddenly alert. The image came to her of an older, rounder version of Aruna, dressed in an emerald sari at the wedding of her other daughter. Gita had a proud, upright bearing despite her lack of inches, and intelligent dark brown eyes that saw everything. Had she given Gita her phone number once? She must have done. 'Is something wrong?'

'I'm afraid there might be. Aruna phoned me, very upset. I think it's to do with her young man, a quarrel of some sort. We could hear that he was there, but we are too far away to do any-thing tonight and I thought perhaps you might be able to help.'

'I'll try to, Gita.' She slid out of bed, wide awake now. What could be going on?

'You live close by, maybe you could ring or visit, find out if she is all right.'

It was a couple of miles to Aruna's, certainly nearer than her friend's parents in Birmingham, so she promised Aruna's mother that she would do what she could, and Gita ended the call, full of effusive thanks and begging Briony to phone her as soon as she found out what was happening.

Maybe Gita was exaggerating the problem. Briony sighed and brought up Aruna's number. The call went to voicemail, so she texted and waited, but no reply came. Then she thought of Gita's anxious voice and reached for yesterday's clothes where she'd left them draped over the back of a chair.

As soon as her car slid into the crescent of old red-brick semis where Aruna lived in a first-floor maisonette, Briony realized that something was up. Curtains twitched at bedroom windows, where light gleamed, silhouetting sleepy inhabitants peeping out. She parked in a miraculously free space and climbed out to hear voices, one angry, the other conciliatory. Pulling her coat round her against the cold, she hastened along the curve of parked cars, and at the sight of Aruna's house stopped dead in shock.

It was Aruna she saw first. Her friend was leaning out of the upstairs window, casting items of clothing into the street. One by one, trousers, shirts, a jacket, flew like diving seagulls to land on the front hedge or the pavement beyond. There was a pause and Aruna's tragic face gazed down, then she vanished inside, presumably to fetch more.

Briony drew back as Luke appeared from behind the hedge, but he was so busy snatching up his clothes and stuffing them into a holdall that he didn't see her. She glanced round as a pair of trousers sailed past her to straddle the wing mirror of a car. Luke caught them up, then opened the rear door and shoved everything inside.

'And don't come back, ever,' Aruna yelled down. She was sobbing now and her words were slurred. Briony, back pressed against the sharp branches of the hedge, was appalled.

'Aruna, for Chrissake,' came Luke's hoarse whisper. 'If you won't let me help you, go to bed. I'll call you in the morning.'

'You can have this too,' was Aruna's drunken reply and a heavy object bounced off the hedge and fell with a soft crunch on the pavement near Briony's feet. She looked down to see a washbag with dark liquid pooling round it.

Luke's footsteps and she straightened to see his anxious face staring back at her in surprise. 'Briony!' he hissed, squeezing her arm as though to assure himself that she was real.

'Can we get some sleep now?' a tired male voice rang out from across the road. Then, above, came the sound of Aruna banging the casement shut. All around, neighbours' windows clicked closed, one by one lights were dimmed and the street returned to silence.

'What the hell are you doing here?' Luke whispered and Briony quickly explained.

He bent down wearily and picked up his washbag by its zip then dropped it into next-door's wheelie bin.

'What happened? Will she be all right?'

'I think so. She's drunk, but not that drunk.'

'I must go and find out.'

'I don't think that's a good idea.' He pulled her back gently.

'Why not?'

'Because, I don't know, she'll throw things at you, Briony.'

Her frustration rose. 'I haven't done anything. She's my friend. What have you said to her?'

He lowered his arm and turned away, mumbling.

'What?'

'Nothing. I said nothing.'

'I'm going to her.'

Luke shook his head, and pulled his car key from his back pocket.

'You go home,' she said, seeing that he had had enough. 'I've got my own car here.'

He regarded her for a moment, his expression hard, unreadable, then he shrugged, opened the driver's door and got in. She watched the car move away quietly, but he did not even look at her and she turned away, miserable.

At Aruna's front door, Briony pressed the bell and waited, shivering, wishing she'd taken an extra moment to put on socks. 'Come on,' she muttered, rubbing her cold hands, but no one came. Finally she dug her phone out and summoned Aruna's number. Four rings and Aruna's bright voice invited her to leave a message. *Am downstairs let me in,* she managed to text with frozen fingers and eventually there came sounds from within, then the door cracked open and Aruna's bleary face peeped out. She seemed to be wrapped in her duvet.

'For God's sake, it's perishing out here,' Briony whispered and Aruna, with difficulty, widened the gap to admit her. Briony followed her friend's bulky figure up the narrow staircase, the billowing duvet rustling against the walls, to where the door to the flat stood open. From inside wafted a strong stink of burnt milk. Briony pushed past Aruna to the kitchenette, rescued the saucepan from the stove and dumped it in the sink, where it hissed and spat. Something warm rubbed against her legs and she glanced down to see Purrkins, Aruna's cat, and bent to stroke him, but he ran off, elusive as ever.

When she turned, there was no sign of Aruna. She filled a glass with water from the tap and carried it through to the cramped sitting room where she found her friend lying on the sofa, wrapped in the duvet. The silent glow of the television illuminated the wreck of the evening. Dirty wine glasses, crisp crumbs, a couple of empty wine bottles. Briony stepped over an open box containing the mangled corpse of a pizza.

'Aruna?' she said to the spray of black hair at one end of the duvet, and Aruna's woebegone face peeped over the top.

She gave a gulp. 'It's over,' she slurred. 'He ... he says it doesn't feel right any more. I want to hate him, Bri, but I don't. I love him.' And she began to sob. Briony put her arms round her and rubbed her back through the duvet until the sobs quietened and Aruna's eyelids started to close.

'Ru, you ought to get to bed,' she whispered. 'Come on.' She helped her sit up properly, made her sip some water, then saw her to the bathroom and from there to the bedroom, trying not to tread on a trail of clothes and towels.

'Did he explain?' she asked her friend, sitting beside the curled-up form on the double bed, but Aruna merely snivelled. 'I'd better ring your mum, it was her who told me to come,' she added. Aruna was too out of it to reply.

Briony went to find her coat, which she'd thrown over the sofa back, picked bits of hedge off it and scooped her phone out of the pocket. Once she'd spoken to Gita and assured her that she'd stay the night with Aruna, she returned to the bedroom to find her friend had fallen into a deep sleep. She made sure she was wedged comfortably on her side, topped up the water glass and left her, gently drawing the door to, then made herself a cup of tea. Her teeth were chattering, from nerves as much as the night chill. She wondered what precisely had happened that evening. It was clear that Luke and Aruna had had a terminal row, but quite what it had been about she didn't know. She hoped that her name hadn't been brought into it, but from what Luke had hinted outside it possibly had. Still, Aruna had let her in and allowed her to help, so she obviously wasn't in too much trouble.

The tea, annoyingly, woke her up rather than calmed her and when the cat crept out from behind the television and crouched to eat the pizza with disgusting crunching noises, she shooed him away and set about clearing up, scraping food into the bin and rinsing out the glasses, turning on the kitchen extractor fan to rid the flat of the burning smell. It was when Briony returned to the sitting room and reached for a dirty plate on the computer table in the corner that she saw a book next to it splayed open face down. She recognized it instantly. It was the guidebook Briony had bought in Tuana. She had forgotten that Aruna still had it. What a happy time they'd had there, *well*, *mostly*, she thought as she picked it up and turned it over, but seeing it was open at the entry about the church she realized she thought about it differently now, because of Paul's letters. The church had been partly destroyed by the departing Nazis, she remembered. How cruel it was for either side to destroy a people's heritage; brutal, senseless, to leave innocent survivors with no future.

Someone, presumably Aruna, had drawn a cross next to one of the photographs. Briony switched on the desk lamp to read it properly and puzzlement washed over her. The picture was of the oval memorial plaque that they'd seen on the wall near the altar. Who had it been for? She stared, tiredness causing the gold letters of the inscription to glitter and dance. It was in memory of a fifteen-year-old boy and had been set there by his family. The text beneath gave an explanation. In the margin was a phone number in Aruna's curling writing, the sevens crossed in her flamboyant manner. It troubled Briony, Aruna's obvious interest in the plaque. A fifteen-year-old boy killed in the Second World War, what, seventy years ago? She read the name again: Antonio Mei. The name meant something to her, but for the life of her she couldn't think what. She closed the book, conveyed the last dirty plate to the dishwasher, then went to search for the spare duvet.

It was just getting light when she was dragged from sleep by a ring on the doorbell. On the front step she found Aruna's parents, short, sombre, weary figures with anxious eyes. They had driven through the night to fetch their daughter home. Inside, Aruna greeted them with the frantic tears of a lost child found.

They waved away Briony's offer to make breakfast, so she tricked the cat into his carrying cage for the journey to Birmingham, gathered coat and bag and took herself home, their effusive thanks ringing in her ears. She drove through early morning streets shining with rain that had turned the autumn leaves to mush. It was Saturday, she was weak from emotion and lack of sleep, and all she could do was fall into bed.

Thirty-nine

By the time Briony woke it was mid-afternoon and the sky was dark with rain. Huddled on the sofa with a cup of hot chocolate for comfort, the trauma of the night before finally hit her and she cried. She felt so alone. What now? Where could she go? No Aruna to talk to. A stab of pain at the thought of her ordeal. She had other friends, of course, but it would involve so much explaining about all the things that had piled up on her recently. Some knew about her work problems and her feelings of fragility, but no one else knew her as well as Aruna. Then there was Luke. She thought of how miserable he must feel, wondered if she should contact him; wanted to, badly. But what would she say and would it be betraying Aruna?

In the end, the place her mind kept returning to was home, by which she meant her father and Birchmere. It was one of those occasions when no matter how grown-up she was, inside she felt like a little girl. She reached for her phone, and couldn't help being disappointed when her stepmother answered.

'I'm afraid your dad's out, Briony,' Lavender said. 'Lunch at The Chequers with Graham – you know, his old friend from the

Chronicle. You sound a little muffled, dear. Are you hatching a cold?'

'No, I had a bad night, that's all. Well, it's true, I'm not feeling great.' Part of her longed to confide in Lavender, who sounded so maternal and concerned, but the other part was too proud. She simply missed her mother even more.

'Why don't you come down here?' Lavender sounded so kind that Briony felt like crying again. 'Today if you like. Your bed's still made up from your last visit. And we're not doing anything tomorrow.'

Suddenly she caved in. She'd been invited to a house-warming party at a colleague's tonight, but she didn't feel like going. 'I'll come,' she told Lavender, 'but I hope you don't mind if I'm not very lively.'

'Of course we won't mind. It sounds as if you need a good rest.'

It helped to be doing something practical, packing an overnight bag, clearing up so that she didn't have to come back to a mess. As she straightened the books and papers on her desk and reached for her phone charger, she noticed the cigar box of letters and after a moment's hesitation scooped it up. The box of mementoes her father had given her was stowed under a bookshelf and she took that too. Perhaps it was time to talk to him.

When an hour or so later Briony drew up alongside the mock-Tudor semi, Lavender must have been looking out for her because she came out at once, hugged her and helped her inside with her things.

'Your father's not back yet,' she said, setting down the box in the living room. She stretched and rubbed the small of her back, though the box hadn't been heavy. 'You know how he and Graham are when they get together. Why don't you sit down and I'll make tea.' She was wearing old navy-blue trousers and a matching gilet over a thick jumper with burrs stuck in it. Briony pointed out one that had caught in her hair. Lavender glanced out of the window as she rescued it to where a line of plastic sacks stood limply on the back lawn. 'I was trying to clear up leaves with that new machine, but they're so soggy I gave up.' She sounded weary and moved stiffly as she went into the kitchen, and Briony felt a stab of sympathy.

'Why don't I make the tea?' she said, following and taking the kettle from her, and for once Lavender let her, though only to turn her attention to the biscuit tin instead, laying fingers of shortbread out on a plate.

'Sorry it's not home-made. I don't know where the time has gone this week.' She did sound forlorn, Briony noticed with concern. Lavender pulled out a chair and sat down at the table, massaging her temples with finger and thumb. Briony brought the mugs of tea over and sat opposite.

'How are you, darling?' Lavender asked, trying to be bright.

'Not too bad. It's you that seems a little tired.'

'Don't worry about me, it's been a long week, that's all.' They sipped their tea and nibbled biscuits in companionable silence. Briony felt more relaxed than she expected, glad that she'd come. It was home, after all, somewhere you came back to when things had gone wrong in the big wide world and you felt alone.

'I think I'm basically all right,' she told Lavender. 'Just suffering from lack of sleep. Oh, and a bit upset about something.' There, she'd done it now, but there was a softness about Lavender today that invited confidences. Her stepmother raised her eyebrows and nursed her mug, waiting for her to go on.

'A friend of mine . . .' And before she knew it she was telling Lavender about Aruna and how upsetting the break-up with

Luke had been to witness. 'The trouble is,' she confided, 'I'm worried that I might be part of the reason for the break-up and it's not because of anything I've actually done.' She explained that Luke appeared to be drawn to her.

'But if it's his fault, then should you feel guilty?'

'I don't know, I just do. Maybe I shouldn't have been so friendly with him. Perhaps it encouraged him without realizing.'

'That's what my parents' generation would have said, Briony. I'm sure it wasn't your fault at all. These things happen in my experience. If their relationship is meant to be then it will mend. Maybe it will help if you stay out of their way for a while. Only they can work out if they want to be together.'

'Yes.' Briony imagined that Lavender was right, but then Lavender said something very shrewd.

'But perhaps you don't want it to mend.'

She stared at her stepmother. 'What makes you say that?'

'Briony, love.' Lavender put out her hand and touched her stepdaughter's fingers. 'It's the way you look, dear, when you talk about this boy.'

'He's my age, Lavender, hardly a boy.'

'Man then. Don't interrupt. You like him, don't you? I can see it in your eyes. He's someone special.'

For a moment Briony stared at her stepmother, her thoughts spinning like wheels on a fruit machine. Which stopped suddenly like an answer falling into place. 'What if I do?' she said bluntly. 'I would never steal my best friend's boyfriend, don't you see.'

Lavender sighed. 'Of course you wouldn't,' she said softly. 'Not on purpose. But maybe you won't have to. I'm a great believer in things happening as they're meant to. After all, look at your father and me. We'd both lost people we loved deeply. You know, I thought I'd never learn to trust a man again. Then along came your father, the most trustworthy man I've ever met, and I'm lucky enough to have him.'

Lavender really loved her father. Briony knew this, of course, but seeing the soft light in the other woman's eyes, she felt a sudden rush of warmth towards her that she'd never felt before.

'And he's lucky to have you.' She smiled at Lavender's pleasure. 'Perhaps I'll keep out of their way as much as possible, then,' she sighed. Though that might not, she privately acknowledged, prove easy to do.

'Did Grandpa Andrews really never talk about any of this, Dad?'

'He died so long ago, but I don't remember him doing so. He certainly didn't want to be interviewed about it for the paper.' Martin finished poking sticks into the wood burner and hauled himself back into his chair.

With the leaping firelight making the cut-glass wall lights sparkle, her father and stepmother's living room was a welcoming place of a winter's evening, especially with Lavender's mushroom risotto and an apple crumble lining the stomach. Briony stroked the fluffy tabby cat that lay stretched on the sofa between her and Lavender, flexing its claws in its sleep.

On the coffee table lay the contents of the box of memories, which she had been going through with her father and Lavender, showing them Sarah and Paul's letters and telling them everything that she'd learned. Of course, Dad had already heard her account of visiting Norfolk and meeting the Andrews and the other Westbury people, but not anything about the letters from Paul. He'd looked through them with amazement.

'That is quite a love story you've uncovered,' he said.

'Yes. I want to know what happened to them. It's so frustrating not to be able to find out.'

'Paul and Sarah,' he said softly. 'Let's go over what we last know of them again. Paul, we've left in the Villa Teresa in Tuana late in 1943. Harry was with him and so was Ivor Richards. Harry obviously returned from Italy alive.'

'So did Ivor, but we don't know about Paul. The records are blank.'

'Surely they'd say whether he died in service or was demobbed.'

'Neither. I can't say definitively, but I'm fairly sure I've searched in the right places.'

'Right.'

'So the last thing we know about Paul is this.' Briony passed her father the note from Paul that she'd found in Harry's memory box.

'*Dearest Sarah . . .*' Her father read it aloud. He turned the scrap of paper over, but the reverse was blank apart from the black smudge that had come through from the front. He shook his head and passed it to Lavender. 'OK, so it seemed that Paul survived and expected to meet up with Sarah. Except it seems that she didn't receive this note that was supposed to have been delivered by Harry.'

'So perhaps she never knew he was coming back. Never saw him again.'

'It would rather suggest it. I'm sorry, love, I know how much you have invested in this.'

'Why wouldn't Harry have delivered it?' she wondered.

'What are the options?' Her father's old journalistic skills were coming into play. 'One, Harry didn't meet up with her for some reason. Two, he forgot to give it to her. Three, he didn't want to give it to her.'

'Why would that be the case?'

'Maybe your father thinks Harry was in love with her,' Lavender spelled out.

'Something like that.'

'Yes.' Briony knotted her brows as she considered this. Nothing in the letters had made her think that. 'Perhaps Ivor leaned on him,' it occurred to her suddenly. 'Ordered Harry not to give it to her.' She tried to imagine a situation in which this might have happened, but it didn't seem possible. Harry had sounded more sympathetic about Sarah to Paul than to Ivor.

'Oh, this wears my brain out,' she sighed.

Her father had brought downstairs the oldest of her mother's photo albums and she began to turn the thick black pages. It was sad, she thought, that there were no photographs of her grandparents' wedding and she wondered why. There were plenty of their daughter, though, Briony's mother. Jean, a tiny bundle, her face peeping out of the folds of a knitted shawl, her mother with her calm face and a halo of fair hair gazing down fondly at her. Crawling, her chubby face one big gap-toothed smile; a toddler with a ribbon tied in her unruly fair hair; with her father at three or four, paddling in the sea. Jean always looked so happy in these photographs, knowing she was precious and loved. That was the kind of person she grew up to be, too, Briony's beloved mother. Briony blinked furiously as distant memories began to flood in. Being taken to view a litter of squirming spaniel puppies in a neighbour's kitchen and her joy when her mother said they were to have one. The scent of hot damp linen as her mother ironed sheets in the steam-filled kitchen with *The Archers* on the radio.

'Briony?'

Briony started and looked up at her stepmother.

'Are you all right?'

'Mmm. Just thinking.' She closed the album, realizing that it might be difficult for Lavender if they dwelled so much on Briony's mother. That must be why she appeared a little wan. Instead she selected one of the old wartime photographs from the box. Her grandfather was recognizable despite the way he screwed his face up against the light. Paul, she supposed, was next to him, a tall dark-haired man with dancing eyes, and that was Ivor, lighter in build and classically handsome with fair hair and regular features, his moulded lips unsmiling. She'd no idea who the other three men were. *The Three Stooges*, it said on the back, which simply wasn't helpful.

It was when she was getting ready for bed that it struck her to investigate the drawer underneath, to see if there was anything further that was relevant to her search. She knelt to edge it open, but there was only the box of her mother's old school books. She pushed the drawer back, then slipped in under the duvet, her feet finding the comforting warmth of the hot-water bottle her stepmother had left there. Dear Lavender. Lying there in the quiet darkness, thoughts of Aruna and Luke returned to haunt her. Perhaps she should have texted Aruna to ask if she was all right, but Lavender might have a point, that she should leave well alone. Would Aruna expect it, though? Briony brooded over the previous night's events, and remembered again the guidebook that she'd found in Aruna's flat. Why had Aruna been looking at it? And it came to her that the answer to the mystery lay in Italy. What had happened in Tuana, in the Villa Teresa, where Paul had last been heard of?

The wartime film footage Mariella had given her! Briony slid out of bed with a shiver, pulled her laptop out of its case and returned to bed with it, hoping that tidy Lavender hadn't switched off the house wifi. No, its symbol above the toolbar glowed steady. The internet drop-file she wanted came up easily and soon she was watching the images that she'd first seen in that stuffy living room on an Italian summer evening. The stricken plane wheeling in the sky, the devastation of the war-torn valley, then in through the gates of the Villa Teresa, through the ruined garden, to where the two men were unloading boxes from a truck. She froze a frame to study their faces, then let it run on to the soldiers playing cards, concluding that three of the cheerful faces were the 'Stooges' from the photo in her grandfather's box. Finally, the pale walls and tiled roof of the villa itself came into view and – who was that? She stopped the film and edged it back a tiny bit. There, in the window. She reached and switched off the bedside light so that the image gleamed more sharply. Could that be Ivor, standing at the window, watchful expression, hands on hips? The face was in shadow, but the man's jacket was buttoned up smartly and he bore himself proudly. Possibly it was him, she reckoned, and moved on. Now, the busy hoe and the gardener working it, the shock again that this was Harry, the springy hair, laughing eyes and tanned narrow face, so like her brother Will's. Definitely her grandfather. But where then was Paul?

The picture flew away in its ragged tail of ribbon and the screen darkened. Once more Briony slid the marker back to the scene where the truck was being unloaded, but though she examined each face again, and those of the card-players, there was no sign of Paul. Perhaps he hadn't been around that day, or – why hadn't she thought of this before? – perhaps he was the cameraman! There had been another occasion when he had been taking the picture, when was that? As she shut down her laptop, laid it on the bedside table and settled down under the duvet, she remembered being with Robyn Clare in her lovely apartment in Westbury Hall studying the photograph of the household in 1939. She'd looked for Paul then in the line-up of family and servants, but Robyn believed that he had taken the picture and could not therefore be in it.

As she lay waiting to fall asleep, Briony remembered the last letter of Paul's that she'd read. It alluded to something terrible that had happened that meant he and Ivor were in trouble. She wondered again what it could possibly be.

Forty

April 1944

The spring brought hope after the long winter in the mountains. Only rarely now did a rime of frost glitter on the mud when Paul stepped out in the early mornings, and this quickly melted away under the fierce young sun. He and Harry and Private Sullivan, one of the Three Stooges, so-called because they'd been billeted together in Naples and since proved inseparable, had started to dig up a plot of land in a sheltered area in the back garden of the villa to grow vegetables, though so far there wasn't much available to plant. He had been watching Harry with some concern, but the man had only suffered one further serious bout of fever, soon after Christmas, and periods of gentle activity in the warming air seemed to be doing him good.

They were two of a dozen men living at the Villa Teresa under Ivor Richards' iron control. A rock-steady Scot named Sergeant John Fulmer commanded another six down in Tuana itself, occupying the Town Hall, where they'd turned the big reception room with its solemn portraits of past dignitaries into an ops room and dormitory, much to the chagrin of the current mayor, a retired bank manager with a distinguished wave of iron-grey hair and a proud, Roman face. His officials were now beset by people from all around with lists of insoluble problems and there was only one small office in which to receive them and nowhere to hold meetings or entertain. Still, the presence of the soldiers at least meant the town received shipments of food and other supplies, though these had been irregular over the hard winter, so it was difficult to do more than grumble.

On this particular April day, Paul and Harry used the last of the petrol to drive a truck down to Tuana. Supplies from Naples had arrived the night before, a welcome relief now that the weather had improved and some of the roads and bridges had been repaired. They assisted in distribution of foodstuffs to the eager, jostling local women, entrusted medical supplies to the nuns at the convent, as there was no doctor now living in the town, and handed out sacks of seed and animal feed to farmers or their widows, with the guidance of local officials.

There was a local boy Paul had seen before, who was fascinated by the British soldiers, and whom the mayor had introduced as his grandson. 'I help, I help,' Antonio said today, his dark eyes flashing. He was fifteen, a tall, athletic, good-looking boy. His father, the mayor's son-in-law, had been taken prisoner by the British, but his family appeared sure that he would eventually return safely. 'I want to fight *la Germania*,' the boy explained, 'but they say too young, too young. So I help you, yes?' He lorded it over the women and children who scrambled for tins and dried goods, upbraiding them if they tried to take too much, which made Paul smile as he ticked items off a list. Inevitably, Antonio would manage to scrounge a few extra items for himself as payment. It was difficult, very difficult, to deny him.

Paul and Harry replenished their petrol tank and packed their truck with the troop's own allocation of rations.

'Was there any post?' Paul asked hopefully of the driver of one of the lorries, a burly Cockney corporal, as he finished unloading goods into one of the storage barns.

'Post? What's that, gov, when it's at home?' With a grin that split his chubby face, he went round to the driver's door, reached behind his seat and brought out a grubby, bulging pouch. Paul seized it, eyes gleaming, carried it along to the Town Hall and tipped the contents out onto a desk. Soldiers crowded round to help sort the parcels and letters, cheered by the sight of these links with home. Paul's heart leaped as he picked out an envelope addressed to himself in a certain familiar handwriting and slipped it into his breast pocket. Harry, he saw, did the same with another, then they stuffed a dozen more letters and packages for the men at the villa back into the bag to take with them.

Outside, they waited as five handcuffed German prisoners were led out of the tiny jail and loaded into one of the lorries. Then the air filled with shouts of farewell as the convoy of vehicles moved on its way back to Naples. Paul gave a coin and a wink to Antonio, then he and Harry climbed back into their own truck.

All the way up the winding lane to the villa, Paul thought of the letter in his pocket, wondering what Sarah would have to say. It was two months since the last one had got through and he hoped that she'd had his reply. Beside him he was aware of Harry taking his own letter out, reading it quietly, then folding it and replacing it again, an uncertain expression on his face.

'Who's it from?' he asked.

'Jennifer,' came the reply, but when Paul asked if there was any news, Harry ignored him, instead shouting out a warning of a particularly large hole in the road.

When they arrived back at the villa, Paul left the Stooges to unpack the truck and, whistling to himself, strolled round to the back garden, where he sat on an old tree trunk, tucked a lighted cigarette between his lips and slit open the letter.

He'd read it through quickly and was thinking about its contents when he heard someone emerge from a door behind. It was Ivor. Paul rose to his feet at once, wary, but the captain had not come to give him an order.

'News from home? Who's that from then?' There had been nothing in the post for Ivor, not even from his mother. Paul almost felt sorry for him.

He folded the letter and said uncertainly, 'It's from Sarah. She's the only one who writes to me.' That wasn't quite true. Very occasionally a postcard from Horst, his chum from Pioneer days, arrived, but he hadn't heard from Horst for several months now and didn't like to think about why.

'I suppose that must be the case, yes,' Ivor said, frowning. Paul did not like the frown, nor the expression of dislike in the other man's eyes. 'She writes to me sometimes, of course. What does she have to say? No, don't worry if it's private.'

It was private, of course, but maybe it was simply news from home that Ivor craved, and it was unkind to deny him that. 'Sarah is well, that is the best thing,' he said, tucking the envelope into his pocket. He would carry it with him for a while, then wrap it up in oilcloth with the others in his kit, a precious packet he'd managed so far to keep dry. 'She is a little worried about her sister, who has not been so good.' Sarah had not mentioned the nature of the illness, merely that Diane had been low in spirits, but becoming a little brighter. That was good. Perhaps she'd recovered from that terrible business with the baby, which Sarah had confided in him about. He sensed from the letter, though, that they were all more cheerful at home now that the war had turned in the Allies' favour.

'A funny sort of girl, Diane.' Ivor leaned against a eucalyptus, filling his pipe. 'Damned pretty, mind you, but deep. Yes, deep.'

'I'm sure you're right.' Paul wasn't going to discuss Diane with Ivor of all people, but it was safe enough to agree with him on that point. Even Sarah couldn't get the measure of her sister. Paul secretly wondered whether Diane was a shallow person rather than a deep one, but she was certainly enigmatic and he sensed her disapproval of him.

Ivor lit the pipe and puffed at it. 'You know ...' he started to say and Paul waited in trepidation. 'No, it doesn't matter.' A cloud of smoke filled the air. 'What was it like in town today, Hartmann? Any trouble to knock on the head?'

'Not really, sir.' Paul emphasized the sir. 'We locked up some of the dry goods as usual. The women find this difficult. They seem to think we're keeping it for ourselves.'

'Ridiculous. I hope you didn't take any nonsense.'

'No, sir, of course not. The mayor's young grandson, Antonio, was there. We asked him to explain to them about rationing it. That we don't know when the next convoy will get through.'

'And the prisoners?'

'Like lambs, sir.'

Paul didn't like the lingering look of dislike. 'I expect you feel sorry for those Jerries, eh, Hartmann?'

'Not particularly, sir. Except that a civilized man should feel pity for any prisoner.'

'What do you talk to them about, eh? Not ways to escape, I hope.' He gave a dry laugh.

Paul paused a moment before he replied. 'Of course not. You know what I do. Deal with any complaints or reasonable requests. Reassure those that are sick.'

'Of course you do, of course you do. I'm watching you though.'

Paul felt rage course through him. He guessed that Ivor didn't seriously believe that he would assist German prisoners to escape, but that he enjoyed tormenting him. He also enjoyed running down the enemy in his presence, calling them pigs and bastards. Paul tried very hard not to take the bait, but every now and then his anger bubbled up. Harry had found him outside the other night, where he had come to let off steam.

They'd stood together under the dark trees, smoking to keep the midges away. Harry had not been able to say much, merely expressing sympathy, but Paul appreciated the fact that he'd tried. Harry being here helped ground him. They could share memories of Westbury, though they'd hardly known one another there. To Harry, Paul had merely been one of the gardeners at the Hall, but now they'd become close friends. Harry's kindness was one of the good things about this war, though he sensed that Ivor despised this virtue in Harry as he despised Harry's malaria and his shellshock as weakness.

'Richards wasn't a bully at school, you know, rather the reverse. He has a sensitive side and the big louts spotted it, went straight for it. Now he's getting his own back on the world, I reckon. You mustn't let him see he's got to you or he'll have won.'

This was sensible advice, but what Paul would never let on to Harry was how much the image of Sarah, conjured in the air between them, fed Ivor's bitter dislike. Harry was too happy-go-lucky, too much the optimist to think badly of anyone much, which was why everyone liked him, but these were also qualities that undermined his authority in the field. Harry was no leader of men and preferred it that way.

That night they'd ended up being joined by the Stooges, chatting and laughing as they stood together in a clearing gazing up at the icy stars, trying to identify the constellations that pierced this foreign sky.

Several nights after Sarah's letter arrived, Paul was woken by a commotion. Someone, Sparky Webster, by the voice, was bidding them get up. 'There's a problem down in Tuana,' he heard the man say. Paul wriggled out of his sleeping bag, pulled on his jacket and felt for his boots. From the other rooms he heard curses as the men scrambled to readiness.

Outside, staring across the valley, Paul saw that the little town was full of dancing lights. A distant crack of gunfire echoed all around, making them hurry. He fired up one of the trucks, Harry the other. The men piled in and they were off, slowly bumping and lurching down the winding track that clung to the hillside, the shaded beams picking out the ruts and potholes. It had been their first job here to clear the route of mines.

When they drove through town a few minutes later, the streets were empty, though lines of light glowed at the edges of many a window shutter. They found two of Sergeant Fulmer's platoon prowling the square, puzzled chaps wondering where their pals were.

'What the hell's going on?' Ivor Richards barked at them.

'We don't know, sir. A lot of noise like running footsteps woke us up,' said one. 'Sergeant Fulmer's having a look-see. Told us to stay here. Something strange is going on, that's for sure.'

'What were the shots about?'

The two men peered at one another in the greyness. 'That was the Sergeant. It was to get everyone off the streets. Don't think anyone got hurt. Anyway, it seemed to work.'

'And which way did Sergeant Fulmer go?' One of the

squaddies pointed past the damaged church towards a gloomy maze of streets beyond.

'You stay here,' Ivor said to Harry, 'with you, you, you and you. Keep order and look after the vehicles. The others come with me. No lights or we'll be walking targets for snipers.'

Paul followed Ivor, rifle at the ready, out of the square down the stony streets where the reflection of moonlight on limewashed walls lit their way. From time to time he was sure he saw a shadow, or heard a scrape of falling masonry, but when he paused to take stock there was nothing. At one point a whisper reached his ear, the sound of frightened breathing, but when he flicked his torch on and off, there was no one caught in the glare, so he wondered if he'd imagined it. He stumbled over rubble, the remains of a portico, followed Ivor round first one corner and then another, then heard his muttered curse. Several figures loomed out of the darkness and he felt the pit of his stomach drop. When he heard Sergeant Fulmer's deep voice call out the password, relief spread through him.

'It's the storage barn, sir,' Fulmer was telling Ivor. 'The doors are locked, but we think they've been in there. Someone swiped our key.'

There was no need to ask who 'they' were. Paul was used to the townspeople being lumped into one suspect mass, 'their' strange customs, 'their' impenetrable language, 'their' passionate emotions, 'their' cunning or cowardice or superstition, this was how Fulmer and Richards spoke to one another about the local people, and most of the soldiers went along with it. Paul did, too, on occasion, when faced with frustration and failure on both sides to understand each other.

They set off once more until the street petered out into countryside. Here stood the black shape of a stone barn with metal doors on which had been set a large padlock. It was inside that supplies of food and seed corn had been locked.

In the absence of a key, Ivor Richards stepped across and ordered Paul to stab down at the padlock with the butt of his rifle and, when this didn't work, he brought out his pistol and shot it apart. He prised open the double doors and a slice of a moon shone in on – nothing. It was empty.

For a moment they stood there amazed. 'How did they get the key?' they asked one another.

'Let's go,' Richards shouted in a voice full of rage. 'The damned idiots. How do they suppose we're going to last till the next convoy?'

Nobody answered. Nobody liked to suggest that perhaps they'd been too hard on the locals, too mean with the rationing, but the difficult winter had made it necessary. Yes, it was hard to see children go hungry, but better to go carefully with what they'd been given, to eke it out with what they'd gleaned from the ruined harvest, the few animals that hadn't been slaughtered or requisitioned. So they'd thought. This was the people's revenge, though perhaps by their theft they were only hurting themselves.

'Right,' Richards said. 'We'll spread out, knock on the doors. Search everywhere. We can't let them get away with this. Round up anyone who gets in our way.'

A low hum of alarm started in Paul's head. They were supposed to be protecting these people who had suffered so much, not treating them as the enemy.

'Get on with it.' Richards' cry was almost a screech. Everybody snapped to attention and set off in groups, muttering to each other as they went. A hammering on doors could soon be heard, the growl of British voices, Italian ones raised in response, the odd squeal of outrage, a baby crying.

'What are you waiting for, Hartmann?'

Paul stared at Richards, then turned on his heel and followed the others. He could hear Richards' angry breathing close behind him. Up and down the streets the soldiers were bringing out boxes of the missing rations. A truck was fetched from the square to load with them. Paul witnessed a woman who would not let go of her stash until a soldier wrenched the packets from her, begging her pardon. At another house the family would not open the door and Harry stood outside arguing with them. Richards snatched Harry's rifle and smashed his way in. The mother and her three terrified young daughters were made to stand in the street as two soldiers fetched the boxes out. Only then were they allowed to return.

'We'll have to drive everything up to the villa,' Richards shouted to one of the Stooges, who was edging the truck up the street. 'Can't trust them with it all down here.'

Hostile eyes followed them everywhere. Paul hadn't felt such enmity from them before, a mute accusation that they were taking food from children's mouths.

'There's someone skulking down there.' Richards led the way along a tight alley with overhanging buildings where the darkness thickened. When they paused, the sound of fleeing footsteps could be heard. 'Who's there? Show yourself!' Richards shouted. The footsteps faded.

'They've gone,' Paul said, hoping Richards would give up, but he was ignored. They rounded a corner and ahead the cobbles glistened with moonlight. A row of pots burgeoning with shrubs lined the wall of a shuttered villa. Paul's eye slid past scattered outbuildings to see the edge of the hillside itself, glimpses of a ruined olive grove, the valley, a pit of darkness, beyond.

A clink, like a loose tile sliding on stone. Richards sank

behind the shelter of the shrubs and Paul followed his example. Light gleamed from the pistol in Richards' hand. 'Sir,' Paul whispered. 'Whoever it is ... they might not be armed.'

'Shh,' Richards interrupted. At the same moment he glimpsed a shadow fly along the ground beyond the end of the alley, heard a pebble bounce. Richards scampered to the corner of the villa, where he pressed himself against the wall and ducked his head round. 'Nothing,' he hissed to Paul. 'Stay back.' Paul saw the man's hand tighten round his pistol. They waited for some time, absolutely still. There was only the sough of the breeze and the faraway bleat of a goat. The light was dimming as cloud wreathed the moon, and then they saw him.

A bulky figure separated itself from the silhouette of an outhouse and set off running along the hill's edge, its strange shape appearing to be caused by the heavy box it was carrying. 'Hey! Stop, you, *presto!*' Richards tore after him, Paul loping in his wake.

The runner, he saw, was only a lad, his head encased in a bandana. He cast a look over his shoulder at his pursuers and it was close enough for Paul to see terror in his great dark eyes. The youth abandoned the box, zigzagged away through the rubble and veered back towards the town and now Paul caught his profile in the brightening moonlight. Recognition struck him like a sickening blow. It was at this exact moment that a gunshot split the night and the boy was lifted briefly into the air before slumping to the ground.

'No, Antonio!' Paul sprinted over to the boy, but there was nothing he could do. The mayor's grandson lay lifeless, blood spreading from the wound in his temple.

He rose slowly and turned to stare, horrified, into Richards' face. The man was deathly pale, his lips raised in a brutish expression, the eyes glittering. Then the colour flowed back and realization softened his gaze. Paul licked his lips and pushed his helmet back with his hand. Richards still held the smoking gun loosely at his side. His hand trembled slightly.

'You ... bastard,' Paul managed to say. For a long moment they stared at one another. Richards was first to break his gaze.

'He was looting. He'd know the price.'

'He was a boy. Just a boy. There is no weapon, where's his weapon?' The Paul he'd once been would have felt a prickle of tears. He badly wanted them to come, to feel human, but instead he simply felt numb. That's what the war had done to him. He dug into his chest pocket for his handkerchief, shook it out and laid it like a shroud over the boy's head, a futile gesture, but he made it all the same. Then he shouldered his rifle and walked away with weary step. Before the streets of the town swallowed him, he glanced behind. Ivor was still standing there motionless, staring down at the body.

Forty-one

Briony closed the door of her car with a weary gesture and looked about her. Westbury Hall was a dour place in December, the wisteria above the entrance a dead thing, the winter trees bordering the car park black and dripping from the misty rain. She shivered, wrapped her parka more closely round her and walked slowly up to the entrance.

'Kemi, hello.' The heavy door shut behind her. It felt surprisingly cosy in the high-ceilinged hallway, where Kemi, seasonal in scarlet skirt and jacket, was hanging gold baubles on a tall, slender Christmas tree.

'Hi, Briony.' Kemi grinned back. She appeared reassuringly the same as ever, except as they exchanged pleasantries her eyes darted continually to her left hand where a ring Briony didn't remember seeing before dazzled out of the gloom.

'Is that new?'

Kemi held out her hand, delighted the ring had been mentioned.

'Last week,' she said proudly. 'We were going to announce it on Christmas, but in the end TJ didn't want to wait.'

'Well, congratulations,' Briony said, thinking she wouldn't have been able to make a decision like that when she had been twenty-one.

'Thank you! You've come to see Mrs Clare, haven't you? She told me.'

Briony had written to the old lady in the end. The reply had been penned in the same flowery hand as the card she'd received from her during the summer, the writing even more quivery than before, but there was nothing shaky about the tone of it. She'd be 'delighted' to see Briony again and so would Lulu, who was 'very grateful' for the time Briony had looked after her. It was extraordinary that Mrs Clare had survived so well the trauma of the summer, she thought, as she knocked on the door of the ground-floor apartment.

It was Avril who inched it open, nudging Lulu back with her foot. 'Come in, won't you? Lulu, bed.' Safely admitted, her parka whisked away by Avril, who withdrew to the kitchen, Briony greeted the wispy-haired old lady who sat in the armchair facing the window. It was a shock to see her, she seemed sunken, diminished, but her blue eyes shone as guileless as before and she had no trouble remembering Briony's name.

'Don't mind if I don't get up.' Mrs Clare's voice was slurred. 'I have to use this wretched thing now.' She touched a walking frame that stood at one side of the chair.

'The pattern on it's very pretty,' Briony said. Someone had wound decorated plastic tape round the metal.

'That's my granddaughter's sense of humour. They sell the stuff in Liberty. Isn't it marvellous what you can get now?'

'Isn't it?' Briony drew up the easy chair positioned nearby and glanced through the window. 'The garden looks colourful with all the berries.'

'I think so, though it's not at its best. Still, I like to sit here and remember.' She sighed. 'I'm afraid I live in the past these days. It all seems much clearer to me.'

They gazed out of the window together onto the dank garden with its winter shrubs and straggly lawn. The shape of it was clearer in winter. It was carved up by four paths that met at a central fountain, the beds that surrounded it spiked with the torsos of rose bushes. Beyond the garden, an arc of trees stood sentinel against pewter skies where rooks drifted like flakes of ash. The bleakness of the scene endowed it with a special beauty and it was pleasant to sit in the warmth with the scent of hot butter and mince pies.

Avril brought in the tray, the delicate tea plates accompanied by miniature paper napkins with scalloped edges and a holly berry design.

'What are you both doing for Christmas?' Briony asked. They talked about families and traditions for a while. Briony bit into pastry that melted in the mouth, tasted the sharpness of fruit and licked icing sugar from her lips as she listened.

Mrs Clare's son and daughter-in-law were coming up and taking her to lunch at a country hotel. Kemi had ordered a few things online on her behalf because she didn't like to go out. 'She is a good girl. Has she told you about her engagement? She brought her young man to meet me. He has some strange name and is rather peculiar-looking, with one of those shaved hair-styles that seem fashionable, but he speaks very nicely.'

Briony managed to hide a smile at Mrs Clare's acidity. When Avril had retreated to the kitchen once more, she asked after Greg, to be told that as far as she knew he was well, but he hadn't been to see her lately. She spoke disapprovingly, which made Briony wonder whether he'd displeased her in some other way. She set down her plate, dusted some sugar powder from her skirt and edged the conversation round.

'I've been doing quite a bit of research since I saw you last. I was sent another collection of letters, you know, this time written by the gardener cousin we talked about, Paul Hartmann, to Sarah Bailey.'

'Letters,' Mrs Clare mumbled through a mouthful. 'I heard something about that.'

'Did Greg tell you?' Briony was surprised.

'Yes. The whole thing has upset his father by all accounts. You know it's all very well this digging around in other's lives, but it doesn't do any good. To some of us it's not history, it's personal. We lived through it. It was a terrible time and some people were put into situations they would never have faced in peacetime and we can't entirely blame them for things they did.'

Briony blinked in surprise at Mrs Clare's heartfelt bitterness. 'Greg's father, he must be older than I thought if he fought in the war.'

'No, no, he was born after it ended, but *his* mother only died a few years ago and he doesn't want the family reputation ripped to shreds.'

'Ripped to shreds. Why should it be?'

'Because of that man Hartmann. Well, what did he have to say for himself in these letters of his?' Robyn Clare fixed her with her watery blue gaze and Briony sensed again the change wrought by her illness. The guardedness had gone, she'd become more direct.

Briony began to explain, haltingly at first, then with more confidence. All the time she watched Robyn Clare, interested to see the surprise in her face.

'Sarah and Paul were friends, but then they fell in love.'

'I didn't know that at the time, though I heard it later. Mrs Bailey was very displeased, I was told, not that I cared about *her* finer feelings. Paul's father was German, you see, even though he was related to my mother.'

'Yes, I know that, but he was totally loyal to Britain. He wanted so much to fight against the regime responsible for his father's death. But Greg's grandfather ...'

'Poor Ivor.'

'... he was jealous of Paul because he loved Sarah too. And Paul was unfortunate enough to find himself in the same unit as Ivor Richards. Ivor became his commanding officer and treated him unfairly.'

'A lot of nonsense. It was Paul who was insubordinate, caused Ivor all kinds of trouble.'

'And you learned that from ... ?'

Mrs Clare's eyes were furious. 'Everyone round here knew it. Ivor had a terrible time, was nearly court-martialled, you know. Think of it, the shame, especially for his poor parents. As it was, he was given a dishonourable discharge. His army career was ruined. All because of that German man. Paul Hartmann.'

'But what happened? What had he done?'

'A young Italian boy was killed. He'd been looting, Ivor said. Something like that. These things happen in wartime, of course, but in this case there were complaints. The boy had been a relative of someone important.'

Briony suddenly remembered the memorial in the church in Tuana. 'Was the boy's name Antonio?'

'I have no idea. All I know is that Ivor hated Paul. Said he'd left him to take the blame.'

Briony frowned, wondering why the young Robyn Clare had had no room for compassion for Paul when, after all, he was her flesh and blood. She thought then of the group of friends she belonged to: Ivor, Jennifer and her brother Bob, Harry and the others. Perhaps the bonds of friendship were stronger than her relationship with this strange distant cousin who'd become the family gardener. That must be it.

'But what exactly had Paul done?'

'What had he done? Lied, I don't know. Gone against the word of his commanding officer.'

'Do you know the circumstances?'

'No. Too long ago and it wasn't spoken about. Major and Mrs Richards were devastated, we could see that. You have to understand how it all was. So many families had suffered loss. Others came back from the war having experienced things beyond ordinary comprehension. The only thing to do was to carry on as normal. There wasn't all this talking nonsense that there is today. It wouldn't do any good going over and over the unpleasantness. No, people tried to put it behind them and continue their lives as best they could.'

'What happened to them all after the war?' she asked and Mrs Clare's eyes clouded.

'Initially we were simply relieved that the war in Europe was over, that Hitler was dead, but then the news came out about those dreadful camps, and the fighting was still going on in the Far East and there were the hydrogen bombs in Japan.' Mrs Clare was rambling now. 'Many local men had been sent over there and many of them never came back. There was poor Bob Bulldock, who came back from Germany in 'forty-four ...'

'And Paul? And Ivor? The Baileys?'

'Dear oh dear, you do ask a lot of questions. My mother discovered my father's affair with That Woman and we didn't come down here much. Then all of a sudden we heard that *she* was marrying again, she'd taken up with one of her husband's old army pals, some old lover of hers, I wouldn't be surprised. She moved to Suffolk, I believe. Didn't want to be too far from her daughter.'

'You mean Sarah?'

'No, no, Diane, of course. A funny girl, Diane. I'm sure I have the wedding photograph somewhere. Stand-offish until the day she died. I can't think why Ivor married her.'

By the time Briony left Mrs Clare the light was beginning to fail and the ground beneath her feet already crackled with frost. Away to the west, beyond the village, billowing cloud cover was blushing a peachy orange. She had a two-hour drive back to London before her, longer if the traffic was sticky, but something held her here. Perhaps she'd take a little walk first.

Loneliness tracked her like a black dog's shadow as she followed the path down towards Westbury Lodge where she'd stayed four months before. It was shut up, forlorn, it seemed to her, as she peered through the windows, thinking all sorts of thoughts about Paul who'd lived there once, about Luke and Aruna and the laughter they'd shared, about Greg, who'd come to find her.

Greg. She wondered if she'd ever see him again, whether she wanted to. So his grandmother had been Diane Bailey. When Mrs Clare had told her, she'd been stunned into silence. It was odd that he'd never mentioned Diane's name and she wondered why. How had the marriage come about? Can't get one girl, marry the sister, that was not uncommon in life. Briony thought about the photograph Mrs Clare had found for her in an old album. Diane had been pretty, in a doll-like way, with large, wide-spaced eyes and a tiny mouth in a heart-shaped face as she hung on Ivor's arm. Ivor, in a civilian suit, looked proud as he faced the world, but Briony wondered what they were each thinking behind their smiles for the camera.

What was that? A movement at an upstairs window broke her thoughts. She caught her breath, but then she knew it for the reflection of a tiny bird. There it was, behind her, flitting from tree to tree. This place spooked her. She moved on.

The door to the walled garden creaked open and she stopped, first astonished and then dismayed. The smooth summer lawns had been torn up as though by a giant mole. More likely a digger. Greg and Luke had been at work. To one side lay a pile of brand new pipes, blocking the path. The irrigation system, waiting to be laid. Why was Greg doing this? It must be expensive for a pet project. She remembered his plan for a nursery and a farm shop. For a while she stared round at the desolate scene, then turned away. She didn't belong here any more. Where did she belong?

As she pulled the gate to, the softness of the light drew her further along the path towards a copse of trees. She guessed where this led and suddenly she wanted to see it. She walked on and there it was, the pond, dark and sullen, the willows bending over it like mourners trailing their hair. A stench of something rotten, stagnant, made her nose wrinkle. It was only of vegetation, she told herself, the breakdown of dead leaves and muddy water. She remembered the story of the child who'd drowned here, Robyn's brother, little Henry, and she shuddered. Perhaps it had been an enticing place to a small boy then, with trees to climb and glimpses of the speckled backs of fish, a flick of a tail on the surface. It would have been easy to lean too far from an overhanging branch and to slip ... She could see him in her mind's eye, his small head disappearing, his feet sinking in the deep mud at the bottom, weeds catching at him, drawing him down to darkness and silence.

She'd turned to go when her phone vibrated in her coat pocket. She dug it out, surprised that there was a signal, and read the caller's name with shock, let it ring twice, three times, before she found the will to answer. 'Hello?' The phone was cold against her ear. 'Aruna?'

'Are you alone?' Aruna's voice sounded accusing.

'Yes,' she said slowly. 'I'm in Westbury actually. What about you?'

'Westbury? Why?' Aruna asked, ignoring Briony's question.

'I've just seen Mrs Clare. She's recovering from her stroke and said she'd see me.'

'Still chasing red herrings?'

'Yes, if you mean Paul and Sarah. Nothing fishy about them as far as I know.' Where was this conversation going?

'I should say thank you for helping me the other night. I was a bit out of it.'

Out of it was an understatement 'You were upset, you poor thing.'

'I suppose you knew what it was about.'

'Your mum told me the bare bones and then you mumbled a few things. Otherwise, no, I don't know the details. Aruna, I think I may understand what you're getting at, but it's simply not true.'

'What? What isn't true? How can you know what I'm talking about?'

'Hang on, this is getting way too complicated. Are you OK?' She was sure she had heard a snivel. 'Oh, Aruna, I'm sorry.'

'Why did you do it?'

'Why did I do what?'

'Take him away from me.'

'Aruna, this is nonsense. I didn't. I haven't done anything. Except exist. That's all I've done. I don't know what Luke has told you, but nothing has happened between us. I've been trying to stay away from him so that nothing did.' She realized instantly that this confession was unwise.

'So you did know how he felt. You must have done something to make him feel that way.'

'I can't think what, I'm sorry.'

'Is that all you can say, that you're sorry.'

'I don't mean sorry in that I'm guilty of anything, just sorry in that I am sad about what's happened. I hate it that you're unhappy.'

'You knew how important he is to me. I told you.'

'Yes, you did. And I was happy for you, that you'd found someone.'

'I expect you were jealous.'

'No. I really wasn't. It may not be normal, I don't know, but I was pleased for you. Genuinely. You were my friend.' Were. 'Are.'

There was a silence, followed by another snivel.

'Aruna, it's really not my fault and I don't know how I can mend things. It's between you and him and since I don't even know what he said to you ...'

'He said ... just that, oh God, that he had tried to think of us being together the rest of our lives and he couldn't do it any more.' Aruna started to sob.

'Where are you now? Still at your mum's?'

'No, I came back to London. I have work, don't I, not that I can concentrate much at the moment.'

'Do you want me to come round? I should be back home early evening.'

'I'm going out for a meal with Mike and Zara. And I ... if he ...'

Aruna's voice had begun to fade in and out. 'The signal's bad. What did you say after Mike and Zara?'

'I asked Luke if he wanted to come, but he didn't.'

'Oh, Aruna.' She remembered how her friend had thrown all his possessions out of her window and felt embarrassed that Aruna could misread Luke that much to think he might want to make up. Briony knew he wouldn't, that Aruna shouldn't have treated Luke like that. And the realization that she knew Luke intuitively, better than Aruna, finally made her feel guilty. Aruna's voice wavered in and out of hearing. 'I'm losing you,' Briony spoke into the handset, but she was talking to a slab of glass and metal. She waited in case Aruna rang back, then tried to call her, moving about to pick up the signal, but to no avail. Finally, she pocketed the phone, feeling miserable. Aruna didn't want to see her and blamed her for the break up and yet ... There was something else, too. It was that it didn't sound as though Briony had figured as much as she had feared in Luke's parting with Aruna. On the one hand that made her feel less responsible, but on the other it made her wonder if she was wrong to imagine Luke's feelings ... Except Aruna had accused her of—

'Damn,' she said aloud and squeezed her eyes tight shut for a moment in an attempt to banish her spinning thoughts.

From a nearby bush a bird started to sing, a beautiful full-throated liquid sound, its evening aria, then, looking about, she glimpsed him, a cock robin, whose beady gaze rested on her as she listened. All around, the twilight deepened, birds sang in distant trees as they settled for the night. Clouds were thickening overhead. It was time to go.

It was while she was on the motorway back to London, hunched forward in her seat to see past heavy rain blurring the windscreen, that Briony realized another source of unease. She hadn't had a chance to ask Aruna about the guide to Tuana and her interest in Antonio's memorial. How had Aruna learned about the link between Paul and Ivor and Antonio? Perhaps it was connected to the man in the car who had spoken to her outside the Villa Teresa that day. Aruna, being a journalist, would not have been able to resist following the scent of a good story.

Forty-two

Briony was late into college on Monday morning after a break-fast meeting with her publisher, and two young female students with rucksacks on their backs were sitting on the bench outside her office like patient snails, bleary-eyed from the long term.

Inside, she sifted quickly through the post she'd snatched from her pigeonhole, noting a cheap white envelope addressed in a familiar round hand, before dumping it all on her desk as the first of the students entered. She sat down tentatively on the sofa, laying her essay on the coffee table. Briony joined her with an inward sigh, picked up the pages and began to read.

Although the girl's written work was always excellent, with her pale mask of make-up and voice too tiny to hear well, the advice she most needed was to have faith in herself. It might have been her own younger self sitting there, Briony mused, and resolved to give this girl the support that a lecturer had once given her. 'Trust yourself,' the woman had urged her. 'You have grown strong wings, now fly.' It wasn't so much the words themselves as the sense that the woman was there encouraging her, believing in her. This was the legacy she could pass on to her own students. She smiled at the girl and congratulated her on her work, and for a moment the young woman's nervous expression was transformed by a smile.

At lunch break – a sandwich at her desk – Briony closed the door against visitors and finally, fingers trembling a little, slit the flimsy envelope and pinched open the single slip of paper inside. The message was short, but it was enough. There was a telephone number given. For a moment her hand hovered over the handset on her desk, then she snatched up the receiver and pressed the buttons. When the call was answered, there was some scuffling at the other end before a quavery old man's voice spoke. A voice she knew from the tapes in the Norfolk Record Office.

Derek Jenkins lived on the third floor of a small block of flats on a modern estate Briony reached by the Central line going east towards Essex.

'Hold on, I'm coming.' A muffled voice, then a frail man in his eighties with shaking hands admitted her to the stuffy cheerfulness of his living room.

'Nice to see children having fun,' she said. A picture window looked out on a green where toddlers played on a blue-and-red climbing frame while mums laughed and chatted close by.

'It's as good as the telly, isn't it? Even me grandsons are grown up now and I miss having kids around. Me and the wife, we wanted lots of them, but in the end only our Lindsay came along.'

'How many grandsons do you have?'

'Just the two, Euan and Ashley. That's them.' Derek nodded at some framed photographs on a narrow mantelshelf above an electric coal-effect fire that whirred away quietly. One of the young men wore a mortar board and black gown, the other, a real rogue, grinned from his seat astride a huge motorbike, the helmet under his arm.

'You must be proud of them,' she said.

'I am. If only Pat was still around to see 'em. Ten years she's been dead and I miss her every day.' He hobbled over to the huge television, which dominated a corner of the room, and indicated another photograph hanging on the wall nearby. 'Can you lift it down?' he asked, 'I'll only drop it.'

She obliged and together they examined the colour print of a friendly-looking woman, somewhat stout, sitting behind a garden table spread with sandwiches and an elaborately decorated birthday cake. 'That was her seventieth,' Derek sighed. 'And the next year she was gone.'

Briony murmured how sad this was and obediently returned the photograph to its hook. Leaning attentively in the easy chair where he bade her sit, she learned through gentle questioning about Derek's life, his mother's death in a bombing raid, his eventual return to London to live with his father, how he gave up school at sixteen for a series of jobs he hated, the short, failed marriage before he met Pat, then forty years as a telephone engineer. 'I can't say I liked every moment of it. I stuck with it for Pat and Lindsay's sake. But you haven't come because of any of that. You want to know how I got the letters.' He fixed her with his bright-eyed gaze.

Briony nodded and he settled back in his chair and closed his eyes. For a moment Briony was worried that she'd tired him, but then he opened them, glanced at the portrait of his wife Pat as though to seek her reassurance and began to speak.

'I liked Miss Sarah the best of them, apart from Mrs Allman the cook, she was very motherly. Mr Allman had died in the Great War and they'd never had any kids theirselves. She used to say it was like having her own boy, looking after me. As for

Mrs Bailey, she did her best, that's all I can say. She was good to me in her own way, but she didn't like it if I cried and she had quite a tongue in her head. She wasn't used to boys who walked mud into the house and were hungry all the time. Miss Diane was dainty and pretty in the way of one of them china dolls she kept in her bedroom. But my mate Alf's ma said Miss Diane wasn't right in the head, so I stayed out of her way.'

Forty-three

Derek had liked it in the country well enough, though he was frightened of the noises at night, the creak of the floorboards and the strange cries, that Alf told him were devils, but which Miss Sarah said were foxes. Foxes being strangled more like.

They'd been very kindly to him when the news came. It had been 1943, just before Christmas; he'd hated Christmas for years afterwards. It had been a direct hit; his mum would have been killed at once, his dad told him when he came down to see him, as if that was a consolation to a young boy who'd lost the person he loved most in all the world. His dad told him to be a brave big boy and to stay with the Baileys because he was working nights and sleeping at his sister's in the day, and what with her kids, too, there wasn't room for Derek. And so he'd stayed in Westbury until the end of the war when his dad found them lodgings and wanted him home. Thirteen he was and settled in Westbury, but he hadn't any choice. You did what your dad told you then.

Miss Sarah said she'd come up in the train with him and

make sure he met up with his father. She took a small suitcase with her, said that she'd stay with her aunt, make a proper trip of it.

She hadn't spoken much on the train, but had stared out of the window at the passing landscape, her eyes dreamy with her thoughts, some of which must have been happy ones, for then she smiled, but at other times when he glanced up from his comic she appeared troubled. He wondered what she was going to do in London, but wasn't bold or interested enough to ask. Boring old shopping, he supposed. Women liked to shop. He remembered the battlelight in his mother's eyes when she arrived home with a bargain, and blinked away tears at the memory.

When they reached Liverpool Street Station, his dad wasn't there so they hung about a bit on the station concourse, then Miss Sarah said he was to look after their cases while she went to the convenience.

Derek waited with the luggage, his own holdall, Sarah's suitcase and, over his shoulder, a long-handled cotton shopping bag of the same dull brown as his jacket. From this she'd extracted a vacuum flask and a greaseproof paper packet of sandwiches which they'd shared for their lunch on the train. He watched Sarah's sturdy figure disappear into the ladies' waiting room and continued to scan the crowds for a jaunty bow-legged man with his hat pushed back above an open face, but Dad was nowhere to be seen. Hanging above the concourse was a great clock with heavy roman numerals that marked the time with ponderous hands. Dad was already fifteen minutes late. Derek watched a pigeon alight on top of the clock and set about cleaning its wings.

A slurred male voice behind him made him jump: 'Hey,

young man,' and he turned to see a stranger, some gent who must be down on his luck, for he was ill-shaven with dark circles under his eyes and wore an ill-fitting suit and cheap shoes. Derek's nose wrinkled at the alcoholic fumes on his breath.

'You're with Miss Bailey. C'n you give her this?' Despite the slurring, there was something about his voice that made him think of Westbury. He glanced at the crumpled envelope the man held out and drew back. The bloke wasn't wearing gloves and Derek felt a shudder of revulsion at the livid scars across his hand.

'She'll be back in a minute, sir. You can give it to her yourself,' but the man's eyes darted nervously in the direction Miss Sarah had gone.

'No, that wouldn' do. Jus' give it t' her, there's a go' lad.'

Derek had been drilled to be polite to his elders so he accepted the envelope. When the bloke rummaged in the pocket of his trousers and brought out a coin, he received it automatically. Then the man tipped a finger to his hat brim in a clumsy salute and stumbled away.

'Sir, who shall I say ...?' Derek called, but the man merely gave a dismissive swipe of the hand before he was swallowed by the crowd. A minute later, Miss Sarah could be seen walking quickly towards him. She reached his side smelling lightly of a flowery scent as though she'd visited some foreign land.

'Still no sign of your father then?'

He shook his head and held out the letter he'd been given.

'Where did you get this?' She examined her name on the front and her blue eyes rounded and her cheeks drained of colour. He thought she hardly heard his explanation. He watched her slit it open with her thumb, pinch open the scrap of paper inside and heard her sharp intake of breath as she read it. Her eyes met his, unfocused, then she craned to see the great clock where the first pigeon had been joined by another. Dad was twenty-five minutes late now and his heart fluttered like the birds' wings.

'Derek!' His dad was barrelling towards him out of the crowd, a short, heavily built man in working clothes. He ran, felt Dad's rough hand round his shoulders and pressed his face briefly against his father's coarse cheek.

Sarah came over, a wild look in her eyes. 'Mr Jenkins, we're very glad to see you.' She held out her hand and his dad shook it.

'Much obliged to you, miss, and beggin' pardon for the lateness. An unexploded bomb in Lime Street, and the bus weren't goin' nowhere. Shanks's pony all the way and my chest ain't too good.'

'He walked, Miss,' Derek explained, seeing her puzzled expression. 'Did the bomb go off, Dad?' he said in a nervous voice, thinking again of his mother.

'I'm dreadfully sorry to be rude,' Miss Sarah cut in,' but I have to go. Derek, be a good boy, won't you? I'm sure we'll meet again some day.'

'It's very good of you to 'ave 'ad 'im,' his dad said.

'It was a pleasure, always a pleasure,' she said, and bent and kissed Derek, and again, that flowery scent and he felt himself blush. Then she took up her suitcase and was off, the crowd parting for her busy figure to pass. She was gone.

'She was in a hurry,' his dad said, a little affronted.

'I thought you weren't coming,' he whispered, glancing up at his dad and, to his shame, he felt tears flood his eyes. He dashed them away with his hand and as he did he felt the weight of the bag on his shoulder and a tremor of horror passed through him.

'Dad, she's forgotten her bag.'

'That's a shame. What's in it?'

They opened it and peered in. There was the battered

vacuum flask, something wrapped in cloth that turned out to be a pair of shoes, much repaired, and underneath, a cardigan wrapped round something that felt like a book. Nothing valuable then.

'Women's things. We'd better take it with us, I suppose. Come on, nipper, or I'll be late for work.' He seized Derek's suitcase and laid a guiding arm around his shoulder. 'It's just you and me now, but we'll do our best, eh?'

'And he did do his best,' the old man Derek told Briony. 'Until the lung cancer took 'im. Just like it took King George. Dad were proud of that, strange, innit? Lived just long enough to see the Queen's coronation on the telly. I rented it for 'im special cos 'e couldn't make it to the Mall. We sat and watched it together.'

Briony smiled to picture this, then she said, 'But what about the letters?'

'They were in Miss Sarah's bag, but we didn't find them till months later. Dad washed out the thermos, but the bag hung behind the door of our room till we got used to it being there. We kept meaning to get it back to her, but somehow it never happened. Then one day when we were on the move again, I took a proper look inside. Found the box wrapped up in the cardigan, but it was all too late then.'

'Too late?'

'Time had sorter passed on. You remember being fourteen.'

'Yes,' Briony sighed. She did remember, but not in the way he meant. She'd been that age when she'd lost her mother.

'It was years and years before I went back to Westbury. And by then the Baileys were long gone from Flint Cottage. There is one thing, though, that always puzzled me. That bloke at the station. When he went off, he threw something away on the ground. I picked it up.'

'What was it?'

'A train ticket. To Westbury.'

Briony was silent for a moment. 'Why is that important?' she said finally.

'He'd bought a ticket, but didn't use it.'

'Oh, I see.' She was still puzzled. Then she opened her bag and said, 'Mr Jenkins, I know it's a long time ago, but do you recognize any of these Westbury men?' And she handed him the photograph of Ivor, Paul and her grandfather Harry that she had brought with her from her grandfather's box.

Mr Jenkins peered at it frowning, changed his spectacles and examined it again. He started to speak, then paused and looked up at her with a shrewd expression. 'I can't be certain,' he said, pointing to one of the men, 'but I think that's him. The gent I met on the station that day.'

Her eyes widened. 'Paul Hartmann?'

'No, my dear. That one's Hartmann. I remember him all right, but it wasn't him that day.'

Briony took the photograph back, examined it and stared up at the old man, unable for a moment to understand what this meant.

'You'd better keep clear of Westbury. You're not wanted there, do I make myself clear?' Ivor's last words to him at the demob station still rang in Paul's mind as he watched the passing English countryside through the grimy window of the train.

'What did you say?' he asked Harry, who had finally stirred from the stupor into which he'd fallen as soon as the train had started. Paul had noticed with compassion how the rays of sunlight playing on his friend's face emphasized the lines around his eyes, the shadows of exhaustion. Then, ignoring the high-spirited banter of the others in the carriage, he had retired into his own thoughts as the train bore them on towards London.

'Have you decided?' Harry's bleary eyes were on him. 'What'll you do.'

'You heard our friend Richards,' Paul said, leaning back in his seat. 'I don't see much point in returning to Westbury. It would only cause trouble.' They'd send on his mother's paltry possessions if he asked, he supposed. Once he had an address for them to be sent to. Otherwise his pay would keep him going for a short while until he found a job.

'You'll have a hard time here being a Jerry. No references from Sir Henry after what happened. Go home to Germany, Hartmann.' Ivor's voice sneered inside Paul's head.

To some extent Ivor was bluffing, he sensed that, but there was a strong likelihood of truth in everything he said, too. He wouldn't feel comfortable going back to Westbury, but he didn't know where else to go. And if Sarah's feelings about him had changed after what had happened ... although even Ivor hadn't been so low as to make such a judgement ... then he'd be on his own. A German on his own in London after a bitter war, especially with all the shocking news coming out of his homeland now ... how could they, his own countrymen ...?

'I'll find some digs in London,' he told Harry. 'Don't worry about me.'

Harry studied him without emotion. His hand went to his chest, feeling for a front pocket that wasn't there in this new suit, then he rolled his eyes and searched inside the jacket instead, finally locating his cigarettes. Paul took one from the proffered packet and for a while they both smoked in silence.

'I tell you what,' Harry said finally. 'I'll stay in London a few days. We'll go about together, shall we? Have a few drinks. I don't feel ready to go home yet.'

'I don't mind if we do that,' Paul said, though the pain and desperation in the other man's eyes disturbed him. The war had changed Harry more than any of them.

They shared a gloomy room in a cheap hotel in Earl's Court. It wasn't much with its view of the back of another building, its bare floorboards and the ever-present smell of boiled cabbage wafting up the stairs, but it would do.

'We won't be here much, look at it that way,' Harry said as he dumped his bag onto one of the rickety beds. 'Shall we try that club round the corner first?'

Paul remembered the suspicious way the proprietress had glanced at him with her darting eyes and pursed lips, and he gave the wardrobe door, which fell open all the time, another kick. He couldn't help comparing the room with the humble attic he and Sarah had shared in Kensington and his heart ached for that night of happiness that seemed so long ago. 'I'll meet you there in an hour,' he told Harry, 'I have something to do here first'.

When Harry had left, he went down and bought some writing paper, envelopes and a stamp from a very old lady who answered when he rang the bell on the desk. Upstairs, he borrowed the bulb from the ceiling light, fitted it into the bedside lamp and in its circle of meagre light wrote to Sarah. It was so long since he'd heard from her and he had no way of knowing whether she'd received his letters, so he was unsure what to say; then after much thought he whittled the pencil end to a new sharpness with his penknife and decided to keep it simple.

My dearest Sarah,

   I hope I'm right to send this to Westbury as I'm not sure where you are now. I hope that your mother might forward it. As you can see from the address I'm back in London and would

*very much like to see you. I will be here for a few days at least,
but after that letters can be sent poste restante in the usual
way. Needless to say, I feel exactly the same about you as ever
(and dare to hope you still feel the same about me!). I think of
you with love every day.*

    *I trust that your mother and sister are both well. I assure
you that I am in good health and full of hope for the future –
our future!*

    I remain yours,

    Paul xxxx

He read this over, altered the second 'hope' in the third line
to 'imagine', breathed a brief prayer as he folded it into the
envelope and licked the stamp. If he didn't hear back over the
following few days then he'd have to think about what to do
next. As far as he knew, the Baileys still didn't have a telephone.

On his way to meet Harry he dropped the letter into a post-
box that leaned like the Tower of Pisa from a cratered pavement.

It was early afternoon, three days later, that he returned to the
hotel from the labour exchange, where he'd spent a fruitless
morning queuing only to be treated with rudeness by the
matronly woman behind the desk when he reached the front
of the queue. He knocked softly and opened the door of their
room, to find that Harry was still sound asleep and snoring, and
the room smelled rancid. Paul regarded him morosely, but then
everything for him was coloured by the dismal fact that though
he asked downstairs on every possible occasion if there were any
letters or telephone messages, he had not heard back from Sarah.

His bed gave a monstrous creak as he sat down on it, which
caused Harry to stir. He blinked in the dim daylight, then
noticed Paul and pushed himself up to sitting with a groan.

'Wha' time is it?' Harry's forehead, Paul saw, gleamed with moisture.

'Two.'

'Have you been out?'

'Yes. No luck. As soon as they see my papers ...'

'Cretins.'

'No, I understand. It's to be expected.'

'You're a better man than I am, Hartmann.'

'No, I'm not. Listen, Harry. Last night, well. You can't carry on like this. You've got to go home. Your folks will be wondering what's happened to you.'

'They won't.' This said in a distant voice.

'Haven't you informed them you're back?' Paul, who had no family now, was shocked.

Harry muttered some excuse, then rubbed his nape with a shaky hand and yawned loudly. He eased himself out of bed, pulled on his trousers, dislodged a ragged towel from the end of his bed and shambled off to the bathroom. In his absence Paul lifted open the window and stood in the welcome draught of fresh air listening to the sounds of the city and thinking of all the reasons why Sarah would not have answered his letter. *One, maybe she hadn't received it.* She was away possibly. Or ill. Or ... No, he'd have heard if it had been that. *Two, she had received it but she didn't want* ... Hell, his mind didn't wish to go there either. He sighed sadly and turned back to survey the room. It was a horrible place, he hated it and the proprietress hated him, he could tell from her refusal to meet his eye now when he spoke to her. The sooner he moved, the better, but he didn't dare yet in case Sarah tried to contact him. And then there was Harry.

If he stopped being obsessed with his own concerns for long enough, then he had to admit that he was worried about Harry. They'd both taken their fill of drink over the last few days. He'd followed Harry from a bar in the servicemen's club to pub to dance palace and nightclub in his friend's restless quest to lose himself in noisy crowds and alcohol.

Last night, he distinctly remembered sitting glumly on a bar stool in a club downstairs in Piccadilly watching Harry, tight as a butcher's boy, count precious notes out onto the counter to buy whiskies for a load of squaddies and their girls whom he'd never met before in his life, and who would undoubtedly melt away once their benefactor's money ran out. Paul had lost his patience before it got to that point, though, seizing Harry by the collar and marching him out. The walk home in the cool night air should have sobered him up, but he'd been too far gone for that and Paul had ended up half carrying him back to the hotel.

Harry returned from the bathroom, looking slightly the less worse for wear. Rather than hang around while he dressed, Paul took up his hat. 'I'll see you at the place on the corner,' he remarked, referring to the greasy spoon they'd eaten in regularly, and left.

In the café, he ordered fish and chips and when it arrived he ate it slowly, but by the time his plate was empty Harry still hadn't appeared, so he paid the bill and returned to the hotel. There was no one on the desk in the hall when he passed, but he was too concerned about Harry to think of ringing the bell again to ask if there was any post for him, so he took the stairs two at a time and tried the door. It opened, and he was relieved to see Harry there just sitting on the bed. He'd dressed and combed his hair and held his hat in his hand. He glanced up at Paul's entrance and said gravely, 'You're right, of course. I've decided to go home.'

'I'm glad,' Paul said, surprised but relieved at the same time. As he watched Harry slowly pack, he came to a decision. 'Would you take a letter for me?'

'Is it for Sarah? Yes, of course.' They hadn't discussed the matter at all, but then they didn't need to. Harry knew how much Paul's mind dwelled on her.

'I want to be sure it reaches her. If you have a chance to go to Flint Cottage and give it to her yourself ... into her own hand, then at least I'll know ...'

Harry nodded, so Paul took a fresh piece of paper, thought for a moment, then quickly scribbled a few lines on it. He sealed it in an envelope. Harry rose and took it and slipped it into his inside pocket.

They smoked a final cigarette together and spoke desultorily of this and that. It was hard to part after so long a time they'd spent together, so many hardships shared, so often that each had helped the other.

'I will see you again?' Paul said, but when he glanced up he was surprised to see that Harry's eyes shone bright with unshed tears.

'Of course, old man, of course,' Harry said. They shook hands very firmly and clapped each other on the back.

'Convey my regards to ... everyone,' Paul said and Harry nodded, pressing his lips together firmly.

Then, without looking back, Harry took up his case and left, closing the door quietly behind him. All the warmth of the room went with him.

The very same evening, Paul was faced by the furious proprietress when he came back to the hotel after his meal. 'So your friend's gone now, has he? Well I want you out too in the morning. We didn't go through six years of hell to have one of you living here. If my sister ever hears I took in a Jerry, I'd never know the last of it, what with my nephew dead and gone. Out, I say, out.'

It was the venom in her voice that was worse than the words

themselves. Paul opened his mouth to say that he too had fought for this country, he'd risked his life time and time again, but the expression of hatred in her eyes told him it would be no good, she wouldn't listen.

Hamburg. It was that simple word in his identity documents together with the soft consonants of his accent that held him back here. He had no family who wanted him, his home city lay in ruins, he had no job and, worst of all, he feared he'd been abandoned by the woman he loved.

Reaching his room, he threw himself down on his bed in the gathering darkness and struggled against despair. Not everyone was like the woman downstairs, he told himself. There would be somewhere he could go to live and find work, he simply wasn't sure where it was yet. If only he could speak to Sarah. Never had he felt so lost, not even in the dark days after his mother's death. Despite all attempts to keep it at bay, deep loneliness overwhelmed him. It seemed that the whole world had rejected him. Eventually he did the only thing he could think of, something he hadn't done for years. He got down on his knees by the bed, folded his hands and tried to pray, whispering the old words from his childhood. He waited, but there came no answer and he wondered if anyone was up there listening anyway. Still, he felt more calm.

After a moment, he became aware of a hardness digging into his knee, the head of a nail, he saw, and in shifting painfully, almost lost his balance. He shot out a hand to steady himself and it hit something solid under the bed. His suitcase. He dragged it out, thinking at least he could pack and be ready for the morning.

It was a cheap affair that they'd given him at the demob centre, made of a material akin to thick cardboard. He set it down onto the bed, sprang the catches and opened the lid. His few possessions were there, a couple of books, the framed photograph of his parents that had accompanied him across continents among them. He wrapped the photo up safely in a sweater, then went to the wardrobe and began transferring the few clothes he had; socks, spare underwear, a shirt he'd bought using a few precious tokens. He jammed the wardrobe door shut then opened a drawer, took out his hairbrushes and shaving kit, felt for his notebook and sat down hard on the bed in surprise.

There was a wad of paper caught between the pages of the notebook, an identity card, he discovered, and a folded document. Puzzled, he opened the card to see Harry's photograph staring out at him. He'd left them behind. Why? An uncomfortable feeling began to grow inside him. He examined the passport and found a slip of paper tucked in it like a bookmark. The scrawled writing was unmistakably Harry's.

I won't need these any more, so make what use of them you can. Sorry, old man, I'm not as tough as you are. Harry.

Sarah's taxi was crawling west along the King's Road before she realized that she'd left her canvas bag with Derek and a bolt of dismay shot through her. The letters, her precious box of letters! Since she'd planned to stay with her aunt for several nights, she'd brought them with her for comfort. She leaned forward to tell the driver to turn back, then checked herself. They'd be long gone now, Derek and his father. Her mind whirled, then she sat back in her seat, trying to calm herself by smoothing out the note that Harry had left for her; according to what it said, the unknown man at the station had been Harry. It should be possible to get her letters back, surely someone would know the Jenkins' new address. She had visions of herself walking the streets of the East End trying to find them. *A few days*, that was how long Paul said in the note he would be at the hotel, and the date on it was two days before. Suppose she missed him? The traffic was moving so slowly. She refolded the note and tried to relax.

Paul. She hadn't heard from him for several months, and now Ivor had come home with a horrible tale. There had been rumours and in the end she'd confronted him about them. Paul had disobeyed Ivor, his senior officer, and ended up getting them both into deep trouble with the authorities. The people in the little Italian town where they'd been stationed had risen up against the garrison, refused to cooperate with them any longer. There was a story about a boy who'd got shot, and Ivor was vague about this. Paul might have been to blame. To be honest, Sarah didn't entirely understand Ivor's story, there was some false note to it, but he'd refused to discuss it any further. The war was behind them now, over, and everyone was trying to pretend that things could go back to normal. Normal, *pah*. She'd been glad to have an excuse to get away for a night or two. Her mother was fidgety, Diane was fidgety. But Paul was back safe in England. Her heart soared

She leaned and tapped on the glass and the driver slid back his square of window. 'Can't you go by a side street or something?' she asked.

'Sorry, lady, not till after the next junction.'

She sat back and closed her eyes, trying to stay calm, then opened them and glanced at Paul's note once more. He mentioned a letter he'd sent her a few days ago. She'd never received it, which was odd, but then the post was odd sometimes.

Inch by inch they moved forward, past the roadworks, then finally they were through and the driver was swinging the car right down a long shadowy street. Sarah's heartbeat quickened and she felt light-headed with anticipation.

*

The hotel was a shabby place crushed between a flyblown café and a boarded-up shop. A sign that read *vacancies* swung on its nail as she pushed the door open, somewhat gingerly. Her shoes scraped on dirty floorboards and the odour of cabbage added to her disgust. This was a place of a different order to the hotel in South Kensington where she'd stayed with Paul all that time ago. At least that had been clean.

An old harridan with gimlet eyes glanced up from behind the narrow desk where she was adding up a column of figures on a scrap of paper and fixed on Sarah in disbelief. 'Yes?' she said suspiciously.

'I'm looking for a friend who's staying here.'

'A *friend*, is it? What's the name of this *friend*?' She brought out a grimy guestbook from a drawer and began to leaf through it.

'Hartmann, Paul Hartmann.'

'Hartmann ...?' The woman folded her arms and leaned forward over the book, her expression disdainful. 'Yes, he was here, but I asked him to leave. I put up with him when the English gentl'man was with him, but I wasn't having any fingers pointed at me, so I sent him on his way.'

'Where did he go? Did he leave an address?' She barely understood what the woman was saying, but caught her hostility all right.

'What's a nice young lady like you want with a Jerry?'

'He may be German, but he fought for this country,' Sarah said hoarsely. She'd lost him. Her legs felt weak, her mind was reeling and she put a hand on the wall for support. Then she picked up her case and headed for the door. She'd wrenched it open when the woman called:

'Hang about, love, I didn't say he *had* left an address.' Sarah's shoulders sagged and she looked back at the woman, wearily.

The proprietress shot her a mutinous glare as she pulled her cardigan more tightly round her shoulders. Then she ducked down and fished about to a sound of rustling paper. 'But I didn't say he hadn't, neither.' She popped back up and held out a scrumpled envelope. Sarah snatched it from her and smoothed it out, saw with a soaring relief her name on it in that familiar handwriting. A circle of damp had made the pencil fade, and a scent of rotten apple confirmed her suspicion that it had been consigned to a waste-paper basket.

'I didn't think anyone was coming for it,' the woman mumbled.

'You didn't wait long to find out.' As Sarah turned away, the woman sniffed and muttered, what were things coming to.

Once outside she crossed the road and sat on the steps of a sooty brick chapel in the shade of a tree and tore open the letter. It was written hastily and bits were faint because of the apple core, but she could just about make out the words. *Dearest Sarah, I'm to go in search of new lodgings. There's a small park up the road, towards the underground, on the right, just before the bombed-out houses. I'll try to be there in the afternoon at 4 in case you come.*

Which afternoon? There was no date on the letter. She glanced at her watch, brushed an earwig from her case and set off up the street, thinking she saw the ruined houses he meant. It was a quarter to four. She passed a butcher's shop where a tow-headed lad in a striped apron was placing a sign in the empty window. Ominously, it read, *Sorry, no meet.*

Cursing the weight of her case, Sarah broke out into a clumsy run.

Forty-four

In Cockley Market high street, Briony walked up and down, looking at the window displays, but noticing little beyond the repeated message that Valentine's Day was on its way. The minute hand of the clock above the sign on the old coaching inn only crept, as much as she willed it on. She'd taken a day off and started from London in good time in case of traffic, but the traffic had been easier than expected and parking spaces plentiful. There was no market in Cockley on a Wednesday, that must be the explanation. The result was she had a whole thirty minutes to kill. Opposite the inn, she came to the café where she'd once seen Aruna. There was a table free in the window with a good vantage point, so she pushed open the door, thinking she'd warm herself up with a coffee.

As she lingered over a cappuccino, she thought again of what had brought her here, how Derek Jenkins had identified the man in the photograph whom she knew to be her grandfather as Paul Hartmann, not Harry Andrews at all. Did that mean that the drunken man at the station was Harry? Paul, Harry and Ivor – those were the names on the back of the photograph, so if 'Harry' was in fact Paul, was 'Paul' Harry? She and Derek discussed this for some time, and an idea came to her that made her prickle all over. How on earth could she prove it?

When she'd arrived back at her flat that afternoon, she tried some aimless searching on the internet that turned up nothing, before ringing her father's landline, then his mobile, and finally her stepmother's. No answer from any of them, which was frustrating. This didn't stop her jumping into the car and driving down to Birchmere, her eyes dazzled by a most beautiful sunset. She found the house shrouded in gloom and rang the bell. Only the tabby cat appeared and rubbed itself against her legs as she waited on the doorstep.

Her phone rang. 'Lavender? I'm in Birchmere. Where are you?'

Lavender was irritatingly vague. They were waiting somewhere for an appointment, Briony gleaned that much. Yes, of course it was all right for her to let herself in. She knew where the spare key was, didn't she? Did she mind very much feeding the cat?

She found the key under its pot, and when she gained access she filled the cat's bowl with kibble, then raced upstairs to her old room and dragged open the drawer under the bed. 'Jean's schoolbooks.' That was the only box she hadn't searched.

She worked quickly but carefully, flicking through the exercise books she took out and stacking them to one side. As the box grew emptier, her spirits lowered. With the final book in her hand, she examined the few items left at the bottom, but there were no documents about her mother or grandparents at all, no old passports or birth or wedding certificates, only a thin hand-made black evening bag decorated with jet beads. She sat back on her heels and brushed back a lock of hair, disappointed. Who was her grandmother? She'd be able to check, of course, in the public records, if she could find out her full name and dates, but everybody called her Molly. She picked up the evening bag. Its jet beads sparkled. Rather lovely, she thought, unbuttoning it. There was something inside, a comb, a handkerchief and a piece of soft thick card, with a pretty design, decorated with flowers and little songbirds, one holding a red leaf in the shape of a heart. A Valentine's card, then. She opened it and gave a sharp intake of breath. Inside, written in thick black pen, in handwriting she recognized, were the words, *My dearest Sarah, Forever mein Herz.*

As she finished her coffee, Briony's attention was caught by the arrival of a sleek grey Jaguar car. As she watched, it slowed, then turned and swept under the arch of the coaching inn past a sign that read, *Customers car park.* On some instinct she rose, slipped on her jacket, left coins for her coffee and went out, crossing the street and entering the inn by its heavy, iron-studded front door. Inside, she found herself in a comfortable old-fashioned lounge bar that smelled richly of beer and gravy and old wood. It was empty apart from a group of red-faced old men in identical navy blazers, crests on the pockets, and a pair of mature, beautifully groomed ladies who were poring over lunch menus at a table in the window. At the bar, a tall, thick-set man in a charcoal-coloured overcoat was ordering a drink. When he turned and regarded her questioningly, she felt a little shock of recognition. Clean-shaven, short dark hair with a touch of grey, smoothed back over his head, this was the man she'd spotted with Aruna. He was also, she realized, the man she was here to meet – Greg's father, Tom Richards.

'Miss Wood. Briony.' He stumbled over the name.

'Yes.' She moved towards him and held out her hand. For a moment he hesitated, then he shook it, his hooded eyes not meeting her gaze.

'I'm glad to meet you at last,' she said in as level a voice as she could muster. 'We have a good deal to talk about.'

And at last he looked directly at her. 'What'll you have to drink?' was all he said.

Tom Richards could pass for sixty, she thought as she studied him while he ate, though she knew he must be ten years beyond that. He was a whisky and soda man, taller and more solid than his son, but there was that same tightness about his moulded mouth, a wariness in his eyes. A man of few words and fixed opinions, he was not what her father would call clubbable. At some point in his life he'd learned to be suspicious, grudging even.

After he'd bought their drinks, they'd been ushered to a comfortable corner of the quiet, sun-filled, thick-carpeted, wood-panelled restaurant beyond the lounge bar. A carvery counter sizzled and steamed along one wall where chefs plated for them glistening roast meat and potatoes, fluffy Yorkshire pudding and brightly coloured vegetables, all topped with rich brown gravy.

'Just right for a winter's day,' remarked Tom Richards as he spread his napkin and tucked in. He'd restricted his remarks so far to the business of the food. Briony, who was nervous and didn't really want hers now that it was in front of her, picked up her knife and fork and tried a small mouthful of meat. The salty tenderness burst upon her palate and suddenly she was hungry. She sliced another piece, dipped it in the gravy and ate that, too. All the way here she'd thought about what to ask this man, and now that they were companionably eating she couldn't think of how to break the silence. It was Greg who had brokered the meeting, but she'd told him firmly that she didn't want him there himself. They'd both gang up on her, she'd believed, and she refused to be bullied any more. She wanted the truth and sensed she'd be more likely to get it out of Mr Richards if it was just the two of them together.

Tom Richards flagged down a passing waitress. 'Another of these,' he said curtly, pointing to his empty glass.

Briony, her mouth full, shook her head at the waitress's enquiry.

It was only after his second whisky had been served and drunk and he'd eaten every morsel on his plate that Tom Richards slid his knife and fork together, tossed his napkin on the table, then sat back in his chair to regard her properly, as though noticing her for the first time.

'That's better,' he said and cleared his throat.

Briony laid down her cutlery and pushed her half-finished meal from her. 'Mr Richards,' she said, running out of patience. 'Tom.' They were related, after all.

He met her eye with a shrewd gaze. 'You don't look a bit like my mother. I thought you would. You are her grand-niece after all. Which makes us cousins.'

'And you knew all along.'

'No. Greg only told me that you'd come asking questions, that you write books about the war. I had no idea of a family connection. It's come as much of a shock to me as I imagine it is to you. So now you know. My father, apparently, was a bully and a coward, maybe a murderer, too. But I saw little of that. My parents were very happy together, and my mother and me, we were devastated when he died. Only sixty. That's young now.'

'That would have been . . .'

'Nineteen seventy-three. I was twenty-five. It was a great blow to my mother. She lived into her eighties, doted on me and her grandson, you know. Greg and she were very close, like she and I had been. Now, I know what you're going to ask me.'

Briony raised a quizzical eyebrow.

'How I learned the allegations about my dad. It was after both *his* parents had died. His mother, Margo, lived till ninety, you know, died in 1980 when I was in my mid-thirties and Greg was a boy of three or four. I was left with the job of clearing out Westbury House, where Greg lives now. There were some letters I read that my dad had sent home from the war, then I found a newspaper cutting. None of it squared with anything I'd been told and it ate away at me. I didn't like to trouble my mother with it, but in the end I did and she told me how Dad had been unfairly accused and what a bastard, forgive my French, Paul Hartmann had been.'

'And you believed this version?'

'In all honesty, I felt hers might not be the only viewpoint. I had a lot of time for my dad, but he had a side to him that was hard as nails. Of course, she swore me to secrecy. She wanted me to destroy the evidence I'd found, but I'm afraid that I didn't. I became a bit obsessed by it. After she died, I went out to Tuana to poke about, though I stayed quiet about who I was. There are long memories there and I learned enough to realize that whatever the truth was Dad hadn't told Mum all of it. But I kept my promise to her. I didn't tell a soul, not even Greg. Until you came along trying to find things out. Then I had to. I needed Greg on my side.'

'And Aruna?'

Now Briony had surprised him. He looked at her warily.

'I know you spoke to my friend,' Briony said. 'It was you I saw here with her, wasn't it, in the café?'

'I wasn't going to bring her into our discussion,' he growled, 'but since you have, yes, she caught on. She met someone during your holiday in Tuana who told her about the British soldiers' war crime, and then Robyn Clare alerted me after you visited her that first time.'

'Oh, but why?' Briony felt a lump of dismay in her throat. It wasn't only Aruna who'd gone behind her back. She'd somehow trusted Robyn.

'You'd better ask her. Anyway, your friend Miss Patel is a journalist of some sort, isn't she? She believed she was interviewing me, but the truth is, it was the other way round. I wanted to find out what she knew, to put her off the track a bit while Greg dealt with you.'

'This is all ridiculous,' Briony whispered almost to herself.

'It may seem so to you, but this is my side of the family whose reputation is at stake.' His eyes flashed dangerously and Briony felt with a chill how important this matter was to him.

'And what about mine?' she said in a low voice. 'Don't they count in this?'

For a moment his smooth face was like granite, then he pressed his lips together and gripped the table edge as he leaned forward in a deliberate manner. 'It would be best for both of us, don't you agree, to let the matter lie now?'

Briony's mind whirled with confusion. The instinct to tell the truth was strong in her, but could he possibly be right? 'I don't know,' she said, drawing back in her chair. 'I'd have to think about it.'

He nodded, but his expression remained grim.

'Will there be anything else? Dessert? Coffee?' The motherly waitress cleared their empty glasses.

Briony shook her head. 'Just the bill, thank you.'

'No, I insist,' he told Briony. 'We are, after all, family.'

She shrugged and let him pay.

Family, Briony thought, as she drove away through the bleak countryside towards London. What did that actually involve? Tom Richards meant nothing to her, she couldn't say she even liked him, but still there was a link between them that meant they were bound together in some ancient, crooked way, the hidden ties of blood. Diane had been his mother, after all, strange, enigmatic Diane, whom she only knew from her grand-parents' letters. How unhappy Diane must have been as a girl, soaking up the tensions of her parents' marriage, traumatized by the death of her baby brother, the responsibility she'd mis-takenly felt for her father's death, then giving birth to a stillborn baby during the war. Yes, she had some sympathy for Diane, and for why she should have wanted to hide the truth about her husband.

The trouble was that the secrecy, the unhappiness, had been passed down the generations. Her cousin Tom was not an easy man, close, defensive, and Greg, a different sort, had used his charm to deceive. He'd also stolen from her. Briony squeezed the steering wheel in anger at the memory of how he'd tricked her out of the letters.

Still, she didn't have much other family and she couldn't wait to tell her father about it all. She'd ask his advice, she decided, as she took the slip road up to the dual carriageway, into the dazzle of the westering sun. What she was less certain about was Aruna. Why had her friend betrayed her in this way? Was she right, that the journalist in Aruna had caught the scent of a story, or was it merely that strange, manipulative side of her friend revealing itself again? She remembered how Aruna used to take things of hers without asking. That it had been Aruna, too, who had set her up for that television show with Jolyon Gunn, where Briony had found herself out of her depth. Briony had always given Aruna the benefit of the doubt, but she couldn't do that on this occasion. And perhaps Aruna had always felt vulnerable about Luke.

She wondered if their friendship would ever recover from this, whether the bonds between them were strong enough to hold. They'd always assured one another that they'd never let a man, any man, come between them, but this was before they'd met Luke.

Luke. Briony felt the strength drain out of her at the thought of him. Perhaps the whole struggle with Aruna was for nothing and neither of them would hear from him again.

Forty-five

Briony drove down to Birchmere to see her father and step-mother the very next evening, taking all the letters with her and Paul's final note sent via Harry and, after supper, spread them out on the floor of the living room. It took a long time to explain everything clearly. The faded pictures of the young Harry in Westbury, when placed beside the face of the men on the scrap of film on her laptop, were incontrovertible evidence. Briony's brother Will did not look like Harry It was, rather, the wary, dark young man who shared Will's features and that man must have been Paul Hartmann.

'Is it really possible,' Martin Wood asked unhappily, 'that Paul was, um, your mother's father? I'm simply trying to think all round the question. The whole thing seems so ... dramatic.'

'Look.' Briony opened the old family album and together they studied the photographs. The face of the man who called himself Harry Andrews was almost definitely Paul's. 'I've seen a photograph of Sarah's sister Diane, too, and she does remind me of Granny.' She pointed to a black and white photograph of Jean's christening. There was her grandmother with an expression of joy, holding the bundle that had grown up to become Briony's mother.

'But your Granny's name was Molly.' Briony's father was having difficulties coming to terms with this.

'I don't understand how someone official didn't find out what they'd done.' Lavender, who had said very little so far, spoke gently.

'If there wasn't a photograph on Harry's identity card then it must have been easy,' Briony told her. 'Or perhaps Grandpa managed to change it. And there was general confusion at the time anyway. People must have had to ask for replacement cards for all sorts of reasons.'

'Who is this?' Briony's father was looking at the christening photograph and pointed to a woman standing close behind Briony's grandmother.

Briony screwed up her eyes. Lavender rose and opened a drawer in her writing desk in the corner and brought back a magnifying glass. 'I use it to read small print. The leaflets that come with my medication are awful.'

Briony wondered what medication Lavender was referring to, but was too caught up with the matter in hand to ask. Under the magnifying glass the face became clearer. She was a middle-aged woman with a proud expression and the tightest of smiles as though she wasn't used to smiling. A delicate hat crowned her coiffed greying hair. Only one side of her body was visible, but the glimpse of her elegant, corseted figure contrasted with Sarah's soft curves. 'Do you suppose,' Briony said, 'that this is Belinda, Sarah's mother?'

'They don't look very alike,' Lavender said. 'Except maybe something about the eyes.'

If Belinda Bailey had been there at the christening, Sarah had obviously kept up the family ties. Though there was no sign of Diane anywhere. Was it loyalty to her new husband, Ivor, that had kept her away, or had the sisters fallen out? Belinda might have been married again by the time of Jean's birth, but if so her husband hadn't merited a place in the photograph, if indeed he'd been present. There were so many stories that had been lost and which Briony saw no way to recover. The type of stories that aren't documented but passed from mouth to mouth as family myths and legends. Who snubbed whom, who was jealous, who fell out but were later reconciled.

'So Will and you have a whole new family,' Martin said, a little too brightly. Briony had described Greg and Tom to him.

'I don't think we'll see much of them, though Will is welcome to if he wants.'

She'd promised to get back in touch with Tom, though. She supposed she wanted to reassure him that she wouldn't allow his father's name to be dragged through the mud. 'Do you think I'm doing the right thing, Dad? By not ever writing about Ivor's crime? My next book involves writing about Italy, but I've thought of a way of being general about it if needs be, presenting it as part of a number of incidents that showed British soldiers under terrible stress.'

'In my work, too,' Martin reminded her, 'sometimes I had to make that sort of decision. I know you're a person of integrity, love, but perhaps in this case you needn't broadcast specifics like names.'

'It's not as though I'm deliberately hiding anything,' she agreed. 'I'll keep all the letters and finish my transcript, and if a scholar wants to look at them, I expect I'll let them.' One day, after Tom and Robyn were dead, and perhaps with Greg's agreement, she might do something more with her grandparents' love story, a radio programme, for instance, though maybe not with Aruna, but for now, was it worth hurting people close to her by exposing the full tale?

Briony's mind roamed to Italy, to Tuana, where a memorial plaque on the wall of the church symbolized the endurance of a past wrong still felt by the community. Perhaps she had some duty there and this made her uncertain again. There were people still alive who remembered young Antonio. Sometimes truth must be exposed even though it hurt, to allow reconciliation to take place.

She sighed as she closed the photograph album, still uncertain of what she should do.

When she looked up it was in time to see her father reach out and squeeze her stepmother's hand. 'Are you all right, love?' he said and Lavender nodded and gave a watery smile.

'Of course,' she said, bravely.

'What's wrong?' Briony asked, frowning, remembering the mention of medication. Lavender had never talked of needing any before.

Lavender sighed. 'We weren't going to say anything until we knew for definite. I have to have a little op, that's all.'

'Why?' Briony felt a growing alarm. She remembered thinking that Lavender had been so tired recently.

'They say it's nothing to worry about. A little repair to one of the heart valves,' her father murmured as though he were speaking about a car. But she could see the anxiety in his eyes.

'Oh, Lavender,' she whispered and went to put her arms around her stepmother. 'You should have told me about it before.'

'I didn't like to,' she whispered. 'Your dad's worried enough as it is. I didn't want to make you and Will worried too.'

'That's nonsense, Lavender. We care about you too, you know! Don't shut us out.' She felt a rush of love for her stepmother that she'd never felt so intensely before. She remembered, too, how her mother had said little about her illness and how this had added to the shock of her death.

'That's lovely of you, Briony.' And they hugged each other tightly again.

The following day Briony walked into Birchmere, noticing as ever how much had changed since her childhood. The big supermarket was new, the White Hart pub, scene of many a Saturday night gathering, was now called the Mulberry Tree, and there were three sets of traffic lights where previously there had been none. Still, there was enough to make her feel connected to the place; the classical portico of the bank, the clock tower looming above the main square, the bright canopies of market stalls and, where the shops petered out and the common began, the mere, fringed with birch trees and now securely fenced. Briony walked round it, smiling at a sturdy toddler with its father throwing bread to the ducks, before her memories beckoned her down a lane that led from the common into a grid of residential roads behind the high street. She hadn't been this way for years and tried to remember the order of the roads, which were all named after trees, a connection maybe to the name of the town. Ash Grove, Hickory Avenue, Willow Way ... then she came to Chestnut Close and her heart quickened. She turned down it.

It was a cul-de-sac and much shorter than she remembered it, though the detached family houses of a 1930s style were still impressive. Number 4 was half-hidden by a privet hedge, but when she stared up at the white-painted house she was reassured by its villa-style shutters and decorative balconies. It was where her grandparents had lived. Something was different, though. Some of the garden had been asphalted over to make room for cars, though there were none parked there today.

On impulse, she walked up the drive and rang the doorbell, listening to it resound through the house, but though she waited a couple of minutes there came no answer, so she turned away with a mixture of disappointment and relief. What she would have said to the current inhabitant she'd no idea.

As she left, she caught a glimpse of the back garden through the wrought-iron gate and couldn't resist going to look through the bars. It was large, she'd forgotten that, and the beds were heaped with spring flowers and shrubs and she remembered how beautiful it had been, how often she'd visited to find Granny out there weeding the beds or in the greenhouse with her pots. There had been a plant she'd been particularly proud of which grew clusters of pink and white flowers, each one like a small trumpet. That's what Briony had called it, she remembered, the fairy trumpet bush, but Granny had called it by another name, and now this came to her. It was a *Hibiscus syriacus*. Was it still there, she wondered, and had it anything to do with the cutting Granny had brought back from India? She felt suddenly heavy with sadness, burdened by confusion about her childhood past, now lost to her, and withdrew, suddenly glad to leave the house and its secrets.

She walked away, back to the busyness of the town and the present. It would be good, she thought, to spend the rest of the day with her father and stepmother, to whom she suddenly felt much closer. Lavender's operation would be a fairly routine one, but it clearly worried her. Briony had learned something important. Any distance that had existed between her and Lavender had been closed over the last few months and she understood that she loved her stepmother more dearly than she would ever have believed. Lavender could never replace the memory of her mother in Briony's heart, but then she had never tried to do that and never would. What she had done was to make them all a family again.

Forty-six

The last few days of March were petering out and teaching was over. It had been an extraordinarily busy term, especially with the conference, which had gone better than she dared expect, but now she was coming up for air, Briony ached to get away to look over the proofs of her book. Her stepmother had had her operation and was recovering well, so Briony was free to get away. On a whim, she rang Kemi to find out if Westbury Lodge was available and habitable. Kemi said it was, then called her again an hour later to say that she had checked with Greg, who had enthusiastically agreed. What was more, he was refusing to charge her any rent.

Briony put down the phone and sighed, wondering if she'd done the right thing. She badly wanted to revisit Westbury in the light of her new relationship to the Lodge, and it was a good place to work, but she wasn't sure she was ready to see Greg again. It was kind of him to let her stay for free – he was obviously keen to show he was sorry – but she was still suspicious of his motives and not sure she wanted to become mixed up with him. Anyway, the arrangement was made now. She'd go down later today and stay for four nights. There was a tight deadline for her to return the proofs to her publisher.

How welcoming it was to arrive at her gingerbread cottage after a rainy drive from London. It was beautifully cosy, too, because central heating had been installed. A fire had still been laid in the living room, there were milk, eggs and bread and butter in the fridge, and wine and biscuits had been left on the kitchen table. Avril's touch, she thought, having learned that Robyn's carer also looked after the Lodge.

The first night she lay awake between sheets scented with herbs, getting used to the creaks of the furniture again and new sounds, the groans and clangs of cooling radiators. The place felt safe, tranquil, and now she'd discovered her family links to it, she felt as though she belonged there. It was with this thought in her mind that she drifted off into a deep and dreamless sleep.

It wasn't the next day, but the one after that Briony was sitting at her laptop, deep in the queries on her proofs, when she was dragged out of her absorption by the sound of men's voices. They sounded distant and came and went, blown, she supposed, by the breeze, but one, she became sure, was Greg's. The other was quieter, more measured, with rhythms that were familiar, but it was impossible to hear what either was saying. Her curiosity got the better of her, so she saved her document, grabbed her parka from its hook in the hall and let herself out into the misty afternoon.

There was no one to be seen, but when she followed the voices, she found herself at the door of the walled garden. Warily, she pushed it open and glanced inside. There, on the far side of what still looked like a building site, were two men, standing together examining a computer and discussing whatever they saw on its screen. Greg was describing a shape in the air with his finger to make some point. The face of the other man, who wore a beanie hat and a thick jacket, wasn't visible, but then he glanced up and, with a jolt of surprise, Briony realized that it was Luke.

Her first instinct was to retreat, but it was too late, she'd been spotted.

'Briony?' Greg strode in his wellingtons across the muddy ground, and though she tried to keep her eyes on him she was all too aware of Luke rooted to the ground behind him and staring with surprise. 'How are you?' Greg leaned in to kiss her on both cheeks. His hand cupped her elbow and he drew her forwards. 'Were you trying to avoid us?'

'Not really, it's just ...'

'Step round this bit, you'll avoid the worst of the mud. Come and see. We're discussing the layout of the beds.'

Up close, Luke looked at her as though he couldn't believe his eyes. He tucked the tablet under his arm as he came forward to greet her. They slid naturally together into a hug, but quickly pulled back. 'I didn't know you were down this way,' Luke mumbled.

'I ... forgot to say.' Greg's expression could only be described as sheepish. For a while they all swapped polite pleasantries.

'How are your parents, Luke? I thought about ringing them while I was here, but ...' The rest of her sentence died on Briony's lips. What would have been more natural and indeed polite in normal circumstances than to have offered to drop in on them? But circumstances were not normal and there was no point in pretending they were.

Luke nodded as though he understood. 'They're both fine, thank you.' He drew the tablet out again and flicked the cover open and came closer in order to show her the plans for the garden. The daylight was grey and the screen bright, so she could see fairly easily where everything was to be planted.

'Over here, flower beds, there, herbs, and these, yes, will be the vegetable beds.'

'It's like the diagram on Mrs Clare's wall, then.'

'That's right, but with some extra bits from Sarah's letters.'

'Luke's pricing up the plants for me,' Greg explained, 'and then we'll put in an order.'

'I won't stop you, then. Come and have a cup of tea when you've finished.' Briony felt her smile was pasted on as she looked from one to the other. She was holding them up, obviously, and left them to return to her own work. When she sat down at her desk again, she found it difficult to concentrate, half expecting the men to arrive any moment. In the end she gave up trying to work, went into the kitchen and filled the kettle and laid three mugs on a tray.

When the doorbell rang, she opened the door to find only Luke waiting on the path. He pulled off his hat, ran his hand through his mane of hair and grinned in that old Lukeish way that made her gulp.

'What have you done with Greg?' she asked lightly.

'He got a call. I think he was in the middle of some deal. Anyway, said he had to go.'

She let out a long slow breath. 'So you'd better come in.'

Inside, she couldn't help but be aware of his presence filling the hallway, the scent of rain and earth and soap that came in with him. He hung up his coat, followed her through to the kitchen and leaned against the counter, watching, arms folded, as she made the tea and dithered about, returning the milk to the fridge before she'd even poured it.

'I hadn't known you were coming down,' he said again. 'I'm sorry if I seemed a bit stunned.'

'I hadn't known you'd be here.' That was, on the face of it, true, but she felt her cheeks pink up because there had always been the likelihood. 'How often have you needed to visit the garden?'

'It's seemed like every weekend lately, but actually it's not. Greg said he would be about today and that it would be a good time to meet.'

She nodded, secretly thinking, *Thank you, Greg*, as she gave him his tea and they went through to the living room, where she moved some books from the sofa so he could sit down. He did so carefully, as though aware of all his movements.

'I don't think I've seen you since . . .' He broke off.

'Yeah,' she said, remembering that awful night where she'd encountered him on the street outside Aruna's flat, picking up his sodden washbag.

'So how are you?' He looked up, giving her a lopsided smile.

'Yes, not bad.' She felt like crying inside, their words were so stilted. 'I came down to do some work. It's funny, though, I feel sort of attached to here, like I belong. Does that sound crazy?'

'Completely mad,' he said and they both laughed and the atmosphere lightened.

'There's an awful lot to tell you, if you've got the time. About Paul and Sarah, I mean, and Harry Andrews.'

'I have the time. But Greg let slip some of it. He says you and he are cousins or something? He's trying to view you in a new light. Sounds weird.'

She nodded, sure now that Greg was stepping back, allowing Luke to have his chance.

'He knows about Aruna, too,' Luke went on. 'He must have done the whole time.'

'Because she was asking questions?'

'I got it all out of her. About the man she'd met in the flash car outside the villa, who told her about the British soldiers who'd murdered Antonio. She started to make her own investigations and approached Greg behind your back. I still don't know why.'

'I think I do,' Briony whispered. 'She can be like that sometimes. I don't know if it's jealousy, but she can play these power games.'

She thought about all the times that Aruna had interfered in her life. The awful TV show . . . She also didn't want to discuss any of this with Luke. That seemed a low thing to do.

'She loved you though, Luke. Still does, by all accounts.' She felt she had to say this, to be fair to Aruna.

Luke said nothing, but sat with both hands cradling his mug staring down into his tea. 'It's over,' he muttered finally, 'and she knows it.'

'Luke, Aruna blames me, but I don't know why.'

'Don't you?' he said, staring up at her, his eyes narrowed, his expression serious. 'You really don't know?'

'What?' Her voice was faint.

'You haven't "done" anything, but Aruna sensed the truth anyway.'

'That . . . things weren't right between you?'

He sighed, placed his mug on the table and sat back in his seat. 'Are you being deliberately obtuse?'

She flinched at his tone of frustration, then was angry. 'Stop talking in riddles. Luke, listen, I first thought things couldn't be right between the two of you when you came here on your own that day. There was something . . . different about your behaviour. I thought, well, that you were being flaky and that sort of thing really hacks me off.'

'And that's not me, Briony. I'm not like that. It's just I'd started to realize properly . . .' He was sitting up straight now, and his look was fiery, the red lights in his toffee-coloured hair glinting. 'I don't know how to say this. I'll only get it wrong.'

The room was full of a charged energy. Slowly, Briony put her tea down, rose and went to sit beside him on the sofa. It felt like the bravest thing she had ever done. 'Tell me,' she whispered. 'I'm listening.'

He smiled, his eyes brightening with amusement. Very gently he reached out and took her hand. 'Close your eyes, then, and I'll tell you.' She did as he bid.

'The day it happened, when the three of us first met, I was, if you remember, pressure washing a patio I'd been mending. Horribly wet and noisy it was. Suddenly someone taps me on the shoulder, making me jump, and I turn to see this pretty cool chick who's babbling on at me about a lost cat.'

'I was not babbling.'

'OK, asking me, then. I turn off the water and we have a chat about this mog, and all the time I'm thinking how nice she looks, and it's touching how upset she is for her friend, and I'm glad that it's so easy to help her because I'd been hearing meowing from the place next door all afternoon.'

'Poor old Purrkins, he must have been terrified getting stuck like that,' Briony said, relishing the sense of warmth creeping up inside her.

'And I made some appalling joke about cats' nine lives and you laughed and you have such a great laugh, Briony, have I ever told you that?'

She shook her head. Luke's grip tightened on her hand, she felt his warm breath on her cheek.

'But the next thing that happens is that another cool chick arrives, this petite little thing, and she is really upset about her cat and she definitely does babble away. And when I shimmy over the fence and push the cat flap so the mog can get out, she's so grateful, almost crying with relief, and she hugs me and invites me over to supper.'

'I remember,' Briony gave a grim sigh.

'But wait. When I get back over the fence, there is the first chick and it's like the light has gone out inside her. She's all frosty, just thanks me in this polite voice and gives me a polite smile. Then the second chick, who's invited me over, asks you, too, but it's like she's tossed you some ball invisible to the likes of me and you catch it and say, no, you're busy that evening and smile warmly at your friend. Then you give me a nod and off you go.'

'That is really how you saw it?'

'Oh yes.'

'I just thought you were bowled over by Aruna, just as so many men are, so I left you both to it. No one wants the plain friend hanging about.'

'Plain? Plain? That's how you see yourself?' Luke took Briony's face in his hands and looked at her with exasperation. 'The trouble with you is that you don't believe in yourself.'

'I do,' she tried to say, but they were already kissing.

'Oh my god, you're beautiful,' he stopped to say, then they kissed again and Briony found herself melting into him with an astonishing sense of letting everything go. A terrific burden had been lifted from her.

'So are you,' she whispered when they drew apart, and she felt the prickle of tears in her eyes.

They lay down together on the sofa, face to face, and he pulled the comb out of its knot and stroked her hair, soothing her. 'I first began to feel doubts when we were in Tuana,' he said, 'and was rather ashamed of myself. After all, I was fond of Aruna, and she was great. It was all great, but there was still you. The truth didn't properly hit me until we came down here in the summer. Aruna was being grumpy about something and my mother dropped one or two telling comments. It just made me think.'

'My darling friend called me a witch, I seem to remember.'

'In your gingerbread cottage. Yes, you're very witchy. You've certainly put a spell on me.' Once again he stopped to kiss her.

'I don't know what to do about Aruna,' Briony whispered. 'We can never be friends again. Not like we were, anyway.'

'No. It would be difficult.' They were silent for a moment, each lost in thought. 'But let's forget Aruna for a bit.'

'But I feel so guilty.'

'Don't. Think about the ways in which she's hurt you.'

'She wouldn't have meant to.'

'You're a good-hearted woman.'

'No, I'm not, I just hate falling out with people. Luke?'

'Still here.'

'Have you got to go anywhere this evening? I mean, will you stay here with me?'

'That's the best offer I've had all day,' he said, and they laughed and held each other close.

Forty-seven

Tuana lay sleepy under the afternoon sun as Briony and Luke strolled hand in hand through the main square, he with his jacket draped over his shoulder, she in the stylish pale green dress he'd picked out for her in a Naples boutique and a soft straw hat that framed her face. Here was the pavement café with its scattered tables and chairs where she and Aruna had rested, even the same waiter, clearing the table where they'd sat. It was odd coming back, for the memories were mixed ones. Luke hadn't wanted to, but Briony had persuaded him. She still ached for Aruna, but needed to see the town with her new knowledge of what had happened here, to think about it all and what it had meant for her family. To gain some kind of peace about it.

'I really don't remember going in here,' Luke murmured, as she mounted the steps to the church.

'You must have done.'

He shook his head. 'I was at the dentist when you went, remember? And the other times we came it was to shop.'

She pushed open the wooden door and they entered the cool

gloom, their footsteps echoing in the high-ceilinged space. Soft flames from a rack of votive candles drew her to the altar. 'There it is,' she whispered, and pointed with her sunglasses to the oval plaque on the wall next to the altar rail.

'Antonio,' Luke read aloud and his rich voice bounced from wall to wall until they heard the whole place whisper the name, *Antonio, Tonio, onio.*

'*Sorry*,' Luke said more quietly, and Briony, selecting a narrow candle from the box beneath the votive, shot him a smile. 'Do you think that does any good?' he asked, watching her place it in a holder and light it.

'It's symbolic. It was my relatives who were responsible for the boy's death. I can't imagine there's anyone left alive to say sorry to.'

'Maybe you're right.' He didn't appear sure, but at least he was trying to understand. She reached out and briefly squeezed his arm.

They left the church to its memories and its dreams and stepped out into the sunshine again. Briony unfolded a tourist map. 'The town hall's down this way,' she said and set off down one of the narrow streets that meandered off the square, Luke obediently in tow. They found it, but there wasn't much to see, it being a rather plain edifice with a round arched double doorway that was locked, so they continued on until they came to where more recent properties had caused the town to creep out across the hillside. Briony shaded her eyes against the sun and looked around for a building that might have been the barn where the town's wartime rations had been stored, but wherever it had been it must have gone. Instead her gaze swept the valley and up to where the shoulder of the mountain rose steeply above the town. It should be there somewhere, yes, that was it.

'Hey.' She nudged Luke and pointed to an ochre blob among the dark mass of trees, waiting until he saw it.

'The Villa Teresa! Still there!'

'Hope so. Shall we go and see it? We've got time before we're due at Mariella's.'

Luke leaned in and kissed her. 'Your call, my love.'

The road out of the town was one they hadn't taken before, winding up the hillside, at times so narrow that Briony, who was driving, held her breath that something wouldn't be heading down the other way. Occasionally there were turnings off, sometimes signposted, sometimes not, but she followed her instincts and carried on. Eventually, just as they were cresting a hill, dark trees on either side of the road, she paused at where a gravelly lane led off downhill. On an ancient broken sign she made out the word 'Teresa'.

'Go for it,' Luke said beside her and she turned the wheel. The trees thinned out and she tried to avert her eyes from the spectacular view of the valley in order to negotiate the sharp bends in the road. Eventually, they arrived at the point where a year before she'd reached after climbing the hillside in search of the villa. She and Luke exchanged glances, anticipation mounting. She drove on slowly, noticing every detail of the way. There was where Aruna sank down in pain at the side of the track and Luke stuck a plaster on her foot. There was the brief glimpse of Tuana before the bulk of the escarpment swallowed it again. Here was the corner beyond which she'd see the locked wrought-iron gates of the villa. She rounded it and stopped the car abruptly.

'Luke! What's going on?' Before them the old gates stood wide. The turning circle was ploughed by deep wheel marks. Further marks scored the drive.

'No idea.' Luke lowered a window to admit a blast of hot air. 'I can't hear anything. Shall we go and look?'

They walked furtively up the drive towards the villa through a garden as rampant as ever, to be astonished by the sight of metal poles reaching up above the greenery. The sound of tinny music reached them, and male laughter. 'What on earth?' she hissed to Luke. But then they passed the barrier of trees and stopped in astonishment at the scene before them.

Three burly workmen were sitting on boxes around a make-shift table playing cards. The scene was so much like the old war footage of the soldiers nicknamed the Three Stooges that for a moment Briony was confused. But a very modern sports car was parked to one side, and the house beyond could hardly be seen for scaffolding and sheets of plastic, but here and there she could glimpse the signs of repair: new rafters, part of a metal joist.

'Who's doing this?' she gasped.

'And are they supposed to?' Luke growled.

The men hadn't seen them, they were so intent on their game, and so they left them to it and tiptoed back to where they'd left the car.

'Well,' Luke said, glancing behind him. 'That was a surprise. What should we do now?'

'Go to Mariella's,' Briony said grimly, opening the car door.

They returned to the winding road, which they continued along until they came to a fork and took the left-hand option down the hillside. Though they looked for a turning that might lead them to Mariella's house, they must have gone past it, because they found themselves at the café by the graceful bridge over the river.

'I'd forgotten how pretty it is. Shall we walk up to Mariella's from here?' Briony suggested, stopping the car outside the café.

'If we can get something to drink first? I'm not ready for a climb.'

'Good idea. I'll text Mariella to say.'

In the welcome shade of the café there was no sign of Signor Marco, the balding proprietor. Instead a generous-sized woman with a roll of greying hair served them, his wife, perhaps. She spoke little English but beamed at them a great deal as though to make up for it. They sat outside under a bright umbrella and she brought them ice-cold lemonade. They sat quietly, hardly feeling the need to talk, they were so at ease together. Briony's thoughts drifted back to the year before, the unease of their holiday here. She would never have guessed that things would have changed in this way. Here she was, her book finished, ready to be published in October. She knew she'd have to find the courage to step out into the world to give talks about it, maybe even on TV, the radio. Although she was nervous, she was determined to try. Her promotion had come through, too. Luke had already started proudly introducing her as a professor, even though she wasn't strictly one until the new academic year. And the biggest thing of all that had happened was Luke. It was he who filled her with a happiness that she'd never known before. They were still taking things step by step, learning to trust one another, but the bonds between them were strengthening. His parents had been tactful, but warmly welcoming, and Martin and Lavender, too.

A young Italian couple had come in and came to sit at the table beside them. Signora Marco came across with bottles of Coke and greeted them with kisses and endearments. The young man was assured, elegant in a crisp shirt and jeans. Briony glimpsed an expensive-looking watch on his wrist, noticed the sleek phone on the table. The girl was lovely, blooming with youth and graceful, shoulder-length dark hair in a middle parting, a pretty sundress riding her thighs. She appeared faintly familiar, probably like one of her students, that must be it.

'Who did you think that pretty girl was like?' she remarked as they left the café.

'What pretty girl?' Luke replied, quite seriously.

'The couple sitting next to us.'

'Oh them. I hardly noticed.'

Briony laughed.

The path up to Mariella's house was as onerous to climb as Briony remembered, and the dog barked as fiercely as before, but this time Mariella met them at the gate, embraced them both and ushered them inside. The kitchen table was spread with a cloth and plates of dainty cakes and biscuits. There was the fragrance of brewing coffee. 'Sit, sit down,' she bade them and set about pouring syrupy dark liquid into tiny cups.

Briony couldn't stop herself asking straight away. 'We went to look at the Villa Teresa. What's happening there?'

At this a great smile spread across Mariella's face. 'You have already seen,' she said. 'I wanted to surprise you. The answer is *l'amore.*'

'Love?' Briony said, not understanding.

'My daughter is to marry Piero Mei.'

'Congratulations!' Briony said politely, something teasing at the edge of her memory. Mariella's daughter, a quiet, solemn girl stowing linen in a cupboard.

'Please, you don't understand. It is the Mei family who wanted the Villa Teresa. All these years. And now Chiara and Piero will marry and the Villa Teresa will be theirs.'

And suddenly it all made sense. 'The girl in the café just now, remember?' she told Luke excitedly. 'I thought she looked familiar. She's changed so much in a year, Mariella. I didn't recognize her.'

'She is twenty-one now, *cara*, but yes, you're right. Love has made her beautiful – and a little, how shall we say, advice from her mama! And Piero, his father, he pay for the villa.'

As Mariella talked, Briony gradually realized that the Mei family – she'd not heard the name on the memorial plaque pronounced correctly before – were young Antonio's. It had been Antonio's father who had returned to Tuana after the war and initiated legal proceedings against Mariella's grandfather for possession of the Villa Teresa!

'Like the Montagues and the Capulets, a very Italian ending,' as her father would put it later with a twinkle in his eye, bright and cheerful now that Lavender was restored to health.

Luke and Briony stayed at Mariella's for a couple of hours talking about everything that had happened, the story behind the tragedy of Antonio, how Briony had found out about Paul and Sarah and poor Harry Andrews. Briony supposed that they would never discover what happened to Harry in the end. He had disappeared into the dusty ruins of London, just one more victim of the conflict that had destroyed the lives of so many.

They left Mariella with fond goodbyes and a promise of an invitation to the wedding, though Briony was nervous about whether they should attend, given all that had happened.

'I will speak to Signor Mei. I want peace with everybody now.'

This idea meant so much to Briony that she embraced Mariella all over again.

When she arrived home after their holiday and she popped into college to collect her post, there was a letter waiting for her from Greg. *My father asked me to send you this, which he found some time ago in my grandmother's papers. He said you'd guess what it means.*

He thinks it makes sense of something she once said, about falling out with her sister.

Greg had enclosed an envelope addressed to Sarah at Flint Cottage in Paul's distinctive handwriting. It had been torn open long ago. Briony withdrew the letter inside and read it quickly, then read it again. *My dearest Sarah*, it began. ... *I'm back in London* ... A peculiar feeling came over her and for a moment she found she could not move. When her thoughts began to flow again, everything began to fall into place.

This was the letter Paul had sent after his return to London which Sarah had never received, his last letter home. Diane must have taken it from the doormat. But why? Diane had never liked Paul, she remembered him hinting that in another letter. Also – her thoughts roamed – perhaps Diane was jealous of her elder sister, who was loved by Ivor, the man Diane was eventually to marry. Or perhaps her twisted intention was to help Ivor? Unhappy, enigmatic Diane. Whatever the answer, she had nearly spoiled Sarah's happiness. Whether Sarah ever suspected this, it was impossible to know, but maybe Diane felt guilty about it for the rest of her life and that's why she hardly saw Sarah again.

Briony refolded the letter and slid it into her bag. She'd keep it with all the others, she decided, and if she and Luke were lucky enough to have children, one day, when they were old enough, she'd show the letters to them and explain how Paul and Sarah, Jean and Martin, she and Luke, and all the children, were each part of an ancient love story that goes on and on and will never end.

Forty-eight

The park Paul had mentioned in his note was a glimpse of green between two terraces accessed through a narrow passage littered with broken glass and overgrown with weeds. It was little more than an oblong of grass bordered by flower beds rampant with blue and white blooms of creeping plants, but someone tended it, for it was neat and clean, and the grass kept short. An ancient wooden bench had been set on the verge on one side, but there was no sign of Paul. Sarah walked across and sat on the bench, her case propped next to her. Her view was of abandoned gardens of ruined houses, but they were peaceful and she liked the way that nature was reclaiming them. She enjoyed the hazy sunshine seeping through the ruins and the warmth of it on her upturned face as she waited, knowing of nothing more that she could do.

Minutes passed. Four o'clock came and still she waited. Her anxiety began to build. Then she turned at a sound. An elderly man wheeling tools in a barrow hove into sight from the alley. He was a comical figure with his pot belly and his gaping waistcoat and his homely weathered face. He nodded to her, selected a large fork and began to clear dead foliage from one of the beds, dumping each load in the barrow.

It was a quarter past four and a cold breeze had risen. Sarah stood and walked across to him. 'Excuse me,' she said and he halted his work, leaned on his fork and doffed his cap, wiping his face with his sleeve.

'Yes, miss.'

'Is this the only park in this road?'

'It's the only one I know of.'

'Thank you.' She started to go back and sit down, but he spoke again.

'You waiting for someone?'

'Yes. A friend. It's a pleasant place to wait though. You look after it beautifully.'

The man fitted his cap back on. 'I like to keep it shipshape. Molly used to like this place. My wife, you know. That was where we lived before the bomb hit.' He nodded at one of the ruined houses. 'She died in hospital three days later. I come here to think about her.'

'I expect the work is soothing,' she said. 'My father used to call me Molly when I was little,' she told him. 'I had a toy barrow I used to trundle about. *"Look out, Molly Malone's coming,"* he'd say. After the song, you know.'

'"*She wheeled her wheelbarra through streets broad and narra*", I know that one all right.' The old man chuckled.

He returned to his digging and Sarah sank down on the bench once more. He had merely taken her mind off her anxiety for a minute or two, but now all hope was leaching away. Her head swam and her mouth felt dry. *He isn't coming, he isn't coming.* How long should she wait? The stupid song played in her mind. *Her ghost wheels her barrow / Through streets broad and narrow . . . Molly, sweet Molly, sweet Molly Malone.*

A shadow fell across the grass and she glanced up to be dazzled by the sun. She shaded her eyes and there he was.

'My darling.'

A glimpse of a worn face before she threw herself into his arms and he held her tightly, his quick warm breaths on her neck. 'I thought you weren't coming, I thought you'd never come,' she gasped.

'I said half-past four, it's not that yet.'

'The note said four, here, oh there's a smudge. Four-thirty, how stupid.'

'Never mind, I'm here now. Still the same Sarah?'

'Same as ever.'

A polite cough behind them. The old man, she'd forgotten him.

'Glad he found you then. I'll be off now. Goodbye, Miss Molly.'

They watched him stagger to a compost heap in a far corner and tip the barrow, then he wheeled it away along a path between the ruined houses she hadn't noticed before.

'Why did he call you that?'

'Oh, we were just talking about his wife and my father. I rather like the name Molly, don't you?'

'Molly.' He smiled and looked thoughtful. 'I think it suits you. Darling, there's something important I must explain.'

Acknowledgements

Great thanks, as ever, are due to my agent Sheila Crowley at Curtis Brown, my editor Suzanne Baboneau at Simon & Schuster, Maisie Lawrence, Sue Stephens, Pip Watkins, Hayley McMullan and Bec Farrell and all their colleagues who work so hard on my account, and copyeditor Sally Partington.

I am indebted to my friend and garden designer Juliet Bamber, whose patient advice about plants has once again plugged considerable gaps in my knowledge, and to historian Frank Meeres at the Norfolk County Archive, who kindly read the manuscript.

My husband David is always a source of encouragement, as are my friends and family, particularly my sons, Felix, Benjy and Leo, my mother Phyllis and my mother-in-law Elizabeth.

I would also like to thank my readers, especially the ones who write and ask when the next book is coming. I find this tremendously supportive.

*Why not read another stunning novel
from Rachel Hore ...*

The House on Bellevue Gardens

Here, through the imposing front door of Number 11,
is a place of peace, of sanctuary and of secrets. It is
home to Leonie; once a model in the sixties, she came
to the house to escape a destructive marriage and now,
out of gratitude, she opens her house to others in need.

Rosa, Stef and Rick are running from their own problems.
They have all found their way to Leonie's home, each
seeking refuge and searching for a new start.

But then Leonie discovers that the house, which has
provided sanctuary for so many, is under threat.
And now she must rescue the place that saved
her all those years ago ...

**SIMON &
SCHUSTER**

Hidden behind a busy street in north London, Camden way, is a tranquil garden square. You might pass it without suspecting its existence. Its terraced houses are white-iced like giant wedding cakes. At some point in its history an unknown individual named it Bellevue Gardens. Many of the houses have been divided into flats. Their glory days are long past, but once they were the homes of well-to-do middle-class families whose fathers were lawyers or bankers, whose children played on the trim back lawns or in the square's wild garden, under the vigilant eyes of their nannies, whilst their mothers took tea in one another's drawing rooms and organized dinners or charity whist drives and changed their gowns several times a day. The bourgeois world of an age long gone.

There's not much more to say. In the Eighteen Nineties, Oscar Wilde visited friends at Number 13. A blue plaque states that a famous Edwardian actress once lived at Number 34. A row of three houses on the north side still bears scars of the

Blitz – misshapen chimneys, patchwork roofs, angles twisted out of true.

Sometimes, when Leonie Brett arrives home late on a warm summer's night, she finds it easy to forget the ranks of parked cars, the distant grumble of London traffic, and imagines instead sparks flying from horses' hooves as they strike the flagstones, bright clinks of harness and the rumble of carriage wheels. The music and laughter drifting through an open window might be a party from another century, when young girls with stars in their eyes danced in white dresses with coloured sashes, as fresh and lovely as flowers.

Despite its current shabbiness, Leonie believes that her house, Number 11, must once have been the most splendid in the square. It stands at the centre of the left-hand terrace, its single doorbell an indication that it hasn't been turned into flats. It also has a grandiose portico, which makes it look particularly welcoming. She remembers one day, over forty years ago, sheltering under this from the rain as a frightened runaway, of setting her bags down in the hall and wandering the spacious, high-ceilinged rooms with their neat square fireplaces and shiny parquet floors. How grand the house was then, with its ornate mirrors and damask sofas, its heavy mahogany furniture, such a nuisance to polish. There used to be old paintings on the walls, but over the years these have gone to pay bills.

The kitchen is still the heart of the house, but now splashes of paint and tea stains mar the lovely oak table, and candles jammed into empty wine bottles that drip stalactites of wax. The garden was landscaped in an Italianate design. Now it's a blissful wild paradise, with only a series of hedges to remember its formal past.

How safe the place made her feel, how quickly it became

home. Over the decades her feelings for it have grown deep roots. Through everything that's happened since she arrived, the tears, the joys, the things lost and the things found, all the people who have come and departed, it's still her sanctuary, her foxhole, and she hopes it will be always.

One

Leonie

2015

It had been a day of memories, so many of them crowding in, a day of laughter, but sadness, too. It was always like that with Trudi, Leonie reflected as she walked home from the tube station. She loved seeing her old friend, which happened only infrequently. Trudi being always impossibly busy, off visiting her married daughter in New York or holidaying in Florida, but her company, though invigorating, could also be exhausting.

As she turned down the street of shops and offices that would bring her eventually to Bellevue Gardens, Leonie smiled at the thought of something said once by one of Trudi's ex-husbands – there had been three of them. It was that Trudi saw herself as the star in her own show, and everyone else was simply the audience. He had spoken with bitterness, and although it wasn't the full story – Leonie had usually experienced Trudi's considerate and generous side – there was more than a grain of truth in it. Trudi had always been a drama queen. Even now she was in her seventies her life lurched from intrigue to crisis – or so she liked to make out. Today, for instance, at lunch in her Chelsea duplex, with its wonderful views over the river, Trudi, her green eyes bright with excitement, had told her that her new downstairs neighbour – who with iron-grey hair slicked back *must* be a retired gangster – had been sending her flowers and chocolate truffles from Fortnum's, and simply *wouldn't* be put off. When Leonie enquired wickedly whether Trudi had tried hard enough, her friend's green gaze turned dragonish. 'And how is that old crosspatch you keep in your basement? Really, darling, you and your lame ducks.'

'They're not lame,' Leonie retorted. 'They walk perfectly well.' Except Bela, perhaps, the ageing Kashmiri lady who shuffled about in slippers because of her bunions. 'Some of them are down on their luck, that's all.'

Leonie frowned as she walked along. Although she and Trudi were still very fond of one another, it was funny how differently their lives had turned out since the time they'd shared lodgings together with another girl over a shop on the Edgware Road all those years ago. There was Trudi, well-heeled and well-travelled, recently installed in her new luxury apartment overlooking the yachts of the marina, and here was she, Leonie Brett, rounding the corner into her Georgian garden square, as she must have done thousands of times before, and never tired of doing, coming home to the house she had shared with so many friends over the years.

This evening the square was scorched by the flames of a spectacular sunset. So beautiful. She stopped to admire the shapes of the budding plane trees against the sky, the stately houses glowing a peachy orange in the dying sun. It was always so peaceful, this secluded square. From the garden in the middle came the lush warbling of a blackbird, no doubt assuring the other avian residents that everything was all right with their world.

As she crossed the road towards Number 11 her heart gave a little jolt of satisfaction to see its bohemian tattiness; the house was like a louche Cinderella between more splendidly attired sisters. The neighbours – mostly young professionals who had snapped up the converted flats – might frown at its dilapidated paintwork and the weeds growing from its gutters, but she loved the house with all its faults. It had become her home at a time of crisis in her life and, in turn, she'd opened it to others who'd needed a safe place.

She squeezed between two closely parked cars and paused on the pavement in surprise. For a fox was trotting along towards her, a vixen by the slightness of her. It stopped dead a few feet away, its obsidian eyes shining in the gathering dusk. For a lasting second they stared at one another, the lady and the fox, before the animal turned tail and fled.

There were far more foxes than she remembered there being in the past. They played extravagantly and noisily at night and left their toys on the lawns, old shoes, bits of tennis ball, once a pigeon's wing. Gardens were their playgrounds, dustbins their food baskets, burrows under sheds or brambles their homes. Just as her house had been a bolthole for many people. Leonie watched with sadness the vixen's brush vanish through the railings of the square's garden. It was as though the beautiful creature with its wildness had taken something of hers with it, and for a moment she thought of her grandson Jamie. Another wild creature who'd run from her and disappeared.

She searched her handbag for her keys as she climbed the steps of Number 11, scooped up a plump packet propped in the porch, and wrested open the door. Oh the sense of relief that always arose when she stepped inside. She sniffed the air as she pressed the door shut behind her. She loved the old-wood-and-polish scent overlaid by the fragrance of the lilies in their vase on the heavy hall stand and, today, a strong top note of turpentine.

Studying the label on the parcel she saw it was for Bela's husband, Hari. More of his bewildering range of health supplements, no doubt, by the lumpy feel of its contents. She set it down on the stand and leafed through the fresh pile of mail. The electricity bill and some circulars, a letter for Peter, the 'crosspatch' who occupied the basement flat, and, as ever, post for inhabitants long gone. A clothes catalogue for Jennifer, the resting actress with her silent small daughter, who had moved to Cornwall a year ago. A postcard of the seafront at Frinton for sweet old Norman, who'd retired from his hospital portering a few weeks back and gone to his brother's in Newcastle. She set these aside for forwarding and looked for something from Jamie. It had been her birthday last week and she'd hoped that he might have remembered. Perhaps he had, she tried to reassure herself, but the effort of getting together a card and a stamp was more than she could expect of him.

She sighed and turned over a stiff manila business envelope, then tutted under her breath on seeing the solicitor's name printed across the top. It would be another complaint from next door. She knew what it would say. A structural repair to the party wall, blah, blah, blah, and how would she pay for that, she'd like to know? She swept the other unwanted post into the top drawer and slammed it shut, but the manila envelope she dropped down the back of the stand in a gesture of defiance. Out of sight, out of mind, she told her reflection in the mottled mirror. Yet as she hung her coat on a hook and went through to the kitchen something troubled her. I'll think about the letter later, she told herself. It was her tried and tested way of dealing with impossible problems. Sometimes if you left them to stew for long enough they solved themselves one way or the other. As she filled the kettle, her thoughts moved again to Jamie. Sometimes they didn't.